SHALLOW WATER, DEEP LIES

DEEP LIES

BRETHREN OF THE COAST: BOOK ONE

MARK ALDRICH

Wallace Street Press • Kill Devil Hills, NC

Cover Design: Chris Sorensen
Proofreading: Gretchen Douglas
Formatting: Chris Sorensen
Editing: Amy Gillespie
Author Photograph: Justin Patterson Photography

ISBN#: 979-8-9871069-4-5

Published by:

Wallace Street Press
P.O. Box 211
Kill Devil Hills, NC 27948

To my very own gang of OBX lifers. It's a rare thing to find and keep friends through the many seasons of life, and I am grateful for you all. In this all too transient world, it is a great comfort to know that our lifetimes of memories still matter, and that we laugh at least as much now as all those years ago when we began.

James, Theresa, Kristin, Chris, Frank, Catherine, Amy. And, of course, Robin, the first to leave and forever held in our hearts.

And also
My brother, Stephen Aldrich. His love of the Outer Banks allowed mine to be reignited. This book, and likely all of my books, would not exist without him. He is one of the finest people I know and I am grateful for him.

CHAPTER 1

Tyler Lueck turned his white Jeep Wrangler left onto Buffalo City Road, heading into the Alligator River National Wildlife Refuge and its hard-packed dirt and gravel roads. Even as he made the turn, he knew he had taken it too fast and cursed himself. Not for the first time this morning. Last night, instead of stowing all of the company kayaks at the conclusion of the last group tour, he'd tied them up and left them floating in the inlet just under the bridge at the dead end. He'd known he shouldn't. But the tour had run late, and he had a date with Catherine to get to back in Nags Head. A second date. Arguably more important than the first. The weather forecast had been clear, so he had nothing to worry about other than a curious bear wanting to play with the boats. That had seemed unlikely.

Still, he'd only been with Outer Banks KayaX for a few months. It was his ticket to sticking in the Outer Banks for the summer ahead. Maybe longer, if he played his cards right. It hadn't even been a difficult workday. Crowds were light in early April and the group had only been six paddlers. The reason they stayed out late was the afternoon had been unseasonably warm. As a result, the wildlife was active. Very... Bears galore had come out. He still found it hard to believe that the area had such a huge population of black bears, but there was no arguing the point when they stared back at you. They'd seen a fox, two beaver, a handful of cottonmouths, and the stars of the day, more than a dozen alligators. From cautious youngsters only a foot or so long to the king of the swamp, Stumpy, who had lost part of his tail in some inter-gator tussle long ago and came in at over twelve feet in length.

The tourists had been skittish at first. Those gators look a heck of a lot bigger when you're in a kayak at water level and see them returning your gaze. But Tyler knew the real hazard was the cotton-mouths. They normally stick to themselves, but a careless hand dipped into the water could be a problem if it scared the wrong snake. He'd warned the party about that repeatedly, but one man had continually forgotten, and Tyler had to keep on top of him. Jaime.

His mind shifted back to the road ahead of him. The morning fog hadn't burned off yet, and for a moment he lost his bearings. He passed the turn for Sawyer Lake Road where his favorite little gator lived. No time to dawdle, though, so he hit the gas, and the Jeep jumped forward.

The morning mist was fogging his windows, and he had to roll them down, his dark auburn hair dancing in the new breeze. For a split second, in his peripheral vision, he saw a figure standing just inside the tree line. Tall. Impossibly tall. He had to calm the adren-aline surge that came. Just a bear. Out foraging like a bear should do and startled by the roar of the Jeep in the otherwise calm morning.

He was close to the creepy hunter's shack and his nerves always kicked in here. No one really knew who stayed there. Or when. But whoever it was had built a little footbridge over the canal on the left side of the road. A little ramshackle thing. Just a few planks really, but they had made it retractable. A drawbridge for the mystery squatters who dared to wander into the swamp. The shack looked as if it would fall down any minute, boards askew and jutting out at impossible angles. But the walls were adorned with the skulls of small woodland creatures, which just added to the grim tone. A satellite dish perched on the roof seemed incongruous but pointed to ongoing use.

Tyler didn't slow as he passed it. Almost to the boats. He might just get away with this. He cursed himself and vowed never to cut corners again. This job was too important. And the date with Catherine had gone too well to jeopardize staying put all summer. Maybe longer.

He pulled into the cul-de-sac at the end and parked. Before he even jumped down out of the Wrangler, he heaved a sigh of relief. There they were. Right where he'd left them. Blue-white kayaks bobbing where he'd tied them. Like clouds bobbing in a watery sky. And the two brightly colored red ones.

Two? There should be three.

And then he noticed. They weren't exactly where he'd left them. It was as if someone had shaken them about and then thrown them back into the water. A couple were overturned. One had grounded itself on the bank of the water.

"No, no, no," he muttered to himself as he ran over to them. "Stupid, stupid."

He began drawing them in as fast as he could, but not so fast that he didn't keep an eye on his surroundings. Early mornings were prime gator and bear times. And snakes. Yeah, they're usually more scared of you than you are of them. Still.

He pulled the kayaks clear of the water and dragged them to the trailer that the company sometimes left here overnight in the early season. He counted again. Dammit. There was a red kayak missing.

What the hell had happened here last night? No one was allowed into the park after dark. People tried, he knew that from the stories he'd heard from his buddy, Justin Vollmerhausen, who served as a park ranger for the refuge. There were enough cameras and patrols to discourage most trespassers. What could have happened then?

More importantly, where was that kayak? He didn't even want to think how much would come out of his paycheck to reimburse the company. If he was able to keep his job. Big if.

With the other kayaks stowed, he turned back to the water. He scanned the shore and noticed some of the grass had been trampled. As if something had been dragged out of the water. Or...into the water? Weird.

Something caught his eye. Something light colored and wafting on the incoming tide. Something that led his eye back to the bridge.

He caught his breath and scampered down the bank, careful to make noise and shuffle his feet. The last thing he needed was an encounter with the local wildlife. Just maybe the missing kayak was under there and all was not lost.

He craned his neck to see under the span, leaning precariously out over the water. There. A sliver of red poking out from under.

"Yes!" he shouted, and a trio of turtles slid from a nearby fallen tree.

He took off his shoes and left them on the shore, then carefully lowered himself into the water. He wasn't a huge fan of doing this here by himself. It flew in the face of all the safety training he'd been given, but this was the only way to get himself out of the jam.

It had capsized somehow and was listing to one side. He reached the tie-line and started to draw the kayak out into the sunlight. It was heavy. Heavier than it should be. He gave a hearty pull, and the boat shuddered before starting to ease its way out. Probably just snagged on a sunken tree limb.

As he drew it closer, those nerves of his began to jangle again. Something was off. How did the boat get upended? Why was it wedged under the bridge? Especially with the tide running.

Something was in there. Tyler could see it now. As he pulled the kayak, whatever was hidden inside thumped against the hull noisily. It echoed from under the bridge.

"What the hell—" Tyler murmured.

A gator would have made itself known by now. And no snake would make sounds like that.

With the line in hand, he struggled up the bank, but when he tried to get the kayak to dry land, it proved too heavy. In the water he could move it. Nothing doing on dry land.

He scrambled back down and grabbed hold, giving a heave to right the boat. The kayak resisted, until finally, and oh so slowly, turning right side up.

Tyler froze at what he saw. Then slowly crab walked himself back up the bank. His mouth slack and words failing.

There, wedged into the cockpit of the boat was a man. A dead man. A very dead man.

"Not good, not good," he said to no one in particular.

He tied the rope off to a nearby branch and stood.

How? Why? What to do?

He raced to the Jeep and grabbed his phone to call Ranger Justin. He'd know what to do.

Damn. No signal. He knew that with all the time he spent here, but still. A signal right now would be very helpful.

He walked cautiously to the edge of the water.

"Hey, buddy," he said. "Can you hear me?"

But the figure wedged into the kayak was long gone, as the blue hue of his skin attested. He looked to have been an average visitor to the Banks. Sandy hair, now plastered to his head. Green t-shirt, shorts. A blue baseball cap at what would have been a jaunty angle under other circumstances. Middle-aged. Forties but reasonably fit.

"I'll get help," he continued. "Don't go anywhere."

Then he cursed himself again. Stupid.

He climbed into the Jeep and revved the engine, tearing back up the road toward the highway and a phone signal.

Whoever that was in the kayak was not one of his group from yesterday. Thank God. More than that, though, was the certainty that he had never seen the man before.

———

Curt Stephens climbed out of his forest green 1969 Chevrolet Chevelle in the parking area on Hayman Boulevard. The nighttime damp was hovering close to the ground, even here near the beach. If not for that, he would have taken the 1965 Mustang convertible. Time enough for that in the summer months ahead. He crossed the beach road and climbed the recently replenished dune toward the sound of the surf.

Checking his phone, he saw that it was 6:21. Ten minutes to go until sunrise. Perfect. He'd found that the minutes just *before* the sun broke the horizon often yielded the best photos.

He climbed down the far side of the dune and wandered south a few hundred yards to get a clearer shot of the Avalon Pier. Some of his best sunrise pictures had included the pier. Watching the dawn was one of his daily habits. He'd started when he first relocated to the Outer Banks, and assumed it was a phase he'd outgrow. He hadn't. All these years later, it was still how he began each day.

There were a few reasons for that. He felt part of a devoted few that appeared every morning to greet the new day. There was the guy with the blue cap and travel mug of coffee. Unlike the others, he never took pictures. Just showed up at the last minute, strode onto the beach, nodded hello to anyone else there, watched as the sun breached the horizon, turned and disappeared back to the road. Curt knew nothing about him and had never seen him anywhere else on the Banks, which now that he thought about it was odd.

There was Marie, who often appeared at the last minute, her lumpy, lovable dog in tow. She always stopped to talk, and she and Curt had developed a comfortable friendship over time.

There was black-SUV-woman, who arrived early, walked her two dogs for a good twenty minutes along the sand before returning to the walkway through the dunes and the parking lot.

There was the elderly couple who always watched the dawn hand in hand. Curt caught himself. They probably weren't *that* much older than he was. He just dressed and acted much younger than his forty-seven years.

Along with the regulars were the usual blow-ins and tourists. He'd seen couples having beach blanket picnics at sunrise. Or who had clearly been up all night, teetering along the edge of the Atlantic with a champagne or wine bottle clutched tightly and giggling like children.

So, yes, he valued feeling connected to these people, many of whom remained nameless to him, which seemed somehow appropriate. But more than that, he enjoyed feeling connected to the Banks themselves. It was a grounding reminder of why he had come here to begin with. The simplicity and natural beauty of the barrier islands was easy to lose sight of when you spent every day surrounded by it. Work, bills, neighborhood squabbles, seasonal storms, rising costs. They all fought to steal the joy that had brought him here, and starting each day with this simplest of reminders let him touch that, even briefly, before launching into the day ahead.

If he knew little about his fellow sun-greeters, he was sure they knew as little about him. His daily uniform of long board shorts—green today—a printed t-shirt advertising a local brewery, flip-flops, and sunglasses perched atop his head, holding back his shoulder length auburn hair, made him look the stereotypical midlife-crisis beach bum. Few would guess that he was in charge of a significant real estate and stock portfolio. In fact, that was how he had been free to relocate here.

He was also the acknowledged unofficial mayor of the Outer Banks. Nothing happened here without him knowing about it, and no one crossed him intentionally. He was firm, but fair, and as much as he loved the relaxed life here, he knew it was precarious and needed protecting. There were other, even more buried, secrets within him, and had the others on the beach been slightly less focused on the rising sun, they may have noticed that his green eyes were troubled this morning. But they didn't.

Curt took out his phone and began to take a few photos of the sky as the sun threw up a tapestry of purple and orange, announcing its arrival with ribbons of cotton candy clouds. Slowly, the sky shifted to a deep red. Slowly, it lightened. Heading toward pink, eventually.

Even preoccupied, Curt marveled at the celestial show. Every morning here was different and spectacular in its way. Today was especially breathtaking. What did they say about red sky in the morning?

He put his phone down, admonishing himself to spend less time behind the camera and more in the moment. He had a big day ahead of him. A day that would affect him and possibly his beloved Banks for a long time. He had to get it right. And he was the only one who could.

At 6:31 exactly, the sun broke the horizon. Blazing red in the fringe of cloud cover that sat on the horizon, as it so often did here on the edge of the ocean. Spectacular. And lighting the sky anew in a brilliant crimson. He turned to his left and caught Marie's eye. She smiled at him, raised her eyebrows, and nodded to the sunrise. Following her gaze, he noticed a small pod of dolphins lazily cruising south toward the pier. It didn't happen every day, but seeing dolphins always seemed to be a sign of good things to come. He smiled and watched Marie wander over the dune back to her Jeep.

Blue cap guy had loitered longer today and was still on the sand when Marie disappeared. If he was still here, it must be a truly remarkable start to the day. He raised his travel coffee mug in a toast to Curt before also turning and trudging up the dune and into his day.

Curt sighed. Yup. This is why he did this every day. Not everyone could understand, but it was important. It mattered. To him.

His reverie was cut short when his cell phone vibrated. Startled, he nearly dropped it but recovered to check the screen. Incoming call from Deputy Roger Goldstein of the Manteo Police Department. Not who he would have expected to hear from. Not on a Tuesday. And at this time of the morning, it was definitely not good news.

Tyler paced by the side of his Jeep. After making a call when he got to the highway, he'd gone back to the scene. The victim. But he couldn't settle there and ended up needing some distance. He'd moved back up Buffalo City Road to wait for Ranger Justin there. He just couldn't stand by...it. Him. The body. The first body he'd ever seen, actually. He couldn't stop staring at it. And the more he stared, the more freaked out he became. And the more he imagined the poor guy staring back at him. Accusing.

If he hadn't left the kayaks out overnight, would that guy still be alive? Was he somehow to blame?

He realized he'd stopped close to the creepy trapper shack. It was almost as bad as the body, sitting there silent and menacing. He didn't have signal here, either, so he quickly drove further up the track to the corner with Sawyer Lake. He still didn't see his little alligator pal, but he'd much rather wait for the gator to show up than whoever frequented the cabin of animal bones.

He heard an approaching vehicle and stopped pacing to face the highway. A moment later Justin's familiar forest green Park Ranger pickup came into view, kicking up a plume of dust behind it. The early morning mist was gone, and the day was heating up. In more ways than one, Tyler thought.

"Ah, shit," Tyler muttered as he saw another vehicle close behind the Fish and Wildlife truck. It was a police cruiser. Looked to be out of Manteo. Tyler shook his head. He could pretty much kiss his job goodbye. Although what had he expected? Somebody was dead.

He pushed off the hood of the Wrangler and gave a wave, realizing as he did that there was no way they could miss him. There was no one around for miles. Except for dead guy. And shady hunters in the swamp. Suddenly he was glad to see them, and relieved to see Justin's familiar freckled face and close-cropped hair lean out the window as he pulled alongside.

"Damn, bro," Justin said, aiming for levity and falling just short. "The season hasn't even officially started and you're killin' off the tourists? Have you thought about a different line of work?"

Tyler tried to muster a smile but produced more of a grimace. "Thought it was going pretty well up until now," he replied.

"Sorry about bringing the cops along," said Justin, with a nod to the idling car behind him. "Roger's a solid guy. Don't worry about him. But we had to call it in. We share jurisdiction over certain things. I'd say a dead body falls in there."

Tyler glanced over and saw a white-haired man of indeterminate age half fold his lanky frame out of the driver's side door. The newcomer had a cockeyed grin that flew in the face of what brought them here and Tyler instantly felt a bit more at ease.

"Hey there, guys!" came a shout from the deputy. "Let's leave my car and that Jeep here and take the F and W truck down. Less tire prints might be our friend. I'll even let you ride shotgun. I love sittin' in the back."

With that the deputy pulled over across the intersection from Tyler and crossed back to Ranger Justin's pickup, clambering into the bed, and standing with his palms on the top of the cab, facing front.

"I'm the king of the world," he called, holding his arms out to his sides in a pale imitation of Leonardo on the Titanic.

Tyler shot Justin a quizzical look as he climbed into the truck.

Justin laughed. "He's a character, but he's good at his job and we can trust him. Can't say that about everyone in these parts. Whaddaya say you show me what's going on down there, yeah? And don't worry. You didn't do anything wrong, right?"

Tyler nodded, emphatically.

"Then no problemo," Justin answered. "Well, unless those trapper creepers are home. That could be a problem. I kid, I kid. C'mon. Let's see what's what."

As the truck kicked up gravel and headed toward the end of the road and the grim scene awaiting them, from the back of the truck Roger Goldstein, his white mane flying out in the wind behind him cried, "There was room on that door, Rose!"

Tyler shook his head and noted that it wasn't even seven o'clock yet.

Justin pulled his truck up on the far side of the cul-de-sac at the end of the road. Tyler slowly lowered himself from the passenger side, while Roger leaped down from the bed with surprising dexterity for someone of his age. Tyler thought of books and covers and made note.

"You don't have to get any closer if you don't want to," Justin said, putting a hand on Tyler's shoulder. "I get it. Just stay by the truck."

"Thanks," Tyler replied, feeling sheepish about wanting to hang back. But he really wanted to hang back. "He's by the kayak next to the bridge there. I got out of there as fast as I could, so I don't know if he's...floating...or..."

"Not a worry," Roger said, stepping up to the others. "We've got this."

Roger led the way with Justin close behind, their work boots crunching along the gravel roadway in the still early morning. Justin, no small figure himself, lengthened his stride to keep up with the deputy.

They reached the bank of the inlet and stopped. There, half exposed under the small footbridge was the red kayak. And there, half out of the boat, was the victim.

"Poor guy," Roger said quietly, taking off his hat. "Lonely place to go." He put his hat back on his head. "What do you see, Ranger?"

Justin tilted his cap back on his head. The sun was climbing, and it was going to be a bright, beautiful spring day. But not for everyone.

"Well, no idea when he died, but if the tide was coming in, that boat didn't drift against the current under the bridge. Someone put it there." He turned his attention to the grass on the bank. "Something was dragged across the grass here. All wrong for a gator slide, though. Bigger. Less uniform."

"The only animal more dangerous in here than a gator did that," Roger said, squinting into the rising sun.

"You mean a human, don't you?" Justin said with a shake of his head.

Roger nodded and grabbed a long piece of marsh grass, sticking it between his teeth and sucking loudly.

"Jeez, you really are a walking cliché," Justin said with a chuckle. "You must read too many crime thrillers."

Chastened, Roger shrugged and dropped his enormous toothpick with a quick spit.

"I was proud of that one," he mumbled. "And, yes, as a matter of fact I do read a lot of them. No accident I ended up in this job."

"All good," Justin replied, clapping the deputy on the shoulder. "And point taken. He had company. And he isn't exactly dressed for a heavy hike. This all just feels off."

"Not bad, Justin," Roger said, with a sidelong glance at the younger man. "Let me know when you want to join the force." He turned to the scene. "No visible sign of injury. So not an animal attack. He's wedged in there pretty good. Could have drowned but drowning victims don't usually push themselves against the tide under a bridge, unless he got stuck once down there. Doesn't seem likely. No vehicle. Unless he hiked all the way in here in the pitch black, someone was with him and took off. That's an OCEARCH t-shirt he's wearing. Shark research group. May mean something. May not. Hate to say it, but it does look suspicious. At the very least. Means more paperwork. I hate paperwork. But I hate murderers even more. What's say you get me and Tyler back to our vehicles, then you secure the area. I'll call it in and get all the necessary parts in motion."

"Should we get him out?" Justin asked.

"Seems harsh, but I don't think so," Roger said. "Let the investigators investigate. You'll be back in under five minutes. Just keep him safe until they get here."

CHAPTER 2

Curt felt as if the beautiful sunrise had been weeks ago as he was cruising north on the bypass. This was a vital day, as Roger Goldstein fully knew. He'd called the deputy back as soon as he'd reached his Chevelle. The car boasted some serious safety and comfort improvements, and he was using his hands-free feature as the distinctive hot rod growled past the morning traffic.

"Roger," he called into the speaker, "I can barely hear you. What's that noise?"

The response was barely audible, garbled by what sounded like a rushing river.

"Yeah…—orry. In Justin's —uck, lots of wind. Bad —ervice…" Roger responded in fits and starts.

"Whatever," Curt replied with frustration. "You know what's at stake today, Rog. I need you to handle this for now, whatever it is, but I need to know *exactly* what's going on as soon as you do."

Suddenly the phone line cleared, and Roger Goldstein's voice blared into the car with the improved connection. Curt scrambled to lower the volume. A little Roger could go a long way.

"I'll be damned," Roger said with only slightly lowered volume.

"That weird hunter shack must have Wi-Fi. Wasn't turned on forty minutes ago when we passed going in. Anyhoo, short version is that we have our first dead body of the season, although we both know it probably won't be our last. Scene is secured, coroner is on her way. CSI is too. Ranger Justin is staying here to keep things tightened up. I'll take the witness back to the station for a statement."

"Thoughts on the witness?" Curt asked.

"Good kid," Roger answered. "Tyler something or other. Just picked up a job at Outer Banks KayaX—stupid name—and worried he's gonna get fired. Can't see any possible way he's involved, but I've been wrong before. We'll see what he says."

"Foul play?"

"Too soon to tell," Roger said. "No visible trauma. Could be a stupid and unlucky drunk who tried to go for a joyride."

"But?"

"But it's foul play," Roger admitted. "Something's off. No visible injuries. No vehicle nearby. Lots of questions."

"Do I need to be there?" Curt asked, dreading the answer.

A pause.

"Nah," Roger finally said. "Your day has a lot riding on it."

"Good," Curt answered. "In that case, I'm back home to get the VW Buzz and then pick up our candidates."

"Pick up the Buzz? You don't have much time. Why do you—ohhh. You took the Chevelle to the beach again, didn't you? You are such a marshmallow."

"I love the Buzz, you know that," Curt said. "But the Chevelle is my baby. Four candidates today, though. Need the seats in the Buzz. And I only have twenty minutes to start picking them up. We'll meet later?"

"Sure," Roger answered.

But there was something he wasn't saying, and given the situation, Curt couldn't pretend he didn't notice.

"What are you not saying?"

"It's just—after everything last fall. Should we be telling the others about the body? Do you think we might have something… similar going on?”

Curt paused, choosing his words carefully. He was waiting to turn left on Helga Street, and he drummed his fingers on the steering wheel. He could hear the nerves in Roger's question, and he knew how he answered could charge or disarm the situation. He just wasn't sure which was the right approach.

“Rog,” Curt began slowly, “that was a very isolated incident. And, honestly, we saw signs before it went haywire. Have we had any signs that anything strange is going on?”

“Other than the body?” Roger asked. “Sorry, that was a bit much. No. No other signs.”

“Okay, then,” Curt said, trying to reassure the deputy. “I doubt we'll ever see anything like that again. And let's hope we don't, because that's not what we do. We take care of everyday, common problems. And that's what this is.”

He hoped Roger couldn't hear the sliver of doubt in his words. He hoped *he* would be able to ignore it.

“Yeah, yeah,” Roger mumbled into the phone. “You're probably right.” A pause. “Well, I'm back at the cruiser with Tyler. I'll keep you posted, yeah.”

“Perfect,” Curt said. “And I'll let you know what happens on my end. Big day.”

“Sure is, boss. Good luck.”

“You too, Roger. Talk soon.”

Curt ended the connection and sat back in his seat. He puffed out his cheeks and exhaled loudly. Last fall. Sean Curley and Dan Trout had arrived in the Outer Banks to rescue a friend. That friend turned out to be more than anyone would have expected. Old secrets had been laid bare, and Curt and his colleagues had witnessed legends and evil come to life. Everything had been at stake. Their islands. Their beliefs. Supernatural things that couldn't be real had been.

The Banks had become the attraction they were in large part because of the colorful history. Curt had always known there was truth in some of the local lore. The Banks were built on stories of pirates, and magic, and mystery, and the paranormal. But he had to operate in the here and now. He *had* to believe the events of a few months past were a one-time event. Even though he knew the truth and that there were people here, now, who were more than they seemed. But they had chosen to lay low and as long as that was the case, Curt would let them be.

If the islands were really as full of otherworldly danger as they had seen, he would need to rethink his entire view of the world and his place in this little corner of it. He wasn't ready to do that. And he didn't have the time today.

So even if he knew there was more out there, he was *sure* that his responsibility now was to keep it away from those who would be most harmed by it. Or those who could fall under their influence. Sometimes you had to keep things from people for their own good.

It was quite a burden for one person to shoulder, but he knew it had fallen to him. He was the only one equipped to meet the challenge. He knew things the others didn't. Had done things they hadn't. Even now, after everything they had been through. He held some secrets close. Very. And if he still had doubts that he was up to the task, that was a good thing. Right? He would never let his guard down. There was too much at stake. Too many would be hurt if he failed.

The car behind him gave a gentle beep and he startled back to the Chevelle and the now-green turning arrow in front of him. He gave a quick wave of apology to the driver following and pulled onto Helga.

He literally shook his head to clear it. Time to focus. The next few hours would go a long way toward keeping the Banks safe. For now.

Roger Goldstein stood next to his cruiser in the parking lot of the Manteo Police Department. He watched as Tyler's Jeep made a left and pulled up next to him. Roger took off his sunglasses and dropped them into the pocket of his uniform shirt. He gave his keys—and there were many—a twirl on his finger à la a Wild West gunslinger and clipped them to his belt. He made note of how heavy they were. Someone had once told him that you could tell how complicated a person's life was by how many keys they carried. He had a *lot* of keys.

"Tyler!" he called. "Let's get settled into an interview room and squared away. I'm sure you want to get home. You've had quite a shock."

"Thanks," Tyler answered. "You could say that."

"Our coffee is horrible," Roger said, gesturing for Tyler to head for the station. "But it's better than nothing. Like pizza. Even bad coffee is good."

"I'm not sure that's exactly true," Tyler said, walking toward the front door. "But I won't say no."

Tyler held the door for Roger who headed up the stairs to the reception desk on the second floor.

A woman sat at a standard-issue office desk behind a plexiglass partition. She looked at first glance to be in her early fifties. Could be older. Hard to tell, but she took care of herself, that was clear. Her graying hair was pulled back into a tight bun. She had a pair of glasses on a lanyard around her neck. Her eyes were a light brown and wide set. She paused her fingers above the computer keyboard as Roger reached the top of the stairs and inclined her head as she noticed Tyler just behind him.

"You're early, Deputy Goldstein," she said, glancing at her computer screen. "Even by your very eager standards."

"I could say the same to you, Mary," Roger replied. "Crime doesn't watch the clock. We answer when called." He tapped his fingers on the plexiglass earning a tut from Mary. "Mary Hallet, I'd like you to meet Tyler—Tyler, what's your last name?"

"Lueck," the young man replied quietly. Clearly, standing in a police station was something he wasn't used to doing and he seemed to be reassessing the seriousness of the situation.

"Tyler Lueck," Roger continued, not missing a beat. "Tyler's had a rough morning. Found someone deceased in Alligator River and is here to help us figure out what happened. Tyler, Mary here has been here longer than me. Which isn't easy to do. She's good people. Still calls me 'deputy,' though. I think she's afraid to get too close to me. I have that effect on women."

"Stop it," Mary protested, shooing Roger away from the partition. "You're horrible."

Roger laughed but noted with satisfaction the flush creeping up Mary's neck.

"I think we'll head for Room One. They must all be open at this hour. Can you have someone bring some coffee in?"

"Of course," she answered. "And that someone will be me. We're the only two here."

"Much appreciated," Roger replied, with a wink. "I'll make it up to you. Do you prefer emeralds or rubies?"

"Yeah, yeah," Mary answered, pushing a button to buzz them into the station proper. "Just horrible."

But she was grinning as she turned back to her computer.

Roger led Tyler down a hallway lit by long fluorescent bulbs overhead, stopping at the first door they reached and holding it open for Tyler.

"Grab a seat," Roger said in as genial a tone as he could muster. "Mary will have that coffee here in a sec. Need anything else? Pastry? I can send out for something."

"No, thanks," Tyler replied, lowering himself into an institutional gray, plastic chair. "I'm not hungry. 'Preciate it."

"Right. Well, let's get this moving and send you home."

"I need to get to work," Tyler protested. "I've screwed up enough already."

"First things first," Roger said, raising his hands to calm the younger man. "Walk me through what happened. Don't leave anything out. Even stuff that seems unimportant might help us."

And so, Tyler did. As he relived the events of the morning, his confidence grew. His voice grew calmer, more focused, and Roger gave him all the room he needed to walk through it.

He finished his account when he reached the point that Roger and Justin had arrived, took a deep breath, and set his hands on the table in front of him.

"Excellent," Roger said, after a brief pause to see if anything else was coming. "Mind if I ask a couple follow-up questions?"

"Go for it," Tyler answered, as the door opened and Mary entered with a tray holding two steaming mugs of coffee and an assortment of cookies.

"Apologies for the cookies," she said. "We don't have many breakfast goodies around here. There's milk and sugar there for you, too. Need anything else, just give a shout."

"Thanks, gorgeous," Roger said as Mary left, shaking her head yet again. "Now, Tyler. Are you absolutely sure you've never seen the man you found before?"

"Positive," Tyler answered. "I took a long look. Longer than I wanted to. But no. Never."

"Okay. Great," Roger said, sliding one mug toward Tyler and claiming the other for himself. He took a sip, winced at the too-hot coffee, and put it back down. "What can you tell me about the group you led last night?"

"That last group?" Tyler asked, putting his hands around the steaming mug. "Not a whole lot, honestly. I wasn't at my best. I was distracted and really focused on finishing up."

"For your date, yes?" Roger prompted.

"Yeah," Tyler said. "Oh, shit. You don't have to talk to her, do you? To Catherine?"

"Catherine...?" Roger left the question hanging in the air between them.

"Dammit," Tyler said. Resting his head in his hands. "You will. Of course, you will. Catherine Barilla."

"Barilla?" Roger asked. "Any relation to the pasta family?"

"No," Tyler said, face still in his hands. "Actually...I never thought about it. I don't think so."

"Not important," Roger admitted. "We'll check with Catherine to get the timeline straight. But don't worry. I'll make you sound like a hero."

"Really?" Tyler said quietly, peeking from between his fingers. "Thanks."

"Yeah, no sweat. Us guys have to stick together."

Tyler's head came up. He was back in the game.

"Yeah, so the group was a bunch of high school friends. A reunion or something. Middle-aged. Had to be in their forties. Guess they've been coming to the Banks for a long time. Didn't really get many details, but the office should have more information. Who reserved and who paid, that kind of thing."

"Yeah, we'll be in touch with them," Roger said. "Anything else?"

"There were six of them. Three guys, three girls. Women. But I didn't have the sense they were couples or anything. Just a bunch of old friends. They were pretty funny, actually. From the little I paid attention."

"This is great, Tyler. A big help," Roger said. He put his pen down on the table and gave the coffee another try. Better. He managed a sip. "This stuff is just awful. Don't tell Mary I said that."

Tyler nodded and gave his coffee a sip. He raised his eyes to Roger in disbelief. "This is *coffee*?"

"That's what they tell me," Roger replied. "One last thing. Did you have any service on your phone back there? Did you notice anything, say, in the area of the shack back there? Anywhere else?"

"No, and not for lack of trying," Tyler said. "Had to go all the way out of the refuge to make the call."

"Right," Roger answered, now tapping his pen on the tabletop. "What I figured. Interesting."

"So...um...can I ask you something?" Tyler said, tentatively.

"Shoot."

"What was with the crazy act, back in the park? All that Titanic stuff and shouting? We get back here, and you seem different. Kinda normal."

"Good question," Roger said, leaning back in his chair, the front legs off the floor. "Couple of reasons. First, that time of day, it's good to make a fuss. Let the bears and gators know where you are so we can all avoid each other."

"Okay, I get that," Tyler replied, nodding. "What else?"

"No service and pretty isolated out there. That damn hunter's shack always gives me the willies. I find if folks underestimate you, you start with an advantage. They think you're a fool, you've already more than half won."

"Interesting theory," Tyler responded. "Have to remember that."

"Hasn't failed me yet," Roger said. "Keep 'em off balance."

Roger's phone buzzed on the table, and he shot an apologetic look toward Tyler as he picked it up, one finger raised. "Just a sec."

"Goldstein," he said into the cell phone. "Justin, yeah, we're just chatting at the station. What's happening on your end? …Uh huh. Cell phone? …Okay. Interesting." He grabbed his pen and began to furiously take notes. "Got that. Keep me in the loop."

"Can you tell me what's going on?" Tyler asked.

"To a point," Roger said slowly. "A wallet was found nearby. ID in the wallet. You ever hear the name Mark Elliot?"

Tyler paused, thought, and shook his head.

"Forty-eight years old. Down here from New York apparently. They checked with his next of kin. On vacation. He's down here for a reunion with some high school friends."

CHAPTER 3

The Chevelle rolled into the driveway on Wallace Street and Curt pulled into the carport. It could rain later, like most days here, so he made sure the car was covered. He put it in park and climbed out, giving it an affectionate swipe before he turned to his new Volkswagen ID. Buzz. It was vaguely reminiscent of the classic VW Microbus from the sixties, which is probably why Curt had wanted it. He loved his classics, and the retro look hooked him right away. But the Buzz was thoroughly modern. And electric. Which appealed to Curt's environmental conscience but was at odds with his hot rod spirit. It had a range of just under 240 miles, which should be more than enough for his local driving. And supposedly it could charge in as little as thirty minutes. He hadn't tested that yet, plugging in each night to the station he'd installed by the driveway. Couldn't argue with the spacious interior and all the perks, though. The infotainment screen was huge, and he could control nearly everything simply with his voice. It really was a perfect beach ride. It was just so modern.

There was seating for five passengers comfortably, which was the reason he'd needed it today. He had four applicants to interview.

They'd advertised the job as relating to tourism and hospitality. In a way that was true, but *if*—and that was a big if—one of them proved qualified, that was when the actual details would be shared. Technically, it was employment. Technically. There was a stipend involved, but this would be a lot more than a job.

He started the Buzz. It always weirded him out how little sound these electric vehicles made. You should be able to hear someone driving near you. The silence was unnatural.

He pulled out of the driveway and checked his notes on the screen. Four candidates. It had been a few years since they'd tried to bring in anyone else. He felt a flutter of butterflies in his stomach. That wasn't like him. But if they found someone, they'd become as close as family to him and the others.

Right. The notes. First pickup was in the neighborhood, just behind Food Lion. Easy enough. Then one in Nags Head. One in Pirate's Cove by the bridge to Roanoke Island. The last one had offered to meet by the public playground in Manteo by Roanoke Marshes Lighthouse. Extra credit to that one for making some effort.

Four candidates.

Josh Brewer.

Theresa Franklin.

Carlito Vega.

Charles Vane.

None of the four knew that Curt was the one in charge of hiring. As far as they knew, he was just a driver. The interview was to start after they'd all assembled in Manteo at the Lost Colony Tavern, which had agreed to open early.

The first stop was at an unassuming house two long blocks off the sound. Josh Brewer was a small, wiry figure with large glasses, a propensity to chatter, and extensive musical and mechanical knowledge, which he was more than happy to share as they headed out to get the next applicant.

Theresa Franklin was waiting in front of one of the old concrete beach houses from before the age of massive McMansions. Curt pined a bit for those older days as he waited for her to climb into the Buzz.

Theresa was compact, athletic, and deeply tanned. Her black hair was cut to just above her shoulders. She walked with confidence and introduced herself with the same. She'd been a lifeguard until recently but had decided to find something a little more terrestrial as she found herself approaching her mid-twenties. Her deep brown eyes took in everything, including Josh sitting in the second row, whom she acknowledged as she sat next to him, then peppered him with questions about what he thought the job would entail.

Josh did his best to keep up but was clearly overwhelmed by the volume of questions and the sheer exuberance of Theresa.

Noted.

Charles Vane was next to be gathered. Curt pulled into the Pirate's Cove condo neighborhood and around to the address he'd been given. This was a pretty exclusive neighborhood, and Curt couldn't help wondering why someone who lived here would be applying for a job with a very modest salary.

Pulling up to the designated condo, a massive young man, easily over six feet, glanced at the Buzz from under a black Iron Maiden hat. He gave a sharp nod of his head, took a final drag on a cigarette that he then dropped and crushed underfoot and moved toward the van. The black hair poking from under his cap looked unkempt. His jeans were torn, but deliberately. He'd paid well for them to look that way. His shirt was the skull and crossbones. Appropriate.

Vane climbed into the front passenger seat, and immediately took out his phone, not acknowledging Curt or the others in the seat behind him. After a brief moment checking texts, he made a phone call and, with the speaker blaring for the others to hear, proceeded to tell whomever he was speaking to that he would be done pretty quickly and that he was sure he'd get an offer. The conversation quickly turned to making plans for the night and only when they had decided to meet at a bar did the voices become quieter, and Vane cupped his hand over his mouth to keep the others from hearing. He never once glanced at anyone else.

Also noted.

It was another ten minutes until the van pulled up in the public parking lot by the small lighthouse in downtown Manteo.

A young man with a shock of black hair looked up from a book he was reading. He smiled and waved at the group emerging from the van and jogged over to the driver's side where he shot out his hand to Curt and introduced himself.

"Hi there," he said. "Carlito Vega. Nice to meetcha. Wow, if I'd known the ride was so sweet I might have asked to get picked up. First time I've seen one of these in real life."

"Curt Stephens. Nice to meet you too. These are Josh, Theresa, and Charles. We're all going to wander over to Lost Colony and get started."

"Sounds great," Carlito answered.

Curt paused to take in the young man. He was under six feet tall. He was athletic but not overtly muscular. Dressed simply. Faded jeans, blue t-shirt, and worn sneakers. His face was friendly and open, but his eyes were keen, and Curt had the impression that not much got past him. He glanced at the book Carlito had been reading. *Strange Case of Dr Jekyll and Mr Hyde* by Robert Louis Stevenson. Interesting.

Curt led the way toward the tavern and behind him heard Carlito engaging the others in conversation. Vane remained aloof, checking his phone. Josh and Theresa were happy to talk with Carlito, but it was clear who was steering the conversation.

Curt climbed the stairs to the main dining room and held the door while the others followed. Vane entered first, eyes on his screen. Theresa and Josh were next. Josh was cleaning his glasses as he went and almost missed a step up, nearly falling.

Carlito, bringing up the rear, shot out an arm and caught Josh, before turning to thank Curt for holding the door.

Inside the door, they were greeted by a blond-haired, fair-skinned, grinning figure. The man opened his arms wide and said, "Welcome! I'm so glad you made it. We've been waiting for you."

Vane thrust a hand out to the man, finally putting his phone in his pocket and engaging.

"Charles Vane," he said. "Pleased to meet you. I'm looking forward to working with you."

"Oh, no," the man began. "I'm not—"

"Nice place you got here," Vane interrupted. "But this can't be where the job is. It said something about tourism."

"No," the man tried to cut in. "I'm just—"

"Oh, right, hi," Josh said, moving up next to Vane. "Where should we sit? I'm so excited."

"Hi, I'm Theresa," she said, lowering her head and glancing up through her considerable lashes.

Carlito stayed back, taking the scene in and glancing questioningly at Curt.

The man shook his head. "Yeah, I'm not running this interview. This is my tavern. I'm just the host."

"The *host?* Are you freakin' kidding me?" Vane blurted. "Is all this just for a restaurant gig? Not worth my time, man."

"Gene," Curt said, stepping forward. "You really didn't need to come down yourself, but it's great to see you."

Gene O'Shea, the owner of the tavern, had shown up to personally greet the group. He'd worked from time to time with Curt and, unlike the applicants, he knew Curt was a man of consequence and that this must be important. While he wasn't entirely sure what it was Curt did, he knew he was likely the most influential man on the barrier islands. And he genuinely liked Curt. A feeling that was clearly mutual.

"Hey!" Gene responded. "It's not every day I have Curt Stephens in the tavern. Happy to be here. And I've got the kitchen up and running. Got them working on some full Irish breakfasts."

Vane turned to Curt, noticeably paler.

"Wait," he said, head cocked. "*You're* going to run the interview?"

"Actually, no," Curt answered. "I already have. Started the moment I picked each of you up."

"What?" Vane fumed. "That's shady, dude. I had no idea that's what was happening."

"That's the point, Charles," Curt replied calmly. "I find you can tell a lot about someone by how they treat people in service positions. No one ever notices the housekeeper. The gardener. The *driver*. You assumed I was *just* the driver. But all fine. I got what I needed." Curt turned to Gene. "We'll just need three of those breakfasts. Much appreciated."

"Three Irish, you got it, Curt," Gene answered, turning and heading back into the kitchen.

"Josh, Theresa, Charles, I thank you for expressing interest in the opening. We only have one availability, at least for now. So, I invite you to enjoy the breakfast here. It's really quite good. We'll keep your information on file and check in with you when something else becomes available. As an added thank you, there is a tab here under my name that you will be able to use through the end of the week. Try the Sticky Toffee Pudding. It's outstanding. I suggest you drop by for some music or trivia too. Gene runs a great place here."

Josh and Theresa were clearly caught flat-footed and quietly murmured their thanks, shook Curt's hand, and made their way to a table.

Vane, however, reacted very differently.

"Wait, you're going with *him*," Vane spat, jerking his head in Carlito's direction. The comment was loaded with unspoken prejudice of all kinds. "You just picked him up. You've barely spoken to him. This is a load of horseshit. You haven't even told us what the job is! And the email said we'd be driven here to our interview. Not that it would be you in the weird-ass van."

"Actually, the email said you would be picked up for your interview. It never specified when it would begin." Curt said, quietly. "I've seen all I need. And you've been told everything you need to know. I hope you enjoy the breakfast. I'll be in touch when the time is right."

"Yeah, you can stuff your crappy breakfast," Vane fumed. "I'm out of here. Bunch of freaks. I'll bill you for the uber back to my place."

Vane threw the door open and let it slam behind him as he stormed down the stairs and back to the street.

"I think this turned out exactly the way it was meant to," Curt said, gesturing for Carlito to head out the door.

Before Curt left, he turned to Josh and Theresa. "You both did great. I meant what I said about being in touch. Carlito here is just a slightly better fit for this position. I really appreciate your time. Sorry for any subterfuge. Just easier to get an accurate read on people this way. You both did very well. Enjoy your breakfasts."

Curt shouted a farewell to Gene before joining Carlito at the front door.

"Want to hear about this job?" he asked. "I don't want to presume anything. If you're still up for it, I have a lot to tell you."

"Sir, I've never been more curious about something as I am about this job," the young man replied. "You lead. I'll follow. I can't wait to hear more."

"That's what I was hoping you'd say. Let's go."

Roger pulled up in front of one of the large rental properties on the beach in South Nags Head. It was five stories tall and narrow. He shook his head as he climbed out of the cruiser. The beach road had been home to shacks and cottages when he had first started visiting. Now it was crammed full of these rental units that were closer to a hotel than a house.

He'd seen some that boasted up to nineteen bedrooms and even more bathrooms. Which made no sense to him. But such was the modern reality of the Outer Banks. You can't stop progress. Even if progress meant losing what had made something special in the first place.

He put his hat on his head, hitched up his pants, and started for what he thought was the front door. Hard to tell with these new places. It was the only door he could see on the ground floor, so it would have to do.

He knew that what he was about to tell the folks inside was going to ruin their vacation. Heck, it was going to change their lives. But that wasn't his fault. Whoever had killed that man in the wildlife refuge—the man they currently suspected was Mark Elliot—these people could have valuable information. And until proven otherwise, they were all possible suspects. His obligation was to the deceased, not to the vacationers inside.

But he hated this part of the job.

He gave a firm knock on the door. The kind of knock that said, "Official business, open up." He had perfected it over decades. He still wasn't comfortable using it. There were times for his folksy manner. This wasn't one of them.

The door was opened by an attractive woman in her forties. The northern forties, if Roger was any judge of these things. And he was. Her blond hair was pulled back and clipped. She wore a black sarong over a black bathing suit, and her skin was deeply tanned. "Oh," she exclaimed after a beat. "Can I help you?"

"I'm hoping so," Roger answered. "Roger Goldstein. Manteo Police Department. I'm looking for a Mark Elliot."

"Mark?" she asked, cocking her head ever so slightly. "Uh. Yeah, sure. His room is all the way up top. Can I ask what it's about?"

The woman looked at Roger with intelligent eyes, and he knew she would be no pushover, if things got hairy. Which they probably would.

"Just part of an ongoing investigation," Roger answered, offering his hand. "Can't say much more than that, right now. Mostly, we just want to check on his well-being."

"I see," she replied, not holding out her hand. "I'm Amelia Langley. An old friend of Mark's. Everyone here is an old friend. High school reunion. Do you have a warrant?"

"No," Roger admitted. "Do I need one? Just wanted to see if he's okay."

Amelia paused, sizing Roger up and making him feel more exposed than he was comfortable being. Maybe the folksy act would have been a better idea.

"I guess not," she said, finally. "We're just here on vacation. Nothing complicated about it. Come on in."

She stood aside and ushered Roger into a small vestibule with a collection of beach towels and flip-flops scattered about. A boogie board with a shark on it was leaning in one corner. Roger took it all in at a glance. Nothing unusual.

"Actually, can you give me a sec?" Amelia asked. "I should let the others know that you're here."

"Makes sense," Roger answered, glad for the chance to look around. He couldn't understand why so many of these new mini-mansions were so narrow and had basically nothing on the ground floor. He supposed it was to have a smaller footprint and maximize the views from higher up. Still, the former New Yorker in him shuddered at the waste of floor space.

Looking at the beach equivalent of a mud room, he found nothing suspicious. Turning the boogie board over—it was a wooden one, a good one—he noticed the initials "RLT" burned into it.

He heard the door at the top of the stairs open, and Amelia's voice called down. "Come on up! Thanks for waiting!"

Roger started up the stairs and noticed the heavy, high-quality carpet that covered them. Damn. He should have gotten into real estate. Or bought a place down here thirty years ago. Woulda shoulda.

He emerged at the top of the stairs to find a hallway with doors on either side and another stairway at the far end. Amelia's face was peering around the doorframe.

"Almost there," she said. "Up one more to the kitchen and living room."

Roger took the next flight of stairs and arrived on the floor slightly winded and wondering when the next physical test for the force would take place. He also finally understood why a lot of these new places had elevators. He wasn't *that* out of shape, but he'd seen some of the folks renting along the beach lately.

Roger emerged from the stairway into a massive open plan space. As he did, he noted that the music that had been playing turned off. Squeeze. "Tempted." Great song.

The kitchen was enormous. Two ovens, two microwaves. Marble countertops. Stainless-steel appliances that all gleamed in the morning sun that streamed through the floor-to-ceiling windows. And the ceiling was a good twenty feet above.

The clearly expensive tiled floor of the kitchen gave way to laminate floors throughout the rest of the space. Quality, but easy to clean and not a worry if it gathered sand during the week's visit.

The living room area boasted an enormous flat-screen TV on the wall. That was a sixty-incher minimum, Roger noted. The space was ringed by a plush multi-piece sectional sofa. Some seats reclined. Some seemed to have storage below. All looked comfortable enough to sleep on.

And on that opulent couch sat five individuals, all staring at him with curiosity and distrust. Hard to blame them. The cops crashing your high school reunion beach trip must be a serious buzzkill.

The smell of coffee and bacon filled the room. Roger heard his stomach rumble, and he realized he hadn't eaten this morning. If any of the others noticed his gurgling, they were too polite to make note. There was certainly no offer of breakfast.

Surprisingly, Roger found his mind recalling that the technical term for a rumbling stomach was "borborygmus." His brain did some very strange things.

The silence in the room was unnerving. There were times silence could be used to advantage, but even Roger felt the weight of this. Down to business.

He cleared his throat. "I apologize for disturbing you folks. We're just trying to locate a Mark Elliot. He's not in any trouble. Just want to lay eyes on him and maybe ask a question or two."

One of the men sat forward in his seat and folded his hands in front of him. He, like all the others, was in his forties. His sandy hair swept back off his forehead and gave him a younger look than some of the others. His eyes were keen, and he was confident. His very expensive watch almost called out to Roger from his left wrist. "Hi, *Deputy*." There was just enough emphasis on the word to raise Roger's hackles, but the man immediately de-escalated. Point made. "Francis Silver. I can assure you that Mark's upstairs asleep. And if there *is* any problem, I'm his attorney of record."

Amelia pushed off from the kitchen counter where she had been leaning. "I'm sure there's no need for anything like that. Can someone go wake him up? So we can get this all settled?"

"I'll go," one of the women said, standing. "I'm Cathy Policella."

She spoke quietly, but firmly, and walked to a door on the other side of the room that opened to another stairway. She was elegant, controlled. Observant.

Cathy paused at the door and turned back to Roger. "He's up in what we dubbed the crow's nest. All the way up top. Probably why he could sleep through all of us clattering around the kitchen. I'll be right back."

Roger nodded and took in the others. He had to admit, they didn't look like the kind of people who would be mixed up in anything untoward. To his very practiced eye, they looked to be exactly what they were supposed to be: a group of middle-aged friends on a week-long beach trip to the Outer Banks.

As they waited for Cathy to return, the others rose to introduce themselves.

First came an olive-skinned man with shoulder length dark hair, pulled back into an impressive man-bun. He wore thick glasses and the universal outfit of Banks vacationers—cargo shorts, a t-shirt for a Tex-Mex place called Joe T. Garcia's, and sneakers. No socks. He loped over, a grin on his face. "Jaime Aldredge," he said offering his hand, seemingly to the disapproval of Francis Silver, who huffed and sat back on the sofa. "Just another of the high school gang. Can I get you anything? Coffee? Breakfast burrito?"

"Coffee would be great, thanks," Roger answered, taking Jaime's hand. "Much appreciated."

As Jaime moved into the kitchen area, the last woman rose and walked cautiously to Roger.

"Hi," she said simply. "Terry Bracken. You have kind eyes. Anyone ever tell you that? Huh." She paused and stepped back. She was the shortest of the group. Light brown hair bobbed short. Roger noticed a crystal on a chain around her neck. Her fingers sought it out and rubbed it lightly as she considered Roger further. "But I wouldn't want to get on your bad side." Another pause. "Sorry. Sometimes I talk too much when I get nervous. I'll just go help Jaime."

The last of the group approached Roger. Dark hair, with a shock of white hair that had been swept back off of his brow. He had startlingly blue eyes, slightly guarded behind rimless glasses.

He smiled, but the smile didn't quite reach his eyes. "Christopher Deisler. Chris is fine. Thanks for checking up on our buddy. Hopefully, this is a misunderstanding, and we can all get back to our days in a sec. Been coming here all my life. Never seen the slightest problem. At least, nothing beyond kids being kids. And that was a long time ago for any of us."

While Chris perched on one of the stools that ringed the breakfast counter, Roger took in the group as a whole. They were bright, alert. They seemed pleasant enough. Which meant, if something else was going on here, it would be even harder to get to the bottom of it. With friends that went back as long as these did, there were bound to be undercurrents to discover. Histories going back decades. And a tendency to circle the wagons to protect their own. Or settle old scores. God, he hoped they weren't involved. It all sounded so… complicated.

The door to the upstairs opened and Cathy came quickly into the living room.

"Guys," she said. "Mark's not upstairs. And his bed hasn't been slept in."

Looks were shared around the room. In the kitchen, Jaime spilled coffee on the counter and swore quietly.

Carlito climbed into the VW Buzz and settled in while Curt started the van and pulled out of the parking lot in Manteo. He turned left and headed back over the Washington Baum Bridge toward Nags Head and where the morning had begun before Carlito had joined the process.

"If you don't mind," Curt explained, "I'm taking you back over to Kill Devil. Probably best to put a little distance between us and Charles. No need to fan the flames. I have a nice quiet place for us to talk."

"I'm literally along for the ride," Carlito replied. "Just give me a place to sit and a job description. I'm good."

Curt glanced over to the young man. "I knew I was making the right choice with you. Why don't you tell me a little about yourself while we're on the way. More than just the details from the online application."

"Yeah, sure," Carlito said. "Not a whole lot to the story. My family is like a lot of others. Been coming here as long as I can remember. I fell in love with the area, and I graduated from school last year. Spent a few months at home with mom, helping her get used to me being a grown up for real. Then wanted to just take some time for myself. Not a gap year. Just a gap. No real question I would do it here."

"Where'd you go to school?" Curt asked.

"Oklahoma," Carlito said, with a small shake of his head. "Dad was a big Texas guy, so of course I had to rebel and become a Sooner. I don't regret it, but I do think I'd do it differently if I had it to do over."

"Your mom? Where is she?"

"She's back in Texas. I spent a lot of time in Virginia. Dad worked in politics, but we eventually headed back to the rest of the family in Texas."

"You mentioned going home to your mom," Curt said, quietly. "Where's your dad?"

"Good question," Carlito answered. He shifted in his seat and looked out the window, watching the morning sun glistening on the water of the sound as they crossed the bridge. "He went to Mexico with a friend of his. They were always doing things like that. Off on a road trip with no real planning. They ended up in a town called Zacatecas. This was a while back. Cell service wasn't great back then. Especially in the mountains. They just...disappeared. My mom tried everything to find him, but nothing worked. I know I'll go down myself and try at some point. But it's been so long. I think he's just gone. Last we heard, he was getting on a bus to Mazatlán. It's a long, dangerous drive. The bus got there. But no Dad. And no sign of his friend, either."

"I'm sorry about that," Curt replied after a pause. "Let's talk more about that later. Maybe I can help."

"Sure," Carlito said. "Although a lot of people have tried. A *lot*." He put his hand on the window, still cool in the morning air. "I wasn't going to mention that, but you asked."

"I did," Curt agreed. "Thanks for trusting me."

The van turned right and jogged over to the beach road when they had crossed into South Nags Head. Traffic was light. In another month, it would be bumper to bumper as the tourists arrived. Like most vacation destinations, the Outer Banks had an uneasy relationship with the visitors who kept their economy humming. Hours-long waits at restaurants, standstill traffic, and higher prices arrived with the vacationers, and the locals bemoaned all of those things while padding their checking accounts to get through the slow winter months.

But today, all was quiet, and within fifteen minutes, Curt turned left into the parking lot of Swells'a Brewing. He parked in front of the main door and the strangely silent motor stopped. He missed the growl of the Chevelle.

"They aren't open yet, but I know some people," Curt said, flashing a grin at the young man. "It's early for a beer, but they have some good seltzers, and a great space upstairs where we can talk undisturbed. You okay with this? Well, crap. I didn't even ask if you're old enough to drink."

Carlito couldn't hold back a laugh. "Yeah, I'm twenty-two. We're good. But I think I'll just go for one of those seltzers if that's good?"

"Of course," Curt assured him, climbing out. "I'll be doing the same."

When they reached the front door, Curt fished a sizeable set of keys out of his pocket and let them in.

"Sage!" Curt called, though no one was visible in the taproom. "It's Curt, just so you know.

A young woman, early thirties, popped up from behind the bar, brushing strands of curly light brown hair out of her eyes.

"Curt," she said, staring plainly at Carlito. "Just finishing up some inventory. What can I grab you?"

"Couple of seltzers will do us fine," Curt answered, leaning on the counter.

The woman rose and reached into the coolers behind her and emerged with two bottles in hand.

"Hope lime is okay," she said, setting the bottles on the bar. "We're due a delivery later today."

Her tightly curled hair fell around her face, and she kept shooing it away. Her eyes were keen and rarely left Carlito as he stood uncomfortably under her obvious gaze. She wore a blue-and-white patterned shirt, loose at the neck, and a pair of comfortably worn yet stylish jeans. She kept reaching under the bar with her left hand until a wet nose shoved her hand aside and an auburn-furred dog set her paws atop the bar and fixed Curt and Carlito with a stare from ice-blue eyes.

"You're early," Sage said, turning to look at Curt.

"I am," Curt agreed. "Things were pretty clear once we were all in the same place. Upstairs open for us?"

Finally, Sage smiled.

"That's cool," she said. I'm glad to hear that. Right, Riley?"

She fluffed the dog's ears, and both she and the dog seemed to relax. Sage leaned across the bar top and offered a hand to Carlito.

"Sorry," she said, with a shake of her head. "Bad manners. I'm Sage. This is Riley. If you see me, she's usually not far away. Welcome."

Carlito looked from Sage, to the dog, to Curt, clearly confused.

"Uh, thanks," he finally blurted. "I really don't know what's happening, but I appreciate it?"

"Let's head upstairs," Curt said, gently leading Carlito toward a set of wide wooden steps to their left. "You'll get it soon. You know, it might be warm enough to sit out on the deck. I think it's going to be a good day."

"Me too," Sage answered, heading back to her inventory, while Riley kept those piercing eyes fixed on the two men as they ascended.

Curt led the way out into a bright, airy space looking out over the bar below but motioned for Carlito to head out the double doors to a deck that looked out over the street below to the houses and doors across the way.

Curt emerged and settled into one of the barstools lining the area. The morning had turned from the misty damp of earlier to a bright, rapidly warming spring day. The sound of the surf, just over the dunes and out of sight, seemed to soothe both of them. The pleasant sting of salt air settled onto their skin as a scoop of pelicans glided overhead on their way to the water.

Carlito watched the birds sail overhead before turning back to Curt and noticing that he had placed a folder on the ledge in front of them.

"I hate to ask this," Curt said, pulling some pages out of the folder. "It will make sense in a few minutes. Would you mind signing this non-disclosure agreement?" He slid the papers toward Carlito along with an elegant silver pen. "Boilerplate stuff. Straightforward. Honestly, it's as much for your protection as ours."

Carlito sat back in his stool, considering the paperwork in front of him.

"That's a bit of a surprise," the young man said, finally. Reaching a decision, he took the pen and signed. Curt turned the page and pointed to a few more places needing initials. "But now I'm *really* curious. Gotta find out what I'm about to get into."

"Thanks," Curt said, taking the papers and replacing them in the folder. He opened his seltzer and hoisted it in a toast to Carlito, who did the same.

"Now the good part," Curt said, sipping his drink. He turned in his stool and looked straight at Carlito. "Have you ever heard of the Brethren of the Coast?"

CHAPTER 4

Roger Goldstein settled the vacationers and asked them to take a seat. Reluctantly, they shuffled to the sofas, whispering amongst each other.

"I'm going to need you to tell me *exactly* what happened last night," Roger said in a tone that left no room for debate. "Leave nothing out. No matter how small, or embarrassing, or seemingly pointless. I need it all."

The assembled group burst into talk all together before Roger gestured sharply for them to be quiet.

"I know this is a shock," Roger said, hands up to try to calm everyone. "Just because we found your friend's information with the deceased, doesn't mean it's him, although the odds are not in his favor. We'll need someone to come identify the body."

"I'll do it," Chris said. "I'm a vet. I'm used to dealing with things like this."

"But it can't be him," Cathy said loudly. "Not Mark. He was *just with us.*"

"Then where is he?" Terry exclaimed, slapping a pillow next to her on the sofa. "Why isn't he upstairs?"

"This is a nightmare," Francis muttered from one end of the couch.

Once again, they all burst out. Talking. Denying. Crying. Shaking.

"One at a time," Roger declared, loudly. Randomly, he turned to Jaime. "You first."

"Sure," Jaime said quietly. "But...uh...my burritos are about to burn. Can I turn off the oven?"

"Yes. Go," Roger said with a roll of his eyes. "I'll come back to you. Amelia, you're up."

Amelia stood and began pacing. She fiddled with a ring on her left hand, spinning it idly while she considered what to say.

"We all went out for some mid-afternoon cocktails," she began. "Everything closes early here now, and we're not used to that, so we opted for an early start. We headed to Bad Bean. Some appetizers and such."

"Good choice," Roger said. "Not the normal tourist type of spot."

"Not our first time here," Amelia shot back. "We know our way around. But, anyway, we were only there for a while. Our sunset kayak trip was six until eight, so we hit the road by just after five. Mark, though, decided to skip the kayaks. Said he was still tired from the trip the day before."

"And he came here from?" Roger asked.

"New York," Amelia answered. "It is a long drive. His was the longest trip."

"Except for mine!" Jaime called from the kitchen.

"And you came from where?" Roger asked, turning toward the kitchen.

"The great state of Texas," Jaime answered, grinning from the open oven where he was wrestling a tray of burritos onto the counter.

"You flew up, and I picked you up at the airport," Chris cut in. "Technically your trip covered more miles, but Mark's lasted longer."

"Touché," Jaime said over his shoulder, setting burritos on a platter.

"Okay, back to last night," Roger said, pointing to Amelia with his pen.

"Right. I thought it was strange that Mark bailed. That type of thing is usually right up his alley. He loves nature. Photography."

"And he lives in New York? Interesting," Roger said, making a note.

"He travels for work," Amelia replied. "A lot. He's a theatre critic. Covers shows all over the world."

"That does make sense," Roger agreed. "So, he stayed? I assume he had his own car with him?"

"Yeah, we took three cars for exactly that reason, so no one would get stuck," Amelia said. "It's in the driveway. Was there when we got back. That's why none of us gave it a second thought."

Cathy rose and crossed to the front of the house, looking out a window.

"It's still there," she announced to the room. "The blue one, right?"

"Yeah," Francis said, standing and crossing to her. "A Forester. Yup, right where it was when we got back."

"He had been talking to that other guy at the bar," Terry said. "Remember? Did anyone catch his name?"

"Nope," Amelia said, trying to regain control of the conversation. "I guess they met way back in the day on one of his beach trips. I didn't recognize him."

"He did seem distracted after that," Chris added. "I didn't catch the connection, but I did see them talking again when we were leaving."

"We'll talk to the folks at the restaurant," Roger said. "Maybe they can point us in the right direction."

"You know, now that we're talking about it," Terry said, "we had a system. All the car keys were to be left on the counter so no one could get blocked in the driveway. Are his keys there?" She pointed to a table at the top of the stairs.

Cathy walked over to sort through the various keychains assembled there.

"I see yours, Amelia," she called over, holding a set of keys on a NASA rocket chain up. "And yours, Chris. Here's Terry's set. Mine. No, actually. Mark's aren't here."

"This keeps getting worse," Jaime said, now leaning on the breakfast bar in the kitchen.

"I just want to make sure I have this all straight," Roger declared. "You last saw him just after five yesterday as you all left for the kayak outing in Alligator River. Mr. Elliot stayed behind and was talking to someone he had met on an earlier beach trip, but not someone any of you recognized?"

The group responded with bobbing heads and agreement.

"When you arrived here last night, you saw Mr. Elliot's car in the driveway and, seeing his bedroom light off, you assumed he had already gone to sleep?"

"That's right," Amelia said. "We stopped at Fish Heads on the way back for something more substantial to eat. The place on the pier?"

"I know it well," Roger replied. "You folks really do know your way around the Banks."

"Well, by the time we got back it was pretty late," Amelia pointed out. "If Mark really was tired, it made sense to us that he would have turned in early."

"I see," Roger said, nodding. "I'm going to take a quick look at his room upstairs. If he was that tired, maybe he forgot to put his keys on that table. Maybe. None of you move. I'll be right back."

Roger headed up the stairway to the crow's nest. As the door closed behind him, he heard the hushed murmur of voices start up in the living room. Hushed, but urgent. And panicked. Which could be perfectly normal under the circumstances. Or it could be something else.

He quickly took the stairs and opened a door at the top, stopping to appreciate a glorious view out over the dunes, the beach, the ocean, and to the horizon.

"I should have been a theatre critic," he said quietly to himself before taking in the rest of the room.

A canvas duffel bag sat on a chair by the bed, unzipped, with a cascade of t-shirts tumbling out of it. All colors. Most with logos from local beach businesses. Some of which had been gone for years. This guy really had taken to the Outer Banks.

The bed was untouched. Mark Elliot hadn't slept here last night unless he got up extremely early and made his bed. And left his car in the driveway. There were no discarded personal effects anywhere, The bedside table lay empty, except for some postcards. Roger turned them over. Blank. Must have bought them to mail. Who sent postcards these days?

Roger opened the closet and it, too, was bare.

No phone. No keys. No wallet. Nothing.

He descended the stair and paused again by the door at the bottom. The voices on the other side continued. The only things he heard clearly amongst the murmurs was the word "No!" clearly cutting through. He thought it was Amelia.

He opened the door and instantly silence fell.

All faces turned expectantly toward him. The expressions ran the gamut. No one knew if they should hope that the keys were there or not.

"No keys," Roger said, bluntly. "Not much of anything, really."

"Well, that's not good," Cathy whispered to no one in particular.

"Who drove his car here, if he didn't?" Chris asked.

"That, sir, is the question of the moment, isn't it?" Roger replied, eyeing each of the group in turn.

No one moved, and for just the barest moment, Roger's cop instinct picked up on the slightest fracture in the group's unified front. Someone knew something they weren't sharing. He'd dig it out of them. He always did.

"Chris, since you volunteered, I'll need you to come identify the body later. I'll leave you all my number. And you *will* give me yours. I hope it goes without saying that none of you should leave town."

"Are we suspects?" Terry asked, her voice jumping an octave.

"Too early to say," Roger said. "Let's find out who our victim is, first. But I will say, you should be prepared for the worst."

"No," Amelia declared. "Mark would never let anything like this happen to him. Ever."

"Let's hope you're right," Roger said, putting his hat back on. "But someone's dead. And we'll get to the bottom of it."

"Thank you, Deputy," Francis stepped forward and offered his hand, trying to make amends for his prickly start to the encounter.

"Mhm," Roger replied, taking the proffered hand briefly. "I'll be checking out your stories. I'll let you know when I have more questions."

Down in the driveway, he walked past Mark Elliot's Forester. Cupping his hands on the driver's window he checked the ignition. No keys. Whoever had driven the car to the house had taken the keys with them, unless he had missed something in the house. And he didn't miss much.

As he climbed into his cruiser, he looked up to see the entire group watching from the front window. All but one. He paused to look more closely. He was right. Jaime was missing. And just as he realized that he saw a shadow passing up the stairs to the crow's nest.

Carlito looked blankly back at Curt. "Brethren of the Coast?" he finally asked. "Nope. No clue."

"Good," Curt replied. "I'd be a little worried if you had. Secret societies are usually secret."

"Okaaay," Carlito said. Leaning back in his stool and crossing his arms over his chest. "Is this some pyramid scheme or something? I hope we haven't gone through all this just to sell subscriptions to a website or something. 'Cuz if that's it, I'm not interested."

Curt chuckled. "Far from it, I'm happy to say. The Brethren of the Coast is a centuries-old group. Dedicated to keeping watch over specific regions. The whole thing started in the sixteenth and seventeenth centuries when pirates were in their heyday. Most of them came from decent backgrounds and were privateers, meaning they had been hired by governments to harass their enemies in times of war. They had a stamp of legitimacy, but the more attention they attracted, the more their ranks swelled with...let's say, less scrupulous types. They formed a syndicate. Their own system to police themselves and hold their captains and ships to a set of standards."

"Pirates? Syndicate?" Carlito asked, pushing his stool back from the counter. "Look, I'm a brown-skinned kid from Texas. I've got no family or friends here. I want nothing to do with crossing the law. That won't turn out good for me. I'm gonna have to say no. But don't worry, I won't say a word. Let's just act as if this never happened."

"No, no, no," Curt said, quickly, and raising his hands, "you've got it backwards. We're the good guys. Look, the pirates—buccaneers—whatever you want to call them, tried to stay on the right side of things. Their code wasn't designed to make them better people, though. It was designed to keep the ships running smoothly. Nothing more. Eventually their ranks filled with adventurers, treasure hunters. All kinds of nationalities. Freed slaves. Lots of outlaws. Basically, the Wild West on water. Any code they had created for themselves became impossible to administer. The wars that had given them legitimacy were resolved, and with no seal of approval from any of the governments that had supported them...let's just say the baser elements won out and the Brethren slid into pure no-holds-barred piracy. They entered the Golden Age of Piracy, which is what most people think of when they think of pirates."

"Yeah," Carlito said, settling back onto his stool. "Interesting history lesson. What's it got to do with why I'm here?"

"Direct," Curt replied, nodding. "I like it. The original Brethren—

the ones who tried to hold onto something bigger—operated all over. Caribbean, Gulf of Mexico, Atlantic. Some even further, but that's where they were most influential. When their code fell out of favor, some of them saw the chance to make something better and went underground. They held to their code. Expanded it. Made it better. And created chapters to safeguard their homes. Their families. What they believed in. In a funny way, they were the polar opposites of what the pirates became. And while piracy had a relatively short moment in the sun, the secret Brethren kept on. The Outer Banks were always a magnet for thrill seekers and less-than-honest types. That made the Brethren chapter here one of the most active. And important. And it's still active today."

Carlito shook his head, laughing. "What you're trying to tell me is that there is a secret society here that—what?—fights bad guys and protects the weak? So, wannabe superheroes or something?"

Now it was Curt's turn to laugh. "Oh, God, no," he said. "Far from it. We're just some folks who want to do what is right and look out for a place and people we care about. Nothing special about us."

"Isn't that what the police are for?" Carlito asked. "It's not like we're still in the eighteenth century. Things have evolved a bit since then."

"True," Curt admitted, standing and looking out over the dunes. "But the police have certain...limitations. We don't. And we have a heritage to uphold. A tradition. Not every wrongdoing rises to the level of the police. Something can be legal, but still *wrong*."

"And we're back to breaking the law," Carlito replied. "Not interested, Mr. Stephens. I can't get involved with stuff like that."

"I promise you," Curt said, "we never break the law. And the police know about us. Mostly. You won't have to worry about that."

"Why me?" Carlito said, turning to Curt. "I'm practically still a kid. And it's not like I grew up here. I don't fit into what you described. I have nothing to offer any secret crime fighting club."

"I think you do," Curt replied. "I think you have all of the qualities we look for. And to be brutally honest, our numbers are the lowest they've ever been. We need to get younger. For the Brethren to survive. And for the Brethren to adapt to changes in the world. In case you haven't noticed, I'm no spring chicken. And before you get any smart ideas, I can still very much take care of myself when I have to. But I'm charged with looking after the long-term health of the Brethren. And more importantly, to ensure the Banks are protected."

"What does that mean?" Carlito asked. "How low are the numbers?"

"Right now, there are four of us," Curt answered. "No way to sugarcoat it. We need reinforcements. That's where you come in. Hopefully."

"Is this a job?" Carlito questioned. "What are we talking about here? Do I get paid? And what exactly will I be asked to do?"

"Good questions," Curt admitted. "It's not a job in the usual sense of the word. So, it's more of a stipend. It's not a lot. We all still work jobs. But there are...perks. And you won't worry for money. As for what you'll be asked to do, well, there's no way to answer that. One week it may be shutting down a ring of shoplifters. Then a month later it could be making sure Tugboat Joe over in Colington has enough food for the week and a ride to the doctor. We take it as it comes."

Carlito sat staring over the dunes, while Curt stood beside him doing the same. A police cruiser rolled slowly past on the beach road below them. Curt gave a barely noticeable nod of his head, and the car flashed its lights before passing the Ramada across the street and continuing north. Carlito made note of the exchange.

"I'm going to have to think about it," the young man finally said. "It's a lot."

"Totally understandable," Curt agreed. "Take all the time you need. Only thing is I need your answer before you leave. That's not to rush you, mind, just because we have to come up with another idea if you choose not to sign up."

"I'm assuming that wouldn't be Charles Vane?" Carlito asked with a small laugh.

"Um. No," Curt said. "Although, despite his less than magnetic personality, he does have some interesting qualities. But you're right. It's a big decision. It's a beautiful morning. Sit here. Let me know what you decide."

Curt moved back into the building and held the door for Riley who was padding out onto the deck to soak up some sun. She plopped down next to Carlito and fixed him with her ice-blue eyes as Curt let the door shut and headed downstairs.

He reached the bar area and Sage was by the front door hanging some of the brewery's new merchandise. She turned to Curt.

"And?" she asked.

Curt shrugged. "Could go either way. He's good. Exactly what I was hoping for. But it's a big ask. Can't blame him if he says no."

Sage nodded and crossed to the side door on the far side of the bar, opening it and letting in a massive white Great Pyrenees who crossed to Curt and, huffing, fell to the floor at his feet, displaying his belly and demanding a rub.

"Banks, you are shameless," Curt said, dropping to a knee and obliging the dog.

"Seltzer?" Sage asked as she crossed behind the bar.

"Yeah," Curt answered. "Please. But if this drags on too long, I'll probably need something stronger."

Sage nodded as she slid a bottle of seltzer down the bar.

"There wasn't an option number two?" she asked.

"Not one I was comfortable with," Curt admitted, staring down into the display case at the far end of the bar. Inside the case some sort of Frankensteined animal had been stuffed, cobbled together and posed. "What the hell *is* that thing anyway? Fox? Coyote?"

"I have no clue," Sage admitted with a laugh. "People love it, though."

"Yeah, well, people are weird."

"No argument there."

Time crept slowly by as the two busied themselves while wait-ing. Sage cleaned the floor behind the bar for the third time. Curt was on his phone, answering email and trying to distract himself. At some point, Riley silently slipped down the stairs and joined Banks in the middle of the floor.

Curt and Sage both looked expectantly at the stairs, but after a moment, it became clear Carlito was not following.

By ten thirty, Curt couldn't contain himself anymore.

"Okay, enough of this, "he said. "Can I get a Pea Island?"

"Pilsner? You got it," Sage answered, moving to the taps.

"Maybe I got this wrong," Curt said, rubbing his face, and tapping his feet on the bottom rung of his stool. "I felt so sure about him."

"You didn't get it wrong," came a voice from the stairs, "but you'd be disappointed if I didn't take it seriously."

Curt and Sage both turned to the stairs where Carlito stood. Both of the dogs jumped up and ambled over to him. Banks rubbed against his legs like a hundred-pound cat.

Curt leaped to his feet. Sage turned back to the beer taps, giving the two some space.

"Does this mean you're a yes?" Curt asked, holding the back of his barstool, his knuckles white.

Carlito nodded and Curt whooped.

"Forget that Pilsner," Curt called to Sage. "Can I get a Jimmy B? We have something to celebrate."

Carlito crossed to the bar and Curt opened his arms wide and gave the slightly embarrassed young man a huge bear hug.

Carlito laughed as he backed up a step.

"So, when do I meet the others?" he asked. "And do I get a secret handshake, or a pin, or something?"

Curt laughed, relief plain in his voice and on his face.

"No pin, no handshake," Curt said. "We'll call a Brethren Council tonight, if you're available. But you've already met one of your new Brethren."

Sage turned from the taps, placed two glasses of IPA on the bar and gave Carlito a little wave while she raised her eyebrows.

"Welcome aboard," she said with a smile.

Five minutes later, Roger Goldstein sat in his idling cruiser in the parking lot of the Two Roads Tavern. His phone pinged and he glanced at the screen, swiping it on and carefully reading the text.

He let out a victory cry and pounded his hands on the steering wheel.

"Yessir!" he shouted. "We are back in business!"

He turned the wheel and started to head out onto the bypass with the thought of joining Curt and the others at the brewery when his radio squawked to life.

A young woman in Manteo had been found unresponsive and was being treated for a suspected fentanyl overdose. She was in an ambulance on her way to the hospital. At the same time, there was a report of suspicious boat activity in the Roanoke Sound Channel between the Bodie Island Lighthouse and Wanchese.

Roger sat back in his seat and exhaled loudly.

"Dammit," he said aloud. "Good thing the kid said yes."

He fired off a quick text to let Curt know of his change in plans, then turned south on the bypass, flipped his lights on, and sped away.

Amelia Langley stood in the deck staring at the beach behind the rental house. She chewed her nails absently, before stopping herself suddenly. She had stopped doing that in college. Of course, she didn't often have friends disappear and turn up dead, so she cut herself some slack.

She continued staring at the surf. A fin broke the surface and dove again. And another. A pod of dolphins. She didn't remember seeing them as often when they'd come years ago. She wanted to take their appearance as a good omen. Wanted to but couldn't quite.

The sliding glass door behind her swished open and she heard someone step onto the deck behind her.

"Mind some company?"

Turning, Amelia gave Cathy a smile. Briefly.

"Of course not," she replied. "Just hoping the sea air will settle me. This whole thing is just unbelievable."

"I know," Cathy said, joining the other woman at the railing. "It doesn't seem real. My brain won't accept it. This has always been our happy place. Mark's, especially. The number of times he talked about retiring here. And now this?"

"Right?" Amelia agreed. "It doesn't seem possible that he'd be with us and then just a few short hours later, he's gone. And how did he end up right where we kayaked? And how did his car end up in the driveway? None of it makes sense."

"Um. Did you happen to see Jaime heading upstairs when the police left?" Cathy asked. "What was that about?"

"Haven't had a chance to ask him yet, but yeah. I saw. They had been up there yesterday afternoon for a while. Just catching up, I assume. But something is up."

"You don't think he had anything to do with it, do you? Jaime?" Cathy mused, turning to watch Amelia's reaction.

It wasn't the immediate rejection she's expected. Instead, Amelia remained still, scanning the sea in front of them. The pause grew uncomfortably long, and Cathy finally fidgeted.

"Do you?" she repeated.

Amelia sighed. "No. I don't. How could he? We were all together. Leaving the restaurant. In the kayaks. At Fish Heads. There's no way. But they do have a history."

"That was a long time ago," Cathy said, tutting. "One bad review of a college production over twenty years ago. No one's even mentioned it in ages."

"True," Amelia agreed. "But no one in our group has been murdered before, either. And Jaime never wrote another play after that. Ever. But no. Jaime would never. None of us would. This has to be some kind of mistake. Something random. The world isn't what it used to be. Even down here."

"I wonder," Cathy said quietly.

"You wonder what?" Amelia finally turned from the railing.

"Mark changed after he recognized that guy at the bar. I know you noticed. I could see you clock it. And then deciding to stay behind? The kayaks were his idea! He's been trying to convince us all to go to Alligator River for years. And then he bows out on the night it finally happens? No. Something doesn't make sense."

"I did see that," Amelia answered. "I guess I just thought he was trying to remember how he knew him. But now—"

"Yeah, now it seems different," Cathy said.

"Everything seems different," Amelia replied. "It's *Mark*. How can he be gone? Like this? I just. I can't."

From inside the house, they heard a doorbell ring and then a commotion from the others. The two women looked at each other.

"The cops can't be back already, can they?" Amelia asked.

"I wouldn't think so," Cathy answered. "I don't know for sure, but I would think they need some time. For...stuff."

The sliding door opened again, and Francis stuck his head halfway out.

"Kirsten is here," he announced.

"Kirsten," Cathy said, blankly. "Oh, damn. Right. I totally forgot. She gets here today."

"Oh, man," Amelia muttered as she brushed past Francis into the living room.

A woman stood at the top of the stairs, a backpack over one shoulder and a rolling bag rocking slightly back and forth behind her. She was tall, slender, assured. She wore long shorts and a Huntley Meadows Farm t-shirt with a horse galloping across it. She pulled a pair of sunglasses off and looked around the assembled group. Everyone stared silently back at her.

"Hi, gang," she said. "Sorry to get here late, but you're kinda freakin' me out. What did I miss?"

CHAPTER 5

Roger pulled his car into the parking lot of the Wanchese Marina, killed the lights and then the engine. Climbing out, he tossed his hat onto the seat and locked up. No sense having to hold it on his head if they were heading out on the water.

What he really wanted to do was head into The Landing, get some shrimp tacos, and stare at the water, but that wasn't in the cards.

He threw a wave at whoever was working the register inside as he walked down the side of the building to the docks behind.

Ha paused when he reached the water and scanned to his left. He knew who he was looking for, and it didn't take him long to spot the familiar figure, leaning against the center console of a twenty-foot Robalo Explorer, a nimble boat well-suited to cruising the sound waters. A wide-brimmed Shelta Seahawk hat was angled down, but as Roger approached a deeply tanned hand reached up and lifted it back. Grier Roleth fixed Roger with a firm stare and tapped his chunky Timex Ironman dive watch. He was small, barely five and a half feet tall, but sinewy and agile. He'd clearly spent a lot of time outdoors, and judging by the way he maneuvered around the small boat, a lot of it had been on the water. Every move was calculated and direct.

As he prepared to push off, he shouted over his shoulder, "Took your time, mister man! Let's hope the bad guys have waited for us!"

"I was all the way up at Two Roads when the call came in," Roger explained, climbing aboard and stowing the bumpers.

"Bit early, isn't it?" Grier cracked. "Even for you."

"Yeah, yeah," Roger grumbled. "Tough morning already. Was up in Nags Head interviewing the friends of the fella we found in Alligator River this morning. Not my favorite."

"Yeah," Grier said. "Heard about that on the radio earlier. Sorry to hear it. Summer has officially arrived, I guess."

"It can go back where it came from, if it's gonna be like this," Roger replied. "Right. What are we headed toward?"

"Not really sure," Grier answered. "Couple of the charters reported a small boat on the back side of Bodie acting suspiciously. Looking for something, it seemed. Kept avoiding anyone who came close."

"Squirrelly," Roger agreed, shoving off from the dock. "Let's go say hi. Another fentanyl case this morning. I'm not in the mood to play nice."

"I get that," Grier said. "Chose the Robalo. The airboat is too loud. Hopefully these guys aren't in a skiff. I pull eighteen inches draft in this, but if they head into the reeds, they could lose us. Maybe. But we would outrun them a hundred out of a hundred times on the water."

"I trust you," Roger said, settling in behind the center console, where Grier had taken the wheel.

"What happened with the kid? Any word from Curt?" Grier asked, guiding them out of the marina and into the sound.

"He's in," Roger said. "Haven't met him, yet. Curt's high on him. Council tonight at eight. Blue Crab."

"Signs of life in the Brethren, yet," Grier called over the engine as he hit the throttle and opened up. "Not dead yet. First good news I've heard today. Let's keep things going. If whoever is out there is shady, I'm in the mood to take them down."

"You and me both," Roger agreed.

Kirsten Carlton sat on the largest of the sectional pieces in the living room, her luggage forgotten where she dropped it as the others had told her about what had happened. She sat forward, her head in her hands, staring at the floor between her knees.

"This makes no sense," she said quietly. "I spoke to him last night. After you had all left for the boat trip. He was fine."

"Wait," Chris said, interrupting. "You talked to him after we left? That means you were the last one of us to talk to him. What did he say?"

"Not much," Kirsten admitted. "He was waiting for someone he'd run into. Someone he'd met here a long time ago. Just sounded like they were going to catch up. Nothing more."

"Did he say where they were meeting?" Terry asked. "Doesn't really make sense that they were going someplace else. We were all at Bad Bean when he saw the guy."

"He said something about it getting loud, so they were going someplace they could talk. I didn't think anything of it. He seemed fine. I was a little distracted. Getting packed," Kirsten said, shaking her head. "How could I have known? I would have paid more attention. I should have."

"You couldn't have," Amelia said. "But I do think we should call the deputy and let him know about this. There's a room on the left one floor down. Why don't you settle in. We'll make the call."

As Kirsten gathered her bags and headed downstairs, Amelia walked to the counter, placed Roger Goldstein's card in front of her and dialed. After a brief pause, she spoke quietly into the phone before setting it down.

"No answer," she said. "Left a message. I guess we wait."

Chris rose and grabbed a set of keys from the table by the staircase.

"I'm going for a walk," he announced. "Need to clear my head. Get some air."

"Company?" Francis asked, and when he sensed Chris hesitate, he waved his hands. "Never mind. Go clear your head."

"No, actually, company would be good," Chris said quickly. "Probably best none of us go too far by ourselves until we figure out what's going on."

"Good point," Francis said.

As the two made their way downstairs and out onto the beach out back, Kirsten could be heard unpacking. Terry had joined her, and the low murmur of their voices was indistinct.

Amelia and Cathy found themselves back out on the deck. Amelia placed her cell phone on the table between their two chairs as they watched Chris and Francis emerge from under the house and head north on the sand.

"Don't usually see those two together," Cathy said, watching the men.

"They made up a long time ago," Amelia said.

"True," Cathy agreed. "But I never got the sense it was completely forgotten. They never seemed the same after. It was over a girl, yeah?"

"It usually is. Well, maybe something like this is the wake-up call we all need to let the past be the past," Amelia said.

Cathy turned to look at Amelia, but the other woman was scanning the waves. After a moment, she turned to the sea also.

"You're probably right," she replied. "Long overdue."

"Probably," Amelia said.

Both noticed Francis and Chris stop on their walk and face each other, both gesturing largely. But neither woman commented. Instead, they turned back to the waves.

The late morning sun was strong. The breeze off the water was cool. It was the perfect late-spring day.

Just over thirty minutes later, Grier throttled the Robalo down as they rounded the southern end of Cedar Point, with Lighthouse Bay coming into view ahead of them. At first, nothing was visible, and Roger turned to Grier to ask if he was sure they were in the right place. In response, Grier held up his hand for the deputy to be quiet. He pointed southeast toward the shore of Bodie Island. There bobbing in the slight chop of the sound was a small boat. Low to the water and moving quickly in their direction.

"Buck up, Bucky," Grier said quietly. "I think we found the droids we're looking for."

Roger grabbed a pair of binoculars from the center console and fixed them on the distant boat.

"You said you didn't want it to be a skiff, right?" he asked. Grier nodded, and Roger grimaced. "Well, I have some bad news for you. Skiff."

"All good," the smaller man answered. "Even if they try to run, they can't hide forever. We can just send some of the rangers in after them."

"I'd rather handle it myself," Roger growled.

"That makes two of us," Grier agreed.

He let loose two short blasts on the boat's horn, signaling that he intended to keep the skiff on the starboard side, effectively keeping them hemmed into the island behind them.

Roger waved his hands, signaling the skiff, doing his best to look non-threatening.

"Looks to be two individuals on board," Roger said, bringing the binoculars up again. "Two white males. Young. Twenties, thirties at a stretch. Couple of poles out but looks to be more for show. They're not fishing."

They were close enough to make things out now, and while one of the figures waved back, the other gunned the outboard motor and the little boat jerked forward quickly. It looked for a moment as if they were about to make a run for it before slowing and coming back around.

A minute later, Grier brought the larger boat neatly up next to the skiff and dropped to an idle and drifted in close.

Roger, still in uniform, stepped to the starboard side and hailed the men.

"Morning, gents," he called. "It is still morning, isn't it?"

"Just barely," Grier replied, checking his dive watch.

"What can we do for you, Deputy?" one of the men called back.

He was the older of the two. Tall, muscular. Sandy hair that hadn't been cut in some time. Green eyes flashed as he propped his sunglasses up on top of his head. He was the picture of cooperation. Which set Roger's radar off. Most people were more nervous when approached by law enforcement. The guy had gone through this before.

His companion was younger. Early twenties most likely, with jet-black hair and sunglasses that stayed firmly where they were. In fact, he remained seated and barely glanced at the boat that had pulled up next to them.

"Just making the rounds," Roger replied. "Safety checks, blah blah. The usual."

"Seems like that would be more of a Park Service thing," the man mused in return.

"Not today," Roger answered, his radar now clanging even more loudly. "My lucky day. Can you show us some ID and let us know what brings you out here today?"

The younger man shook his head and busied himself with a fishing pole at his side. A fishing pole with no lure, Roger noticed, just before he dropped his line over the side.

"Well," the older man said, "I don't think I *have* to do that, but I've got nothing to hide. Name's Ben. Ben Hornigold. Just out here hoping to hook some striped bass. Maybe even some red drum."

Grier nudged Roger and glanced at the stern of the little skiff, and Roger caught his meaning immediately.

"You do know that every motorized craft has to be registered in North Carolina, right?" Roger pointed out. "Doesn't look like yours is, Ben."

"Yeah, that's my bad," Hornigold admitted. "Just popped that outboard on here. This was all manpower until an hour or two ago. I'll get that taken care of."

Hornigold was close enough now to hand over his license and a fishing license for good measure. Roger glanced at them but knew already they would be clean.

"Looks good," Roger said, with a nod. "Your friend there have a name?"

The younger man didn't so much as glance toward Roger and Grier, instead remaining focused on the useless fishing line he'd dropped.

"Charles," he called over. The one syllable conveying just how much he resented the intrusion.

"You have a last name, Charles?" Roger replied, evenly. "Maybe some ID?"

"No ID," Charles shot back. "Didn't expect to need it out here. Last name is Vane."

Roger let the silence between them linger for a moment before speaking. "Good idea to keep an ID with you all the time, Charles Vane. For next time."

Charles nodded once, never looking to Roger.

"Right," Roger said, turning back to Hornigold. "Get that boat registered, and maybe you do the fishing and let Charles there sit it out. Next time I see you, it won't just be a warning. Have a safe day out here."

"Thanks so much, Deputy," Hornigold replied. "Appreciate the warning. I'll get right on that."

"Oh, and next time," Grier called over, "you might want to bait that hook. Works better that way."

Charles shot Grier a look of pure malevolence, but the older man winked and shrugged in response, while Hornigold turned a disbelieving glance on his young passenger.

As Grier kicked his boat back into gear and wheeled about, Roger saw Charles look over his shoulder at Hornigold and say something that caused the older man to cut him off with a sharp gesture.

"If those two are out here fishing, I'm Brad Pitt," Grier said, heading back toward the marina.

"I don't mean to insult you when I say they are definitely *not* fishing," Roger replied. "Coulda sworn I saw them drop something over the side when they made that little run at the shore."

"Yeah, I noticed that too," Grier agreed. "They're up to something. And it's not good. Hard to track a boat with no registration."

"I can put out some feelers about them," Roger said. "That young guy was pretty surly. But, honestly, Hornigold was too slick for my liking."

Grier nodded and waved at a passing fishing boat.

"Yeah, Hornigold is no stranger to the law," Grier agreed. "Hate to say it, though, but I think the young one is going to be a whole different kind of trouble. Something not right there."

"Damn," Roger said, checking his phone. "Body is ready to be ID'd. And—look at that—a message from the reunion gang. They have more info. Now I have to get back there. Should have been able to just meet them in town. Gotta admit, I'm not lovin' this day. Home, James."

"Never ever say that again," Grier shot back, but he was grinning as he gave the boat full throttle. "Think I might get a drink when we get back. Just 'cause I can. Desiree at the marina does a killer dry martini."

"You're a cruel man," Roger said, as the water flew past.

———

Curt Stephens stood at the front entrance of Swells'a Brewing as he watched Carlito walk across the parking lot toward the beach road and turn south. The day had turned warm, and the sun was bright in the cloudless sky, forcing him to shade his eyes. He opened the door a few inches and called after the young man.

"You sure? It's not a problem!"

"All good!" Carlito called back. "I need the air and some down time. I'm used to it. I like to walk!"

As Carlito turned and continued on his way, Curt turned back to Sage, who was still behind the bar, almost ready for the noon opening.

"Stop it," she said. "He's had an intense and extremely weird morning. Probably just needs some time to process. He's fine. He's young. And bouncy."

Curt shook his head and his mop of auburn hair tumbled over his eyes. He crossed to the bar and lowered himself wearily onto one of the stools.

"You worried?" Sage asked. "Second thoughts?"

"Not one bit," Curt answered. "It was obvious he would be the one. You guys will see it tonight. Eight o'clock at the Crab. You good for that?"

"Good for it?" Sage retorted. "I can't wait. Finally, someone who is within twenty years of me. I'm thrilled."

"Shut it, you," Curt replied, smiling, "or I'll send you to your room. And twenty years is stretching things a bit. For me anyway. Roger? I'll give you that one."

"Supposed to be a perfect sunset," Sage said. "Great way to bring him in. You picking up all the stuff from your place?"

"Yeah, I'll have it. Don't worry. This doesn't happen very often. I'm not about to screw it up."

Sage put her cleaning rag on the countertop and reached across the bar, grabbing Curt's arm.

"You're in charge, Curt," she said, fixing him with a pointed look. "Stop putting so much pressure on yourself. Do it the way you think is right. You don't answer to anyone but yourself. We all have total faith in you to do what's right. For the Brethren. For the Banks."

Curt patted her hand with his free hand and gently extricated himself.

"Thanks," he replied. "I appreciate that. And I wish it were that simple. Lost my Uncle Bob not that long ago. Uncle Butch is still around but very much retired, as he reminds me often. My family has been in this for generations. And now I'm the last one still at it. You three, as great as you are, have a different point of view. You were all chosen because you're *good*. You bring something to the table. Me? I inherited it. I'll always have to prove myself. Live up to my family. Two hundred and fifty years of tradition, and responsibility. Of knowing things that no one else knows. Or can ever know. It's...a lot."

"I hear you, I do," Sage said, taking the hint and withdrawing her hand. "But that's too much for any one person to shoulder. Let us help. And, if I don't mind saying so myself, we've been doing a damn good job. The Banks are thriving, and no one has a clue how much we've had to handle to keep it that way."

"Only way to keep it that way is to never let up," Curt said with a slap on the bar top as he stood. "Thanks for the pep talk. I'm good. I'll be home getting ready for the next few hours if you need me. Who's covering for you tonight here?"

"Sheldon," Sage answered. "Bean was busy."

"As long as you're covered," Curt said. "See you then."

He walked out to his sea foam-colored VW Buzz and silently reversed out of his space and turned north on the beach road. The opposite direction Carlito had taken just a few minutes ago.

Banks, the big Great Pyrenees, crossed to the front door and pressed his wet nose to the glass, watching Curt leave. Riley, of the piercing blue eyes, stayed where she was on the floor behind the bar, unbothered.

Roger pulled up to the now familiar rental house in Nags Head. He noted a new car in the driveway, an older Acura. Well looked after. Virginia plates. He snapped a picture of the plate with his phone. Probably wouldn't need it, but you could never tell. If he *didn't* take the picture, he'd regret it later.

He climbed out of the cruiser, his legs a little achy, a little shaky. Despite living on a string of barrier islands, he rarely got out onto the water, and he wasn't used to using those muscles. And he reminded himself, he wasn't a young man anymore. He wasn't *old*. But his decathlon days were behind him. Long behind him. Like in another life behind him.

He massaged his lower back for just a moment when he stood up straight. Then kneaded his thighs. Damn. A mess.

He walked up to the front door and gave a loud knock. Now that he'd seen the layout of the house, he realized how hard it must be to hear the front door from the living room two floors above. To his surprise, it was opened quickly by Amelia, who had seemed to assume the lead in things.

"Hi, Deputy," she said. "I saw you pull in. Please come in. We had another friend get here this morning. In all the confusion, we forgot she was coming. I think you'll want to talk to her."

"Lead on, MacDuck," Roger replied, without thinking.

Amelia stopped halfway through, turned around, and shot him a puzzled look, before grinning.

"You're funny," she said. "I didn't think deputies were funny."

"How many deputies do you know?" Roger shot back.

"One," she answered with a laugh and turned to lead the way upstairs.

When they emerged into the large, open living space, Roger took stock of the room. Terry and Cathy were seated at the dining table, a plate of crudités and two open bottles of sparkling water in front of them. Not seltzer, Roger noted, sparkling water, and he was reminded that these were no college kids at the beach. These were adults. He'd need to keep that in mind.

Francis was in one corner, a laptop open on a coffee table in front of him. He was wearing headphones and seemed entirely oblivious to anything else in the room.

Chris and Jaime were nowhere to be seen. Roger glanced out the glass doors to the deck, but no one was there. He was struck, as he paused to appreciate the ocean just feet away from them, that it was a shame to be dealing with death and violence in such a beautiful spot. A place where so many came to get away from exactly this kind of thing. And yet, here they were.

Amelia crossed to the breakfast bar where the newcomer had risen from her stool. Amelia stood next to her and introduced her.

"Deputy, this is Kirsten Carlton," she said, gesturing to the woman. "Another of our gang. She had a commitment up home and wasn't able to get here until this morning. Kirsten, this is Deputy"—she paused to glance quickly at his name tag—"Goldstein. He's leading the investigation. He's funny." She smiled as she moved to the dining table and joined the other two women. "You two have a lot to discuss."

"Hi, Ms. Carlton," Roger said, motioning for her to resume her seat at the counter. "I'm sorry to meet you under these circumstances. I know it's all a shock and we're doing everything we can to get to the bottom of it. I promise you. Now, the message I got said you had some new information. Let's start there."

"Yes," Kirsten began, tentatively. "I'm not actually sure how much of a help I can be. But I was on the phone with Mark last night after the others left to go on the boat trip. He sounded fine. Had run into someone he knew from a long time ago. I had the sense it was someone from down here, not back home."

"Did he mention any names?" Roger asked.

"No, sorry," Kirsten replied. "Said they had some catching up to do and were going someplace quieter. He didn't say where."

"Okay, that's fine," Roger assured her. "That's actually a huge help. We can narrow it down by the time of night. Ask around. Was there anything else?"

"I don't think so," she said. "I wish I could think of something. Actually, he did mention where they had met before, but it didn't make much sense. He said something about a puffin. That can't be right. But that's what I heard."

"Puffin?" Roger said, quietly. "That's weird, all right, but every piece of information is a help. Puffin...Anything else?"

"Just that I can't believe this is happening," Kirsten said shakily. "We're a bunch of kids from the suburbs. Stuff like this doesn't happen to us. And Mark never hurt a single soul. He had settled down a lot in the last few years."

"And before that?" Roger asked, his interest piqued.

"The normal stuff," she said, backtracking. "Dated around a lot. Stayed out late. But nothing out of control. Just guy stuff, you know. Not even that. Young person stuff. Every single one of us in this house did the same dumb stuff. You know what? Forget I said anything. Totally irrelevant."

"Maybe," Roger said. "Maybe not. Like I said every little thing might be a help. Thanks for all of that. If I think of anything else—or if you do—just give a call. I suspect this won't be my last visit here."

Roger rose from the stool and cursed his aching muscles to himself.

"Now, as unpleasant as it is, I need to find Chris," he said. "We need him down in Manteo. Won't take long."

"Actually," Amelia said, rising from her seat. "I've decided to go with him. We talked about it. No single one of us should have to go alone. We drew straws to see who would go."

"Guess you lost?" Roger replied, stowing his pad and pen in his back pocket and getting ready to leave.

"I won, actually," Amelia answered. "We're a close group. I think we would all go if we thought it wouldn't be too much."

The others all nodded in agreement. Except for Francis, who remained engrossed in his computer screen. Roger thought he may have to reconsider some things about this group. Again.

Chris emerged from the stairway, waving his hands.

"I'm sorry," he said, quickly. "Got caught up in a vet emergency. Had to talk them through it. Comes with the territory. An owl buzzed a car on the Colonial Parkway. Clipped its wing. Driver said it came out of nowhere, All good now. Short rehab and back to the forest she goes. Anyway, I'll be ready in five?"

"Glad the owl is okay," Roger said. "I'll be down at my car making a call. You two head on down when you're ready."

Roger was calling Curt before he'd even stepped out from under the carport at the foot of the house.

"Curt, sorry to bother you," Roger began. "I know you have a lot to do for tonight, but we've got some new info that needs checking up on. And I'm starting to think this case may be one for the Brethren anyway. These folks have been coming here for decades and something just feels...off."

"Slow down, Roger," Curt replied. "Take a breath. I've got time. Plenty of it actually. Hit me with what you have."

"Another friend was actually on the phone with our victim last night after everyone else left Bad Bean for the kayaks. Said he was going someplace quieter. Any chance you can check with some of the spots along that stretch? Maybe Bad Bean south to...whaddaya think? Nags Head?"

"I can do that," Curt replied. "A few come to mind. Hell, they might have even gone to Swells'a. I'll check with Sage. Lucky 12, Goombays. Probably too loud that time of day, but I'll follow up. Also, have you talked to Bad Bean to see if they have any CCTVs?"

"You read my mind," Roger said. "That was my next call. That could tell us a lot."

"I'll take care of it," Curt said. "You focus on getting that victim ID out of the way. Those poor people have a tough time ahead."

"Will do," Roger agreed. "Appreciate it. If something shocking comes up, give a shout. Otherwise, I'll just see you tonight. Might get there a little before eight. Stake out some good seats for sunset."

"Helluva day," Curt said, before hanging up.

Roger turned at the sound of the door opening and gave a quick wave to Chris and Amelia as they emerged into the driveway.

"There's really no need for you to drive us," Amelia said. "If I drive, we'll save you a return trip."

"Are you sure?" Roger asked. "I was just thinking if you were upset—"

"We'll be okay," Chris replied. "We're prepared for anything. And we might need some time to ourselves after."

"If you say so," Roger said. "I could use the time on the other end. Lots happening."

Chris and Amelia climbed into a BMW M3, a very sleek and very expensive sports car. Amelia was driving. Roger shook his head.

"I should have asked *them* for a ride," he muttered to himself, climbing into his cruiser.

Roger pulled into the parking lot at the police station, parked, and killed the engine. Next to them sat the department's Humvee, and Roger couldn't help but think of when he had used it a few months back to come to the rescue of Sean Curley, Dan Trout, and the other "unusual" guests they'd had. What a time.

Amelia and Chris pulled in next to him and they met between the two cars.

"What's up with that monster?" Chris asked.

"Bought it surplus," Roger replied. "Mostly use it for tricky rescues and such. Honestly, it usually just sits here and gets us attention."

"You ever had to drive it?" Amelia asked.

"I have," Roger answered. "But that's a story for another day. Look, I need to nip into the station for a sec. Got a message from our receptionist I have to check on. Then we'll walk over to the funeral home just across the street. Really, less than a minute. You all can stay here if you want. Do whatever you need to do to get ready."

Roger walked briskly into the station, up the stairs to the front desk where Mary Hallet sat.

"You took your sweet time," she said, when she saw Roger reach the top of the stairway.

"Did you miss me that much?" Roger teased. "Good things come to those who wait, you know."

"Get over yourself, Casanova," she said, playfully swatting at him. "And it's nothing like that. Crazy Lynn Vollmerhausen called again. Swore she saw those lights over the water again last night. She and that equally crazy husband of hers are asking for someone to come out to take a statement."

"Not this again," Roger said. "The nutty bear people. Wonderful. Guess I should count my blessings it's been a couple months. And Bill's not that bad. But how the two of them ever raised Ranger Justin, I'll never know. Let them know it's a busy day, but we'll get someone to swing by their trailer midafternoon. Hey, let's get Russ to do it. He still owes me ten bucks. Smooches!"

"Smooches yourself! Russ Wahl will not be happy with that. Why don't I just ask Chief Brady to do it, while I'm at it?"

"Good idea!" Roger answered. "He owes me *twenty* bucks!"

He hustled back down the stairs before Mary could find something to throw at him.

Back outside, he gathered Chris and Amelia and crossed the street to what looked like any of the other Tudor influenced houses along the residential street. Only a small sign out front identifying it as a funeral home gave away its true nature.

Roger led the two inside where he huddled briefly with someone at a desk in the first office they reached. She nodded and rose leading them down a hallway, before turning into a room to the left. She paused at the threshold and looked back at them.

"Roger," she said, "I know you've been through this before, but I just want you two to know if you feel faint or dizzy, there are chairs around the room for you. And please know that we've been incredibly respectful throughout the process. That's one less worry for you to have."

With that, she stood to the side and ushered the three into a large, tastefully decorated room where a table stood in the center under a gentle, but focused light. A figure lay there, under a sheet that had been pulled up and over his face.

"Let me do this," Roger said, as he stepped to the side of the table and took the edge of the sheet in his hand. "You let me know when you're ready."

Amelia and Chris shared a glance, took each other's hands, and nodded to Roger. He gently pulled the sheet down, revealing the face of the victim on the table. His sandy, reddish hair had been combed and his face looked almost peaceful. If they hadn't known better, he could have been asleep.

Amelia let out a small cry and found her way to a chair.

Chris shot a hand up to his head, first covering his mouth, and then grabbing a handful of his own hair. He, too, let out a strangled sound, and nodded his head. Then shook it.

"Yeah," he said quietly, turning to Roger, then the woman in the doorway. "That's not Mark. I've never seen this man before."

CHAPTER 6

Curt was pulling into the parking lot of Bad Bean Baja Grill. They opened at eleven and the lot was already full. The combination of excellent food, great service, and an authentic OBX beach vibe had made them popular with locals and tourists alike. For his purposes, Curt just wanted to be able to chat with the manager on duty. Most places had some sort of video monitoring system these days. If they could identify whoever Mark Elliot had met, they could at least start to run details down.

He stopped to bring up Elliot's social media pages. Thankfully Elliot was old enough to still have a Facebook account. Curt doubted he could navigate any of the other sites. He found some decent pictures of Elliot and screenshotted them, saving them to his photos. That done, he turned off the Chevelle and started to open the door when his phone rang.

Roger Goldstein. Cripes, he hoped it wasn't bad news again. He answered with a clipped, "Roger."

"Well, nice to talk to you too," Roger replied, but his voice was missing its usual levity. "So, I have some news. Do you want the good news or the bad news?"

"I don't want any more bad news at all," Curt grumbled. "Give me the good."

"You got it," Roger replied. "Mark Elliot is not the dead guy."

Curt paused. Then sat a moment longer.

"Shit," he said finally. "What?"

"Had a couple of the friends come down to ID him," Roger answered. "Definitely not Elliot."

"Who is it, then?" Curt said wearily.

"No clue," Roger admitted. "Just getting to work on that."

"I guess that's good news for Mr. Elliot," Curt said. "But then what's the bad news?"

"My caseload just doubled," Roger said. "Now we have a missing person *and* a dead John Doe."

"Right," Curt said. "Seems like all roads still lead through Mark Elliot. I'll try to find out who he was with last night. Guess you have to do all that police stuff you get paid for. Not my territory."

"Right you are, Curt," Roger agreed. "We're running prints now. Checking any traffic cameras to see if we can get a hit on who might have been in the refuge after dark. I wouldn't say we're all the way back at square one, but close."

"You really know how to brighten up my day, you know that?" Curt said. "Talk to you when I have something."

"Yessir. Just leave the policing to me. You go find me someone to talk to."

Curt signed off and headed into the restaurant, where he finally ran into some good luck. Pam Roberts was managing today. She lived near him over by the sound and they had a longstanding friendship. She knew better than to ask too many questions, which would help things along. Even better, she let him know that they did indeed have cameras covering the bar and tables. And another on the parking lot.

They sat together in the crowded back office while Pam fast-forwarded through the video of the day before.

"What time do you think?" she asked. "Four o'clock and on?"

"Good place to start," Curt said. "Will be a larger group to start with most leaving just before dinner. We're looking to see who this fella stayed to talk to."

He held up his phone for her to see and scrolled through a few of the pictures of Elliot.

"Right, pretty distinctive guy," Pam said, with a nod, scrolling through the video. "There! There's the group. And...there he is. Blue and purple Wave Riding Vehicles shirt. Vintage by the look of it. I don't think they've had that design since the nineties."

"Mr. Elliot has either been coming here a very long time or he has a serious OBX fixation," Curt mused.

Pam continued scrolling and they watched the group of friends move through their happy hour celebration. Curt felt more than a little intrusive as he watched the genuine care that they had for each other play out in fast-forward. There were zero signs of anything out of the ordinary. As personal as it was, it was something that played out in living rooms, barrooms, and restaurants along the Banks virtually every day. This is where people came to reconnect and escape their own realities. Which is what made the entire situation even more upsetting.

As the clock neared a quarter past five on the video, Curt raised a hand and asked Pam to slow down. Elliot seemed distracted by a well-dressed man who came striding through the front door. His outfit set him apart from most of the other patrons. Dark dress pants, a button-down shirt with sleeves rolled very neatly to just below his elbow, and leather dress shoes. The only pair of non-sneakers or flip-flops in the bar.

"Well, hello there," Curt said quietly. "Who do we have here?"

On the video, Elliot was staring at the newcomer, who was scanning the crowd, seemingly looking for someone. Francis gave Elliot a playful shove to the shoulder to bring him back to the group conversation, but it was clear that Elliot was otherwise occupied. Amelia, ever the organizer, checked her watch and began to round up the reunion group, presumably in preparation to head out for the boat tour.

It was at this point that Mark Elliot separated from the others and approached the well-dressed man and tapped him on the shoulder. When the man turned, he was clearly expecting someone else, and immediately looked surprised to see Elliot there.

Elliot leaned in close and said something in the man's ear that caused the nattily dressed man to lean back against the bar and cock his head. After a moment, he seemed to recognize Elliot and nodded his head while extending his hand. At this point, yet another man approached the well-dressed man from his other side. There was no lack of recognition as the two shook hands.

Elliot excused himself and jogged over to his friends who were waiting next to the door by now. He gestured back in the direction of the man he had approached and there was much gesticulating as he clearly was bowing out of the group activity. Francis and Chris clapped him on the shoulder before heading out. Amelia stood her ground a bit longer, trying to convince Elliot to change his mind with no luck. Cathy and Terry gave him quick hugs and shrugged a question to him, but he remained where he was. Jaime was the last to leave. He conspicuously didn't shake Elliot's hand and left with a decided air of frustration. Or anger?

What Elliot was unable to see happening behind him, was the other two men in a suddenly heated conversation. Mr. Fancy Pants had his back to the camera, and the other man was largely obscured behind him. One thing was clear, though. They disagreed about Elliot's presence. Finally, Fancy Pants gestured sharply, indicating that the discussion was finished. He turned and leaned over the bar, motioning for the bartender to take his order. Quite rudely, Curt thought, before touching Pam's arm.

"Freeze it, there, please," Curt said quickly.

The video stopped suddenly, and the second man came into focus as the other leaned over the bar. His sandy hair was unkempt and leaked out of the sides of the blue hat on his head. His bright green t-shirt had the upper portion of a logo peaking over the other man's shoulder. His skin was fair, but he'd obviously spent a good deal of time in the sun. Other than that, he looked as if he could be related to Elliot.

"Can you zoom in on this thing?" Curt asked.

"Let's find out," Pam said, hitting a few keys on the keyboard and suddenly the screen filled with a slightly more pixelated version of the man. The hat, now fuzzy but legible, was angled over his face and advertised a restaurant called Coastal Cactus. The shirt was clearly from one of the many Brew Thru locations that dotted the islands. They were ubiquitous and locals and tourists alike wore them constantly. But that hat.

"Coastal Cactus," Curt said. "Rings a bell. You?"

Pam nodded. "Been gone quite a while now. Pretty popular back in the day."

"And Elliot has an old-school WRV shirt," Curt said, tapping the screen. "These guys go back a ways. Can you keep it going. Slowly. Let's see if—"

Pam let the video move, frame by frame, and then—

"Bingo," Curt said, as the man looked up at the arriving bartender and his face came into view. Curt took a screenshot of the man and had Pam scroll back to get another of Fancy Pants when he entered. "Let's see how this plays out."

The video jumped back to full speed, but little else happened. Elliot returned to the bar and joined the two men, all three having a beer before Elliot gestured that it was hard to hear each other. The other two nodded in agreement, and after settling the tab, they made their way to the exit and out into the early evening. The time stamp showed it was just shy of six o'clock.

Curt scanned the crowd that was left.

"See anyone else you know? Anything suspicious?" Curt asked.

"Looks like any other happy hour. Lots of regulars. A few irregulars. Couple of Manteo's finest were at a table. Some tourists. Nothing out of the ordinary."

"Really?" Curt asked, surprised. "I don't see anyone."

"Mary Hallet and Officer Wahl were at a table. Don't think they ever went to the bar."

"Huh. I'll check with them to see if they noticed anything off. Any cameras out front?" Curt asked.

"Just one in the lot," Pam answered.

"Worth a look," Curt said.

They scrolled through the exterior video but saw nothing of interest. The men exited, got into their cars, headed south, and that was that.

"You've been the biggest help we've had yet. Appreciate it. How's business?" Curt asked.

"Always packed," Pam replied. "And the season is just getting started. If I save enough money this summer, I may just finally disappear to a beach somewhere quieter."

"Wish you luck," Curt said. "But hope you don't go anywhere. Banks are better with you here."

"Yeah, yeah," Pam said, pushing Curt toward the office door. "I know better than to ask you to keep me posted. I'll have to read about this in the papers like everyone else. But if you need anything, you know where to find me."

"Indeed, I do, Pamela," he said, before she shooed him out the door. "I'm going, I'm going!"

Pam closed the door behind him, and he headed out to the Chevelle in the parking lot. The engine roared to life, and he sat for a moment, texting the photos of Fancy Pants and his friend to Roger with a note asking if they looked familiar.

He hadn't made it to the exit before his phone rang. Roger.

Curt answered with a simple, "That was fast."

"Where did you get those?" Roger asked, all business.

"That's who Mark Elliot ran into at Bad Bean," Curt answered. "Well, the slickyhead guy was. The other guy showed up after. Why?"

"Because that *other* guy is our dead John Doe," Roger explained.

"The plot thickens," Curt said.

"It does indeed," Roger said. "Where are you headed now?"

"Swells'a," Curt said. "See if Sage knows either of these guys. Or if we got lucky and they actually went there last night."

"Great," Roger replied. "I'll talk to the friends again. Show them these pictures. First, I might have to go by the Vollmerhausens'."

"Let me guess," Curt said, turning left out of the parking lot. "Lights over the water?"

"You know it," Roger said. "Trying to pass it off to Russ or Johnny, but I may get roped into it."

"Are you sure there's nothing to it?" Curt asked. "I mean…"

"Shut it," Roger answered. "Even if there is something to it, they definitely don't need to know. But I'm sure it's nothing. They've been claiming they see them for years."

"Still—" Curt said.

"Curt," Roger interrupted. "We agreed to keep these things under wraps. Just go and get some more evidence. I wouldn't be mad if you just solved this case. I have other things to do."

"Will I get a raise?" Curt asked, as he swung onto the bypass heading south.

"Sure, we'll double what we pay you," Roger said.

"And double nothing is nothing," Curt pointed out.

"Can't get anything past you," Roger said. "Talk later."

Curt shook his head and turned on the stereo. Despite everything going on, it had tuned into a beautiful day. Jimmy Buffett sang "Breathe In, Breathe Out, Move On," and Curt let the music carry him down the road.

Roger was following Amelia and Chris back to the beach rental. Again. They had immediately called the rest of their group to give them the news that the dead body was, in fact, not their friend. The feeling of relief had been so genuine that Roger had let it go. He knew that he would be bursting that bubble when they all sat down to discuss their now presumed missing friend. But missing was a helluva lot better than dead, so he gave them their moment.

Once again pulling into the now familiar driveway, he jumped out and headed in behind the other two. As he passed Elliot's car, he glanced into the window and stopped suddenly. Something was different. The glove compartment was slightly ajar, and some of the papers inside had gotten jammed when it had been closed. It hadn't been like that before. Had it? No, definitely not. Someone had been in there. And looking for something.

Dammit. This case was quickly going from sad and unfortunate to complicated and annoying.

He slipped on a pair of nitrile gloves and tried each of the doors. Still locked up tight. A new question now for the friends waiting for him inside. Could one of them have found the keys and taken a look around their presumed-dead friend's car? Possible, but they seemed smarter than that.

Could one of them be hiding the keys for some as yet unknown reason, and had gone looking for...something? Possible, but troubling.

Or could whoever had dumped the car here the night before have come back to clean up after themselves? Murder was, at least for now, off the table as far as Elliot was concerned, so it could even have been Elliot himself who had been here. Could he be running? Scared?

Nothing for it but to head in and start asking questions. At least they'd had a few minutes to celebrate. Time to solve this crime.

Roger slipped off the gloves and put them in his back pocket. Shaking his head, he walked to the door, paused, and let himself in.

When he reached the second floor living space, the friends were buzzing with energy. The fear and grief of earlier this morning had been erased and they all paced and burbled with ideas and hope.

Roger appreciated that and planned to put it to good use.

"Okay, folks," Roger said loudly, "I need your attention and your thinking caps. I'm thrilled that Mr. Elliot is not the person we fished out of Alligator River, but the fact is that now we have to shift to him being missing. So, in a way, we are starting all over. If I can get you all to take a seat, I have some new questions for you. Let's start with, do any of you know if Mr. Elliot had any enemies. Someone who wanted to do him harm?"

"He's a theatre critic," Cathy pointed out. "Enemies is a very long list, although I wouldn't think any of that would follow him here."

"You'd be surprised," Roger said. On a hunch, he shot Jaime a glance and was rewarded with a deep blush and quick look out the window by the other man. That enemies line had hit a nerve.

"Let's focus a bit, yeah?" Roger went on.

As the group made their way to the seats, an uncomfortable silence fell over the room. A gull cried as it wheeled past the deck and veered over the water. The dishwasher quietly sloshed incongruously in the kitchen, a subtle reminder that life stops for nothing.

As the friends nervously looked to each other, a new reality settled in: if Elliot was missing and out there somewhere, they would need to be part of the solution. And they were all suspects now. Again. Still.

Roger took out his notepad, settled onto one of the barstools, and fixed each of them in turn with a look.

"Right," he began. "The first twenty-four hours in a missing person case are the most important, and we've lost a good sixteen of those thinking this was a murder. Or at least death by misadventure. We have to make up time."

Francis raised a hand. "What do you need to know?"

"We'll come back to the enemies list. First, did any of you find the keys to Elliot's car? Maybe they were in his room? Or somewhere other than your key table?"

Heads shook around the room. Muttered denials.

Terry looked at Jaime. "You went up to his room this morning. Did you find anything?"

Jaime looked around the circle at his friends, panic in his eyes.

"I just wanted to see if I could find something to help," Jaime said, quickly. "The whole thing feels unreal. I—I don't even know what I was hoping to see. It's Mark, though. I thought I might notice something others had missed."

The room remained silent. No one stirred.

"To answer your question," Jaime said to Roger, "no. I didn't find his keys. I found nothing."

"Well," Roger went on, "then I'm going to need your help finding out who went through his car in the last few hours. And we need to figure out *why*. I'll have one of my colleagues out to go over the car shortly." The friends looked quickly to each other but were silent. "Now, we haven't found a phone. I'm assuming Mr. Elliot had a cell phone. I'm guessing it's not in the house?"

"Pretty sure we would have seen it by now if it were here, but I can call it," Terry said. "Although I don't know many people who leave their ringers on these days."

"Worth a try," Roger agreed.

Terry took a phone out of her pocket and tapped the screen a few times.

"It's ringing," she said, keeping the phone to her ear. The room fell silent, everyone listening for any tell-tale ring or buzz. Nothing. "It went to voicemail pretty quickly."

"Yeah, wherever that phone is, it's probably shut off," Roger said while making a note. "We'll get onto the phone company and see if we can pin down its last known location. Now, about those enemies. Anything any of you need to tell me?"

Shifting of feet and strained silence followed. The dishwasher buzzed signaling the end of its cycle.

"I'll start," Jaime said, finally. "You're all thinking it, anyway. Mark and I had a falling-out toward the end of college. He was just starting to get into writing reviews, and I had written a one act for a playwriting class. Let's just say he didn't like it."

"And that caused the falling-out?" Roger asked.

"No," Jaime answered, throwing his hands in the air. "Me

punching him in the face did that. But this all happened a long time ago."

"I see," Roger said, taking more notes. "Quite the emotional response. Anything else you all should tell me? Any broken romances in the group?"

There was no pause this time, the entire room burst into laughter.

"Sorry," Cathy said, quickly. "But no. That has never been an issue. We're all happily married."

"Any reason none of your spouses are here?" Roger asked.

"A no-spouse reunion," Chris replied. "We don't get tired of our old stories, but they do. It's as much for their sake as ours."

"Any tension any of us ever had with each other is long gone," Amelia said. "We were young together and did some dumb stuff, but we're grown up now. We've all settled down. Mostly. We chose to be here together because we love each other. You won't find any deep dark secrets between us."

"I'm gonna be honest with you folks," Roger said, standing. "I don't think of any of you as suspects, at this point. You all have alibis. And your kayak guide backs up your version of things, at least for the first part of the night."

The deputy walked to the large picture window at the front of the house and looked out over the driveway. Elliot's car was at the top of the driveway, meaning half of it was under the house in the carport. In other words, the front seat wasn't visible from the window.

"Seems to me," Roger said, tapping on the window with his pen, "that you wouldn't see someone in the front seat from here, but you would definitely see someone coming and going. No one saw a thing?"

He turned to face the group, but no one spoke up.

"Right, that's what I was afraid of. Another officer will be out to look over the car soon. If you think of anything, and I mean *anything,* you call me. Amelia, can I have a quick word?"

The others shared a confused look as Amelia followed Roger down the stairs. She returned within a few seconds.

"Nothing to get worked up about," she said, closing the door behind her. "He may send someone over to look at the area around the car. Consultant, or something. Have to say, he seems to be proactive about this. Thankfully."

She went to the kitchen and poured herself a glass of iced tea before heading out to sit on the deck.

Roger left the way he came and paused as he passed the car in question. He looked in the passenger side window, careful not to touch anything. He was shaking his head as he walked back to his car. This time he didn't bother looking back at the house.

Curt pulled into the Swells'a Brewing parking lot. Again. Early afternoon on a Tuesday pretty much guaranteed that the taproom was quiet, which is exactly what Curt found when he entered. Sage was seated behind the bar, scrolling on her phone. There were no patrons, but her two dogs were curled up by her feet, Banks snoring contentedly and Riley with her ears on a swivel, missing nothing.

Sage, not looking up from her phone, said, "You know, you could have just sent me the photos and saved yourself the trip."

Curt chuckled as he took a seat opposite her at the bar. "Where's the fun in that? But, yes, I considered it. On the off chance they were here, I wanted to be able to see the video myself. And I just got a call from Roger who has a favor to ask of you. Case related. And lastly, why would I deprive myself of your sparkling company?"

"Mhm," Sage said, dubiously, putting her phone aside. "Somehow I think options A and B had more to do with it."

"I'm hurt, Sage," Curt replied. "You doubt my sincerity?"

"Yes," she said. "At least twice every day. But your ulterior motives are usually for the best. And at least you fessed up this time."

Curt bowed his head and gestured a *mea culpa.*

"I've been doing some digging on Carlito Vega, our newest conscript," she said, tapping her phone on the bar top.

"I don't think we should call him a conscript," Curt admonished.

"Call him whatever you want, but that kid has an impressive track record. Medal-winning long-distance runner. Scuba certified. Majored in history. Minors in government affairs and literature."

"I didn't choose him accidentally," Curt said. "All of the candidates had upsides. His were a little more varied and, well, up."

Sage nodded and grabbed a bag of chips from a basket at the end of the bar.

"What?" Curt asked. "You're not saying something."

"I just wonder if he's really going to stick around here," she mused. "He's so young. And has so much going for him. Seems like he'd be ripe for a summer season and then off to greener pastures."

"Funny," Curt said. "Roger said the same thing about you not that long ago. And yet, here you are."

"Carlito has a lot more going for him than I ever did," she responded. "I'm a beach bum deep down. This guy could run for governor in a few years, and I wouldn't bat an eye. In fact, I'd vote for him."

"Me too," Curt agreed. "But we just have to see how it plays out. I had to choose the best. Now we hope he buys in. And, if not, how great would it be to have the governor as an ally?"

Sage raised her hands in surrender. "Your call. And he is impressive. I've said my piece. So"—she opened the chips and popped one in her mouth while fixing him with a raised-eyebrow look—"what can I do you for?"

Curt pushed his phone across the bar and flipped it over for her.

"Push play. I've cued it up for you," he said, shaking his head at her. "The guy with the sandy hair in the group at the top is Elliot, our now missing person. He meets a well-dressed guy just before the group leaves. Then a third man joins before they all leave. Any chance they came here? Supposedly they were looking for someplace quieter."

"You saying we don't do a good business?" Sage quipped. "Because I'll have you know that even on a Monday—"

She stopped suddenly and lifted the phone closer, using two fingers to expand the photo.

"Oh ho," she said quietly. "I see the new guy. And...now the third one is there. Mr. Big Shot is Todd Lawton. Surprised you didn't recognize him. Mover and shaker in the hospitality world. Didn't live here full-time until recently. He's the lead on the big new Irish tiki place that's set to open south of here. Word is it's costing an arm and a leg and way over budget."

"Irish tiki bar?" Curt asked. "Haven't heard a thing. I don't like that. I'm supposed to be up on everything. Irish tiki? Weird concept. But whatever. So big bucks. If he only moved here recently, how did he know Elliot?"

"Apparently, he's a long-time blow-in," Sage answered. "Been coming here all his life. Made a killing with restaurants up and down the east coast. But this is his dream. Open here and retire on the Banks."

"A little young to retire, no?" Curt responded.

"Not when you've made the money he has," Sage said. "But the other guy is where it gets interesting. That's Kevin Keegan. Been a bartender up and down the beach for over twenty years. Makes sense they'd know each other. No idea how Elliot would fit in, though."

"And they didn't come in here?"

Sage shook her head. "Not last night. Lawton and Keegan have been here plenty, though. Usually sit outside or upstairs."

"Interesting," Curt said, pulling his phone back to him and watching the video again. "If they didn't come here, where would they have gone?"

"I'd say Lucky 12 or maybe even to the new place. Supposed to be close to ready."

"I'll look into both, thanks. Can we step outside for a sec?" Curt asked with a glance toward the side door.

"Sure," Sage said, giving Curt a curious look while dropping a cleaning cloth on the bar and moving toward the door.

Once they had both seated themselves at a picnic table in the side yard, the dogs once again at her feet, Sage leaned forward on her elbows.

"What's up?" she asked. "This cloak and dagger stuff isn't like you."

"Funny," he said. "Seeing the video from Bad Bean got me thinking. Cameras everywhere. Just felt a little less...observed outside. If nothing else, it would be harder to hear what we're saying out here."

Sage nodded. Slowly.

"Okay. So?"

"Roger asked if you could take the dogs to the rental place our reunion folks are in when you finish up. He's hoping the dogs may be able to pick up a scent. See if our missing person was with his car when it was left there. One of the group, an Amelia Langley, will be waiting for you with something of Elliot's to give them the lead. It's not a bad idea. Right now, we have the three guys leaving Bad Bean and then—poof—nothing but one dead body and one disappeared guy. If you can handle that, I'll track down Mr. Lawton. He's the only one who can answer these questions."

"Not a problem," Sage said. "But don't you have things to do to get ready for tonight?"

Curt tapped his phone to check the time.

"Shit, yeah, I do," he admitted. "I'll take a drive by this new tiki place, see what's what. Maybe I'll get lucky and find our man. What's it called?"

"Angus McTiki's," Sage said, laughing. "Irish pub and tiki bar combo."

"Saints preserve us," Curt said with a faux Irish accent and a shake of his head. "I guess I've heard worse ideas. Can't remember any, but I must have. When you get to the house in Nags Head, Russ

Wahl may be there dusting for prints and such. That would actually be a good thing. Means you can get inside the car. If I don't talk to you, I'll see you at eight. Big night. We'll have to put this aside as much as we can. Make Carlito feel welcome."

"I'm on it," Sage said, rising.

"This is such a mess," Curt said, quietly, before also standing. "I have no clue how these three end up together, but Lawton is the key. We have work to do."

Sage stood in the doorway as Curt's Chevelle rumbled out onto the beach road.

She reached absently down and ruffled both dogs' ears.

"Not sure what we're getting into here, pups, but I have a bad feeling."

When her shift ended at four, Sage gathered the dogs and headed out to her Ford Bronco. She'd traded her old one in a few months ago and now drove a brand-new Big Bend edition. The Outer Banks edition had felt a little too on the nose. She'd gotten Eruption Green Metallic with a black roof, and she was in love with her new baby. But the more she drove it, the more she realized that what she really wanted was the tricked-out vintage Bronco that Dan Trout was driving when he came through town last fall. She'd tried to buy it off of him, but no luck. She just may have to fix one up herself.

She punched the address into the GPS and headed south toward Nags Head. Fifteen minutes later, she was pulling into the driveway of the house and shaking her head at the sheer excess of it all. She'd been coming to the beach here since she was a child. It had been her family's getaway of choice. She remembered when there were only a smattering of small hotels and motels and most of the houses were older. Most of them barely shacks made for the simplest of shelter. Most people came and spent all day on the beach, coming inside only to sleep and *sometimes* eat. Now everyone who came expected luxury. More bathrooms than bedrooms—which made no sense to her—and Jacuzzis with views of the ocean. A dozen bedrooms, each with picture windows facing the water. God, she sounded like an old person, even to herself.

She got out of the car and approached the door under the house. Before she reached it, a pretty blond woman opened the door and shut it quietly behind her.

"You must be Sage," the woman said. "Amelia Langley. Deputy Goldstein asked me to meet you. I brought this." She held up a worn Wolfe Tones t-shirt. "It was Mark's favorite shirt. He saw them with his dad and brother a while back."

"Was?" Sage asked, pointedly.

"Is!" Amelia exclaimed. "*Is* his favorite. I keep doing that. We were all so prepared for the worst. I'm having a hard time adjusting."

"I get it," Sage said. "You all have had quite a day."

Sage gently took the shirt and called Riley and Banks over. She knelt and held the shirt out for them to sniff and they both obliged.

"Find this, guys, okay?" she said to the dogs gently. "Go. Find."

She let them both off their leads and kept a close eye on them while still talking to Amelia.

"They've been through this before," she explained. "Trained in search and rescue. Both really good, but Riley is special. If your friend was here, she'll pick it up. Just don't tell Banks I said that. He's sensitive."

Amelia laughed, then tried to cover it when she realized that Sage was serious.

The dogs circled the car, noses to the ground. Banks stopped for a moment and both women leaned in, but he quickly moved on after pawing the sand at the edge of the driveway. He then wandered off and marked his new territory by peeing on the front lamp post. Riley was more focused and seemed to follow something before turning suddenly, looking at Sage, and sitting down.

"I'm going to keep at this for a few more minutes," Sage said, calling the dogs to her and showing them the shirt again. "But early indications are that your friend didn't bring the car here himself. Or at least didn't walk away from the car. You might want to fill your friends in."

Sage gestured to the window above the driveway, where five faces were staring down at them.

Amelia shook her head and said she'd be right back. As she retreated inside, a dark blue Ford Police Interceptor SUV pulled into the driveway. Sage waved hello. It couldn't be Roger; he would have given her a heads-up. Chief Brady wouldn't be out for something like this. That left Russ Wahl. She liked Wahl. He was a genuinely good guy and a mountain of a man. He was friendly and open, until you pushed him too far, and then watch out. She'd seen him clear a parking lot of a rowdy group of bikers in under five minutes, sending them all packing with not much more than bruised egos and a newfound respect for the local police.

Wahl climbed out of the SUV after parking behind her Bronco.

"Rog dragged you into this?" he called as he strode toward her. "What's up, Banksy? Hiya, Riley!"

Banks romped to him and jumped, putting his paws on the man's midsection, which said something about how tall the officer was. For her part, Riley stayed back but allowed a gentle wag of the tail to be her hello.

"Never can tell if Riley likes me or not," Wahl said, and laughed, rubbing Banks's ears.

"Let's just say, you'd know if she didn't," Sage replied. "And yeah, Roger dragged me in. How did you get stuck in it?"

"To be fair, your dogs are the best on the beach," Wahl said. "Don't tell our K-9s I said that. I'll deny it. And it was this or heading over to the Vollmerhausens' to talk about orbs over the water. I chose this."

"Smart man," Sage replied, chuckling.

"We need to get in there, huh? Let me grab my Slim Jim. Won't take a sec."

Wahl went to the SUV, retrieved a long, flat strip of metal. He carefully slipped it between the window and the door and after a few seconds of moving it back and forth he stepped back and indicated the car with a flourish.

"Voilà," he declared, slipping on some gloves and opening the door. "Roger didn't say exactly what he wanted me to look for. I know you're not department, but...?"

"Your guess is as good as mine," Sage admitted, craning her neck to look inside. "Anything that tells us something about where he was last night, I guess."

Wahl slid into the driver's seat and opened the glove compartment. Rifling through the papers, he shook his head. Nothing out of the ordinary. Next, he turned his attention to the console between the front seats.

"Interesting," he muttered, holding up something for Sage to see.

Leaning in she saw it was a bar coaster. The kind bartenders put under a drink. Something she was all too familiar with herself. It was the inexpensive cardboard variety, as much promo item as bar protection. Printed on it was the logo for Lucky 12, one of the beach road bars.

"And yet another," Wahl said, holding up another coaster. This one was flashier. Made of higher quality materials. It bore the picture of a leprechaun standing on a stool to give a hula girl a kiss on the cheek over the name "Angus McTiki's." Wahl shot a questioning look to Sage.

"New place," she explained. "Not open yet. He was seen with one of the owners last night before he disappeared."

"Well, I'd say this qualifies as a clue," the officer said. "And wouldja look at that." He reached forward and removed a set of keys from the ignition. "Did not expect to find these here."

"That's a pretty obvious one," Sage said. "Surprised Roger didn't notice those when he was here."

While Wahl was distracted in the front seat, Sage took a quick look in the back. She fished through the seat back storage pocket. She glanced at Wahl, feeling slightly guilty for literally going behind his back. But only slightly. One of the benefits of being in the Brethren of the Coast was not being bound by local laws. As long as they didn't get caught. The goals were the same—the safety and protection of the Banks and their citizens—but they used different methods to get there. She knew she was here for more than letting her dogs take a sniff.

Her hand fumbled along something in the pouch. She quickly pulled it out and dropped it into her pocket. She knew without even looking that it was a cell phone. She thrust her hand in again. This time she pulled out a smart watch.

"Not much else I can find up here," Wahl announced, climbing out of the car. "No sense dusting for prints after all that fog this morning. Probably wiped the exterior clean. I'll bag the coasters and keys and get back to the station and start running things."

The weight of the electronics was heavy in Sage's pocket, but she knew if she turned them over it would end up back in evidence with the police. That would slow their whole process down. They needed to find this guy. Fast.

"And if my dogs are right, and they always are," Sage added, giving a short whistle to bring them in, "he wasn't even here when the car was dropped off."

"Well, shit," Officer Russ Wahl said.

"Eloquent, as always, Officer Wahl," Sage shot back to him as she loaded the dogs into the Bronco and strapped them in. "I'll let Roger know what's what. Good luck. Hope you find this guy."

"You and me, both," Wahl said, heading back to the police SUV.

Amelia Langley's was the only face pressed to the window above.

CHAPTER 7

Roger pulled his cruiser off Shipyard Road in Manns Harbor and onto the rocky path leading to Lynn and Bill Vollmerhausen's double-wide trailer nestled on a lot with a shockingly good view of the Croatan Sound. It was a lot that the blow-in millionaires in Manteo would kill for, if they knew it existed. Out here, with nothing but trees and the local wildlife as neighbors, the Vollmerhausens were guaranteed at least a few more years of splendid isolation. Roger stopped to drink it in for a moment, and felt the weight in his heart when he realized the developers would surely arrive all the way out here soon. But for now...

Lynn Vollmerhausen appeared from behind the trailer, her tiny form on a massive riding lawnmower. She didn't notice Roger, reaching the end of their lot and swinging the tractor around for another pass. She disappeared behind the trailer, emerging a moment later on the other side, before turning again and repeating the process. She was hunched over the wheel, as intent on where she was steering as any NASCAR driver. Her dark brown hair whipped out behind her, and Roger was momentarily impressed that she could coax that kind of speed out of the mower.

Bill, her long-suffering husband, appeared at the front door and waved at Roger from the window. He motioned for Roger to head on in. He was a big guy. Tall. Muscled. Moving into middle age. He had tight, curly blondish hair. It bore all the hallmarks of a long-ago ginger, now settling down as the years crept by.

Roger reached the door and Bill opened it, offering a big, meaty hand in hello. The sound of Lynn on the mower Dopplered as she rode back and forth in the back "yard." In reality, it wasn't a yard, but a small swath of forest floor that had been adopted by the couple and tamed into something slightly less wild than the surrounding forest and marsh.

"Sorry about Lynn," Bill said, shaking Roger's hand. "She's a little fixated on the plot lately. Probably runs that mower over it at least three times a week. Not really even any grass back there. She's mostly kickin' up dust and scaring the squirrels, but it makes her feel better, so what's the harm, right?"

Roger laughed as he passed into the trailer proper and stopped to appreciate the space.

"Wow, Bill," Roger said. "This place is something else. I haven't seen it in a while. It's gorgeous. And so much bigger than it looks from the outside."

"Yeah, we get that a lot," Bill replied, amiably. "We like it here. Quiet. We've got the water right there. Lots of critters come to visit and not many people do. Just the way we prefer it."

Roger walked to the back of the trailer, which was essentially a series of floor-to-ceiling reinforced windows looking out over the small clearing out back—currently being scoured to the dirt by Lynn and her John Deere—and the Croatan Sound twinkling in the afternoon sunlight just beyond. The trailer itself was well appointed. The living room was filled with Love Sac modulars aimed to make the most of the view. An enormous television was mounted on the wall to the left with a pellet stove below it and off to one side. The open kitchen was all gray marble and stainless steel. Roger was pretty sure the appliances were all new. And high-end. Sub-Zero if he wasn't mistaken. The exception was the range, which, as something of a gourmand himself, Roger recognized as a La Cornue CornuFé. That would set someone back fourteen thousand. Minimum.

Roger turned back to the wall of windows. A sliding door opened up onto a deck. Roger gestured toward it.

"Should we get Lynn in here and find out what's what?" Roger asked, unable to hide a quick gasp as he noticed the back deck was home to an Aquatica Downtown Infinity Spa. That would run another twenty-eight thousand.

Bill saw Roger's dismayed look at the spa.

"Not as expensive as you would think," Bill said, quickly. "I know a guy. Perk of being a building inspector all those years."

"I take my hat off to you," Roger said. "You have it made back here. Just don't let too many people know about it."

Roger also happened to know that the Vollmerhausens had invested wisely. This was one of a number of trailer sites they owned. They were the unofficial mobile home king and queen of the Outer Banks. They made a mint every summer and then cut deals for locals to stay on their properties for less in the offseason. It made them very popular in certain circles. Actually, if those other places were anything like this, Roger thought he might just give them a call in October when things started to slow down.

Bill walked out onto the deck and waved his arms, calling to Lynn. She was wearing a massive set of bright pink headphones, and it took two laps of the yard and Bill crossing down the steps to get her attention.

When she finally noticed Bill, she began to wave him off until she noticed Roger standing in the doorway to the house. She threw her hands up in the air and quickly cut the engine, hopping down from the big mower, stripping off a pair of work gloves and marching with purpose toward the deck.

"Well, look who finally decided to show up!" she called, wagging a finger at Roger. "I guess late is better than never, but I'm sure glad we didn't have an emergency that needed help right away. Don't just stand there with your trap hanging open, get inside before you let every mosquito in the county in. Good lord, man, who raised you?"

Roger backed quickly away from the door and Lynn clomped past him and into the kitchen. The work boots she wore must have been Bill's, because she looked like a toddler playing dress-up.

"Stop staring at the boots," Lynn called over her shoulder from the refrigerator.

Yes, they're Bill's, but he never does any work around here, so someone should get some use outta them."

Bill arrived at the door, rolled his eyes to Roger and gave him a what-can-you-do shrug.

"Roger, have a seat," Lynn went on. "How does some iced tea sound to you?"

Roger replied in the affirmative before he noticed Bill frantically gesturing for him to say no. Too late now.

"Excellent," Lynn crowed, rummaging in the massive fridge before entering the living room with two tall glasses of a murky, brown liquid.

"Mushroom tea," she announced, putting one mug in front of Roger and the other in front of Bill, who grimaced. "Good for your stress levels, inflammation, digestion. Bill needs all of those. Some nights, I've considered sending him to the deck to sleep. Smells worse than the local bears if he eats wrong."

Bill hung his head, quite pointedly not touching the glass. Roger cursed himself internally. He hadn't been here in a while and had forgotten that Lynn adhered to some strict and less-than-delicious dietary restrictions. He wouldn't make that mistake again.

He looked timidly at Lynn before taking the glass and a very small, experimental sip. Not as bad as he expected, he raised the glass in a salute to her. This was significantly better than the pizza she had once served him that lacked cheese. And sauce. The so-called pizza dough did have plenty of seeds and grain-like lumps. It hadn't been bad, per se. It just hadn't been any kind of pizza.

"Look, Roger," Lynn said. "We've danced this dance before. I tell you we saw more of the orbs out over the water. You tell me it's swamp gas. Or a drone. And don't you bring up the Brown Mountain Orbs again. We're nowhere near Brown Mountain. And that's no swamp out there over the sound. So, I want you to take it seriously this time."

Bill was watching Roger with his mushroom tea and cautiously pulled his to him and took a small sniff.

"Lynn, first off, I'm sorry for the delay," Roger replied. "We've had a helluva day, and I've been running in all directions since the sun came up."

Lynn's manner softened. Slightly.

"We heard all about it," she said. "Dead guy down the road in Alligator River. That poor girl taken to the hospital with an overdose. Whoever is bringing that poison into our neck of the woods needs to be put away. How is the girl?"

Roger looked to Bill in surprise. They were very well informed.

Bill shrugged. "Police scanner," he explained.

"Ah," Roger said. "We think she's going to be fine, but a long road ahead of her. And you know I can't really talk to you about the situation in the refuge. Ongoing investigation."

Lynn guffawed. "You, Roger Goldstein, are the last person I need to get information from. I probably get all the news ten minutes before you do. Right. Enough chitchat. What about our orbs?"

"Walk me though this," Roger said, taking out his well-used notepad. "When. Where. What did they look like? What were they doing?"

"About time you took this seriously," Lynn replied with a shake of her head. "This was last night. Must have been after midnight. We had a couple bears wandering through, and I like to stay up and talk to them. Nothing weird. I don't get close or anything."

"Good," Roger said, looking at her and Bill with admonishment. "Bears are dangerous. And wild. And should be left alone."

A couple years back, it had come out that Lynn and Bill had been feeding the sizeable local bear population. And though it was done with good intentions, it had been pulling the bears out of the refuge and closer to the more populated areas. And when Bill had been chased into the house by a rambunctious boar, Roger had felt the need to intervene. They'd been known as the "Crazy Bear Couple" in certain circles ever since.

"Not the point of the story, Roger," Lynn continued. "These orbs were thicker and brighter than ever before. They were moving past away from Alligator River direction. Most were a dull yellow and hovered just over the water, but every so often a few would take off up high, then come down again a few minutes later. But what really got us was when the blue ones showed up. Those were everywhere. They seemed to be under the water, racing back and forth. When they turned up, those yellow ones hightailed it off. Damnedest thing we've seen in a while. What do you have to say to that?"

Roger sat for a moment, chewing his pencil and looking from one to the other of his hosts.

"Don't suppose you got any photos of all this?" he asked.

"I knew you'd want that," Lynn said, wagging a finger. "Bill, show him."

Bill dug his cell phone out of the pocket of his faded work jeans, tapped the screen a few times, and turned it toward Roger and handed it over.

Roger took a quick look and shot them both a glance. "If I scroll back, will there be more?"

"Yeah," Bill affirmed. "I know the quality isn't great, but we worked with what we had."

Roger swiped through a few more photos and was surprised to see exactly what they had described. The first time in their many claims of orbs that they had provided evidence beyond their word. It was the series of pictures with the blue streaks under and above the water that caught his attention most. The rest he could explain. Somewhat. But those? Not as straightforward.

"Send those to me, if you would?" Roger said, taking a few more notes before standing and putting his pad in his back pocket.

"Did you feel that, Bill?" Lynn said, with a hoot. "That chill that just blew through? That must have been hell freezing over. I do believe old Rog is finally taking us seriously."

Roger shot her the friendliest dirty look he could muster before heading to the front door.

"I always take you seriously, Lynn. But this time you gave me something we really like in my line of work. Evidence. And yes, I am going to do some digging to see if I can get to the bottom of it."

Lynn was still laughing as she exited through the back door. The sound of the mower starting up reached the two men before they got to Roger's cruiser.

"I know she can be a pain in the ass," Bill said, shaking Roger's hand, "but she always means well. And this time, there really was something weird happening out there. I wouldn't steer you wrong on that."

"I know, Bill," Roger replied, shaking the other man's hand. "Those photos show something strange. I'll work on it."

"Appreciate it," Bill said, stepping aside as Roger got into the car. "Quick question," he said, before Roger closed the door.

Roger nodded as he started the engine.

"Did you really like that tea?"

Roger paused, drummed his fingers on the steering wheel, and turned slowly to Bill.

"No," he admitted, "but I didn't hate it as much as I thought I would."

Bill nodded and pursed his lips.

"Let's make a deal," Roger said, throwing the cruiser into reverse. "Never ever invite me over for pizza night again, and I'll never squeal on you when I see you at Duck Donuts or Kill Devil Custard, yeah?"

Roger laughed at the look of shock on the other man's face and pointed at his own eyes and then at Bill, letting him know that he'd been watching him.

He was still laughing when he pulled out onto the road again, but his laughter died as he drove off. There was something very worrying about those photos. Something else to bring up at the meeting of the Brethren tonight.

Grier Roleth was anxious. Fidgety. Something about the encounter he and Roger had experienced with the two so-called fishermen earlier in the day just sat wrong with him. He'd spent most of his life traveling the world and had found himself in plenty of dangerous situations. From great white sharks off the coast of South Africa to outracing angry hippos in Tanzania to tracking and relocating tigers in India, he had seen a lot and had realized early on that he'd much rather tangle with any of those creatures than his fellow man. Men were duplicitous, vengeful, mendacious, self-serving schemers. Not all of them, of course, but enough to make him wary when his internal alarms went off. His instincts were hard earned. He didn't ignore them.

After Roger had left, Grier had gone to the bar but decided against the martini he had teased his friend about. He wanted a clear head. And he wanted another look at the area those two shady boaters had been. He had settled on a hot tea, a habit he'd picked up from his time overseas. One look at Desiree attempting to steep the tea leaves properly—no tea bags for him—he had gone behind the bar to show her himself. Not her fault, he realized. He must be the only weirdo to ask for hot tea here. He knew they only stocked it for him. And Desiree was sharp as a tack. Smart. Pretty. Funny. He knew a lot of the regulars came just to spend some time chatting with her. Himself included.

But it was while the tea was steeping that the itch became more than he could take. Those two out on the water had been up to something. Something no good. And he didn't put up with that. Not in his Outer Banks. He was a member of the Brethren, after all, and if he could get to the bottom of it and take some pressure off of Roger, who had already had a bad day for the ages, he would.

Desiree shot him a dismayed look as he ran out to his boat and came back with his BrüMate travel mug. He poured his tea, gave Desiree a peck on the cheek, thanked her profusely, told Will in the corner to call a cab and not drive home, and dashed out the door and to his boat.

He fired up the Robalo, threw off the lines, and headed back out. He checked under the console and patted his flare gun in its case, before checking one of the lockers and making sure his RIFFE Marauder Speargun was in pace, with his mask and fins nearby. It had cost a pretty penny back in the day but had proven worth it many times. He had no doubt he could handle himself, and most definitely those two knuckleheads they'd run into, but preparation was the key to success.

Another thirty minutes out, and he found himself cruising toward the back of Bodie Island. There was no sign of the skiff or the men who'd been in it, but something still felt off. The wind had died, and the water was calm. Too calm for his liking. And then he noticed. No birds. No bird calls. No fluttering of wings. No birds diving for the fish he knew were under his boat.

He cut the engine, letting the boat coast for a moment. Listening. Nothing. Too much nothing.

And then something metallic glinted in the sun from under some of the brush on the shore. Something that didn't belong there. Something like a skiff.

He dropped a couple of drift socks off the cleats to slow down and took a look at the shore through his binoculars. He couldn't be sure it was the same boat, but there was a small boat beached and hidden under some loose branches and scrub. Even if it wasn't connected to what they'd seen here earlier, it didn't belong there, and he would have to call it in. He let the boat drift closer hoping to spot some sort of identifier.

A less experienced boater may have drifted straight into what his peripheral vision caught just in the nick of time. Something sat just under the water. He couldn't tell what it was, but he could tell it was trouble, and he grabbed one of his gaffs. Luckily, most places in the sound were relatively shallow, including this one, and he was able to use the gaff to shove the boat away from whatever lay concealed. As he passed, he used the gaff to explore what the object was and drew it back up with a heavy mesh fishing net, weighted to hover in the water just below the surface. If he, or any unsuspecting boater, had passed over it, the net would have snagged the propeller, disabled the boat, and caused a heap of trouble.

"I don't think so, assholes," he muttered, as he pulled the net into his boat and stowed it behind him. "Not cool."

He fired up the engine and let it idle for a moment, fixing his binoculars on the beached boat. He was just in time to see it disappear further up the bank, pulled out of sight.

"Not this time, losers!" Grier shouted toward the island. "We don't put up with that kind of stuff around here!"

The only answer he received was the crack of a rifle shot.

"Aw, shit," he muttered, diving for the console. "We don't put up with that either!"

He punched the throttle, retrieved the drift socks, and the Robalo rose up quickly in the water, its wake rising and headed to the shore.

There was no second shot, and Grier allowed himself a deep breath as he put more distance between himself and the island, while cursing himself for not taking any pictures. Even a blurry shot may have given them some clue. He looked to his left and knew his Nikon DSLR was in the cupboard there. Within reach. Stupid.

But he did have the improvised net trap on the deck behind him, and that would count for something. Hopefully, that would give them some leads.

As he headed back to the Wanchese Marina, he looked behind him and saw nothing moving on the shore. He'd half expected to see someone racing out after him. That rifle—and to his ears it was bolt action and nothing semi-automatic, thankfully—would have been a problem. He had the flare gun, spear gun, assorted knives...but nothing along those lines. Had never felt the need for one. But times change.

He grimaced. He had definitely not made Roger's day easier. Quite the opposite. But at least they had some more information. And knew that they were definitely not imagining things. Something underhanded was going on in the sound around their beloved Outer Banks. And that would not stand.

This time he would allow himself one of Desiree's martinis. But just one. The Brethren met at eight.

CHAPTER 8

Curt turned the Chevelle into his driveway on Wallace Street and pulled it forward into the carport under the house. He let it idle for a moment and leaned his head back on the seat. He turned the AC on high and angled one of the vents so he got more of the blast of air. Even though it was still spring and not particularly hot outside, he always ran warm. His AC ran year-round and therefore was one of the first upgrades he'd made to the car. Money well spent, as far as he was concerned.

He'd struck out at Angus McTiki's trying to find Todd Lawton. The work crew hadn't seen him today, but the foreman took a card and promised to make sure it got to Lawton. Curt may not have known about the project, but those contractors definitely knew who Curt was. Just his presence there had made them a bit squirrelly. That was a red flag if ever Curt had seen one. He'd make sure to keep an eye on that location. If Sage's rumors of cost and timeline over-runs were accurate, that's when corners got cut and safety took a back seat to expediency. That wouldn't do.

With a deep sigh, Curt cut the engine and heaved himself out of the car. Damn, that AC had felt good.

He let himself in through the door to the carport. Passed the washer/dryer and paused outside of the room he'd had built downstairs. That wasn't exactly right. The room had existed when he bought the house, but he had it winterized and secured. It was by far the most well-appointed room in the house now.

He knew he'd have to go into the room before he left for the meeting of the Brethren later, but he needed to sit down for a few minutes. This had been a rough day, and only one of the things, the interview this morning, had originally been on his schedule.

Jeez. That interview was that morning. It already felt like a week ago. No wonder he was tired. He trudged slowly up the stairs and let himself into the main floor of the house.

It was a simple cottage. What the locals called a "beach box." One main floor on pilings to protect from flooding and storm swells. Three bedrooms. Two and a half baths. And a large great room that combined the kitchen, dining room, and living room under a vaulted ceiling with a three-quarter wraparound deck facing the street and his neighbors.

He had certainly accumulated enough money at this point in his life to buy a larger house. A fancier house. A house on the beach, or in a gated community. But he loved this house. He'd gotten it before all the successes had rolled his way, and it represented a simpler time in his life. This had been his castle when he first moved in. A lifelong dream achieved. He knew his neighbors. He enjoyed the quiet. He even enjoyed the late afternoon walks to the sound to watch the sunset over the water, usually surrounded by friends. This house *meant* something to him.

He poured himself a glass of iced tea and wandered out front onto the deck, settling into one of the big chunky deck chairs. He waved as one of his neighbors, Bob, walked by. There would be no sunset for him today. If the Brethren meeting started at eight, he had things to prepare. And some more decisions to make. He'd also be there early to prepare. It had been quite a while since they had welcomed a new member, and he expected to be out of practice. Anticipated some nervous flutters. Not just for him, but for the others, as well.

He felt the weight of centuries of tradition on his shoulders. He, Roger, and Grier were getting older. The future would belong to Sage. And hopefully Carlito. And then to whomever they found to fill the ranks. Back in the day, there had been dozens of Brethren at any given time. The fact that they were down to four—hopefully soon five—had to be addressed. These numbers were just not enough to safeguard the entire Banks. If they spread out across the islands the way they should, they would never see each other.

People had forgotten all about the Brethren, and maybe that was for the best. They had once been a poorly kept secret, and their very existence went some way toward keeping people in line. But over the years, the Banks attracted more and different people. And along with them more and different threats. Threats that were often unseen or difficult to detect. As society changed, the Brethren had to change with it.

Curt knew he wouldn't win many street fights. Or challenges on the high seas. His brain was his most effective weapon. It had served him, and the Brethren, well for a long time. He was the last in his family to take up the mantle, unless one of the younger generations decided to join. Something that looked less and less likely with each passing year.

That weighed Curt down also. All of the tradition and loyalty and history would fade. Unless he chose wisely and was able to instill it in those who came along.

And it all started in earnest tonight. Sage had joined when the older generation had been in their primes. No thought of leaving. Of growing old. But times had changed. And quickly.

And he knew there were still choices to be made. How much and how quickly would he share with Carlito? How much of what he'd done did he need to confess to the others. Roger suspected. Grier too, he thought, although Grier would give him space to admit it. Sooner or later, Roger would force the issue. Probably better to get ahead of that, if he could.

For tonight, though, he knew the pair of daggers and the boarding hook were mandatory. As they always had been. The ornate daggers were rumored to be passed down from none other than Blackbeard. Although, to be honest, he wondered about that. The boarding hook had a murkier provenance. It was certainly from the Golden Age of the Caribbean Pirates, and tradition labeled it as coming from Blackbeard's final ship, *The Adventure*.

The daggers represented the Brethren's willingness to fight in close quarters. To be exposed and risk the ugliness of staring your enemies in the face. To witness the consequence of battle firsthand.

The boarding hook, used by pirates to snare enemy ships and hold them still, or pull them close to board, represented taking the fight to those who would harm the Banks. The Brethren were bound by no laws or rules other than their directive to protect their home. If that meant that sometimes they bent, or even broke, local laws? Then so be it. Someone had to be willing to do it.

Although, they went out of their way to avoid that happening. Most of the time.

There were various papers and parchments that served as the Brethren's library and chronicles. Those would be shared, as well. They played less of a direct role in their business these days, though.

And then there was the final relic. The deep heavy chest of stained wood and iron banding that held the most rumored and potentially dangerous of the Brethren's traditions. That was what had him pensive today. That was the decision he dreaded making. It was also the decision he had made months ago and not truly faced. Yet. The decision he had taken upon himself.

He sipped his tea in the late afternoon sunshine. Bob returned at the end of his walk. Headed home. Curt waved again. And Bob had no idea that Curt was feeling the siren song of a centuries-old chest rising up from his ground floor. A chest that, once the secrets were shared, would change so much. Would change everything.

Roger pulled the cruiser into the station lot. He'd been eyeing the time and was annoyed at himself for getting drawn into the Vollmerhausens' stories. But something about the way they'd described those orbs, and the timing of them, was setting off internal alarms. He'd have to talk to Curt about all of this. And he suspected that was going to be a difficult talk. There was already so much they'd avoided saying. It couldn't go on forever.

He patted the department Humvee as he passed it in the lot. Probably one of his finest moments, at least in his own mind, had been when he drove it roaring onto the grounds of Bodie Island to save his friends during their last case. One of his finest moments but no one other than his fellow Brethren would know what he'd done. That had to be enough.

He took the stairs to the second-floor reception area two at a time. He'd had a long day. A stressful day. But he knew he had to report to Chief Brady before clocking out. And that knowledge did nothing to lessen his anxiety.

Johnny Brady was a fire hydrant of a man. Five foot seven on a good day, he was bald as a cue ball and as hard as one. At least until you got to know him, which very few people managed to do. His brown eyes would drill a hole straight through you and he had a habit of staring at a person silently until they buckled under the accumulated pressure and spilled whatever he was after. As a life-long Manteo resident and the oldest serving officer on the Manteo force, he'd gotten to his current position through sheer grit and determination. He was big trouble in a small package. And he was waiting for Roger.

Slightly out of breath, Roger reached Mary Hallet's front desk and leaned on the counter, wheezing ever so slightly.

"Why Roger," Mary cooed at him, "no need to get down on your knees for me. I'm a practical woman. Wine and roses will do just fine."

Roger peered up at her. This was new. Usually, he was the one lobbing flirtation at her and she was the one swatting it away. He wasn't sure how to react to this change in the order of things.

"Mary," he said, between uneven breaths, "if I thought getting on my knees would have worked, I'd have tried it years ago."

Mary laughed, and it was a deep chesty laugh. A sound he'd never heard from her.

"Should have known I couldn't throw you, Roger," she shot back, "but it was worth it for that look on your face. Enough chitchat, though. Brady is waiting for you in his office. And let's just say he seems annoyed."

"Just annoyed?" Roger asked, as Mary hit the buzzer to let him into the station proper. "Must be my lucky day."

Roger tapped twice on Mary's plexiglass divider as he opened the door and started back. She tapped twice back. Their usual routine.

"Oh, Rog!" she called before he got more than a few feet through the door. "Any news on the poor fella from Alligator River?"

"Why Mary," Roger replied over his shoulder, before turning back in her direction. "You know I can't talk about those things with you"—he mouthed the word *no*, before changing direction—"but now that you mention it, it did come up that you and Russ were at Bad Bean last night. Your personal life is your own, and I'm setting my jealousy aside for the moment. Just wondered if you saw anything unusual when you were there?"

"Well, what a strange thing to bring up," Mary replied, leaning back in her seat. "Can't imagine how, let alone why, that would come up. They had some new beer from Seven Sounds and Russ felt pity for an old lady and took me along. But no. Nothing unusual. Good food, a beer, a margarita, and off we went home. To our separate homes, I might add. Silly."

Roger nodded his head, thinking, and started back again toward the chief's office before stopping, remembering his manners.

"Thanks, Mary," he called back to her. "I appreciate you. Next time you two should invite me along. I have a very sophisticated palate."

With one last wink, he disappeared into the depths of the station. Two right-hand turns and a last left brought him to a door with "Police Chief John Brady" stenciled on it. It was worn. Flaking at the edges. It had been there a long time. Roger paused in the doorway, put his arms on either side of the doorframe and took a deep breath.

Just as he raised his hand to knock, he was greeted by a high-pitched shout from within.

"I can see your feet under the door frame, you great sizzling numpty!"

Roger shook his head, opened the door, and walked gingerly into the small office. It was warmer than usual, and Brady seemed more at loose ends than the average Tuesday. His tie was loose around his neck. His top button undone. He had a pair of reading glasses perched atop his head. If he'd had any hair, it would have been tousled.

"Sit, Goldstein," Brady barked, "and try—just try—to explain to me why you chose today—the day we got called to a body in the wildlife refuge—to waste time taking a statement from the damn crazy bear couple of Manns Harbor. It's at least the fourth time this year they've called about those damn orbs. You don't get paid to piss your time away making the local nut jobs feel better about their imagined little green men sightings! Explain yourself!"

Roger took a seat across the desk from Brady. There was barely room for him to cross his legs, but he managed. He was always surprised at how cramped the chief's office was. Every possible surface was covered with folders, and forms, and manuals. Two citations for distinguished service were on the wall to Roger's left, but they were almost entirely obscured by tall file cabinets, which he was sure were filled with yet more files and forms.

The one redeeming quality of the room was a large window that looked out over a massive tree drooping over the expanse of grass outside the front of the station.

"Well?" Brady growled.

Roger relaxed slightly. All in all, this was the chief in a good mood.

"Sir," Roger began in a measured and reasonable tone, "we needed someone to process the missing guy's car in Nags Head. Now you and I both know that Russ is much better suited to that than I am. He did take that forensics course a couple years back. Russ seemed the better bet to do that right. And since we were now shifting to a missing person case while we wait for more details on our John Doe, I figured I'd tackle the Vollmerhausens. Given that they're on the water over that way, I thought maybe they might have seen something to help us in our investigation. And, before you say anything, I don't mean orbs or ghosts or aliens. I just mean someone out on the water late last night. Seemed like the best use of time, under the circumstances. Sir."

Brady deflated behind his desk. His Napoleon complex fading into just a tired middle-aged man at the end of a long day.

"Dammit, Roger," he said, reaching into one of his desk drawers and pulling out a bottle and two shot glasses. "If you'd just told me that to begin with, we could have avoided all of this tension. You're right. Russ is the one for that job. And you can handle the nuts like nobody. Here. Have a shot with me. Red Breast. Twelve year."

"Just one, sir," Roger said. "I have things to do tonight."

"Good for you," Brady replied, pouring two generous measures and sliding one glass across the desk. "Anything interesting from the loonies?"

"Maybe, but doubtful," Roger answered, silently toasting Brady. "I'll have a report for you on your desk in the morning."

"I know you will, Rog," Brady said with a nod as they both tossed back their whiskeys. "Best damn officer we have. Just never come for my job. 'Cuz you might get it."

"I like exactly where I am," Roger shot back. "Plan to stay here until I hang 'em up."

"Sorry for the numpty crack," Brady said, sheepishly, as Roger rose and headed to the door. "Long day."

"I heard that," Roger called as he reached the hallway and headed back the way he had come.

Piece of cake, Roger thought, as he checked the time again. He knew how to handle Brady like no one else. It had gone so quickly, he even had time to go back to his little cottage, shower, and pull himself together for tonight. Brethren Council.

———

Curt arrived at The Blue Crab Tavern on Colington Road early. It was only seven o'clock. Sunset wasn't for another forty-five minutes, and the Brethren Council wasn't due to begin until eight. But Curt knew he had things to prepare. Not least of which was himself.

He entered through the front door and waved to RG behind the bar. She was the owner and long-time bartender and had become as much a fixture in the bar as the well-worn pool table and the vintage beer signs that adorned the walls. Vintage being a polite term for old. More than a few of the beers advertised hadn't been brewed in years. But the Crab was known for being out of step with current trends. That's one of the reasons it was so favored by locals and long-time visitors to the area. You wouldn't find the latest mocktail, or espresso martini, or the hottest glitter beer. They served the tried and true, with an occasional surprise thrown in. It was cash only. No frills.

And it was home to a throng of locals who struck newcomers as rough around the edges. Not by accident, either. Though they happily looked out for each other, they were completely aware your average tourist could find them intimidating. Some turned around and hightailed it. The ones who stayed, usually found themselves a part, if temporarily, of the extended family.

Curt had long ago become one of the regulars. He saw Bullfrog, so named because he could mimic the sound of a bullfrog better than an actual frog, in his usual seat on the corner of the bar. He was joined by Tugboat Joe, who had done a long stint in the merchant marines and come back with some interesting stories. He also wore two teardrop tattoos on his face, just under his right eye. They were both filled in, and street lore claimed that anyone who had those tattoos was guilty of killing an enemy. But Tugboat Joe was soft-spoken and gentle. If those two tattoos represented his committing two murders, they were either from another very different time in his life, or an exaggeration meant to keep trouble away. No one had ever asked about them. No need.

Curt dropped a fiver on the bar and was about to order a Fat Tire when he remembered they had changed the recipe. He asked for a Lost Colony Flounder Pounder instead, a clean light beer brewed not far away in Stumpy Point. Normally, he would want to keep his head clear, but they were the Brethren of the Coast. Descended from pirates. You didn't conduct official business without something to quaff near at hand.

He thanked RG, told her to keep the change, and nodded toward the sliding doors to the back deck. She nodded in return, and assured him that at twelve minutes to eight, when the sun had fully set, she would call any other patrons in from the outside. Curt reminded her that he would buy a round for the house as an apology for any inconvenience and she gave him a wink.

RG didn't know exactly what the Brethren did, but she knew Curt was important, a loyal patron, a good person to have on your side and always looking out for the community. That's all she needed to know. All she *wanted* to know.

Curt let himself out onto the back deck and allowed himself to soak in the view for a moment. It never ceased to amaze him that the one last dive bar on the Banks also boasted what was likely the most soul-stirring view of the sunset over the sound. And most people who passed through the area had absolutely no idea.

He watched as an otter left the shore off to his left, cruising out for some late day fishing. Judging by the size of the splashes around the deck, he'd picked a good night for it. He did have some competition. A great blue heron was wading across the inlet, slowly, ever so slowly, moving through the water, patiently scanning for dinner. Judging by the echoing sound of another heron nearby, the good weather had brought out the local predators. It never failed to surprise Curt that such an elegant, graceful bird as the great blue had such an ugly and undignified *grak* of a call. Mother Nature had a sense of humor.

This was Curt's Outer Banks. Where he felt most at home. Most relaxed. Most peaceful. And these were the Outer Banks he had sworn to safeguard.

He heard the sliding doors open behind him and wasn't the least bit surprised when he turned to find that the second arrival was Carlito.

The young man gave a tentative wave, awkward at finding himself alone again with Curt after the morning they'd spent together.

Curt saw that Carlito's hands were empty and raised his own to stop the youngster from getting any closer.

"March back in there and get yourself a drink," he announced. "We don't do this without something to toast each other. Stick to beer, if you don't mind. You'll be happier that way. And grab something light for Roger while you're at it. Just have them put it on my tab."

Carlito flashed a shy grin, nodded, paused to say something, and then thought better of it and retreated to the bar. Curt laughed. Yeah, he'd made the right choice.

Roger was next to arrive, choosing to enter the deck through the side door that led to the parking lot. He'd changed out of his uniform, but he knew the regulars were aware he was a cop, and he limited his inside time as much as possible to cut them some slack. No sense setting them on edge. Eventually, he'd drop in to say hi. But best to give them a chance to realize he was here. Of course, he was off duty and couldn't care less about what they got up to, but allowances had to be made.

Before he'd even reached the table under the pavilion where Curt had seated himself, Carlito appeared with a PBR, a Yuengling, and a Mother Earth Brewing Reef Keeper IPA.

Roger turned to Curt with a look of surprise.

"I know you said you liked him," Roger said, "but I didn't have him pegged for a triple fisted drinker. Way to make an impression, kid."

Carlito, confused, turned to Curt, who patted him on the shoulder and ushered him to the bench next to him.

"Take it easy, there, Roger," Curt replied. "I sent him in to grab you a beer, since I know you usually come around the side."

"Well, thank you, kind sir," Roger said, as Carlito handed him the Yuengling. "How do you explain that third beer, then?"

Curt turned a questioning look to Carlito.

"Oh, yeah, this," he answered, holding up the IPA. "You told me Sage would be here. She said the dogs are always with her, and I figured she'd probably not bring them through the bar. She works at the brewery and a lot of beer people like IPAs, so I took a chance. Um. Is that okay?"

"It's better than okay," Curt said. "It's perfect."

"Smart," Roger admitted. "You may have actually gotten this one right."

"Carlito, meet Roger Goldstein," Curt said, by way of introduction. "One of your soon to be fellow Brethren of the Coast. Roger, meet Carlito."

"Pleased to meet you, sir," Carlito said, offering a hand to the deputy.

"My father is sir," Roger said, taking the proffered hand. "I'm just Roger."

Sage's arrival was announced by her dog Riley bounding around the half-open gate to the parking lot. Riley immediately bypassed the table where the men were seated and raced to the edge of the deck where the otter had just paddled by. She stuck her nose in the air and whuffed.

Sage came through the gate next, with the big, galumphing Banks in her wake. Banks, unlike Riley, headed straight for the table, nosed each of the men in salutation, and plopped down by Curt.

"Carlito already grabbed you an IPA," Curt told her. "So have a seat. We just need Grier, and we can get going."

"Kid's already making me look bad," Roger said, grinning.

"Don't blame him for your shortcomings, Rog," Sage shot back, accepting the IPA from Carlito and nodding her thanks.

The sound of an approaching engine reached them, drifting across the otherwise still water of the sound by the deck.

"And if I'm not mistaken," Curt said, gesturing in the direction of the sound, "our final member will be arriving by water soon. Relax, Carlito. This will be easier than you think. And then we have a few things to talk about. We're going to put you straight to work."

"You'll find that's the norm around here," Roger said before talking a healthy pull on his beer. "But the glamour and fame make up for it all."

Carlito looked to Curt in confusion.

"Ignore him," Sage said. "He thinks he's funny. You'll be great."

As Grier's little Robalo boat rounded the end of the cove where they were perched, Sage reached across and clinked glasses with Carlito, who toasted the table at large and leaned forward onto the table.

***

Back at the rental house, the reunion friends had gotten restless. The news that Mark Elliot was *not* the body that had been found was initially met with relief. Almost celebration. But as the afternoon wore on, they'd started to think about where exactly their friend could be. They had so many questions and no further information from the police. Why was Elliot's car here and who had left it? Where had he gone after leaving Bad Bean? Who was the man from his past who had caught him so off guard that he had backed out of a long-planned excursion with his friends? But most importantly—was he still alive?

By six o'clock, Chris and Amelia had hit the bar and begun serving drinks to the others. Terry and Cathy had shared a bottle of Sauvignon Blanc, Terry dropping ice cubes into her glass with each refill. Chris and Francis had each opened a crowler of Swells'a beer, purchased on their way into town. Amelia, as was her wont, carried a bottle of Malbec with her and planted herself on one of the deck chairs and began scrolling on her phone while the late afternoon sun settled further behind the house. Kirsten joined her with a beer in a life preserver-themed koozie.

The others had settled into various nooks of the living area. The men were debating which bars Elliot would most likely visit. The women, curled on the sofa with their legs tucked underneath them, tried to recall each of the beach trips they had taken since high school.

"He never met any girls here, did he?" Cathy asked Terry. "That doesn't really seem his style."

"Not that I know of," Terry replied. "The boys were always big talkers, but not big doers. There was the one set of sisters in the nineties, but I don't think that led anywhere."

"He almost hooked up with *sisters*?" Cathy asked, incredulous.

Terry laughed in response. "No, no, no. I think he liked one and the other guy from back then—Rick?—liked the other. I may be misremembering."

Chris and Francis had fallen silent, listening to the women, and finally Francis could take it no longer.

"I think it was oh-nine," he interrupted. "Mark liked the older sister, but she was already seeing someone. They flirted, but after the beach they only spoke a few times and then she flaked out. He was bummed, but I don't think it was a major life event."

Jaime, who had been sitting alone at the kitchen table, and

pointedly not drinking, rose and crossed to the love seat opposite the sofa.

"Yeah, he told me about that," Jaime said. "Not really that big a deal. That other time, he and Chuckles went out one night. Can't remember where they went, but Chuckles left later the following day and Mark was definitely off for the rest of the week."

"Why do I not remember this?" Chris asked. "And speaking of Chuckles, where is he? He should have come this year."

"I asked him," Francis said. "He was busy. Still in Northern Virginia but has some high-paying job now. Maybe we should touch base with him and see if he remembers whatever happened."

"Worth a shot," Terry said, leaning forward on the sofa and unfurling her legs. "But I feel like we should be doing something *now*. He's out there somewhere. And we're just here having happy hour."

"And what do you suggest we do?" Cathy asked. "I'm not being snarky; I just have no idea where to start."

"I mean, we could start at Bad Bean and just—ask around. Show his picture. Follow any leads," Terry suggested.

"Isn't that what the cops are doing?" Jaime said quietly from the opposite side of the room. "That deputy definitely didn't ask for our help."

"That deputy doesn't exactly inspire confidence, as far as I'm concerned," Francis replied. "Not the sharpest tool in the shed."

"I wouldn't underestimate him," Jaime said. "I have a feeling there's more to him than meets the eye."

"What makes you say that?" Chris shot back. "He's not exactly keeping us in the loop. If there even is a loop, at this point."

"Because people have always underestimated me," Jaime said quietly. "I think they do the same with him. Gut feeling."

"I mean, even if he is more on the ball than we think, wouldn't it be good if we asked around?" Cathy asked. "The more people looking, the better the odds of finding him, yeah? And we know him. The cops don't. That means we have an advantage."

"That settles it," Chris said, standing. "I'm going out to look for him. I can't just sit here. Not with him out there."

When Chris headed for the table of keys, Jaime rose and cut him off.

"Nope. No how, no way," Jaime said, his hands up to stop Chris's progress.

"You don't want us to help?" Francis asked, incredulous.

"I don't want any of you to drive after having what? A crowler each?" Then he looked at the women. "Or the better part of a bottle of wine?"

Amelia and Kirsten, seeing movement in the living room, came in from the deck.

"What's the word?" Kirsten asked, heading to the fridge for a new beer for her mini life preserver koozie.

"They want to head out and ask questions in bars to try to find Mark," Jaime explained, planting himself in front of the keys.

"I'm not so sure that's a good idea," Amelia replied. "The police are on it. We could just get in the way. Make things worse. I'm on the record as being against it."

"You're also on the record as being mostly done with a bottle of Malbec," Chris said. "So I hope you don't take offense if we make our own decision?"

Amelia raised her hands in surrender. "We're all adults," she said, turning back to the door to the deck. "I think some of us should be here just in case Mark comes back or the police need us. I'm staying. You all do what you think is best."

"I'm going," Francis declared. "I'm a lawyer. I know how to question people. And I always know when someone is lying. Anyone else?"

Terry and Cathy both raised their hands.

When Kirsten looked at them in disbelief, Cathy shrugged.

"I can't just keep sitting here," she said. "I have to try."

Jaime grabbed a set of keys and turned to the others.

"Seeing as I'm the only sober one," he said, "I'll go. This is exactly why I didn't have a beer. Someone has to be thinking clearly. Not sure if it's a good idea, but I know any of you driving is a very bad idea. Come on, then."

Jaime headed down the stairs toward the driveway and, after a moment of looking to each other, the others followed.

Kirsten, left alone in the living room, watched them go and shook her head.

"I knew I should have stayed home," she said to no one, then turned back toward the deck and joined Amelia outside.

They sat in silence for a few minutes. Finally, Amelia set her drink down and turned to Kirsten.

"They're wasting their time," she said. "It's idiotic."

"I guess they just need to feel like they're doing something," Kirsten replied. "I get it. I mean, I get the need to do something. I agree with you on the pointless part."

"I just hope they don't make anything worse," Amelia said, reclaiming her glass of wine.

"I'll drink to that," Kirsten answered, raising her beer in a toast.

The current roster of Brethren had assembled around the table in the rear pavilion of the Blue Crab. Grier's little boat was tied up on the dock just a few feet away, and he had joined the others, shaking hands with Carlito after a formal introduction by Curt.

Curt had taken a heavy muslin sack out of a bag he'd stowed under the table. Very carefully, he'd unwrapped what lay within and placed three items on the table. Two large blades were crossed. They were simple, unadorned, lethal in appearance. While they clearly carried significant age, they had been well tended and looked polished and honed. In the center, where the blades crossed, Curt had laid a large iron shaft with three hooks protruding from the end, looking like a fountain spraying. The hook had a heavy hemp rope coiled intricately around its length. Any functionality it had once enjoyed was gone. This was clearly ornamental. The daggers, on the other hand, looked ready for business.

"Carlito, I think you've met everyone, now," Curt began. "Are you sure you are ready to go through with this?"

"No," Carlito answered bluntly. "But I spent the day thinking it through, and it seems like the kind of thing someone could spend the rest of their life wondering about if they passed it up. I didn't come here to take the same path everyone my age does. I'd have stayed in Texas and gotten an office job if that was my plan. Granted, this is a little quicker than I thought I'd find good trouble, but I'm not into regrets. Let's do it."

"I like this kid," Grier said. "There's some fire in there. We need that."

"Not that anyone asked me," Roger added, "but I agree. Good call, Curt. Welcome, Carlito. Can't wait to show you the ropes."

Sage was leaning against one of the corner posts of the pavilion and raised her beer to the others. "Curt knows how I feel. Welcome, Carlito."

"Carlito," Curt continued, "we're not into flowery speeches and old-time ceremonies. Most of what the Brethren did, and how they did it, has been lost. What we do know has been passed down from one generation to another. These few items are the last known remnants of the original chapter of the Brethren here. Likely they were on Blackbeard's ship itself. Very little else from that time is still around."

The others all turned to Curt, but Carlito, caught in the gravity of the moment didn't notice and the moment passed.

"Place your right hand on the daggers."

Carlito did and seemed to show some nerves. The blades were not just for show, and he rested his hands very lightly on them.

"Do you swear to observe the rules of our chapter? To abide by the equitable distribution of any goods acquired by said chapter?"

"Don't expect any goods," Roger muttered. "I still haven't seen any."

Roger fell silent at a look from Curt.

"Ignore him," Curt went on. "But he's right. We aren't a for-profit group. But this is what little tradition we observe. Do you agree that every member is due an equal vote? That you swear to respect, protect, and support the others? To foreswear theft among each other? Do you acknowledge that gambling for money amongst each other is forbidden? To avoid drunkenness?"

Grier coughed into a closed hand and Sage hit him lightly on the side of the head. Another warning look from Curt.

"Do you promise to devote yourself to the protection and well-being of the Outer Banks and all her people? To place yourself in harm's way if called on? To see your fellow Brethren as family and brothers-in-arms?"

"I hate that part," Sage said. "Sexist."

"Or sisters-in-arms?" Curt added.

Carlito stood frozen in place, his hands still set on the blades.

A moment. Another.

"Is that it?" Carlito finally asked.

"That's it," Curt responded.

"I guess I thought it would feel...different. More words. More swearing. Just more," Carlito said, looking around at the others. "But yeah. Of course I do."

"We're about action," Grier responded. "Words don't serve us so much."

"Welcome to the Brethren, Carlito," Curt said, pulling Carlito into a bear hug. The others crowded in, patting his shoulder. Tousling his hair.

Sage let out a hoot and raised her beer above her head, spilling a significant amount in the process. Roger started to do the same, before remembering something and reaching into a bag he'd set under the table. He drew out a bottle, raised it over his head, and howled at the moon, now just visible on the horizon over the sound.

"Picked this up on my way out of Manteo, seemed only appropriate," he shouted.

The bottle he held aloft had a blue and silver label declaring it to be Kill Devil Rum. It was a white rum, unaged and pure. Roger peeled the foil off of the cork with his teeth and then twisted the cork free of the bottle and taking a long drag straight from the neck. He let out a long, satisfied "Ahhhh" before handing it to Sage who did the same.

"Kill Devil Rum for the Outer Banks Brethren! Only fitting. Welcome, Carlito," Roger said, putting an arm around the younger man's shoulders and beaming as Sage followed suit.

During this, Grier sidled up to Curt.

"The chest is under the table, isn't it?" he asked Curt.

Curt paused before answering. "Yeah, it is. No sense taking chances."

"And when are you planning on sharing it with him?" Grier asked more pointedly than he'd intended.

"As soon as I can," Curt replied. "But not here. Not in the back-yard here at night where Bullfrog or anyone else could wander in. He's Brethren now. I will. Promise."

Grier nodded slowly. "I'll just point out that you were the one who chose this place. If I didn't know any better, I'd think you were putting it off."

"Well, I hope you know better," Curt said.

"Mhm," Grier answered quietly, risking a quick look under the table where the sturdy chest was partially hidden by the trailing edges of the muslin bag. "You can't keep it all to yourself, you know."

But Curt had turned to the others and accepted the bottle of rum.

Grier shook his head before facing the others and joining the celebration. None of them noticed the blue streaks of light racing through the waters of the sound and gathering below the dock that held the table. And the artifacts. And the Brethren.

Amelia and Kirsten were still on the deck as the sun went down. Just after eight, Kirsten got up and disappeared inside the house. She grabbed another beer for herself, peeked out the door and saw that Amelia still had a mostly full glass of wine. She flipped the switch, turning off the exterior lights on the deck, and night settled over their seats like a heavy blanket. Suddenly, the sky came alive with countless stars. With the ambient light gone, and the neighboring houses likewise dark, the night sky had become a patchwork of pinpoint lights.

The mesmerizing rhythm of the waves finding the beach lulled both of the women. The endless stars, like cosmic fireflies, stretched as far as they could see, finally sliding below what must have been the horizon, though the black night made the entire vista one canvas. A few courageous clouds wandered into their view, catching the flickering starlight and sailing silently along, sky lanterns sent from where they could never know.

Kirsten emerged again and took her seat. The two women sat in a comfortable silence. These moments could only be enjoyed here. They were quintessential Banks. Their homes were in Northern Virginia, where strip malls, interstate highways, and gridlock were the order of most of their days. The skies they passed beneath every day crowded with flight paths and black helicopters that thumped their mysterious ways ceaselessly. The stars, the very stars that now winked down at them, were rarely seen and even more rarely noticed. Hidden away, as if offended by what had been done there in the name of progress.

Five minutes passed. Ten. Finally, Amelia tapped her phone screen to check the time. It was later than she'd thought.

"When do we start getting worried about them?" she asked. "They've been gone a while."

"Not yet," Kisten said. "Most places are open until nine. If we haven't heard anything by then we can start to think about it. I'm guessing they went to Bad Bean, then another bar, started talking, and never left. Remember. Jaime hadn't been drinking. So they're okay on that score. They'll be back."

Amelia made a sound that could be interpreted as agreement.

"And then there's Mark," Amelia said, reluctantly. "He's out there. Somewhere. Alone. And we're sitting here having a drink and looking for shooting stars."

"Wherever Mark is," Kirsten answered, "the police can do a much better job of finding him than we can. Look, I get why they felt like they needed to do something, but the truth is, it's just as important for someone to be here. In case he shows up. We're not cops. We haven't got the slightest idea how to find a missing person."

"I know," Amelia said. "I *know*. It just feels wrong. This whole thing feels wrong. All of it."

"I sent him a text," Kirsten admitted. "A few. Just hoping they reach him, and he knows we're worried. They haven't been read yet."

"I did the same," Amelia said. "Left a voicemail too. It all feels so lame. So pointless. I want to do more."

"Let's both send another text," Kirsten suggested. "Then we focus on getting those other nutjobs back safe and sound. In forty minutes, we can start bugging them to come back."

"Right," Amelia said. "One text. A few more minutes of quiet. And then we get in gear."

They both picked up their phones and typed for a moment before they each hit send and heard the whoosh of an outgoing text.

"C'mon, Mark," Kirsten said quietly. "Give us something. Let us know you're okay. Wherever you are."

But their texts disappeared into the night like the clouds drifting between them and the stars. Amelia rose and stood at the railing staring at the sky. Kirsten stared at her phone screen, willing it into action. And the clock marched onward toward nine o'clock. Closing time. And time for the rest of their friends to get back. But in the meantime? Silence.

The celebration over Carlito's joining the Brethren had been short-lived, but genuine. The disappearance of Mark Elliot and the fentanyl case loomed over everything, and they settled in to compare notes and ideas. It didn't take long for them to reach the conclusion that until the autopsy results on Kevin Keegan were returned, they would be flying blind. Their current best bet was to find Todd Lawton, co-owner of the new mega-bar on the beach road. His EZ-Pass had been used on the way north to Virginia today. He had a business to open, so he'd have to be back soon. When Curt had asked around about the dead man, Keegan, he'd mostly been met with blank stares, although one of the bar staff thought his name sounded familiar. Most of the staff hadn't met each other yet. Formal training was set to start the following day, and they were aiming for a soft opening on Thursday. For that to happen, it would mean almost around-the-clock work to put the finishing touches on pretty much everything.

Sage reached into her bag and took Elliot's cell phone and smart watch in a plastic bag, on the table in the midst of everyone.

"Found these today," she said, eyeing Roger sheepishly. "Probably should have let Russ take it back to the station, but I thought we would crack it faster. And before you ask, yes, I think they're Elliot's. I found them in his car."

Roger wagged a finger at her, and the look on his face was stern.

"You could get in a lot of trouble pulling stunts like this," he scolded. "If Russ had seen you, you'd be up on charges. But I gotta admit, you have a point. We'll move on this faster than the red tape at HQ would allow. Password protected?"

Sage nodded an affirmative, and Roger cursed under his breath.

"Actually, I'm pretty good with stuff like that," Carlito said. "Give me a while with it and I bet I can get us into it."

Roger gestured for Carlito to help himself, and the youngster pulled the bag toward him and looked it over, nodding to himself.

"Not a problem," Carlito said after a few taps on the screen. "I can have us something by morning."

"What else?" Grier said, nodding his approval at the turn of events.

Curt told the others that he would stop by the new bar, Angus

McTiki's again tomorrow and be far more persistent in his questioning. Roger let everyone know that he'd been trying Lawton's cell phone throughout the day with no luck. He'd redouble his efforts tomorrow. If Lawton was trying to dodge them, he'd regret it when they caught up to him. And they would catch up to him.

Carlito, who had been sitting silently throughout, absorbing as much as he could, slowly raised a hand over his head. Curt noticed and turned an amused look to the young man.

"You don't need to raise your hand here," Curt said. "You're not in school anymore and, in case you forgot the oath you just swore, we're all equals. If you have a question, just fire away."

"I mean, I guess it's sort of a question," Carlito replied, softly. "Maybe more of a thought. It's just...you have these three guys who were together last night. One shows up dead. The other two? You all seem to be assuming that those two are missing, but there's no proof of that. What if all three of them are dead and you just haven't found the other two yet?"

The table fell silent. The others all looked at each other for a moment. Sage reached under the table to pet her dogs who were curled up at her feet. Roger puffed out his cheeks and grunted. Grier stared at the table in front of him and scratched at the surface. Curt remained fixed on Carlito.

"Well, shit," Curt said finally. "We made a lot of assumptions, didn't we. I hope you're wrong, kid. I *really* hope you're wrong. But you have a point. This is the Banks. We don't think along those lines here. One death alone is rare and bad enough. But we have no proof those two are still alive."

"But wait," Grier broke in. "Elliot's car showed up. That could mean something. And that other one, Lawton, his car was on the road north just this afternoon."

"But no one has actually seen either one of them," Sage said. "Until we do, we have to accept they might be dead. We need to move faster. If they're alive, they could be in some serious trouble."

"Right," Curt said, with a fist to the table. "We get serious tomorrow. Roger, Mary and Russ were at Bad Bean when all this went down. Talk to them?"

"Already did," Roger admitted. "But I'll take a different angle tomorrow."

"Good," Curt said, looking around the table. "What else?"

Roger and Grier shared a look, before Grier sat forward on the bench.

"I know there's a lot happening already, but Rog and I had a run-in on the water with a couple of local guys who were definitely up to no good."

Roger then took up the story and relayed it to the others. When he finished, Grier held a finger up to hold the others for a moment.

"Roger, there's more," Grier announced. "Something just didn't sit right with me, so I went back out after you had left. Just wanted to see the place again. Try to understand what might have been happening."

"And?" Roger asked.

Grier then filled them in on the second encounter he'd had, complete with the submerged net-trap and the shot fired from the cover of the island.

"I thought it was just a warning shot," Grier said, but when I got back to the marina, I found a bullet hole on my starboard side. It was more than just a warning."

"Grier, I know you're used to being on your own, but that's exactly why we need to do those things with at least another member. That could have gone very badly," Roger said.

"You're right," Grier replied. "I know it. I just thought I was doing some recon. Never thought anyone would still be there. Totally my bad."

"Right," Curt said, moving on. "This needs some attention too. Roger, do some sleuthing tomorrow when you're at the station. Best guess?"

"Smuggling something in, I would think," Roger answered. "Given everything going on in town, my money would be on drugs."

"Bastards," Sage spat out, rising to stand at the railing.

Just then, the booming call of a bullfrog split the night. Curt was on his feet in an instant, flowed by Roger.

"What's happening?" Carlito asked, looking in confusion to Sage and Grier.

"That's our buddy, Bullfrog," Grier said, rising. "That means there's trouble inside. And that almost never happens here. The regulars make sure of that."

"This has got to be bad," Sage said, snapping her fingers for the dogs to get to their feet.

Before Curt could reach the sliding door, a massive crash came from inside, followed by a chorus of shouts.

CHAPTER 9

As the time had slipped by, Amelia and Kirsten grew more agitated. The drinks were finished, the glasses put down and not refilled. With the setting of the sun, a late spring chill rode the ocean breezes as they reached them on the deck.

At one point, Amelia had gone inside to grab a light jacket. Not long after, Kirsten did the same, returning with her lucky robe wrapped around her.

When Amelia shot her a questioning look, Kirsten shrugged. "I thought they would be back by now," she said. "I figured we could all use whatever juju the robe can give us."

Amelia nodded in understanding, but remained silent, staring out into the dark of the night. The sounds of the waves reached them, and just at the edge of their eyesight, they could catch glimpses of the ribbons of sea foam that rode the sea into the beach, only to be left behind when the water returned home. In fact, if they looked away from the beach, their peripheral vision undulated with the ocean's endless, mesmerizing rolling waves.

Simultaneously, their phone alarms chimed as the clock turned to nine.

"Dammit, dammit," Amelia said quietly. She snatched her phone from the table and walked through the living room to the large window that looked out over the driveway and the street beyond. The faint lights in the carport sprang to life. Motion sensitive. Amelia stepped involuntarily back, startled.

Kirsten, who had been trailing her across the room, moved faster and reached her, putting a hand on her shoulder.

"You okay?" she asked.

Amelia let out an involuntary laugh. "Fine. The outside lights just came on. Wasn't expecting it. Probably a cat. I'm just jumpy."

"Anything else out there?" Kirsten asked, pulling the heavy robe tighter. "Maybe it was the gang coming back?"

"Nah," Amelia replied. "Nothing moving out there. No cars. Nothing. Just ours down there. And Mark's. Just sitting there like an accusation."

"Right," Kirsten said, "enough. Time to stop waiting. I'm calling that deputy. If they're in trouble somehow, we need to let someone know what's up."

Kirsten crossed back to the kitchen counter where one of Roger's cards had been left. She took it to the couch, curled up in a corner, and dialed.

Amelia remained at the window, staring out. She heard Kirsten behind her speaking quietly into the phone.

"Well?" Amelia asked, with a last glance out front.

"Went to voicemail," Kirsten answered with a shrug. "It is pretty late."

"He said to call anytime," Amelia pointed out. "And it's not *that* late. Let's just hope he gets back to us soon."

"No sense in us going out looking, I suppose," Kirsten said.

"Don't think so," Amelia replied. "Just the blind chasing the blind. But I am going down to turn those lights on for real. I think it will just feel better, and I don't want those motion sensors freaking us out every time they snap on. Me. Freaking *me* out."

She headed down the stairs and made sure the exterior lights were switched on. As she leaned on the door, she heard something scratching along the pavement just outside and snapped the door open.

She jumped back, startled at what she found. And the raccoon she'd startled jumped as well, before scurrying quickly off into the yard. Amelia, leaned on the door frame, laughed at herself, and breathed deeply. Peeking outside to make sure the critter had cleared off, she opened the door and walked along the side of the house to look out at the sky and ocean. Another breath. This one steadier and with the tang of salt in it. She zipped her jacket and walked partway along the small boardwalk that crested the dunes and led to the beach. Stopping at a small pavilion at the top, she leaned on the railing.

Kirsten had exited the living room again, returning to the deck. She had flipped her phone's volume on, something she rarely did. She wasn't willing to miss the call if Roger got back to her. She was giving it until half past before trying again.

She saw Amelia emerge downstairs and cross the deck, heading toward the beach but stopping to...what? Pause? Rest? Think? All good options and understandable.

Both women were staring to the horizon, when a lightning strike flashed across the sky far out over the ocean.

Normally, they would have enjoyed the celestial pyrotechnics, but tonight it felt too ominous. Too heavy.

Following the lightning, clouds began rolling in off the water. Somehow darker than the night around them, they turned off the stars as they approached. One by one, they winked out. Covered by the clouds and the night. It wasn't long before a light rain started to fall, leaving dimples in the sand and angry stains on the decks around them.

Amelia turned and headed back into the house. Outside, a proper storm swept in and soon the two retreated from the balcony to the living room. At exactly half past nine, Kirsten pulled her phone from the robe's pocket and dialed Roger again.

Curt was the first one through the sliding door into the Blue Crab, with Roger and Grier close on his heels. None of them were prepared for what they found. The barroom was a chaotic melee. The locals were pressed to one side of the room, their backs to the bar. The owner, RG, was behind the counter, anger written on her face in a way none of them had seen before.

Bullfrog and Tugboat Joe had placed themselves in front of the older woman, and though they weaved a bit on their feet having been at the bar for quite some time, their faces were determined. Every so often, Bullfrog reared back and let loose a croak that cut through the shouts and threats that sailed throughout the room. The rest of the regulars had assembled around them. Confusion competing with anger in most of their faces.

Facing them from positions around the pool table were four individuals. Three men and a woman. One of the men was dressed in garishly colorful clothes. An orange and red Hawaiian style shirt and purple jeans with shiny gold high-top sneakers. The woman wore faded jeans, holes peppering the legs. And these weren't designer-produced holes. These were good old-fashioned worn places. She wore a black tank top under a denim button-down shirt. Both of the other men were clothed in all black. Jeans, shirt, boots.

They were all planted, legs shoulder-width apart, aggressive, poised for violence. The man in the garish clothes was waving a butterfly knife in front of him, flicking it open. Closed. Open.

Another man held two halves of a pool cue that had been snapped in half. The woman was holding a broken beer bottle, its jagged edges pointed directly at Bullfrog. In front, the youngest of them held a massive hunting knife low, along the side of his leg.

The young man turned to the newcomers, pointed at them and laughed.

Curt, Roger, Grier, and even Carlito, who had entered last, groaned.

"Sonofabitch," Roger mumbled. "Vane."

Curt turned to him; eyes narrowed. "How do you know Charles Vane?"

"He was on the boat I told you about today," Roger said, never taking his eyes off the aggressors. He slowly pulled a Taser from his belt.

"How do *you* know him?" Grier asked, stepping up beside Curt and Roger.

"I interviewed him this morning," Curt said between clenched teeth. "Needless to say, you can see why I went with Carlito."

Charles Vane stepped forward, lifted his large knife in front of his face, and ran his tongue along the blade.

"You *must* be kidding me," he hissed. "All of my least favorite people in one place. Of all the gin joints...Oh, and look, there's little Carlito hiding back there. Guess that job didn't help you grow a spine. This night just took a turn for the better. And the worse. Either way, it's gonna be fun. And I am going to gut you all like fish." He noticed Sage behind the others. "Not you, sweetheart. I have nothing against you. Yet. Except the company you keep."

Roger held Curt back with a palm to the chest and stepped toward Vane and the others.

"What's the issue here?" he asked. "No need to make this worse than it is. Far as I can tell, the only damage is a busted pool cue. So far."

"Yeah," Tugboat Joe shouted from the bar. "That asshole broke it over his knee when we told them they had to wait their turn. That's my lucky stick!"

"You know these people, Roger?" RG called from where she stood. "They're about to get a whooping if they don't leave some cash for that cue and clear out."

The man in the garish clothes actually laughed out loud.

"Old lady," the woman with the beer bottle shouted back, "that stick ain't worth a dime, a lot like this dump of a bar. You lot started this, but we're just as happy with a bar fight as shooting pool."

Curt quietly picked one of the balls off the table but otherwise stood motionless. Sage stood by the door, speaking quietly to the two dogs, keeping them out of the way.

"I've met them a time or two, RG," Roger replied to the bar owner. "Can't say I know them that well. But I'm sure we can figure a way out of this mess."

"This isn't even your patch, *Deputy*," Vane said to Roger. "Your word doesn't mean any more than anyone else's here. So shut it. I'm starting to think you all are following me. Should have known you'd all hang together. Takes a loser to know a loser."

As they spoke, Grier took a retractable baton out of a pocket on the leg of his cargo pants and flicked it open. He hefted it. Curt gave him a quick look.

"Picked it up when I was in the U.K.," he explained. "Took to it pretty fast."

"Handy," Curt replied.

"He's actually right," Roger said under his breath. "I'm not on duty and, even if I were, we're not in Manteo. Best to shut this down fast, unless we want to spend the whole night making statements and filling out forms. But I know this lot. The clown suit is John Rackham. Showy but not much else. Pool cue guy is Ed English. Not like him to cause problems, but he hangs with the wrong crowd. Obviously."

"What about her?" Curt asked, indicating the woman.

"Mary Read," Roger replied. "Nasty piece of work. Probably the meanest of the lot. Watch her. And you know Vane."

"Sadly, I do," Curt answered.

Grier tapped Curt on his shoulder.

"They're on something," he said. "Look at their eyes. Be careful."

It was then that Curt noticed. The four aggressors were practically buzzing with energy, eager for violence.

"C'mon, old folks," Vane shouted at them. "Come *on*."

On the last word, he drove his knife into the side of the pool table, before drawing it back out and scratching down the length as he advanced on Curt and Roger. As he did that, the man with the pool cue halves dashed toward Grier, only to be dropped by a shot from Roger's taser.

John Rackham, of the outlandish outfit and butterfly knife, cursed Roger and made a slash in his direction, the knife flicking faster than eyes could follow. Before he was close enough to do any damage, Grier's baton came slamming down on his forearm. The knife went skittering across the floor and the man sank to his knees, one arm dangling at his side.

"You broke my arm!" he screamed, although he seemed more angry than in pain.

"I doubt that very much," Grier replied. "You'd know if I really put anything into it."

The woman, Mary Read, screamed something incomprehensible and dashed at Sage, who remained behind the others. She hadn't taken two steps before Sage's dogs met her. Nimble Riley grabbed an ankle, while big, goofy Banks transformed into 120 pounds of protective rage. His teeth bared, he planted himself in front of the woman, daring her to come closer.

Mary Read shouted again, and waved the broken beer bottle at Riley, still clamped on her calf.

"You touch one hair on my dogs, and it will be the last thing you do!" Sage screamed.

Whether it was Sage's naked fury or the massive dog snarling at her, Mary stopped in her tracks and began a slow retreat.

"It's so hard to get good help these days," Vane said, laughing as his companions got the worse of their encounters. "Guess I have to do this myself."

Knife held in front of him at eye level, Vane rushed at Roger and Curt, but before he reached them, Curt let the pool ball fly and caught Vane on his chest, just below his throat. Vane stumbled, let out a hoarse wheeze, and sank to one knee, but kept his knife fixed on the other men.

"You are really pissing me off, old man!" Vane shouted when he was able to catch his breath. "That was the last mistake you'll ever make."

He rose and lunged at Curt, the knife carving the air far too close for Curt's comfort.

Suddenly, Carlito appeared behind Vane, and before anyone could react, he had twisted the knife arm up and behind. The knife slid across the floor, where Grier retrieved it and hoisted it, whistling.

"Kid, you are making the biggest mistake of your life," Vane screeched, his voice an octave higher than it had been just seconds before, and spittle flying from his mouth.

"I doubt that very much," Carlito responded calmly, as he steered Vane toward the front door. "You seem to do a lot of threatening and not a lot of doing. So, get out and stay out."

Carlito tossed Vane through the door and into the parking lot where he stumbled and fell face first before skidding to a stop.

Sage's dogs herded the others to the exit, their fight seeming to have left the premises when their leader had been planted on the gravel outside. Lightning flickered across the sky behind them.

"This isn't over!" Vane continued from the ground outside. "Not by a long shot!"

As the Brethren gathered in the doorway to watch Vane and the others limp to a battered pickup truck, Curt called after them, "Looks pretty over to me!"

Grier, appreciating the hunting blade he'd just acquired, held it up and said in a horrible Australian accent, "Now, *that's* a knoife."

Roger cursed quietly, reaching into his pocket.

"My phone has been going nuts since this all started."

He looked at the screen and then shook his head.

"This day," he said to the others. "Our reunion folks have been calling me. Let's hope this is good news, for a change."

He stepped away to listen to his messages and when the others turned back around to face the bar, they were greeted by a round of applause from the regulars and a strangely celebratory bullfrog croak.

Curt looked at Carlito with surprise. "You never mentioned anything about martial arts or whatever that was you pulled on Vane."

"Some things are best not advertised," Carlito answered quietly.

Curt was about to say something else when Roger returned.

"Not good news. Nope," he told the others. "Five of the gang went out looking for their missing friend, and now *they're* missing. So now we have *seven* missing people. Is it too early for me to retire? I gotta go handle this. Call me if those jokers cause any more problems, but my guess is they'll be licking their wounds for a while now."

"Hope you're right," Curt said.

"Need me to tag along?" Grier asked.

"Don't think so," Roger answered. "I'll let you know if that changes. Actually, you know what? Have a beer and relax. You've done enough for today. This is on me."

"Phone's on if anything comes up," Grier replied.

Roger nodded as his phone rang again. He waved over his shoulder as he headed toward his cruiser, and they could hear him answer asking Russ Wahl what he had for him.

The remaining Brethren walked back into the bar and the cheers continued, while RG called out that the next round was on the house and the cheers grew even louder.

Roger hit his lights but left the siren off. This time of night around here was considered late and as far as he knew, there was no imminent danger to anyone. Russ Wahl called to tell him they'd gotten a report of a stranded car on Route 12 on Hatteras Island just north of Coquina Beach. Not far from the Bodie Island Lighthouse, come to think of it. Normally something this routine would be handled by the rangers who patrolled that area, but at this time of night it had been thrown to whoever would answer. Russ had answered.

Given all that had been going on, Russ had thought it wise to let Roger know what was happening. Especially as that stretch of highway was notoriously spotty for cell coverage. Roger had done more than take note. He'd told Russ he'd meet him there. He was hoping that this would solve one of the many missing person situations. And his money was on it being the lost reunion goers.

Russ was coming from Manteo and Roger from Colington, so he expected them to get there about the same time. The bypass was mostly clear this late, and he let the cruiser cruise when he hit the highway.

He called Amelia back as soon as he'd hung up with Russ.

"God, I am so glad to hear back from you," Amelia said, answering her phone. He heard her cover the mic as she explained to Kirsten it was the deputy calling back. "We're out of our minds with worry over here. Can you help?"

"I'm already helping," Roger answered. "We have a stranded vehicle on Hatteras Island. Probably less than fifteen minutes from where you are. I'm betting it's gonna turn out to be your friends. What were they driving?"

Another hand over the mic as Amelia asked Kirsten what Jaime was driving. "Sorry," she said returning, "I'm horrible with cars. Kirsten says he's driving a silver Ford Explorer. Can you let us know as soon as you find out? We wanted to go look ourselves, but that's how we ended up in this position in the first place, so..."

"You did the right thing," Roger assured her. "I'm probably less than ten minutes from the location, but cell service is bad along that stretch, so it could take a little while to get back to you. *Don't worry.* And don't go anywhere. We don't need anyone else going missing. I'll be in touch."

He disconnected the call and sped along the nearly empty highway. He would be there in less time than he'd anticipated. He loved his job. And speeding through the towns with his lights on and cars scattering around him like leaves in an autumn wind was one of his favorite things. His twelve-year-old self was in heaven.

He buzzed past the closed restaurants, candy stores—why were there so many?—surf shops. He knew how lucky he was to live here. Probably why he took his job so much to heart. He got to live in his idea of paradise. And he got to keep the people who called it home safe. Better than he'd ever thought he would have it when he was growing up in Queens, New York. And a far cry from those city streets.

Within minutes, he was turning left to follow the road into the Cape Hatteras National Seashore. As he did, the houses grew fewer, and the night grew darker. He saw Russ pull onto the highway behind him, his lights also flashing.

Together, they drove south, two blue and red strobing specters carving through the deep black of night that surrounded them. As so often happened to him, he became very aware of the vastness around them on this narrow spit of land. These islands that were so vulnerable to every whim of Mother Nature. He could almost feel the expanse of the Atlantic off to his left. It's immensity pressing in on his tiny cruiser, reminding him how truly inconsequential he was. They all were. He rolled his window down and let the sound of the crashing surf serve as his soundtrack.

It wasn't long before he spotted not one, but two sets of headlights in the distance on the opposite shoulder. As he neared, he let out a relieved sigh as he made out that one of the vehicles was a large silver SUV. Ford Explorer.

The other pair of headlights was smaller. Closer to the ground. As he made a U-turn and pulled up behind the car, he recognized it as an old 1970s AMC Javelin. Maroon and well-loved, it was a miracle it still ran. It belonged to Herbie Knight, a local musician, teacher, and hardcore surfer. He was one of the Banks' true characters. What he was doing here Roger couldn't fathom.

Russ pulled a turn just behind him and parked to his rear on the hard-packed sand shoulder. Tides had run high over the last week and the road and sand both showed signs of the overwash that was so common along this stretch.

As Roger climbed out of his car, he threw a wave to Russ approaching from behind and strolled up to the other two vehicles.

"Evening, Herb," Roger called to the owner of the Javelin. "What's the story here?"

Herbie Knight rose from where he'd been kneeling by the passenger side front tire of the big SUV. There was a cluster of people, barely shadows in the on and off of the flashing lights. Herbie came around to the driver's side to shake Roger's hand and nod to Russ. He was early forties with tightly curled, sandy blond hair that he'd let grow long. His easy smile lit up a deeply tanned face.

"Roger! A sight for sore eyes," Herbie replied. "Nothing too serious. These poor wandering ones caught a wet patch of sand and dug themselves in pretty good. Being the very model of a modern neighbor, I stopped to lend a hand. But I think it may be beyond even my considerable talents."

"Nice G & S references," Roger replied. Herbie had a habit of slipping musical lyrics into his conversations to see who could keep up. Roger always gave him a run for his money. "Guessing you've tried pushing and pulling. Let's see if Russ has some traction mats and get these people on their way. Russ?"

"On it," Russ called, jogging back to his car and opening the trunk.

Roger stalked around to the far side of the Explorer and gave a clipped wave to the assembled group there. It was the missing vacationers, and they seemed appropriately chastened at being helpless and stranded.

"You folks have given your pals a lot of worry," Roger said. "And you dragged me out of a bar that was about to get really interesting. Care to explain what the hell you were thinking?"

Jaime stepped forward and answered. "We just felt helpless. Sitting there. Doing nothing. While Mark is out there. Maybe in trouble, maybe worse. We went to some of his favorite places to see if we could find someone who had seen him. It was dumb. But we had to do something. I was the sober one. I drove."

Roger stood back and gestured to the stranded SUV. "You *sure* you were the sober one? And if you were going to his favorite places, why are you here in the middle of nowhere?"

"Mark used to go to Bodie Island and Pea Island a lot. When we struck out at the bars, we thought we'd take a look."

"And you ended up stuck in quicksand how?" Roger asked, arching his eyebrows.

"That's the interesting part," Cathy said, joining them. "We had given up and were heading back to the house when we saw something out on the beach through one of the parking lot entrances. We pulled up here to try to peek over the dune, but you can see how that turned out."

"What exactly did you see out there?" Roger asked.

Francis and Chris had given up on the SUV and drifted into the conversation.

"Lights," Francis said.

"A lot of them," Chris added. "On the beach and out on the water. Looked like flashlights, but there was a boat too."

"Not long after I got here, I saw a truck or something cross from the beach over to the lighthouse entrance," Herbie said, gesturing south along the roadway. "Moving at a good clip, but I was focused on getting these folks out. And whoever was driving was moving fast."

"Right," Roger said. "Let me have a talk with Officer Wahl here. You all were reckless tonight. Leave the policing to the police from now on. Not you, Herb. You were a gem. As usual."

"We meant well," Jaime protested weakly.

"Famous last words," Roger replied. "*Don't move.*"

The group nodded mutely. Embarrassed.

His message delivered, Roger walked back to Russ's vehicle, where a pair of elongated plastic snowshoe-like boards were leaning against the fender.

"You think you can handle this?" Roger asked. "I want to call their friends and give the all clear. I know I can get signal down by the lighthouse. Won't take but a few."

"Yeah, yeah," Russ said. "Do your thing. I just got the new TRED Pros. Been meaning to give them a try. Not gonna be a problem. We'll have them on their way in no time."

"Great," Roger said, already heading to his cruiser. "Make sure to scold them again before they head off. We have enough work to do without having to babysit this lot."

"Heard that," Russ said, hoisting his traction boards over his shoulder.

Roger pulled yet another U-turn and a moment later was on the road that led to the lighthouse. He passed the Park Service field office as he headed up the darkened road, pine trees flanking him on either side. The office was closed up tight for the night. Only the emergency light over the front door gave any clue the building was even there.

A quarter mile later, Roger emerged from the trees into the large circular parking area for the Bodie Island Lighthouse and its museum and gift shop, housed in the old keeper's quarters. He knew that building was closed for the foreseeable future, victim of a recent fire. There were two Park Service vehicles sitting out front. Roger thought that odd but chalked it up to the overflow from all the new construction happening to repair the fire damage.

He pulled into a spot near the hulk of a building and checked his phone. Sure enough. He had service. He made a call to Amelia and Kirsten, assuring them that their friends had been found and would soon be back. He reminded them again to keep out of the way of the investigation, although he knew those two were not the issue.

Next, he gave Curt a call. He knew the Brethren would be relieved to hear that their list of missing people had returned to its more manageable, if unfortunate, total of two. Curt didn't answer, and Roger imagined the others enjoying a well-deserved beer with Bull-frog, Tugboat Joe, and the others. FOMO was a real thing.

As he put the cruiser in reverse to head back to Russ, something through the trees to his right caught his eye. A flash of light. And another. Multiple lights gliding through the trees. Or on the other side of the woods that led to the marshes in the back of the reserve and eventually to the sound past that.

Lights. Floating. Drifting. Almost like—he hated to say it—orbs.

He pulled out of the space and headed deeper into the park instead of back to the highway. He kept the headlights off and used the running lights only. Something or someone was in that direction, and he was tired and fed up with chasing and being chased throughout this very long and annoying day.

When he reached the gate leading to the paths and trails in back, he jumped out and started in on foot, instantly cursing as his feet sank into a mud puddle. The waters really had been high over this way, if the water had gotten this high.

He shook his foot dry and plowed ahead. As he turned a corner he saw, off to his right, white and yellow lights sliding across one of the canals that led to the open water of the sound. He realized Wanchese lay across the sound from here, meaning he was now not far from where he and Grier had encountered the suspicious skiff so many hours ago.

One thing he could be sure of this time was that Charles Vane was not out there. It hadn't been that long ago that he had been sent packing from the Blue Crab. He couldn't have been on Coquina Beach at the same time he had been starting a dustup at the bar. But someone was out on the water. And despite the grief the Vollmerhausens often received, he could see those lights looking like orbs. If you needed glasses.

Roger stood for a few long minutes, watching as the lights flickered through the trees and eventually picked up speed and glided away.

He turned and shuffled back to his car, one shoe and sock squishing loudly with each step he took.

As he headed out of the lot, he stopped by the service vehicles parked by the museum, climbed out and laid his hand on the hoods of both trucks. The larger one was still warm. Someone had been driving it recently. He stepped back and noticed a track of sand it had left on the parking lot cement when it pulled into its space.

Guess those meddling tourists had been onto something.

He made a mental note to check in with Ranger Justin in the morning. The Bodie Island ranger crew needed looking into. Maybe they could find a connection. Something. Because right now, they had a lot of questions and very few answers.

As he headed back out the drive toward Route 12, he saw a pair of headlights headed in his direction. As they approached, he recognized Russ Wahl's cruiser and let out a sigh of relief. He really didn't need any more surprises today.

Russ slowed and stopped next to him and rolled down his window, gesturing for Roger to do the same.

"Find anything?" Russ called over.

"Actually, yeah," Roger answered. "Those high school buddies seem to have been on to something. Spotted some lights out on the sound around back, and one of the ranger trucks had just been driven. I'll put in a call to Justin in the morning, see if any of the staff here have any red flags."

"Good idea," Russ said. "Just FYI, we got those folks out and they headed back to Nags Head. Herbie headed off singing 'Bye Bye Bye.' Didn't have him pegged as an NSYNC guy."

Roger chuckled and was about to put his car in gear and head out when he snapped his fingers and turned back to Russ.

"My mind is like a sieve today," he said. "Been meaning to ask. You and Mary were at Bad Bean last night. When you two left, did you notice anything odd. *Anything?* Everything seems to have started there."

"Well, we didn't leave together, to start off with," Russ replied. "She was still there when I left. I didn't see anything but maybe she did? About halfway through our queso she took a funny turn. Got real quiet. I asked her if she was okay, but she brushed it off. I was surprised she decided to stay. Would have stayed with her, but

Sasha was expecting me back. Just looked like a normal night to me."

"Got it," Roger said, with a shake of his head. "I feel like I'm missing something but am just too damn tired to figure it out."

"Go home, Rog," Russ said, putting his car back in gear. "Been a long day. Start fresh tomorrow. It'll come to you."

"Yeah, you're probably right," Roger muttered, more to himself than Russ.

He drove to the entrance to the park, signaled, and turned north onto the highway. He'd driven for five minutes when something clicked in his mind. Mary had told him at the station that she and Russ had left together. Russ had just made it clear that was not the case.

More than likely, it was just a simple mistake. But something about it seemed off. Another thing to chase down tomorrow. He slapped himself on the neck to keep himself awake. The last thing this day needed was him falling asleep on the drive home.

"Helluva day," he said to himself. "Yessir. One helluva day."

***

At the Blue Crab, a sort of crowd euphoria took over after the ejection of Charles Vane and his cronies. The drinks were flowing fast and free. Curt saw the way things were going and announced that he was paying for rides home for everyone. There was a lull in activity followed by a cheer. RG smiled, shook her head, and locked the front door. This had the makings of a historic lock-in and she knew her till would be overflowing before all was finished.

Bullfrog was ensconced in one corner. A small group surrounded him, including Sage and her dogs, as he gave a step-by-step tutorial on how to make the frog sounds he made. That corner of the bar sounded like a summer morning in the marshes.

There was an impromptu arm-wrestling tournament taking place at the far end of the bar. Carlito, despite his slight frame, was the current champion. As Curt watched, he saw the younger man beat Tugboat Joe, who laughed good-naturedly after and got right back in line to give it another try.

As he looked around the barroom, Curt grew a bit choked up. This ragtag group, with nearly nothing in common beyond their love of this place, filled his heart. Nights like this had been happening here for hundreds of years. And as long as they had been happening, there had been Brethren to safeguard these people. This place.

He was surprised to feel a bit lonely. On reflection, he supposed it made sense. The watchers were always one step outside the communal circle. They had to be, in order to watch.

He remembered the box he'd left outside and quietly moved to the sliding doors and slipped onto the back deck. The blue luminescent lights had increased since they'd gone in to confront the troublemakers. He wasn't surprised at this, and sat on the lowest level of deck, close to the water, took off his shoes and trailed his feet in the water.

Twenty minutes later, Grier appeared at the sliding door and let himself out. Curt looked up over his shoulder and gave a nod.

"Figured you'd be out here," Grier said, joining Curt on the deck, but keeping his feet clear of the glowing water.

"Figured I should check on it," Curt said, his eyes now fixed on the water. "If Vane had somehow stumbled onto the chest before they left, it would have gone very badly for him. I guess that would be one way of solving the problem."

"True," Grier agreed. "But damn hard to explain."

Curt nodded and laughed lightly, trailing his feet through the water. As he did, the lights swirled and eddied around them.

"Does this mean what I think it means?" Grier asked. "Does Roger know? Did it start? Just need to be prepared, you know."

Before Curt could reply, the side gate opened on rusted hinges and Riley and Banks came bounding around to the deck. Riley immediately dashed off to the grassy patch by the side, while Banks let out a deep whuff and ambled over toward Curt and Grier.

Sage came next and stopped short at the sight of the glowing waters chasing Curt's feet.

"Aw, shit," Sage said quietly. "Yup, I knew it. Only thing that made sense after Bodie."

Curt stayed where he was, facing the inlet where Grier's boat was tied up.

Carlito came rushing out the door, panicked.

"Sorry, sorry," he called. "I didn't realize all of you were gone until just now. Did I miss anything? My bad."

Before anyone could answer, they were startled to see the lights blink instantly out. One moment there, the next gone as if it had been a hallucination.

Sage gasped and took two steps toward Curt.

Grier leaned forward over the rising tide and finally dipped his fingers into the now darkened water. He raised his dripping hand and held it in front of him. There was nothing to see.

Even Banks belly-crawled to the edge of the dock and swatted at the suddenly still waters.

Carlito, sensing the charged atmosphere, hesitated.

"Wait," he said finally. "Did I misread this? Should I leave you all alone? Just trying to figure out my place. I can go back inside..."

Grier was the first to respond, rising and wiping his hand on his faded jeans and turning to Carlito. He glanced once at Curt. Saw no response was coming from that direction and walked to the confused Carlito.

"No, you're fine," Grier said. "You one hundred percent belong here."

Carlito gave a relieved smile and nodded.

"He's right," Curt said, rising from the dockside. He grabbed his shoes and walked to where the others were. "There are a few things I need to tell you. Couldn't do it here. Too many eyes and ears around. And you had to be sworn in before I could fill you in. We'll meet tomorrow, and I'll tell all, cool? Maybe at Swells'a?"

"Yeah. I mean, yes. Of course," Carlito agreed quickly.

"That cool, Sage?" Curt asked, turning to her, Banks having rumbled across the deck to plop beside Curt.

"We can make that work," Sage agreed. "I'll wait for confirmation."

The sounds of a guitar began to drift out through the open door.

"Guess they broke into the music closet," Grier said, hoping to take some of the tension out of the air. "Anyone up for a good late-night hootenanny?"

"It's all good, Carlito," Curt said, a hand on the younger man's shoulder. "It's my fault. You'll be up to speed tomorrow. Promise."

Sage called Riley to her and turned to go back in toward the music. She stopped and turned to Grier.

"Who the hell says hootenanny? What are you? Eighty?" she teased.

"Respect your elders, whippersnapper," Grier answered, with a laugh.

Before he went back into the bar, Curt stopped to check on the items he'd left under the table. Satisfied that all was in order, he headed back inside.

Noticeably, none of the Brethren continued drinking. What had happened on the deck had put them on alert.

Bullfrog and Tugboat Joe had climbed onto a small makeshift stage that was set in one corner of the bar, Bullfrog strumming on a guitar and Joe keeping a fairly poor beat on a single snare drum.

"RG always has some spare instruments in a closet behind the bar," Grier explained, sidling up to Carlito. "Have heard some pretty great music here late at night. The Henhouse Prowlers were here last fall for the bluegrass festival and ended up playing after their concert. Great night."

The duo onstage launched into a rickety version of "The Sinister Minister" by Béla Fleck and the Flecktones. It wasn't going well, and the room had begun to return to conversation, when the thump of an electric bass joined the song and pulled it all back on track.

Surprised, the chatter dwindled as people began to notice. The newcomers turned to find that none other than Curt Stephens had found a beat-up instrument in the back and was making it sing. When the song reached one of the most iconic bass solos in popular music, Curt attacked it with precision, confidence, and emotion. All other sound had stopped inside the Crab. Everyone was laser-focused on Curt.

Grier and Sage may have been the only ones to notice, but the makeshift stage seemed to glow with a brighter light than the rest of the room. They took note, but other than a quickly shared glance, said nothing about it.

When the song was finished, Curt stepped off the stage as the patrons all erupted. He crossed to Carlito.

"I'll see you tomorrow," he said, before taking the three Brethren in. "Sorry for all of the confusion. I'll do better."

"Didn't know you could do that," Sage said, gesturing toward the stage.

"Yeah," Curt said, looking down. "I'm full of surprises."

He crossed to the front door, RG met him and gave him a quick, shy hug and thanked him. He grinned and then was gone.

"He's got some secrets, doesn't he?" Sage asked Grier.

"Too many," Grier said, still watching the front door. "I worry about him. He needs to share more. With us, preferably. But someone."

"Hard to keep secrets on the Banks," Sage answered. "Sooner or later, most things come out. Over a bonfire. Over a beer. Gotta let them go. Hold them inside and they will eat you up."

CHAPTER 10

Roger showed up at the station early. Earlier than Mary Hallet even. He sat down at his standard issue desk, reminding himself that it was overdue for a good cleaning. It was piled high with files, reports, and more Post-it notes than he could keep track of. He made a note to talk to Mary about the night she and Russ had been at Bad Bean, tore it off the yellow pad, and stuck it on the top of his desk lamp. Eye level. He should see that no problemo.

The first thing he did was fire an email off to Ranger Justin asking about the staff over at Bodie Island. Someone with access to the government vehicles had been using one late last night. There could be a simple reason for that. But given the way things had been going lately, his money was on something more complicated.

He ran a check on the movement of Todd Lawton's EZ-pass. It was still active and moving around the Richmond, Virginia, area. A quick try of Lawton's phone number went straight to voicemail. If the man was driving his own car, he was avoiding calls. If someone else was driving it? Well, that would lead to a new set of questions.

He checked his in-box and was happy to see that nothing urgent was popping up there. He hated email on principle and avoided it as much as possible. He likely wouldn't check it again until the end of the day. That habit had gotten him into a few jams over the years, but he was a stubborn man.

He pushed his rickety office chair back and stretched his arms. One of the wheels was wonky and moving it about his desk was frequently a bit of an adventure. But it had been his chair for years and he hated change. Stubborn.

He took a moment to just sit. He rarely had the station to himself. And he knew that this was the most peace he'd find today. Looking out the window over the majestic tree out in front of the station, he paused to appreciate the stillness of the morning, the sky still glowing with purple, orange, pink. Even in what served as downtown Manteo, the beauty of the area was never far.

His cell phone began to ring. He cursed. It was barely past seven. Who the hell would call him at this time?

He checked and cursed again. Louder. The Vollmerhausens. He was sure it would be more orbs, based on what he'd seen last night off Bodie Island. He just couldn't face them, so he let the call go to voicemail. He hadn't even had his coffee yet.

This day was already on his nerves.

He ambled over to the kitchen area and turned on the coffee machine. He was much better at drinking it than making it, but desperate times. Mary had always made better coffee than him. Marginally. He thought he did all the same things that she did, and yet the results were so different.

While waiting, he heard the chime of a voicemail arriving on his phone.

"Lynn and Bill," he said, "you'll have to wait a few minutes. Coffee before cuckoos. New personal rule."

Eventually, he poured a steaming cup of coffee. His personal mug that featured the Grinch in his Christmas outfit and sneering with disdain.

"Bah, humbug," Roger said, returning to his desk and reluctantly picking up his phone.

From the direction of the front desk, he heard Mary call back to him.

"It's April, Roger," she shouted. "Save that Christmas spirit for later!"

He chuckled. It was one of their many private jokes. They'd worked together so long; they could practically read each other's minds. He hadn't even heard her arrive. Time to get his head out of the clouds.

He settled into his wobbly chair, leaned back, put his feet on his desk, and promptly almost fell over backwards, thought better of the position, and put his feet back on the floor.

Swiping his phone, he played the message the Vollmerhausens had just left.

His first surprise was to hear Bill Vollmerhausen's voice. Normally, Lynn took the lead on things like this. Roger had always assumed that Lynn was the one who "saw" a lot of these things and Bill just allowed her to do her thing.

His next surprise was to hear Bill announce that the call had nothing to do with orbs. Instead, he was calling to let Roger know that on their morning drive through Alligator River, they had noticed that the creepy shack back by the kayak launch had shown signs of activity. Smoke had been rising from a small pipe in the roof and the turf in front had been chewed up, as if someone had been moving things in and out of the building. They couldn't say for sure, but they thought they had seen a truck of some sort parked behind it. They hadn't gone any closer because...well...it really wasn't their business. But it was unusual, especially given all that had been going on, and they thought they should report it.

"This morning sucks," Roger muttered, grabbing his car keys.

He was headed to the stairs down to the parking lot when he ran into Chief Brady arriving.

"Leaving already, Roger?" Brady asked. "Was it something I said?"

"If only," Roger replied. "The Vollmerhausens just called."

"Leave it," Brady said. "We can hunt their orbs later."

"Actually, sir, they had some interesting information this time. Someone's at the old trapper shack in the refuge. Too close to where we found Keegan's body to let it go, so I'm headed out to poke around."

"Good idea," Brady said. "I'll get on the horn and see if Ranger Justin can join you. Safety in numbers right now."

"Thanks, appreciate that," Roger answered, starting toward the stairs again.

"Roger, I have some news myself," Brady said, holding out an arm to stop the deputy's progress. "You should probably hear it before you head out."

"What now?" Roger asked. He had the distinct feeling he wasn't going to like what he was about to hear.

"Preliminary autopsy results have come back from Raleigh," Brady answered. "Cause of death is what we thought. Drowning."

"That's actually good, though," Roger said. "Makes our job simpler, yeah?"

"You would think so," Brady said, drumming a finger on the door frame. "Keegan drowned. But he drowned in fresh water."

"Wait what?" Roger sputtered. "Fresh water would mean—"

"That he didn't drown in the refuge," Brady said, nodding. "Someone killed him somewhere else and moved him there."

"The water back there can get brackish," Roger replied, arching an eyebrow. "Especially if there's been heavy rain. Maybe I should get a water sample since I'm going that way. See if we can match it up?"

"I don't think that's gonna work out," Brady said. "The water in his lungs was chlorinated."

"Pool water?" Roger asked.

Brady nodded his head. "Sure looks that way."

"Aw, shit," Roger said.

Behind him he heard Mary tut in disapproval.

Curt woke early for the sunrise. But today he headed to the sound instead of the beach. He knew he wouldn't see the sun break the horizon there, but he needed to be away from people. Even the casual friendships with the other sunrise devotees seemed too much right now.

He hadn't slept well. Not that that was unusual for him. But this time, it felt that the accumulation of things going on around him was reaching a crescendo. A breaking point. He'd been trying to handle the most difficult elements on his own. He knew it flew in the face of everything the Brethren were supposed to be and stand for, but every cell in his body was screaming at him to protect those closest to him. Even if he hadn't been able to tell them how much they meant to him.

He drove the Chevelle to the Wright Brothers multi-use trail park, pulled into a parking space, and strolled down to the water's edge. The park was empty. Not even any of the stray joggers who frequented the trail.

A big tree next to the observation deck dipped its branches down to the incoming tide. It had been here as long as he could remember, and he'd always liked it. It somehow had an air of wisdom. And permanence. Others near it had fallen victim to hurricanes or floods. This tree, though, persevered.

The sky was beginning to brighten. Purple and orange growing brighter and brighter. He imagined it was a nice view on the beach and momentarily thought of his friends over there. But he knew he'd made the right choice. He was too preoccupied to share space with them.

There were things he needed to share with his fellow Brethren. Things they needed to know in order to protect themselves. Things they needed to know if anything happened to him. But something held him back, and he knew it could prove dangerous. Maybe fatal.

He trusted them all completely. Even Carlito. It wasn't that. It was his instinct to shield others from danger. And from bad news. But this time he had no choice.

He knew Grier and Roger had suspicions. And Sage, too, if he was being honest. Carlito may end up being the most crucial, though. He sensed something in the young man. Something that could become a powerful addition to their group. Maybe *the* most powerful. And that meant he had to handle this afternoon carefully. The future of the Brethren could depend on how Carlito reacted.

He picked up a loose stick and tossed it into the water, surprising a cottonmouth swimming past. It scooted across the surface before settling back into its natural rhythm.

He was aware of the subtle streaks of blue ribboning through the ripples the stick had kicked up. He saw them more often lately. He knew why. And he knew that was at the heart of him needing to come clean.

He waited until the sun had risen high enough behind him to illuminate the entire sky before he turned back to the lot and his waiting Chevelle. Another car was pulling in as he exited. The joggers had arrived.

***

Grier had slept fitfully. He was worried about Curt. Something was off with his friend. It wasn't the addition of Carlito, although it was a huge shift for the Brethren. But he had been around when Sage was brought into the group, and it had been seamless. Carlito seemed even more suited to the job, if that was possible. No. It was something else. Something Curt was keeping to himself.

Giving up on sleep, at last, Grier rose, made himself some French press coffee, and took the short drive to where he kept his airboat. He always enjoyed taking it out for a spin. Literally. Few things delighted his inner child more than getting the airboat up to speed and skidding across the surface of the sound. He'd had friends when he was younger who had been thrilled at sneaking into parking lots late at night and turning donuts with their cars, spinning in circles and drifting while leaving a trail of burned rubber and skid marks. He knew, now, that his airboat was an even better option. Something about the water, the open sky, the deep thrum of the blades spinning just behind him creating a wall of sound that let him feel he was in a world of his own.

He cleared the marina and opened up the engine. Instinct took over. He knew these waters and islands like the back of his hand. He closed his eyes for just a moment, allowing the rushing wind to whip past him. It almost felt as if he was flying. As much as he loved the ocean, he had come to feel more deeply for the sound. You knew what you would find there. Could count on certain things. Develop a relationship with the landmarks. *Soundmarks?* The islands. The currents. The tides.

Relaxing into his own personal bliss, he allowed his mind to wander to the reasons he had been so unable to sleep. Something was wrong. Well, obviously. There was a dead body, missing people, unsavory folks skulking about on the backside of the islands clearly up to no good. But it felt like something closer to home was off. He knew it came back to Curt. Knew he had to do something about it. But he wanted more than anything for things to be open and smooth between the Brethren. They had become family to him. His refuge. His purpose. In that moment, he understood that those were the reasons he had to make things right. Shine a light on what was hidden. Carlito deserved an honest beginning.

He thought back about the Mark Elliot disappearance. There was something still to be discovered about the childhood friends. He couldn't shake the feeling that something important was buried in their shared history. They just hadn't dug in the right place yet.

He had a thought and decided to follow his instinct. He spun the airboat in a tight half circle and sped back toward the marina.

His first thought was that he would share his plan with Curt.

His second thought was that whatever lay between them needed to be taken care of, because he felt himself fighting a reluctance to trust Curt completely. That had never happened before, and it didn't sit well with him.

His third thought was he wanted another coffee before tackling what he had to face with Curt. Grier was a simple guy. He liked things to be clear. Direct. And right now, things felt very complicated.

Sage woke slowly, but early. Both were unusual for her. She worked nights, and as a result she tended to sleep in. But when she did wake up, she shot into the day straight away. She'd always been that way. The dogs helped that along. By the time she was up, they were ready to ramble. They were outdoor dogs and longed to roam. When she thought about it, she was an outdoor person. Probably why she had ended up in the Outer Banks. She'd never enjoyed the feeling of being penned in. And even a small city like Richmond, Virginia, had felt too unnatural to her. Too much concrete and not enough green. It felt like a trap.

The logical response, in her opinion, had been to head to the one place she knew offered open skies and the few wild places she'd known. The Banks had become a tourist attraction. There was no denying that. And she was more than happy to tap into that as a means of earning her way. But underneath the seafood buffets and t-shirt shops, she could still find pieces of the old Banks. She knew the stretches of beach that would show hers to be the only feet passing along them any given day. She could still take a walk in the woods and sense the past whispering through the forest around her.

But this morning, she felt as if she'd tied one on the night before, and she certainly had not done that. Parts of the evening lingered happily. Curt's unexpected appearance on stage. Carlito's wide-eyed induction into the Brethren, the good-natured ribbing she enjoyed with Roger. And Grier, although she found him a harder nut to crack. There always seemed to be a sliver of him tucked away just out of reach. Fair enough. Everyone was due their private spaces. Roger, on the other hand, clicked with her easily. She knew his folksy, aw-shucks act disguised a whip-smart mind. A keen investigator. But, man, did she have fun with that yokel persona he put on.

Enough woolgathering. The dogs were antsy. Riley was always antsy, but it took Banks a much longer time to get there. And he was there. He sat by the front door, whining in a pitch that no dog his size with any self-respect would make.

She swung her legs over the side of the bed, pulled her also fuzzy hair into a ponytail, grabbed a pair of sweats, a Swells'a shirt, and was out the door in less than thirty seconds.

Her Bronco growled to life as the dogs slipped into the back seat. She fastened them into their Mighty Paw seat belts—she took their well-being very seriously, more than her own—and backed out of the driveway, turning south. Riley fidgeted in her harness. Anxious to run. Banks settled in and enjoyed the ride. The journey was part of the happiness for Banks.

The sun had crested the horizon over the ocean to her left, but she knew exactly where she was headed. The Bronco had the beach road pretty much to itself, and she pushed past the thirty-five mile an hour limit. She wasn't in a hurry, necessarily, but the dogs' restlessness was contagious, and she wanted to feel the cool spring sand beneath her feet.

She cruised past Oregon Inlet, Bodie Island and Coquina Beach, where the reunion folks had stranded themselves only hours before. The open beaches of Hatteras Island opened up as she continued south, until she saw a familiar turn-off. It was nothing to look at from the roadway, but a few minutes down a narrowing trail, led her to a small parking area. Less that that really. Just a space that had been flattened from repeated use. Almost all of it most likely by her.

She unleashed the hounds, and Riley was off like a shot, disappearing down a barely visible sandy path. Her auburn fur billowing in the gentle breeze. Banks, gentle as ever, stayed by Sage, tail wagging. He pressed a damp and grateful nose into her hand, gave her a knowing look, and ambled after Riley down the path and through the tall grasses that surrounded it.

Sage smiled to herself. She locked the Bronco before turning to where the dogs had disappeared. She hated locking the truck, but tourist season was starting and that meant lots of strangers around. Down the path she went, and, after a short walk, she crested a small rise in the sand and looked out over her special place. A wide stretch of sand looking out over the sound. As she had expected, no footprints dotted the beach here. It was hers again. The water rippled in the light breeze. She looked out over the Pamlico Sound and toward what she thought must be Stumpy Point, although she had never been there herself.

Riley was sprinting along the beach, small plumes of sand erupting behind her as she opened up and let her instinct take over. She would stop briefly at times, her nose thrust into the air. Even from this distance, Sage could see the dog's blue eyes flashing in all directions. Banks shuffled along, thrusting his nose into any interesting tuft of grass or decaying driftwood he passed. They belonged here on the Outer Banks as much as she did, Sage realized. And once again, she found herself happy they had each other.

Watching them revel in this place felt almost as if she were running down the beach herself. The tightness around her heart lifted as she watched them. And that made her stop and think about why she was so troubled.

Something was off in the Brethren. She'd never experienced that before. She didn't distrust any of her partners. It wasn't as if she felt in danger. But she did feel that there were currents below the surface that she hadn't identified yet. And while she didn't feel as if it placed her in harm's way, any secrets in the Brethren placed the Outer Banks at risk. And that was unacceptable. This had to be nipped in the bud.

But for now, on this spit of sand between the ocean and the mainland, she turned her attention to her dogs. Her pack. And before she'd thought too much about it, she found herself racing after Riley.

The cool, damp sand felt life-affirming between her toes, and she ran faster. Tousling Banks's fur as she flashed past him, his surprised face jerking up as she chased Riley down the beach.

Banks woofed in surprise and delight. He heaved his massive self after her and galloped in her wake. And all was well for all three of them. For now.

Carlito sat on the hood of the car he'd rented from his landlord. He'd taken the leap, thinking that he would need to be mobile now that he was in the Brethren. It wasn't much to look at, but it would do. An old Subaru Brat. 1987. Red with white racing stripes. To be honest, he loved it. Nothing fancy about it, but it felt like an old beach beater. If it actually ran, he might try to buy it and skip the renting.

Here he was in one of the parking lots that led to the beach on Hatteras Island. He'd arrived long before sunrise, too jittery and excited after last night to sit still, let alone sleep. From his perch, he'd watched as the sky lightened and then broke into the most glorious palette of colors he could imagine. The Outer Banks were the one place that could get him out of bed early. As long as he could remember, he'd been the typical teenager. Sleeping late and staying up late. Mornings had held no attraction for him. But something had changed when he had first come to the islands. Something inside him. Maybe it was just a connection to the natural world around him. He hated to sleep in now. Hated to know he was missing something like this.

Traffic had been basically nonexistent since he'd arrived, so he couldn't help but notice Sage's Bronco when it cruised past his parking lot. He saw Banks with his head poking out of the rear window and he was sure the big dog had spotted him. His massive tail had wagged once before the truck had turned off the highway just past where Carlito watched. But it turned in the opposite direction. Toward the sound.

Carlito considered following her. Saying good morning. Romping with the dogs for a bit. He would have enjoyed it. Truth be told, he'd been a bit lonely lately. He found little in common with most of the people he met in his age group. He hadn't come to the Banks to party or hook up. He wasn't running away from anything. If anything, he had run *toward* this new life.

He was grateful to have found the Brethren. Surprisingly. Yes, he was the youngest. But he felt somehow as if he belonged with them already. And maybe that's why he resisted the urge to follow Sage. The last thing he wanted to do was wear out his welcome before he'd even had a chance to settle into the group. No, he had to ease his way into things. They'd already showed him so much trust and encouragement. No need to push.

He slid off the hood and headed up over the low dune toward the wide beach beyond. The dunes were so much smaller even than they had been on his first visit. The barrier islands were being battered by the elements. Massive efforts were being made to preserve them. But Mother Nature's march had an inevitability about it.

He knew just south of here in the town of Buxton, cherished family homes had been losing their battle with the sea. Many had been swept away. Others had been moved, at great cost, to what was hoped would be a safer location. Safer, but not entirely safe.

Carlito knew that change was coming to the Outer Banks. Proof that, no matter the advancements man made, nature would always have the final word. Maybe the knowledge of that battle fueled his desire to help protect this place. They had enough going against them to have to deal with selfish, foolish people doing selfish, foolish things.

He dropped down onto the beach and walked north, away from Sage's beach on the opposite side of the roadway. A squadron of pelicans glided past, just beyond the breakers. Silently sliding along just inches above the water. They seemed impossibly close, but continued on their way, masters of their world. One peeled off and headed further out to sea, then climbed into the air before turning and flashing down into the water, leaving a sizable splash in its wake before surfacing, something large struggling within its pouch. A moment later, it made its awkward return to the air and sailed after its cohort.

Carlito watched transfixed. A half smile frozen on his face. How could anyone ever get tired of this place?

He continued his way north along the beach, checking his phone to make sure he had service here. He was a member of the Brethren now. He knew that meant they could need him at any moment.

CHAPTER 11

Roger turned right out of Manteo, crossed the Virginia Dare Bridge, which at over five miles just happened to be the longest in the entire state, and into Manns Harbor on the opposite side. He was getting to know this drive better than he'd ever expected. Another ten minutes, and he swung his cruiser onto the gravel Buffalo City Road.

As he left the highway, he saw Ranger Justin's truck just behind him making the same turn. Roger huffed in relief at the sight. With everything that had been going on lately, the refuge had taken on a slightly more sinister air to him. And, if he was being honest with himself, that derelict shack in the back of the preserve had always spooked him. Why was it there? And why was it allowed to *stay* there?

He slowed as he passed the turn for Sawyer Lake Road, lifting himself in his seat to look down into the canal next to the path. Sadly, he didn't see the little gator there that he had come to like. Still a bit cool in the April morning. Soon, he hoped.

He pulled his cruiser up in front of the shack and killed the engine. Something was different. Subtle, but different. He climbed out of the car and waited for Justin to join him.

"We have to stop meeting like this," Roger said, as the lanky ranger joined him in looking at the cabin. "Any word on staff at Bodie Island?"

"Henry Avery is the name of the newest guy. We'll look into him. And we can keep meeting; I'd just rather it not be here for a while. What's wrong with the Lost Colony? If the town weren't so backward, we could've met at 1718 Brewing just down the street. Stupid politicians," Justin replied. "Glad we have Lost Colony, at least. Good beer, and Gene is a hoot."

"Yeah. They screwed that brewery deal up for sure. But tavern it is. It's a deal," Roger agreed. "Next time. For now, though, tell me what you see here. You know this place better than I do. What's going on?"

Justin leaned against the hood of Roger's car and stared for a moment at the shack.

"Well, tire tracks to start," the ranger said after a pause. "Someone didn't want to be seen, though, because they lead around back. Out of sight."

"Interesting," Roger said. "Not too much traffic back this way. Must have *really* wanted to be incognito."

"No back door, though," Justin noted. "So they still had to come around to the front door. That screen door is off the latch. Never seen that before. Someone was in a hurry."

"How do you know there's no back door?" Roger asked, turning to Justin. "You been back there?"

"Maybe," Justin answered with a sly grin. "This one little sliver of land is a carve-out from the park. No one seems to know why, and we haven't been able to track down the private owners. But—and this is just theoretical—if we had probable cause to enter...we could. You know, if we thought someone could be in danger. Or a crime was being committed."

"You've been in that death trap?" Roger blurted.

"Once," Justin answered, with a quick nod of his head. "Couple of the guys and I got curious. It's pretty much what you'd expect. Nasty. We had a quick snoop and got out before anyone was the wiser."

Roger turned to his left and looked down to where they had found Kevin Keegan's body.

"Think we have probable cause now?" he mused. "Proximity to a crime scene. Suspicious behavior."

"Sounds like cause to me," Justin said. "I'm good if you are, Deputy."

Together, the two men approached the shack. The tire tracks led off to the right and around the building. There was no footpath to the front door, so they made their way through the tall grass and weeds that reached all the way to the front porch.

The boards on the porch were loose and felt precarious. Each step they took sent up a squealing creak that echoed around the suddenly ominous clearing.

"Built-in alarm system," Roger noted. "No sneaking up on this place."

"You can say that again," Justin replied with a jerk of his head to the far corner of the porch. Roger followed his gesture and spied a well-camouflaged video camera. The light on the bottom was off, and it gave no sign it was functional.

"Disconnected?" Roger mused.

"Looks like it," Justin answered. "But I wouldn't count on it. Someone wants to keep people out of here."

Justin took a look around the small porch. The skulls of small animals were nailed to the wall on either side of the door. Most appeared to be squirrels and rabbits. Run of the mill small poacher targets. But in amongst them, he spotted a fox, a small gator, and what looked to be a bear. He swore under his breath, took out his phone and began snapping pictures.

"Sonofabitch," he muttered. "Can't turn our backs on this place anymore. Time to clean it all up."

The ranger opened the screen door, which was hanging by only one hinge at the top and tried the front door.

"Locked, of course," he said. "But that's interesting. Three locks, all new but painted brown and red to look rusted from anything other than close up."

"I can handle that, "Roger said, stepping up to the door next to Justin and fishing in his jacket pocket. He took out a small, zippered wallet, opened it, and took out what looked like a long nail file with a sharpened end.

"Officer, I am shocked," Justin said. "Shocked, I tell you."

"Probable cause," Roger said, bending low to get a better look at the locks. "I'm a man of many hidden talents. These locks look tough, but, nah. Piece of cake."

In less than a minute, Roger had dispatched all three of the locks, gave a gentle push to the door, and stepped back motioning for Justin to go in.

"Such manners," Justin said, stepping past the other man and over the threshold.

"Not really," Roger replied. "Could be booby-trapped. You're younger. You can take it."

"You're all heart," Justin shot back, feeling his way into the darkened interior.

It was midmorning when Curt pulled up in front of the already bustling site of the soon-to-be Angus McTiki's pub. A team of landscapers was hard at work on the front lawn and the sound of power tools came from inside. Curt scanned the parking lot and allowed himself a moment of disappointment when he didn't see Lawton's car anywhere. If he were the kind of businessman his reputation indicated, there is no way he'd be absent this close to a major opening night like this.

As he climbed out of the Chevelle, Curt stopped short as the enormity of this project became clear. Palm trees lined the front walkway and the expansive front deck. Exotic flowering plants dotted the property. They were so striking that Curt imagined they must be fake, but as he neared them, he saw they were the real thing.

The structure was immaculate. Every board, every feature, every accessory looked to be carefully crafted, chosen, and placed. It wasn't a huge place, but it was impressive in its workmanship. The building itself looked like a Polynesian hut. On steroids. The vaulted roofline was fringed with palm fronds and the two-story doorway, with massive teak double doors, was flanked by two ten-foot tiki carvings.

Shaking his head, Curt began to approach the entrance before being distracted by a smaller doorway off to the right. It was a simple wooden entrance, painted red, with the words *Angus' Snug* painted in brilliant gold letters on it.

Truth be told, the snug seemed more Curt's speed, so he altered course to head in there when he was brought up short by the buzzing of his phone in his pocket. He looked at the screen and almost declined the call when he saw it was Grier calling. Realizing that was his conscience speaking, he hit accept.

"Grier," he said, "what's the latest? I'm about to head into Lawton's McTiki place. It's impressive. Hopefully, impressive enough for him to show up and oversee things. If he hasn't been kidnapped. Or killed."

"Let me know what you find," Grier said, haltingly. "I wanted to touch base with you before the day got away from us. I'm gonna take the reunion folks out for a spin on the airboat. Killing three birds with one stone, hopefully."

"Go on," Curt said, distracted as he watched another team of workers emerge from behind the building.

"First, it will keep them from getting itchy and finding another way to get into trouble," Grier replied. "Show them the sights, distract them. But I also think there's something more to their whole story. I can't help coming back to the idea that their past here holds the key to what's going on."

"Maybe," Curt said, staring intently at the work crew. "That's two. What's the third bird you're taking down?"

"After what Roger and I ran into yesterday on the water, there's clearly something going on out there. I need to look around again and leading a tour group is a perfect cover. Plus, there will be more eyes to pick up on anything strange going on."

"Sounds good," Curt agreed. "Go for it."

"And Curt," Grier continued after the slightest hesitation. "We need to talk. Today. You need to tell me what's going on with you."

Curt closed his eyes and pinched the bridge of his nose with his free hand. "I know, Grier. I know. This afternoon. Let's meet at the Blue Crab at two, yeah? It will be empty then. Move it over from Swells'a?"

"Fine. I mean it, Curt," Grier said, more terse than he was comfortable being with his friend. "No more avoiding. The truth."

"Yeah," Curt replied, his eyes still following the workers headed toward the front door. "I promise. But I gotta go. Now. Like, right now."

"Curt!" Grier snapped. "Dammit, stop brushing me off!"

"I'm not brushing you off," Curt replied, starting off at a brisk pace. "But this is urgent."

"What could be more urgent than this?" Grier demanded.

"I'm watching Todd Lawton walk in the front door of his bar right now," Curt explained.

"Oh," Grier muttered. "Right. Go! See you at two."

Curt cut the call off and began waving his hand as he chased down the group entering the building.

***

Justin inched his way into the shack, the front door swinging freely all the way open. He reached to the wall on his right, running his hand along the paneling. He fished further along. Higher. Lower.

"No light switch," he said quietly to the trailing Roger. "Given the satellite dish and camera, I thought we might get lucky."

Both men took out their phones and turned on the flashlights. Roger broke left and worked his way around while Justin did the same on the opposite side.

"Well, this answers the power conundrum," Roger said, kneeling to shine his light closer to a small portable generator in the far corner. "Off and dead, far as I can tell."

Justin wandered over to take a look.

"Anker SOLIX," he said, after leaning down to examine the machine. "Not cheap. That solar panel isn't much good in here, but that gas mini attached would do the trick. Empty is my guess."

"Right, let's keep moving," Roger said. "I'd like to get out of here fast in case anyone decides to come home."

"Not a bad idea," Justin agreed, standing and heading further into the shack. "Pretty empty. Looks like someone cleared the place out."

The cabin had one large front room and then divided into two rooms in the back. Justin split right and found himself in the kitchen, although that was giving it more credit than it deserved. A wood camp stove rested in the far-right corner under a grime-crusted window. Despite the filth of the window, the stove was surprisingly well maintained, with a black matte finish and cooling racks attached to either side. He placed a tentative hand on it. Cold. He swung the door open and noted that it had been entirely swept clean. No ashes, nothing. Spotless.

He wiped the window, hoping to clear a space to see out back. Mostly, he succeeded in smearing the dirt into little swirls, but he finally made a tiny spot out of which he could see. The tire tracks that had been called in were clear to see and large enough to indicate a sizable truck had been back there. But whoever had left them was long gone.

The cupboards held a hodgepodge of glasses and mugs, most with chips or cracks. A collection from restaurants and bars from years past up and down the Banks. Kelly's, Coastal Cactus, Puffin Isle, Mako Mike's. There were two plates in only slightly better condition.

There was no refrigerator, but there was a long, low ice chest. Justin poked at it with a boot and was rewarded by a hollow *thunk*. Using his jacket cuff to cover his hand, he tentatively lifted the lid and peered inside. A small puddle on the bottom of the cooler was all that remained of whatever had been inside. And judging by the pungent and very unpleasant smell seeping out from under the lid, this had been where the poachers had kept their catch.

Justin lowered the lid in time to hear a loud crash from the other room, followed immediately by Roger exclaiming, "Sonofabitch!"

Justin raced around the corner and into the other back room where he found Roger seated on the floor and scooting as quickly as possible toward the door.

"Damn thing almost took me out!" he cried, pointing toward a pile of discarded sheets and blankets in the far corner.

Justin stepped past the babbling deputy to get a better look at what had set things off. Coiled in a corner of the musty heap of linens was a reddish-brown snake with bands across its body. The snake looked as surprised as Roger at the turn of events.

"Cottonmouth!" Roger said. "Been on the Banks long enough to see that. Damn, just about gave me a heart attack."

Justin laughed.

"What's so funny about it?" Roger fumed. "This is not the time or place I would choose to cash out. Dammit!"

"Relax, Roger," Justin replied, walking slowly toward the snake, his hands raised in front of him.

"You have a death wish, Ranger?" Roger continued. "Go get a box or something. Don't you have one of those snake net things in your truck?"

"It's not a cottonmouth," Justin said, kneeling and quickly gathering the snake in his hands. "Northern water snake. Easy mistake to make. But this little guy is harmless. He's more scared of you—"

"Than I am of him," Roger interrupted. "I've heard that before. I find that hard to believe. He's huge."

"He's cute," Justin countered. "Just look at him."

"He's gotta be two feet long," Roger complained, his voice lowering.

"Two and a half," Justin said, holding the snake up for a better look. "Poor guy just came in to warm up. I'll bring him outside and we can all go on with our days."

Justin carried the snake to the front door, still swinging on its hinges, and took the few steps down to the forest floor where he released the snake easily into a tuft of brush. In a flash, the snake was gone. Not a sound or a rustle of leaves. Just gone.

Smiling to himself, Justin rose, squinted at the rising sun, and trudged up the steps back into the cabin.

"Easy peasy," he called as he rejoined Roger in the back bedroom, stopping short as he found the officer leaning over the pile of sheets and blankets. "What did you find now, Jack Hanna?"

"Something more useful and a lot less threatening," Roger answered. "I hope."

He turned to Justin and held out a new-looking iPhone in a clear evidence bag.

"Whoever has been using this place cleaned it out pretty good from what I can see," Roger said, taking a closer look at the phone. "But they made a mistake. Even the smart ones always make a mistake."

Roger pressed buttons on either side of the phone and the screen lit up almost instantly. He tutted under his breath before turning the screen to Justin. On it, a tall, middle-aged man with salt and pepper hair and an expensive looking suit, was standing in front of a sign with his arms outstretched. The sign, in bright colors and embellished with tropical flowers and shamrocks, said *Angus McTiki's.*

"Unless this is the greatest coincidence I've ever seen," Justin said quietly, "we just found Todd Lawton's phone."

"I don't believe in coincidences. And now we have two missing people who don't have their phones, making it even harder to track them down."

"And why is it here, of all places?" Justin said. "Was he in here the whole time when we were recovering Keegan's body just down the road? Dammit. We blew it."

"We have it now," Roger replied. "No idea if it was here then. Or if *he* was here then. But let's head toward the highway so I can call this in to Curt. He needs to know."

"Curt Stephens?" Justin asked. "Not your superiors?"

"Curt's working on this with us," Roger said, quickly. "Multi-jurisdiction."

"Oh, cool," Justin said, headed back to the vehicles. "If there's anything I can do, just give a shout. I'm around."

"Thanks, Justin," Roger answered. "You saved my life in there."

The ranger laughed. "Hardly. If anything, I saved that poor little snake. All good. Glad I could help."

As they headed back up the dirt road toward the main roadway and a stronger signal on their phones, neither noticed the security camera on the porch of the shack turn to follow them, a green light now blinking on the bottom of the lens.

Grier had been waiting for ten minutes at a parking lot under Virginia Dare Trail before it turned into the Washington Baum Bridge and headed over to Roanoke Island. He'd headed here after getting off the phone with Amelia at the reunion house. She had accepted his invitation of a morning on his airboat exploring the Roanoke Sound. She'd sounded relieved, and he guessed the group had been getting antsy staying at the house.

The hood of his chocolate brown Volkswagen Rabbit was still warm from the drive over and, combined with the morning sun, was conspiring to put him to sleep. His humble Rabbit was no match for Curt's Chevelle, but that didn't mean it was any less dear to him. In fact, it could be even more as he'd had it since it had been handed down to him by a friend years ago. He'd spent a fortune maintaining it and had even shipped it to Europe once for a road trip the length of England and Scotland. Worth every penny. It was in storage most of the time these days, but the weather was so crisp and clear today, he had decided to break it out.

He kept his large airboat at the small marina here beginning in April of each year. It was handy to lead excursions of students from the nearby colleges and to help out a few of the local tour outfits when the summer season kicked in and demand outpaced their capacities. He didn't mind. He still found the sound endlessly fascinating and liked sharing some of his knowledge of it and watching the guests' eyes light up as they learned about an ecosystem most of them ignored unless they were glancing out the window while crossing one of the many bridges.

This trip would be slightly different. He had every intention of giving them the deluxe tour, but he needed to get to the root of their relationship with the missing Mark Elliot. He was convinced that the clue they were missing lay in their history here on the Banks. They'd all been visiting for decades. Decades of accumulated history with each other, but also with the barrier islands themselves. When bad things happened, in his experience, they often had begun long before. Of course, in an area as transient as this, sometimes random events could spin out of control. But with Elliot running into someone he knew, and the entire group gathering to reminisce, the clues seemed to lead backwards in time.

He watched a couple of the smaller fishing charter boats begin to trundle their way out for the day. It was late for them, already nine, but the time was perfect for a leisurely turn around some of the usual sights.

An older Acura, followed closely by a large silver SUV, appeared, approaching down the ramp that led from the roadway above. Grier squinted in their direction and saw two Virginia license plates. These must be his guests.

Having watched the security videos from the Bad Bean, he had an advantage on the high school friends, and so pushed himself up and off the hood, with more of an ache and old-man sound than he remembered making before and waved them into the open spaces next to the Rabbit.

Four women emerged from the Acura, all of a similar age and dressed casually. Their faces, though, seemed tense. Tight. There was no small talk and no laughter, just some half-hearted timid waves.

The three men who stepped down out of the SUV reflected the same sartorial splendor. Which is to say none. The one noticeable difference was they wore sneakers in place of sandals. And Grier was pleased to see one shirt emblazoned with a logo for the Wright Brothers Memorial. One history buff, at least.

"Welcome, welcome, everyone," Grier called. "I'm Grier Roleth. Marine biologist, traveler, wildlife expert, consultant with the local authorities. I work at the college and help out the police with anything that happens out on the water, so you can feel safe with me. All above board, if you'll pardon the pun. I know you've had a rough couple of days, so Roger—Deputy Goldstein—thought we could get you out of the house, show you some of the Banks you might not see otherwise. But it's not all fun and games. While we're out and about, if anything comes to you about your friend, the night he disappeared, anything, just let me know. And if you see anything that strikes you as odd out in the sound, speak up. So, in a way, you'll actually be helping us look for your friend. I work with the local investigators a lot. One big happy family around here."

The friends all made their own introductions, and after, Grier led them down a ramp onto a floating dock and toward his airboat. The shallow water boat had three benches positioned in front of a pilot's seat at the rear. Grier hopped aboard and lifted a headset from the pilot's chair.

"You'll find one of these on each seat," he announced. "Trust me, you'll want to put them on straightaway. That engine back there could fly a small plane, and it's a lot closer to you here than in the sky. So, save your ears, and pop one on. There's a small button here on the side. Push this if you want to say something. We'll see a lot of interesting things. Don't be shy with questions. This is my jam. I love talking about the sound and all its quirks. Now, do we have anyone who's squeamish on the water?"

Glances all around the group until Jaime tentatively raised his hand.

"I am," he admitted. "Nothing crazy, but—yeah."

"No worries," Grier replied, with a smile. "Look, this airboat is pretty smooth running and it's a calm day. Sometimes I like to open it up and hit some donuts out there, but I'll be gentle. These boats are nimble. I doubt you'll even realize you're on the water once we get going. If you do feel queasy, just raise your hand or push the button and let me know. Sound good?"

Jaime nodded but looked less than convinced.

Grier came back down to the dock and helped each of his guests from the swaying dock to their seats. When Kirsten reached him, he helped her on and noted to himself that he hadn't seen her in the video footage.

With everyone safely seated, he leaped up and into his seat.

"Okay, folks," he said into his headset as the engine began slowly and then increased in speed and noise until even the soundproof headsets were put to the test. "You never know what you'll see out in the sound. Every day is its own thing. Let's go be surprised."

With that, he pulled the airboat out of its slip and pointed it toward the open Roanoke Sound.

"Mr. Lawton! Excuse me, Mr. Lawton!" Curt called, as he hustled to catch up to the group of contractors that was on the threshold of Angus McTiki's.

The group paused and Lawton, the only one in a suit and tie, separated from the others and stepped toward Curt.

"Curt Stephens," Lawton said, extending a hand as he approached. "To what do I owe the honor? You do know we're not quite open yet, right?"

Lawton chuckled at what he seemed to think was a clever joke as he shook Curt's hand. But his smile held no mirth, and Curt found himself instinctively distrusting the man. Curt, who was no stranger to the finer things in life, noticed that Lawton's suit was Italian, handmade, and very expensive. Zegna, if he wasn't mistaken, which meant that suit had run over ten thousand dollars. At a minimum. And it was wildly out of place here in the Outer Banks.

"I realize that, Mr. Lawton," Curt answered with what he hoped was a more sincere smile than the one he had received a moment ago. "I'm here to ask you some questions about two men you were seen with the other night."

Lawton paused. Barely. Most people wouldn't even notice, but Curt wasn't most people.

"Oh, that's odd," Lawton replied, quickly recovering. "I'm afraid I'm a bit pressed for time. Soft opening is this week and still a lot to finish. Deadlines come and go, but somehow there are still details left hanging."

As Lawton gestured back toward the now open front door and the waiting workers, one of the men stepped away from the group.

"Boss?" he called. "We need you in here if we're going to decide on those light globes. Unless you trust us to do it?"

"No, definitely not, Rick," Lawton called back with an apologetic shrug to Curt. "Duty calls. Can this wait?"

"I'm afraid not," Curt replied. "You're a hard man to reach. We've been trying to reach you since yesterday."

"That isn't actually that long," Lawton replied, with a hefty dose of condescension. "You should have checked here. I've barely left in days."

"I did. You weren't here. The authorities tracked your E-Z Pass up to the Richmond area. And you haven't been answering your phone."

"Authorities? Huh. Simple enough to explain, not that I feel I have to," Lawton said, hands spread wide in front of him. "I loaned my car to my cousin. As I said, I'm just here these days and he needed it. His car is in the shop. Family is family, after all. And I'm a wealthy man. I have more than one car."

"And why didn't you answer your phone?" Curt asked.

"Also simple," Lawton answered. "It was stolen a couple of days ago. Probably at Bad Bean or Lucky 12. I really should report it, but it's just a phone."

"Inconvenient time for you to be without one, I would think," Curt said, nodding toward the almost completed bar behind them.

"Like I said, I'm always here and we have land lines and a parade of contractors all trying to get in my face," Lawton said with a woe-is-me expression. "Honestly, it's been a relief. I figured I'd wait until opening to replace it. I've enjoyed the peace and quiet. Relatively speaking. Now can you tell me what this is about? I really do have to get going."

"Sure. You were seen in the company of two men. Kevin Keegan and Mark Elliot at Bad Bean. Both of those men are reported missing, and as you were the last person seen with them, we were hoping you could help us out."

Curt kept the fact that Keegan was deceased to himself. No need to lay all his cards on the table.

Lawton now turned to Curt and fixed him with a stare and knitted brow.

"First," Lawton said, "who exactly is 'we'? I wasn't aware you were employed by the police."

"I'm not," Curt admitted. "I've been brought on board by concerned family and friends. I'm cooperating with the local authorities, though."

"Got it. So not a cop," Lawton replied. "Nothing official about this, then. But that's not really the point. If Kev and Elliot are missing, I'd be glad to help, but I don't know anything about it. I've known Kevin a long time. He's worked with and *for* me in various capacities. We go way back to my days as a teenager visiting. But I don't know Mr. Elliot, at all. He thought he recognized me from years ago here in Nags Head. Honestly? He might have met me, but that was a long time ago and I meet a lot of people. Always have. If I met him when we were kids twenty years ago, or whatever he claimed, I have no recollection of that."

"Right," Curt said, nodding more to himself than Lawton. "But see, we pulled the security video from Bad Bean and saw the three of you leaving together. Now they're both missing, so..."

"Look, Stephens," Lawton replied, brusquely. "I don't know how I can help. We went to Lucky 12 for a quick drink and I took them by here to show them the progress on the place. Kevin was thinking about coming in as a bar manager."

"Was?" Curt asked, eyebrows arched.

"Is," Lawton corrected himself. "He is considering it. I know him. Trust him. I need people like that here. The first few weeks of a new place can make or break it."

"Kind of late to be hiring managers if you open this week, isn't it?" Curt asked.

"It's never too late if it means you get the *right* people," Lawton answered.

"Boss?" Rick called from the doorway.

"Coming, Rick! Dammit," Lawton shouted in return.

While Lawton turned to deal with his contractors, Curt felt his phone buzz and turned away to answer quietly when he saw that it was Roger calling. Curt listened, nodded, and said he understood, before turning back to Lawton.

"Look, sorry, I really need to get moving," Lawton said, with no hint of genuine apology. "Give me a call later and I'll talk things through with you, but like I said, I don't have anything to add. I'd help if I could. Don't like to think of anyone going missing. But don't drag me into it. I can't have any bad PR this close to opening."

"I'm happy to give you a call later," Curt said, nodding, "except for that pesky missing phone, remember?"

"Dammit, I forgot," Lawton said, with a shake of his head. "Just leave me your number and I'll reach out later today."

"Yeah, well, it's not just me you have to deal with now," Curt said, waving his phone at Lawton before placing it back in his back pocket. "That was the Manteo Police Department. They'd like a word too."

"For the love of…" Lawton said, staring at the sky and taking a deep breath. "Why do they want to talk to me? I avoid Roanoke Island like the plague. Haven't been in ages."

"But your phone has," Curt returned. "Manteo PD just found it in a poacher's shack in Buffalo City. Not far from where they recovered Kevin Keegan's body."

Lawton's carefully crafted veneer slipped then, ever so slightly. And no amount of tailoring would have made him look comfortable in his very expensive suit.

***

Grier cruised around two small tidal islands out in the Roanoke Sound. He was surprised at how much he was enjoying himself. The reunion gang was good company. Smart. Asking intelligent questions. He found himself really hoping that they weren't involved in the disappearance of their friend. And the murder of Keegan. He just wanted the nice folks to be what they seemed, for once.

Chris, seated in the front row of the airboat, pointed to starboard, out into clearer water and Grier glanced in that direction, before banking the boat more sharply than he'd intended to head where Chris had indicated.

"Whoops!" Grier said, pushing the button on his headset so the others could hear him while increasing their speed. "Sorry about that Jaime! Over the side, if you have to hurl! Good eyes, Chris! Folks, our resident animal expert spotted some dolphins off in that deeper canal. I'll take us over and see if we can get a closer look without spooking them."

Francis, seated behind Chris, tapped him on the shoulder and rewarded him with a high five. Jaime looked decidedly less enthusiastic as he grabbed the bench to steady himself.

"Dolphins in the sound are not all that unusual," Grier continued. "Most parts of the sound are actually quite shallow, coming in at four feet deep or less. But the dolphins have adapted well and stick to the deeper channels running throughout. In fact, these dolphins spend their whole lives in the sound. Never leave."

Kirsten pushed the button on her headset. "Seems weird to me," she said. "Why would they stay in the sound? The whole ocean is right there for them if they just head out. Why stay cooped up in here?"

Grier looked at her and smiled.

"Another good question," he replied. "The answer is—no one really knows. They just do. And to take it even further, while these individuals stay in the sound, the dolphins just beyond in the ocean rarely come in here. The two populations don't interact. Completely avoid each other."

"Considering they're such social animals, that seems counterintuitive," Cathy chimed in.

"Agreed," Grier said. "Just shows how much we still have to learn about them."

"I went swimming with dolphins," Terry said, with a click of her headset. "In the Bahamas. Long time ago. Don't think I would be comfortable doing that now. The enclosure was pretty small."

"Yup," Grier agreed. "Not the best practice, we know now. Not good for their socialization or temperament. Happily, we don't have anything like that here in the Banks. Oh!"

Grier throttled the boat down and allowed it to slow and settle into the water.

"Now here is something most people don't get to see," he said over the com, lowering his voice. "That dolphin there"—he pointed to the closest animal—"is playing with a puffer fish. I think I've only seen this once, and I was nowhere as near as we are now."

"Playing with a puffer fish?" Jaime asked, relaxing slightly as the boat stopped moving. "Whaddaya mean playing?"

"Seems weird, right?" Grier said, with a laugh and a big grin. "Dolphins are super smart. They do a lot of things we don't really understand, and this is one. Puffers have a toxin that they release in self-defense. Problem is, dolphins know how to get just the right dose. And the dolphins seem to get some sort of high out of it. So, when you see dolphins playing with a puffer fish, they're basically passing a doobie around the circle and all getting stoned."

"That really is one of the weirder things I've heard in a long time," Terry said.

"Nature is endlessly surprising," Chris muttered, eyes fixed on the dolphins.

"Dolphins have a reputation as being these fun, goofy animals," Amelia broke in. "Weird to think of them basically torturing poor little puffer fish."

"That image of dolphins is purely man-made," Grier said, maneuvering the boat again to get a better look at the dolphins. "*We* think of them that way but remember they are pretty much apex predators. And they are very good at hunting and killing. Like any wild animal they do what they have to do to survive. They *look* cute to us. To a squid, or crustacean, or a puffer fish? Not so cute. What we see is definitely not the whole story. Dolphins can be just as vicious as any other hunter."

"Sounds like some people I know," Terry said.

"Yup," Grier agreed. "People do the same thing. What it takes to get by. We're rarely what we seem. That would be too easy."

"What happens to the puffer fish?" Francis asked. "You know, when the dolphins are done?"

"That's one of the strangest parts," Grier said, nodding. "They almost always survive. The dolphins don't even bother to eat them. They just gnaw on 'em, get high, and go on their way leaving some very traumatized puffers in their wake."

"I'm changing my opinion of dolphins," Amelia replied.

"Actually, you're probably just getting a clearer picture of them," Grier said, giving a mock bow. "You're welcome. Hey! Let's leave these delinquent dolphins to their puffer party. There's an island over this way with a little natural cove. I'll give you a crash course on clamming. Hold on, Jaime! Here we go!"

As the airboat revved its engine and began to skim across the water, Jaime gripped his seat tighter and leaned his head over the side to catch the breeze as it kicked up. Just in case.

Roger strolled into the police station, having left Justin back at Alligator River with a request to keep an eye on the poacher's cabin throughout the day. He had caught Curt before he'd left Lawton, and the discovery of the phone had been enough to convince the truculent businessman to come to the Manteo police station later in the day. Roger hustled up the stairs. He had to fill Chief Brady in on developments and get an interview room set up for late that afternoon. The Brethren meeting was at two, so they would have their chat with Lawton at four. Curt would sit in, provided everyone was still speaking to each other after whatever was in store for the secret society's gathering.

He breezed past the reception desk, Mary buzzing him in with a wink and a blown kiss.

"Man on a mission!" she called after Roger. "You got an early start!"

Roger stopped short at the sound of her voice, something itching at the back of his mind.

"Mary, Mary, quite contrary," Roger said, turning back to her. "I had something to ask you—what the hell was it?"

"You have to give me more than that, heartthrob," Mary teased. "I'm good, but I'm not *that* good."

Roger felt the weight of the recovered cell phone in his jacket pocket and his mental logjam released.

"Right," he nearly shouted. "Keegan, Bad Bean, Russ...that was it. You told me that you left Bad Bean with Russ, but he says you stayed after him. And the security video shows you leaving alone a few minutes later. You sat in your car a bit too."

"Why, Roger," Mary cooed. "Am I a suspect? Have to confess, I imagined you putting cuffs on me under different circumstances."

Roger felt his cheeks redden and laughed nervously. This was brazen, even by their usual flirtation standards.

"Don't be silly," Roger stammered, his inner schoolboy making an appearance. Something he'd thought he was long past. "No, no. Nothing like that. Just thought I'd check to see if you had noticed anything else after Russ skedaddled."

Roger immediately turned a deeper shade of red.

"Skedaddled? Who talks like that?" he chided himself quietly.

"Now that you mention it," Mary said slowly, enjoying every moment of Roger's discomfort. "I did stay a sec to finish my drink. Didn't see a thing. Headed to my car and checked my email before I left. Sadly, I didn't have anything from you, but I live in hope."

She played with a strand of hair that had escaped her usually tightly pulled back hair. Roger became even more flustered.

"Right, well," he said, tapping the doorway by his head. "Yup. That's what it was. So...um...let me know if you think of anything. Just text me. Or whatever."

"You clever boy," Mary purred. "All this just to get me to text you? Just come out and ask me, next time."

Roger laughed awkwardly as he turned toward Brady's office, and he could swear he caught a glimpse of a mischievous smile on Mary's face as she got back to work.

Roger felt Mary's eyes on him as he knocked on Brady's door, but when he snuck a peek back, she was on the phone and paying him no mind. He shook his head and stepped into the office when he heard Brady beckon him. Mary wasn't even his type, but she sure could twist him around like a pretzel.

As Roger closed the door gently behind himself, Brady said,

"Whaddaya have for me? Anything to that tip about the cabin in the woods? Creepy freakin' place."

"As a matter of fact, yes," Roger replied, sitting in front of the Chief's desk. "The Vollmerhausens were spot on. Tire tracks, signs of recent visits, an enormous and very dangerous snake, and this."

With a flourish, he removed the bagged phone from his jacket and laid it on the desk between the two men.

"And what do we have here?" Brady asked, sliding the phone over to his side of the desk.

"That there is, unless I'm mistaken which rarely happens, Mr. Todd Lawton's cell phone," Roger said, emphasizing his statement by tapping the desk with each word. "And that puts him just a few yards from our victim."

"It puts his *phone* in the vicinity," Brady cut in. "Let's be careful about getting ahead of ourselves."

"Fair enough," Roger agreed. "How about we get this to Russ and see what we can find. Lawton is coming in for a little chat at four today, so we have some time."

"Now you're talking," Brady said, gesturing to the door. "If this guy had anything to do with it, we'll nail him."

"I don't doubt it for a second," Roger called over his shoulder as he left the office.

"Don't believe you about the snake," Brady yelled through the now closed door.

"Didn't think I'd get away with that," Roger replied as he headed down the hall to have Russ work on Lawton's phone.

Grier was wading through the three feet of water that made up the picture-perfect beach where he had brought the reunion gang. All of them, even Jaime, had jumped out of the airboat when he had dropped his small anchor in the stillness of the little cove.

The visitors were peering intently into the water and shuffling their feet. Every so often, one of them would cry out and thrust a hand into the sand at their feet. More often than not, they rose clutching a clamshell and waving it for the others to see.

Cathy had proven particularly adept at finding some healthy specimens, and she had just come back up holding what was clearly the largest anyone had found to this point.

"Nice one!" Grier called, sloshing through the thigh-deep water to reach Cathy's side. "What you have there is a quahog. That's the biggest you'll find out here."

"Quahog," Cathy repeated. "I've heard of them but definitely never seen one. This is so cool!"

"Fun fact," Grier continued, giving Cathy's find an appreciative heft. "So far, we've found littleneck and cherrystone clams. Those are the smallest two varieties of...drum roll...quahogs! They're all the same type of clam, we just give them different names based on their size. They're used in pretty much every clam dish you can think of. From New England chowder to the fried clams you can find up and down the beach."

"I'm going to put this bad boy back," Cathy said, returning her quahog to the sandy bottom and watching it burrow into the sand. "He's made it this long; seems he earned the right to go on his way."

"Good on ya," Grier replied. "I applaud your generous spirit."

"What's that over there?" Kirsten asked, pointing across the open sound beyond their cove and to the next island over. "Looks like someone has a house there, but that island is way too small, isn't it? And there's no dock."

Grier waded over to where Kirsten was standing, shaded his eyes, and followed her line of sight.

"Duck blind," Grier replied after a moment. "I'm out here so often I forgot it was over there. Hasn't been used in quite a while. Probably looks a lot less welcoming up close."

"Duck blind?" Chris asked. "That looks pretty elaborate for a duck blind. Looks like a full-blown vacation home."

"Yeah, it does," Grier agreed. "Another one of those funny Outer Banks quirks. A while back, there were no real regulations on duck blinds out here on the sound. Well, people being what they are, some folks got the idea to start building the blinds bigger. And more elaborate. After a while, they started to look just like that. Like full on houses. And some people were abusing the system, finding a way to have a vacation home down here without any of the cost and red tape. Very much in the spirit of the pirates and adventurers that settled here."

"What happened?" Francis asked. "Clearly something did. You said that place is falling apart."

"Human nature is what it is," Grier answered with a nod. "One very ambitious duck hunter went as far as to install solar panels and a septic system. Local authorities had turned a blind eye as long as they could. Passed some new regulations and shut down the faux hunting blinds. Now they just sit there. Falling apart."

"The Banks really have always attracted free spirits, haven't they?" Amelia asked, joining the others in looking out over the sound. "But I get it, in this case. Houses down here have gone crazy. Huge. Expensive. If I could have a cheap, off-the-grid place out here to myself? I'd be tempted."

"Remember the first houses we rented when we started coming here?" Terry asked. "Basically, just shacks. Walls, a roof, refrigerator. Not much else."

"And I loved 'em," Jaime said, showing off his latest clam capture.

Grier looked at the clam and gave a wink. "Littleneck," he announced. "Cute little thing."

Jaime gave a shrug and let the little mollusk plop back into the water.

"I think the very first one was called Green Hall," Jaime continued. "The walls didn't even reach to the roof. We had water pistol fights from one room to the other squirting over the walls."

"That OBX doesn't exist anymore," Grier said. "Sad to admit. I wish I'd gotten here sooner to see more of it. You've all been coming here twenty years? Twenty-five?"

"Longer," Amelia admitted. "Scary to think about it that way."

"You must have seen a lot of change," Grier said. "What keeps you coming back?"

"Good question," Amelia replied. "Nostalgia? But no, it's more than that. Shared memories. Escapism. Returning to the scene of the crime?"

Amelia laughed, but Grier took note. An odd thing to say.

"I think," Terry added, "that it's the original spirit of adventure, wildness. Living just beyond the norms on the mainland."

"Yeah," Chris agreed. "Even with all the changes, there's still no place like it. Not in this part of the world. Island life. Even with the McMansions and real estate prices, there's still something romantic about it."

"Remember those big natural grass putting courses from the nineties?" Jaime asked, rinsing his hands in the water at his knees to get rid of the briny clam smell. "I loved those. Only time I've ever golfed. All filled with condos or huge houses now."

"What was the name of that place that had a ship's bar upstairs?" Francis asked. "I sat on a barstool that John Wayne had used. That place was great."

"Windmill Point," Cathy answered quickly. "Gone ten or fifteen years now. Shame. Really unique. The S.S. *United States*'s bar was recreated upstairs. I read somewhere they just moved the old ship to Florida and sank it to make a reef. It's all gone now."

"What other places did we go?" Terry asked. "Gandalf's was on the beach road. I loved Quagmires. Any other places?"

"Slammin' Sammy's had a moment," Francis said. "By George or something like that was good. Oh, Papagayo's! Loved it there."

"What was the place over by the sound?" Cathy asked. "Jaime, didn't you and Mark like to go there for a few years?"

"What was that called? Yeah," Jaime replied. "We loved it for a while. It got a little dicey there towards the end. I missed a couple trips, but Mark kept hanging out there. Next time I was here, it was gone, and he told me he had stopped going because it started bringing in a rough crowd."

"I seem to remember, he had a bad experience there and never went back," Amelia said. "What was it? Something isle?"

"Yes!" Jaime exclaimed, pointing at Amelia. "Puffin Isle. That was it. Made no sense, but it was the only place like it. Amazing sunset views. But yeah. Mark said he saw someone harassing a girl one night and just wrote the place off."

"That's a new one on me," Grier admitted. "All of them are, actually. Fun to hear your memories, though. Wish I could go back in time."

"Don't you just?" Kirsten agreed. "If only life worked that way."

"And as much as I hate to say it," Grier said, looking at his dive watch, "I need to take us back in. I have a meeting this afternoon. Doesn't that just sound so boring after all our talk of adventure?"

The group chuckled as they splashed their way back to the airboat. Before they reached their ride, Grier brought them to a sudden stop, raised his finger to his lips, and pointed toward some bushes near the edge of the island in front of them, where a brilliant blue bird, roughly the size of a sparrow, was flitting from branch to branch.

"Indigo Bunting," Grier said quietly. "Just gorgeous. This is the time of year to see them. A lot of migrating birds actually. April is prime time."

"That is stunning," Kirsten exclaimed in a hushed voice. "I've never seen such a vivid blue before."

"And that's another reason that the Banks will always be the Banks," Grier said. "Mother Nature will always reign supreme here."

The group clambered into the boat, Jaime taking a tumble that drenched him before finally managing to find his seat. Grier fired up the engine, and as they headed back to the dock where their journey began, Kirsten peppered Grier with questions about local birdwatching. By the time they docked, Kirsten had managed to convince Grier to lead another trip to the nature preserve at Pea Island to spot more migratory birds.

Grier didn't seem to mind one bit.

Carlito sat in a corner of the Front Porch Café, his laptop open in front of him and Mark Elliot's phone next to it. He really hoped he could do something with it. He'd been so excited to contribute, he may have overstated his technological expertise. He still believed he would be better than any of the others. Except maybe Sage. She seemed pretty savvy. The others all had their strengths, but he very much doubted that they included being cell phone experts.

He plugged the phone into his laptop and began to run a password unlocking program. He'd entered a few prompts and let it run. It could go through thousands in the time he would have gotten through a handful. He didn't really know anything about Mark Elliot. Only that he'd been coming to the area most of his life and wrote theatre reviews for a living. Not much to go on, but he was hopeful the program would pick up his slack.

He leaned back and sipped his latte. His impostor syndrome had kicked in with the light of day. He had no business being part of the Brethren of the Coast. He was a kid from Texas with no particular skills that would help safeguard the Banks. He wasn't a wealthy businessman, cop, world traveler, or even a bartender with the ears of the community.

He was a recent arrival with no job prospects and no friends. No one knew him, or trusted him, or shared any kind of history with him. He was renting a basement room in someone else's house and doubted his landlord even knew his name. Which is why he was more comfortable spending his time in the café than back at the house. At least here, they smiled when they saw him, something that definitely didn't happen back "home."

Genevieve, who worked weekday mornings here, was the closest thing to a friend he had in town, and they hadn't done anything but exchange pleasantries. She was cute. If he ever managed a job and some confidence, he planned to ask her out. Maybe. Hopefully. She made a mean latte, but that was about the only thing he knew about her beyond her blond hair, green eyes, and elegant way of moving around the coffee shop. He wondered idly if she had ever studied dance? It looked like she had.

Even after his morning stop at the beach on Hatteras, he was still the only person at the Front Porch. People at the Banks either got up super early—the fishermen and such—or super late—vacationers who had stayed up late. So midmorning was a bit of a no-man's-land here and he liked it that way.

Genevieve was stretching to reach a blueberry scone that had gotten stuck at the back of a shelf in the display counter. Carlito was about to jump up to offer to help, when his laptop pinged. The program had done its job, and he was into Mark Elliot's phone. He felt funny poking around someone's personal life that he didn't know but reminded himself that this was to try to find Elliot and hopefully bring him home safe.

He checked and smiled. Elliot's password was "OBXLifer." Not exactly the safest or most secure, but it did show his attachment to the islands. He hoped whatever he turned up would help.

With a guilty glance at Genevieve, still struggling for the scone, Carlito turned his attention to the phone in front of him and started to dig through where it had been and the most recent photos. He would have something to show for his work and hoped it would earn the trust the Brethren had placed in him. That was enough to make him relax. A little.

He cheered inwardly as he saw Genevieve grab the scone. They were both having good mornings.

Roger had his feet up on Russ's desk, watching the lanky officer do whatever it was he did to pull information from Lawton's recovered phone. There was a cable leading from the phone to a laptop. Every few moments, Russ would make a guttural noise under his breath and stab at a few keys on the keyboard of the computer. The phone would be sent to an electronics expert, but Russ got first crack at it.

With each muttered sound, Roger shook his head. He took a bite of an apple pastry Russ had brought in this morning. Not just *any* apple pastry, though: an Apple Ugly from Orange Blossom Bakery down toward the southern stretch of the Banks in Buxton. They were a renowned local delicacy and sold out daily from the bakery before most people were even awake. Apple, and cinnamon, and lard, and all sorts of things that were not particularly good for you were what made them so in demand.

As Roger tucked into the Ugly, his own guttural noises joined those of Russ, though with vastly different inspiration. The silence of the computer work became punctuated by the mmphs of delight and uhhhs of frustration. The symphony of nonsensical vocal percussion became so loud that Mary peered into the office with a question on her face.

"What in blazes are you two up to in here?" she asked. "It sounds like nothing any respectable officer would do in public; I'll tell you that. Oh! Uglies? Why didn't someone tell me."

Mary grabbed one from the box on Russ's desk and started back for the door, stopping short when Brady's voice came echoing down the hallway.

"Did someone say Uglies?" the chief shouted. "You're all fired if I don't get one. Not you, Mary. I need you."

Mary laughed, wheeled around, and with a shrug of disingenuous apology, grabbed another pastry for the boss.

"What can I do? I'd miss you both too much if you got fired," Mary said, as she disappeared in the direction of Brady's office.

Russ had barely lifted his head from the computer screen

throughout the entire episode, and Roger went back to work on the Apple Ugly.

"Why was Sasha all the way down in Buxton, anyway?" Roger asked around a mouthful of apple and dough. "That's not a short drive."

"Mmm," Russ responded. "Friend from school coming through on the way to Ocracoke. High school, I think. Jill something. They met at Orange Blossom before the friend caught the ferry. Thought she was crazy to make the trip, but it seemed important to her." He shrugged a "what can you do" without breaking eye contact with the screen.

Both of their phones pinged at the same time, and they shared a look. That usually meant bad news.

They took a pause to read the alert and then both looked up at the other.

"Our fentanyl patient is out of the woods," Russ said, with a nod. "Long way to go but she should be okay. That's the good news."

"Yeah," Roger answered, "but the bad news is two more kids were brought in with the same thing this morning. This is getting out of control. It's gotta stop."

"It does," Russ agreed. "One emergency at a time. Have to get into this phone."

"I wish it worked that way," Roger answered. "Can't tell those parents we were too busy on another case. And the bad guys don't wait until we can deal with them."

An uneasy silence fell over them both, and Russ focused again on getting access to the phone. Two men with too much to worry about.

"I talked to Mary about your night at Bad Bean," Roger said, coming up for a breath from his baked good, arching his back, and patting his stomach. "These things can't be good for you."

"Quit complainin'," Russ answered. "It was free, and it has fruit in it. It's practically health food. Win, win."

Roger chuckled and nodded in agreement.

"Mary said she forgot that she stayed to finish her drink and followed right behind you," Roger went on. "That sound right?"

"Wouldn't know," Russ answered. "I left, remember?"

"Fair point," Roger replied. "Anyway, she said she didn't see anything of note, so that was another dead end. Worth a shot."

"Always worth a shot," Russ agreed. "It was actually nice hanging out with her away from here. She's pretty cool. Realized I didn't know much about her outside of the office."

"Yeah?" Like what?"

"She used to be married, for one," Russ answered. "Didn't last. Has a daughter but they haven't spoken for a while. No idea why. Didn't want to pry. Been on her own for a long time now. She grew up in Kitty Hawk. Settled there for a while before heading to Wanchese. Got the impression her move had something to do with the marriage ending. Seemed a sore subject. Great sense of humor, though. She did a killer impression of Brady. He'd fire *her* if he ever heard it."

"I'll be sure to ask for it, next chance I get," Roger said with a laugh. "Never knew about the marriage thing. She's always just been...Mary."

"Longest tenured employee here," Russ replied. "Been here even longer than the Chief. That's saying something."

"How long *has* the Chief been here?" Roger asked.

"A long time. More than a decade. That's all I know," Russ said. "The two of them are both fixtures in the station. Can't imagine the town without them. Probably be here long after you and me are gone."

"Probably," Roger agreed. "I'm outta here as soon as I can claim that pension."

"Same here, friend," Russ said, before suddenly jumping to his feet and clapping his hands. "Yessir! That's what I'm talkin' about! I am in!"

"You seem awfully excited about it," Roger noted. "I thought you were our resident tech expert. Techspert, if you will."

"I am," Russ protested. "Compared to the rest of you, at least. But I wasn't one hundred percent sure this was gonna work. And yet"—he splayed his hands in front of him toward the equipment—"victory is mine."

"What are you going to get for me?" Roger asked, rising and crossing behind the desk to look at the screens with Russ.

"All of it, Rog," Russ said, his mood so much lighter than a moment ago. "Where the phone traveled, texts, photos, search history, emails. We've got Lawton right where we want him. If he had anything to do with this, that is."

"You could have told me this was tough for you," Roger said. "I know a guy."

"Yeah, well, I like my job. Keep your guy for something else."

Roger shook his head.

"So insecure for someone so tall," Roger joked, poking Russ in the shoulder.

"Height has nothing to do with it," Russ said, swatting Roger away. "It's good to challenge yourself once in a while. You should try it sometime."

"I'll keep that in mind," Roger replied, his wry smile going unnoticed. "I have a meeting in Colington in a bit. Can you send me whatever you get from the phone, ASAP?

"Colington, huh?" Russ shot back, dragging his eyes away from the screen. "Tell Curt I said hi. And yes. You'll get it as soon as I do. I'll send what I have to the printer now so you can take it with you."

"Thanks, Russ," Roger said, rising and starting for the door. "And thank Sasha for the Uglies. I owe her."

"She'll hold you to that!" Russ called as Roger slipped out and down the hallway.

He kept coming back to the idea of Mary having been married. And a daughter? No reason he should have known, but somehow, he felt a twinge of jealousy that he hadn't. And that Russ had found out before he had. Mary really was a bit of a mystery to him. Even after all these years. He scolded himself for being childish and rushed out the door with a quick wave at the reception desk.

194

CHAPTER 12

Curt arrived at the Blue Crab a half hour before the meeting was supposed to start. The bar wasn't open yet, but RG gave him a key and he pretty much had the run of the place. They didn't need to be inside for this meeting. In fact, it was important they be outside. He needed the half hour to settle himself and think through how he wanted this to go.

He expected Grier, and possibly Roger, to arrive early too. They understood what was happening. They were beginning to get more information on the Keegan murder and Elliot disappearance. If experience was any indication, things would begin to move fast now. And they'd better, because every hour that Elliot was missing brought them closer to a negative result. And Lawton was hiding something. He wasn't sure what, but he could feel it.

There was also the other matter that he knew had to be addressed. No more keeping things from the others. He had to come clean, and that meant bringing Carlito all the way into the fold. And risk losing him, if he couldn't accept the full truth.

He stowed his bag under the bench on the lower dock, making sure it was secure. Then rather than sitting on the bench, he dropped down to sit on the edge of the dock, letting his bare feet trail over the edge and into the rising tide. The water was cool. Some would say cold. April was still early in the season here and many locals waited for the waters to warm further before venturing into the ocean. Here, on the sound, the coming and going of the tides kept the water cooler longer. It didn't bother him. In fact, he enjoyed the pins and needles that the sting of the water sent through his feet and up his legs. It helped him focus.

He laughed to himself that one of his favorite places on the entire Outer Banks was out back of what many considered the last standing dive bar in the area. But the people were genuine, and the view was breathtaking. Especially now, as the sun was coming back around to show itself just across the cove. Winter months saw the sunset hidden further behind the trees, but the spot was coming into its own now. And soon the most intrepid tourists would begin to find their way here, breaking the mostly local spell that thrived from November through May. Not that he minded. He'd made some life-long friends out of summer visitors. Not many, but some.

Fifteen minutes after he'd arrived, Curt heard the hum of Grier's little Robalo boat in the distance and smiled at how well he knew his fellow Brethren. Before the craft had rounded the bend in the shore, Curt heard cars arriving in the gravel parking lot. More than one. He'd been right on Roger wanting to arrive early but had seemingly underestimated Sage and Carlito when it came to eagerness. He was mildly surprised when the gate in the fence opened and all three of them entered the back deck. Limber Riley squirmed through their feet while Banks waited patiently for his turn with a grateful look to Sage as she closed the door behind him.

"I suppose you're wondering why I called you all here," Curt said, rising from the dock, but his attempt to lighten the mood fell flat and he understood why. "Let's all take a seat around the table up top, and I'll get down to business. I'm glad you're all here."

Grier was still tying up his boat when Curt placed his bag on the table and rested his hand on it.

"Before we get to what I have in here," Curt began, "I think we need to get each other up to speed with what we have on Elliot's disappearance. We've had some preliminary reports from Raleigh on the postmortem. And maybe some more information from Lawton's phone?" He shot a questioning look at Roger who nodded in response. "Excellent. And no pressure, Carlito, but did you manage anything with Elliot's electronics? Would be great if we could get that back to Manteo PD, just to avoid any messiness."

"Oh yeah," Carlito answered. "I got in and can tell you almost anything you want to know about the guy. He's a writer, so he has a *lot* online and in notes."

Curt gave the young man a mildly surprised, but definitely pleased, look.

"Great work," Curt said. "Anything new from either of you, Sage and Grier?"

Sage shook her head, but Grier sat forward on his seat.

"Actually, yeah," Grier replied. "I took the reunioners out for some sound side sightseeing this morning. Learned a fair amount."

"Excellent," Curt said, absently picking at a loose splinter on the picnic table in front of him. "I'll go first, just get things rolling. I finally tracked Lawton down at Angus McTiki's this morning. He claims his car was loaned to a cousin and that's who was in the Richmond area. Could be true, and we're checking into that. Maybe a traffic camera or some CCTV can clear it up. He also *claimed* that he had lost his phone the night Keegan died. He tried to play it that it could have been stolen, but subsequent events have made it pretty clear he lost it. More on that in a sec from Roger. As far as Lawton the person goes, I don't trust him. He's slick on the surface, but he was definitely hiding something from me and wanted me gone ASAP. We need to find out more about his past, his current movements, and this new place he's building. Roger? Want to take it from there?"

"It would be my pleasure, oh great one," Roger answered, earning an eyeroll from Curt. "Let's start with Keegan's cause of death. It came as no surprise that it was drowning. The surprise came from the fact that he'd died in chlorinated water, not salt water or even the brackish water you can find in Alligator River."

"So, he was killed somewhere else, and someone moved him to where we found him," Grier said. "So much for anything being accidental here. This was intentional."

"Absolutely," Roger concurred. "There was one contusion on his head that appears to have been administered before he died, but any other trauma was post death. Likely getting him into the water, under the kayak. Maybe even in transport."

"As far as I know," Curt said, "the only chlorinated water I've seen in this investigation has been the pool and hot tub at the reunion house. Thoughts?"

"No, no, no," Grier replied. "There has to be something else going on. I spent the morning with them. I would bet good money they aren't involved. I just don't see it. And it's the beach. A lot of people have pools. Or hot tubs."

"Elliot could have brought people back to the house," Sage posited.

"Possible, I suppose," Roger answered. "We don't have any indication he did, but maybe his devices will shed light on that."

"Murder it is," Curt said. "We need more pieces to the puzzle, though. Roger, you've had a busy day. Fill everyone in on the rest?"

"Yupper," Roger went on. "Tox screen on Keegan will take a bit longer but it's being fast-tracked. And then earlier today. Following a tip about suspicious activity from none other than the Vollmerhausens this morning, Ranger Justin and I paid a visit to that weird shack toward the back of Buffalo City in the refuge. I'll be damned but they were right. Signs of a vehicle or vehicles coming and going. We determined a look inside was called for. Just to make sure no one was in any danger"—he shot a look at the others, daring them to question his reasoning—"and we found that the place had been cleared out. Almost nothing left behind for us. We did find one massive and angry snake who resented being disturbed, and, lo and behold, a cell phone that seems to have been left inadvertently."

"Let me guess," Sage said. "Lawton's?"

"The one and only," Roger continued. "We tagged and bagged it, brought it back to the station, and Russ finished some preliminary work on it just a while ago. Tracking shows that, from Bad Bean, Lawton went to Lucky 12 and ended up at the soon-to-be McTiki's. Up to there, Lawton's story holds up. Then things get interesting. He was there for close to an hour. Then his phone took a drive to the Wanchese marina. Then proceeded to Alligator River and the site of Keegan's body. It stayed there a while. Then made its way very slowly to the cabin where it remained until we found it this morning."

"Lawton is squarely in the picture," Curt said. "No surprise there. Anything else on the phone?"

"Still fishing through it all," Roger admitted, tossing a sizable file onto the table in front of him. "Any help is greatly appreciated. Some photos, for sure. Lawton and Keegan at the Bean. No pictures of Elliot or anything from after Bad Bean. No Lucky 12. No McTiki's."

"Like he was avoiding any record of things," Grier said.

"Possibly," Roger admitted. "Or they were just getting lubricated as they went along and catching up on old times."

"Lawton claims he doesn't really remember Elliot," Curt said. "That maybe they met once a long time ago, but that he meets a lot of people. He did admit that he's known Keegan a long time. They were supposed to work together on the new place."

"Elliot did know Lawton, though," Carlito pointed out. "It was important enough for him to leave his friends and miss out on a planned activity."

"Doesn't seem to add up, does it?" Curt asked. "Anything else, Rog?"

"A bunch of deleted texts," he replied. "Russ is digging into them. We'll get them, will just take a bit. A lot of them seem to be around the time between McTiki's and Keegan being dumped. Russ is taking a look at Keegan's apartment today. We had to wait for a judge to sign off on it. He lived in Wanchese, so should be an easy search."

"Right, we'll stick a pin in that and come back to it," Curt said. "Tell us about your morning, Grier."

"The reunion gang seems to be exactly what they say they are," Grier began, "old friends. Didn't pick up on any underlying tensions or secrets. They were mostly focused on seeing the sound. Loved the dolphins. Clamming. The only thing that stood out was they mentioned that Elliot had a bad experience a while back at a bar that's long closed. Spooked him enough that none of them ever went back to the place. Then it closed making it a moot point. They couldn't remember exactly what had happened. Only that a girl had been harassed."

"Name of the place?" Roger asked.

"They said it was Puffin Isle," Grier replied. "Stupid name for the Outer Banks, but they seemed sure."

A curious look flitted across Curt's face before Roger took out a pad and made a note.

"I'll look into it," Roger said. "Probably nothing. That was a long time ago. Can't say I remember that bar."

"They said it was over on the sound," Grier went on. "Late night spot. Sunsets. Dance floor. Club scene. Nothing really like it anymore."

"Thankfully," Curt interjected. "Anything else from this morning, Grier?"

"That's about it," he answered. "A little editorial, if you don't mind? I like them. I can't see them involved in anything nefarious."

"Noted," Curt said. "Moving on. Carlito? What have you got for us?"

The younger man squirmed in his seat as all eyes turned to him.

"I did manage to get into Elliot's electronics," he began quietly. "A lot of exactly what you would expect, like Roger said about the other one. One difference though is that Elliot *was* taking pictures. Lots of them. Not so much of Keegan. Most of them were of Lawton. And they seemed to be taken when Lawton wasn't watching. Nothing posed. No happy reunion stuff."

"I wonder what he was after?" Curt mused. "He had to have been confident enough that he knew Lawton to spend the whole evening bar hopping with him."

"And his phone seems to follow that," Carlito agreed. "Sounds like it followed the same path as Lawton's phone. Difference being that his stayed on longer. But it made the same circuit. Bean, Lucky's, then McTiki's. Quick stop in Wanchese. And then out to Alligator River. That's where it was turned off. Interesting thing, though, was his health app. The phone and the watch both showed a spike in heart rate when they would still be at the tiki place, then a really quick slowing. Almost would have thought he was asleep, but they were moving around."

"Interesting," Roger murmured. "I'll have to ask Russ if he checked the health app on Lawton's phone. Good work, kid."

"Very good work," Curt agreed. "And we never did find a phone for Keegan?"

Roger shook his head. "Could have gone out with the tide. Probably long gone by now, but the rangers have been told to keep an eye out for anything."

"Good work everyone," Curt said. "Anything on your end, Sage?"

Sage turned sideways on her bench seat to take in the sky to the East of them.

"Not really," she said. "No real word on the street about it. No one's asking questions. Beginning of the season, so everyone is distracted. Maybe that's a good thing. And word hasn't really spread that it's Keegan. He doesn't seem to have a lot of close friends, but he's been around a long time. Alligator River feels a long way off to most locals—which is nuts because its only thirty minutes away—but it will hit home soon enough."

"What the hell did we do before people carried little computers everywhere with them to track their every move?" Roger asked, rising and crossing to the railing. "As a human being, I hate it. As a cop? No idea what I would do without them."

"Well, in this case, it's doing a lot of heavy lifting for us," Curt agreed, joining Roger at the rail.

He turned to the deputy and shot him a quizzical look. Roger read his meaning immediately and gave Curt a resigned shrug.

Curt heaved a mighty sigh and turned back toward the table and the other Brethren.

"Anyone have anything else before I move on?" he asked.

The assembled all shot looks at each other, but no one spoke, so Curt retrieved his bag from the lower dock and set it on the table.

"I guess it's time we got to the heart of today's meeting," he began. "Obviously, all of that other information is vital to this case. But what we're about to discuss runs deeper. This could affect the future of the Brethren. Some of this is known to most of you, but I don't think any of you know everything. And Carlito? Keep an open mind and feel free to ask questions. *After* I finish. This is going to be a lot. Just remember why you decided to sign on."

Curt then reached into the bag and removed a wooden box, slightly larger than a shoebox and sturdy. Heavy, chunky clasps and intricate carvings laced across the top.

Slowly, he began to open the lid.

The reunion friends had stopped for lunch on their way back from the morning jaunt on the water with Grier. Being out on the sound, with the salt air and the brisk breezes had left them hungry and tired. Tired in the good way that followed time outside. The kind of tired that none of them experienced regularly in their forty-office-hours-a-week lives. The kind of tired that reminded them of what their lives had been like when they had spent more time together. More time outside. More time in the Outer Banks.

Kirsten had heard about a horse-riding excursion held over at Coquina Beach on Hatteras and excused herself. She invited the others to come, but they demurred. Coquina was far too close to where most of them had gotten stranded on the sandy shoulder of Route 12. And none of them had the fervor for all things equine that Kirsten did.

The rest stopped at Tortuga's Lie. One of their favorite beach road spots, and one of the few holdovers from their earlier times on the barrier islands. Seafood, great drinks, and a perfect laid-back atmosphere. It didn't hurt that it was directly on the way back to their house.

An hour later, they rolled back out to their cars, pausing in the parking lot, unsure of what their next move would be.

"We could drive the bypass," Jaime suggested. "Keep an eye out for any sign of Mark."

"Good lord, Jaime," Amelia replied. "Didn't you learn anything from your little nighttime excursion? Deputy Goldstein is a nice guy, but if he has to deal with us again, he just might lock us up until this is all resolved. No more Sherlock Holmes stunts."

"Sherlock Holmes?" Jaime countered.

"Excuse me," Amelia shot back. "Some of us read more than the latest University of Texas sports news."

"Guys," Terry broke in, "stop. We're all on edge after the last few days, but let's not turn on each other. That won't help anything."

"She's right," Cathy agreed. "We're all on edge. And we should be. But this is out of our hands for now. Let the police do their policing."

"Hook 'em," Jaime said, under his breath.

"I heard that," Amelia hissed. "Wahoowa."

"Stop!" Chris barked. "Just stop. It's bad enough, without you two going at it."

"Tortuga's has always been one of Mark's favorites," Francis said, absently flipping the keys to his car around his fingers. "And he would have loved that airboat ride. It feels wrong to be enjoying anything while he's still...out there somewhere."

"I know it does," Cathy said. "I know. But if you read between the lines, this morning was their way of keeping us out of trouble. Grier

Roleth mentioned Deputy Goldstein and all the projects they'd worked on together. I think we were right where they wanted us: out of the way."

"I noticed that too," Amelia said. "Look, when we get Mark back—and we *will* get him back—we'll go out on the water, again. After copious celebratory drinks."

"Okay," Terry said. "Did we get all of that out of our systems? Good. What now?"

"Here's a radical thought," Cathy replied. "Why don't we go spend some time on the beach. Or at least out on the deck, by the pool. Sun is out. A little Vitamin D never hurt anyone."

"Good idea," Chris said, climbing into his car and starting the engine. "I could use a little peace and quiet. That's what we came here for, right?"

"It may be quiet, but I doubt I'll feel very peaceful," Francis said. "Not until we get some answers. But yeah. Some time in the sun might do me good."

"Friends?" Jaime asked, extending a hand to Amelia as she turned to get into the other car.

"Of course, you idiot," she answered, pushing his hand aside and drawing him into a hug. "I'm just on edge."

"And you have the reading habits of an octogenarian," Jaime said with a grin. "When we get back, I'll make a list of books from this century you should check out."

"Sure, man-bun," she answered with a laugh. "You're exactly who I would go to for literary suggestions."

"Literary suggestions?" Jaime asked. "Who said anything about literature? You're at the beach. Read something mindless."

"Like your book list?" Amelia tossed back.

"Ha, ha, ha," Jaime deadpanned to her, closing the car door behind him. But the air had gone out of their flare-up, and all was back to relative calm.

Twenty minutes later, the friends had all found their way onto the deck in back of their rental house. Chris and Jaime had settled into the hot tub, arms stretched out on the deck behind them, heads lolling back as the hot water and jets worked their magic and lulled them to a not-quite-sleep state.

The others, Francis, Terry, Cathy, and Amelia had opted for the more bracing temperature of the pool. They propped themselves up on the edge of the pool, resting their heads on their folded arms and facing the beach while the warm springtime sun kept their heads and shoulders toasty. Their legs wafted in the water behind them, weaving random patterns and sending currents out into the pool behind them.

"It's good to be back," Terry said after an extended silence. "Some of my favorite memories are from our times here. I missed it. I missed all of you."

"Me too," Amelia agreed. "I wonder if we'll feel the same after all of this mess with Mark is resolved. If something happens to him, I doubt I could ever come back here."

"Well, *something* has happened to him," Cathy said. "But I have faith we'll get him back. I have to. The alternative is something I'm just not ready for."

"And think of the story he'll have to tell," Francis said. "The story of all stories when it comes to our times here."

"So far, "Amelia pointed out.

"Bite your tongue," Cathy replied. "Once we get past this, I'd be perfectly happy to have nothing but boring and simple from here on out."

"Hear, hear," Terry said.

"What do you think this trip was all about?" Amelia asked. "After all these years, not having done it for a while...what were we hoping for? Reliving our early years? Reconnecting? What?"

"I just wanted to see you all again," Francis answered. "I didn't have an agenda. Just a little escape with some of my oldest friends. That simple."

"But escape from what?" Amelia pushed on. "By our own admission, we're all pretty happy with life. Good relationships. Good jobs.

Nice homes. Why take a week off from all of that, if it's really that good?"

"The past is always going to be idealized in some ways, isn't it?" Cathy said, looking to the sky as a gull glided overhead. "It's past. We can never quite bring it back. We can love our present and still hold a little space for the past in our hearts, can't we?"

"None of us is a blank slate," Terry said. "We're the sum of our parts. Our pasts. Wanting to be here with all of you doesn't mean I'm planning to abandon everything else I've achieved."

"No, I guess not," Amelia mused. "And that's not really what I meant. I guess I just wonder why we keep coming back. No matter how much time goes by."

"No matter how good I have it," Cathy said, "my life isn't what I thought it would be. Back then. Not even close."

"Me, either," Terry agreed. "Maybe it's that sense of possibility I miss. Would love to feel it again."

"There is something sobering about realizing that we're getting older," Francis said. "I never thought about time passing back then. I was just in the moment."

"That's closer to what I meant," Amelia replied. "Maybe that's what I was hoping to feel again."

"And this place," Cathy added. "It seeps into you, doesn't it? It's full of history, and legends, and memories, and ghosts."

"Our ghosts. And others' ghosts," Terry agreed.

"And it's a beach!" Francis exclaimed. "It's filled with fun, and drinks, and youth, and no responsibilities...and...and...and..."

"All true," Amelia said. "Maybe once you come here—if you're like us—you can never really leave it. Not really."

"Maybe so," Cathy said, absently, following a disappearing heron as it headed north.

"And now this whole thing with Mark is part of this place for us," Francis pointed out. "Another memory. A very different one. But a bonding for us, for sure."

"That is undeniable," Amelia said. "My feet are pruning. I'm headed in to shower off."

Terry and Cathy climbed out of the pool and wrapped their towels around themselves.

"Coming Francis?" Cathy asked.

"Thanks, but I think I'll take a walk on the beach," he answered. "Need some sand on my feet. And I need to think about Mark. I feel like I've forgotten things with him—with all of you—that shouldn't be forgotten. Guess I'll go spend some time remembering."

"I get that," Amelia said, giving him a quick hug. "Make them happy memories, yeah?"

"I'll try," he said, as he climbed out of the water, draped his towel over his shoulders and took the stairs down to the sand.

The women turned to the house and passed Chris and Jaime, eyes closed, still reclining in the hot tub.

"Don't drown yourselves in there," Cathy called, as she and the others headed in. "We've got enough to deal with."

Both men mumbled indecipherable responses. Kirsten appeared on the deck above them all and waved a hello, wearing a huge smile. The riding excursion had obviously been a success.

Cathy shot a backward glance, and saw Francis headed north, following the path of the heron, and silently wished him a peaceful journey to their past.

Russ Wahl stopped by the reception desk, the search warrant for Kevin Keegan's apartment in one hand and the remains of an Apple Ugly in the other. He tapped the paperwork on the plexiglass barrier as he headed for the top of the stairs.

"Headed over to your neck of the woods," he said, pointing toward Mary. "Anything I should know about Wanchese that I don't already?"

"Not much to know," Mary replied. "Mostly blue collar. Lots of fishermen, service workers. You know the drill. Getting pricey, though. Like everywhere else. Probably see them headed out for someplace else in the next couple of years. Shame."

"You've been there a good stretch, yeah?" Russ asked, stopping by the stairs and turning back.

"Long time," Mary said. "Seen a lot of change."

"Ever bump into a Kevin Keegan?" Russ shot back. "Longtime bartender up and down the beach."

"Do I look like a hang out with many bartenders?" Mary said with a laugh. "I might know him to see him, but that's the extent of it. I'm pretty tucked back out of the way."

"This guy lived in an apartment above someone's garage," Russ said, glancing at the paperwork. "Near the marina, if I'm right."

"Not near me," Mary replied. "I'm on Friendly Drive. Other side of town. A little rambler. Nothing fancy. And no water views, that's for sure."

"Friendly Drive?" Russ asked with a laugh. "Of course you are, Mar. Makes perfect sense."

"Only good thing that lasted from my marriage," Mary said. "Had been in his family for years. He wanted off the Banks, and I wanted rid of him. Everyone left happy."

Russ paused, then walked slowly back to the reception desk. Mary rarely spoke about herself, and he didn't want to dissuade her by hurrying out. A dead Keegan did not take precedence over Mary.

"What happened?" he asked, haltingly. "Tell me to shut up anytime, but I never even knew you'd been married until the other night."

"No point talking about the past, is there?" Mary asked. "Especially when it's painful. Nah, he wasn't a bad guy. We just had too much water under our bridge. Some things you just can't get past. At least, as a couple."

"I'm sorry," Russ said. "I'm very lucky to have Sasha. Luckier than she is, that's for sure."

"You're not wrong," Mary said with a grin. "But she did pretty well in the deal too. And Luke was okay. We just didn't fit together anymore. Life happens."

"Any idea where he is now?" Russ asked.

"No," Mary said flatly. "I learned when I was very little not to pick at my scabs."

Russ nodded, and looked as if he wanted to say more, but Mary waved her hands in front of her face and shooed him away.

"Your daughter?" Russ ventured.

"That's an even tougher scab. Enough about me," she declared. "If you want to know more it's going to have to be over a margarita at Bad Bean. Now get! You're on the clock."

Russ tapped her plexiglass affectionately and pointed at her.

"You're on, Mary Hallet," he said as he headed once more for the stairs. "Thanks for the chat!"

He emerged from the station and headed across the lot to his cruiser. He preferred the SUVs, but the cruiser was less obtrusive, and he didn't need to let an entire neighborhood know that the police were rummaging through a house on their street. The lower profile the better.

He turned left onto Route 64 and headed toward Manteo. He'd be there in less than fifteen minutes but couldn't get his mind off of the talk with Mary. On a whim, he put Friendly Drive into his GPS and headed there first. He wanted to see where she lived. He couldn't help feeling guilty that it had taken him this long to think about her outside of the office. Really think about her.

Twenty minutes later, he found himself slowly rolling along Friendly Drive until it came to a dead end. He'd only seen one rambler, so pulled up out front of it on his return trip.

It was immaculate. As he'd expected. A large front lawn, manicured to a T, led to a small brick rambler with a carport to the left and a trellis on the small front stoop covered in vines. The brick was painted a spotless white and the shutters a deep forest green. Everything about the house spoke of pride of ownership and respectability. This was old-school Outer Banks. The house built low and solid, before pilings had become the de facto beach defense. For better or worse.

He did notice the name on the mailbox. It was Willis. L. Willis, to be precise. Must be her ex-husband, Russ thought. Hallet must be her maiden name. Strange that she wouldn't have changed it after all this time. But people are complicated. He would ask her about it, but not until they were happily ensconced at Bad Bean with something fruity to drink in front of them.

His curiosity both satiated and piqued, he turned back toward the waterfront and the address he had been given on the warrant for Keegan's place. He pulled up out front and saw that Keegan's apartment was above a detached garage. Not a bad situation actually.

He got out of the car and took a quick look at the main house. The driveway was empty, and it seemed quiet. Not unreasonable to think everyone would be at work on a midweek afternoon.

Russ proceeded to the stairs on the side of the garage that led to a door on the second floor. He knocked once, loudly, and announced himself. Waited. Repeated the exercise.

After another wait, he knocked louder and declared that he had a search warrant. Met by silence again, he tried the doorknob on a whim and was shocked when it swung open.

"Well, I'll be," he muttered as he shouldered the door open slowly and thrust the warrant ahead of him into the apartment. "Police! I have a search warrant for these premises."

Once again, only quiet followed, so he cautiously entered, a hand on his holstered service gun. Two steps into what seemed to be the living room, he stopped short. The entire apartment had been cleaned out. There were a few pieces of standard beach furniture. He saw a few utensils scattered along the kitchen countertop, but everything else looked wiped clean.

He put the paperwork into his pocket. Didn't seem to be any need for it here. Proceeding through the rest of the small apartment, he found it all to be swept out. Not spotless, because the carpets showed signs of rough wear and a few of the stains seemed questionable, at best. But he didn't think there would be anything of value here, which raised even more questions.

He was wrong. His cop reflexes kicked in, and he checked some of the usual hiding spots for anything illicit. In the bathroom, opening the top of the toilet tank, he hit paydirt. And what he found sealed in a plastic bag sent him back to his car, phone pressed to his ear. He'd need forensics here. But first, he had to tell Roger the latest. Everything he'd found in Wanchese.

He left a notice on the door of the landlord's house, the name Avery posted by the door, explaining what had happened. A quick search online revealed the landlord as Henry Avery, a recent hire of the Park Service. He would have to follow up with Mr. Avery. It was the second time his name had come up.

Curt took a deep breath.

"A lot of this will be for Carlito's benefit," he began slowly. "Some might be new to you, Sage. We've never really sat down to have a real talk about this stuff. But here goes."

"Why am I nervous?" Carlito said quietly.

"You'll be fine," Sage replied, giving him a squeeze on the shoulder.

"As you know by now, the Brethren began in the ranks of the pirates of the seventeenth century. When the pirates proved too unwilling to adhere to the principles put forth in the Brethren Code, the group made the decision to continue, but in secret, vowing to protect their various coastal waters and islands. We"—he gestured around the table—"are the modern descendants of the Brethren who swore to safeguard the Outer Banks."

"Nothing new so far," Carlito muttered to Sage.

"He's getting to the good part," she said. "Hold tight."

"You probably know that Blackbeard is the most famous pirate to have prowled these waters," Curt continued. "He was a divisive figure, to say the least. Beloved in his hometown and loathed in most other places. He was finally defeated in a sea battle off Ocracoke Inlet, south of here. That was 1718, long before these states were united, so the Royal Navy was responsible for hunting Blackbeard, and after ambushing and killing him, they beheaded the poor guy, put his head on a pole at the mouth of the Hampton River north of here in Virginia as a warning to any who were considering following his career path."

"Always seemed a bit excessive to me," Roger said, "but I have a soft spot for the old fella."

"You wouldn't if you'd met him in the flesh," Grier pointed out.

Something loud splashed under the deck suddenly, and Curt shot both of the older men a warning glance. Grier crossed to the edge of the deck and looked over, before turning to Curt and shrugging.

"Probably best to hold the commentary for a while," Curt said, eyebrows raised. "Getting back to our story, legend has it that Blackbeard's skull was plated with silver, fashioned into a punch bowl, and spent some time at the Raleigh Tavern in Williamsburg where it was trotted out for special occasions. Also, according to legend, it was eventually bequeathed to a historian, who passed it down through the years to other aficionados. At one point, one of them claimed to be in possession of it and donated it to the Peabody Essex Museum in Massachusetts. That one proved to be a fake. Rumors of it being kept deep in the storerooms of the Smithsonian have persisted, but I can tell you for sure that is not true. The skull disappeared from the history books, but its whereabouts have always been known to a select few. Because the skull was given to the Brethren for safekeeping. We've had it all along."

Curt lifted the top off of the box on the table and lifted out a muslin covered object. Placing it in front of him, he lifted the covering to reveal a large bowl, the base of which was crafted from what was clearly a human skull.

Carlito stood all the way up now and retreated to the farthest railing on the upper deck.

"That is some sick shit there, boss," the young man said. "This was definitely not in the job description."

"You should probably just sit back down," Grier said, motioning to the seat next to him. "Nothing for you to worry about here. Just history."

"You definitely want to be sitting for the next part," Roger agreed.

"Yeah," Curt said, gesturing to the seat. "Because now we're getting to the weird part."

"*Now* it gets weird?" Carlito muttered, feeling his way back into his seat.

"The Banks have a long and very colorful history," Curt continued. "Not just Blackbeard. Hauntings. Legends. Mysteries. Most of them aren't true. *Most.*"

"But some are," Roger said, quietly.

Sage ran her hands through her hair and reached down to ruffle Banks's ears.

"One of those legends is that the spirits of some of the pirates still patrol the waters around us," Curt said, turning to look out over the sound behind him. "In fact, it's said that the streaks of light that we see in the waters are the pirates themselves, either looking for release or still prowling for victims. Some of those lights are just bioluminescence. But some...?"

"Here we go," Grier interjected, earning another look from Curt.

"But Blackbeard? As you would imagine, he's not too thrilled that he ended up passed around as a party favor," Curt went on. "Can't say I blame him. Legend says that when this came to the Brethren, a pact was made. A bargain. As penance, Blackbeard was bound to us. His spirit, along with the crewmen of his that still haunted these islands, vowed to answer our call should we ever need his help. In his own way, he loved the Banks too. It's not such a stretch that he would contribute. Especially...well, with this."

Curt rested his hand on the bowl, and as he did the water under the deck began to crash into the pilings below.

"This is nuts," Carlito said. He looked to Roger for reassurance, but the deputy just looked at him and cocked his head.

"There are conditions," Curt said, raising his hands. "Only the leader of the Brethren can summon Blackbeard. And he can only be summoned three times before the leadership must pass to another member. And after he has served three leaders, his debt is paid, and he's free. And the skull is returned to the sea."

"Free to do what?" Carlito asked. "Not that I'm buying this. This is seriously messed up."

"He's free," Curt answered. "Whatever that means. To find some peace and leave or continue haunting the waters. His waters. Just… free."

"And I guess that makes you in charge of old Blackbeard, here?" Carlito continued, getting louder and almost rising from his seat again. "Tell me? Have you ever called him? Huh?"

The silence that fell was heavy and glances flew from one face to another like gulls buffeted by the wind. Sage rose and crossed to lean on the railing. Grier was still as a statue, eyes fixed on Curt. Roger stared out at the water, focused on nothing.

"Once," Curt answered. Quiet. Eyes on the table in front of him.

Roger shook his head and joined Sage at the railing.

"And what happened?" Carlito asked in a voice rising with anger and confusion. "Did the ghosties come to help you out? Come on! This is all complete bullshit. Just stop it!"

"What happened?" Curt said. "Well, I was alone on the beach when it happened, so whatever I say, no one can confirm. Or deny. All I'll say is that the threat to the Banks—a threat we couldn't handle alone—disappeared."

Curt was answering Carlito, but his eyes flew to each of the others on the deck with him, pleading.

"I didn't want to do it," he insisted. "I had no choice. I was the only one who could do anything. Judgment call. But a lot of people I care about were in danger." His voice fell to almost nothing. "I had no choice."

"Playing with fire," Sage said quietly.

"But we swore to protect the Banks and all who call it home!" Curt exploded. "None of us would be here if I hadn't done what I did."

Carlito's eyes grew wider as he looked from Curt to the others and felt the tension between them all. He couldn't believe what he was hearing, but these people *believed* this.

"This is nuts," the younger man said, slapping the table in front of him. "So, no one saw a thing, and all we have is Curt's word for it? What was this so-called danger? What could be so bad?"

Grier placed a hand on Carlito's shoulder.

"Not right now," he said, gently. "I'll tell you, but not now. Not here."

The water continued to thrash violently beneath them, and the deck began to sway under the onslaught. It could be a passing boat, or the incoming tide causing it. Could be.

"I hope to never do that again," Curt said. "I hope we never have to face anything like that ever again."

When he finished speaking, the water abruptly stilled. No waves, no thrashing. In the deafening silence, Curt quietly wrapped the bowl quickly and stowed it back in its box. He slipped it back under the table.

Roger leaned into Sage, his hand still on her arm.

"He had to," Roger whispered. "You know he did. There was no choice."

Sage seemed to deflate suddenly. Tears were in her eyes.

"I know," she admitted.

"I dunno," Carlito said. "I feel like you weren't totally honest with me. I needed to know this before I agreed to...all of this."

"He has a point," Grier said, fixing a stare at Curt. "Helluva thing to spring on someone just *after* they sign on."

. . .

Curt rose from the table and silently walked to the top of the stairs leading to the lower deck. He moved slowly, with the box tucked under his arm. Curt paused on the first step down. He held the box out in front of him, considering it.

"Okay," he said back at the others. "You, and you, and *you*"—he pointed in turn to Roger, Grier, and Sage—"have known for a long time what this place is. What this box contains. You were there and know I did what I had to do. To save the Banks. To save us. And you" —he pointed to Carlito—"need to listen. Really listen. I told you there was more to come. And here it is. You joined a centuries-old secret society founded by *pirates*. In one of the most storied, mysterious, historic regions anywhere in the world, you vowed to stand between this place and its people and whatever comes for them. To get here, you drove through a town called *Kill Devil Hills*. We have stories of witches, and goat-men, and disappearing colonists, and the aforementioned pirates! It's called the *Graveyard of the Atlantic*! This place is a spiderweb of things we still can't fully understand. These islands are crowded with ghosts. Literal and figurative. Every inch of these islands has witnessed something inexplicable. It's part of this place. Baked in. So, if I have access to something that has been passed from generation to generation to safeguard these Banks and these people? Something that may be a little scary and means taking a leap of faith? Means stepping into a gray area to keep the darkness away? You better damn well believe I'm going to take it! It's not about *me*; it's about what I've sworn to do. And it's about what you've sworn to do. I would hold the devil's hand and follow him to hell if it meant that I could protect the Banks. Because I don't matter. That's what the vow we made means. Sometimes we're called on to compromise parts of ourselves so that others can live unaware of things that would make their blood freeze. That's what the Brethren do. It's what we've always done."

The others stopped where they were, mouths open. It was the most passionate and animated they had ever seen him.

Curt continued down to the lower deck and stood next to the

frothing water; the box still held firm under his arm. He bowed his head and seemed almost to be praying until, slowly, the others understood that he was staring into the waves at his feet.

"I'm not a praying man, but I pray that we are never in a situation like that ever again. Give me drug pushers and a run-of-the-mill murder any day. I can deal with that with one hand tied behind my back. But being Brethren will not always be neat and clean," Curt said, closing his eyes. "If it were that simple, we would have left it to the cops and disappeared. We do what no one else will do. And we do it with no applause or medals or interviews. We just do. And nothing about the Banks is what it seems. That's part of what has drawn folks here for centuries. It's not something you can define, or label. There's something...magical about this place. When you come to accept that, you find yourself willing to believe things you never thought you could. And do things you never thought you would."

Sage moved to the top of the stairs, but paused there, turning back to Carlito. The young man seemed to be paralyzed between joining the others and running for the parking lot. He pushed himself out of his chair but stopped where he stood.

"This is a one-time offer," Curt said quietly, eyes still closed. "Leave. Now. If you can't accept what this is, what it could be from time to time, then go. No hard feelings. No repercussions. No consequences. You will be absolved of membership, and all I would ask is that you never speak of it with anyone. Including me. Because it would break my heart. Other than that? Just go. Any of you. All of you, if that's how you feel. I'll start over and build it all again. But this is it. One chance."

"I'm going nowhere," Roger said, his eyes now on the water in front of them.

"Me, either," Grier said, quietly. "Never a doubt. Here until the end, Curt."

Curt's nod was barely noticeable. His eyes still closed.

Sage took another step down the stairs and turned to look back at Carlito. She shrugged and took the last few steps to stand behind Curt.

"I'm sorry," she muttered. "I should know better. And I trust you. I have to say that. Fear makes people do stupid things. Fear is the mind-killer. I'm in."

Curt broke a small half smile. Roger nodded to Sage. Grier took her hand and smiled.

"Nice *Dune* reference," he said.

"Seemed appropriate," she replied.

Now all four of them were contemplating the water in front of them. It continued to settle and calm, but now the tendrils of blue light were becoming more pronounced. They moved to their own rhythm, in no relation to the movement of the waves.

Carlito hadn't budged. He was stuck in place. He looked to the sky and was surprised to be reminded that it was still a clear, cloudless afternoon in a perfect early-spring day on the islands. With a shake of his head, he stepped to the top of the stairs.

"What the hell," he called to the others. "I didn't come here to flip burgers or rent dune buggies to tourists. I'm in."

"I'm very glad," Curt said, his eyes finally opening. "I didn't look forward to calling Charles Vane."

The others laughed uncomfortably; unsure how serious Curt actually was.

"I do promise you that ninety-nine percent of what we do is basic, earthbound stuff. And we don't go looking for otherworldly trouble. If something doesn't threaten anyone, it's none of our concern. Let ghosts be ghosts. It's part of this place. But that one time out of a hundred? We're the ones that step up."

Roger's phone broke the silence. He fumbled for it and answered, stepping away from the dock's edge and breaking the spell that had held the others in place.

A moment later he returned, a somber look on his face. As if a spell had been broken, the lights in the water were gone and the sound was still as glass.

"Sorry about that," he said. "Russ with some news."

"Do tell," Grier answered.

"He took a look at Keegan's apartment," Roger answered. "Cleaned out. Someone's covering their tracks."

"They could've swept it before we even knew Keegan was dead," Grier said.

"And that would have been bad news for us if they hadn't missed something," Roger said, tucking his thumbs into his belt. "Fentanyl. Hidden too well for whoever got there before us. Enough to keep the beaches going for a month, apparently."

"Well, well, well," Grier muttered.

"Not entirely shocking, from what I've heard," Sage said, with a scowl.

"Right," Carlito said, finally joining the conversation. "I can get on board with fighting that."

Curt turned from the water to look at Roger. He slipped the wooden box into its sack and cinched the top.

"That interview with Lawton just got even more interesting," he said to the deputy.

"Sure did," Roger answered. "Looks like our two cases just became one."

"Are we good?" Curt asked, looking at each of them in turn. "Solid? A team?"

Each of them nodded. Slowly, and with renewed determination.

Curt sat wearily on the bench at the back of the dock, placing the sack gently next to him.

"Thanks," Curt said, turning to the others. "Glad we talked it out. Let's hope life stays earthbound and simple for as long as we're here. And I appreciate you all staying. You *are* the Brethren to me. We are."

"Gotta run," Roger said, nodding to Curt. "I have a shady busi-nessman to question."

As the others all prepared to leave and offered reassurance to Curt, he remained on the bench. And when he heard the gate to the parking lot slam behind them, he finally let out a long, shaky sigh. That had actually gone better than he expected.

CHAPTER 13

As the Brethren, minus Curt, made their way to the parking lot to leave, Roger slowed and raised a hand. The others paused, curious as to what he had to say.

"Okay, friends," he began. "I know that was a lot. It was for me too. But let's try to set it aside for now."

"Easier said than done," Sage replied, taking a few more steps toward her Bronco before slowing and turning to look at the others.

"Oh, I know that," Roger said. "But there's a guy still missing, and we need to find him. Hopefully alive. And time is ticking."

"What are you suggesting?" Carlito asked. "You have someone to interview, but I have no clue what I should be doing next. Other than having nightmares about what I just heard."

"I'm glad you asked," Roger said. "As a matter of fact, I do have a couple ideas. While I've got Lawton down at the station, seems like a good time for someone to apply for a job at that new tiki place. Or even two someones. Maybe get a look around. Catch some unguarded talk among the employees."

"Yeah," Sage said with a glance at her watch. "I can swing by and do that. Curious to see it, anyway. Carlito, wanna tag along? I know you have your own wheels now, but two pairs of eyes are better than one. Sweet Brat, by the way."

Roger shot her a questioning look, and Carlito laughed and pointed out the name on the side of his new/old truck.

"That Brat, not me. And, uh, yeah, I guess," Carlito stammered to Sage. "I've never actually worked in a restaurant before."

"Hey, lookit that!" Roger said, clapping Carlito on the back. "There's something the boy wonder hasn't mastered! Don't worry, though. You don't actually have to get a job. Just snoop. Snap some pics. Eavesdrop. You know, all the fun stuff we get to do. Lawton will be gone, so no need to worry about him. He knows about Curt and me, obviously. Best to keep some cards close to the vest. Those cards being you two and Grier. Never know when we'll need a surprise. "

"Right," Carlito said, suddenly eager again. "That I can do."

"Grier?" Roger continued. "What are you thinking?"

"I'm going by the rental house," Grier answered. "Keep picking their brains. And while I'm there, might as well collect some of the water from the pool and hot tub. That's still the only pool directly connected to the case that we know of. Is it even possible to identify water from a specific pool? I'm thinking about the water in Keegan's lungs."

"It is," Roger said, wagging his hand in a so-so motion. "Not always, but it's worth a try. Good thinkin'."

Grier nodded.

"I'll keep Lawton at the station as long as I can," Roger said, turning back to Sage. "I'd bet you two are good until six. I'll drag my feet as long as I can. Don't like that guy, so it will be a pleasure to annoy him. I'll pull out my golly-shucks act. That'll drive him nuts."

"Sure as hell will," Grier agreed.

"Most definitely," Sage chimed in.

Seeing Carlito's confused look, Grier waved his hands in front of himself. "Be glad you don't know. Just hope you never have to witness it. Truly pathetic. Let's roll."

As Grier ushered Sage and Carlito to their vehicles, Roger clucked in disappointment.

"Why, Mr. Roleth," he called after them in the most annoyingly ingratiating voice, "those are some hurtful words. But I'm sure you don't mean it! Hey! What's your hurry, Mr. Roleth? Hold up, there!"

"Run!" Grier said with a laugh to the others and their cars left a cloud of dust and gravel behind them as they peeled out and away from the Blue Crab.

Grier was second-guessing himself before he even turned onto the beach road. He'd had a good time with the gang out on the water earlier, but was he pushing his luck by showing up out of the blue? He wasn't their friend. Just a guy who had shown them around for a while. No, *they* were real friends. With history. And someone close to them who was missing. And here he was, butting in. Collecting evidence that could incriminate one of them. Or all of them. He'd seen *Murder on the Orient Express*. What if there were old scores to be settled? As nice as they had all seemed this morning, he had been around the block enough to know that people are complicated. And everyone has secrets. Everyone.

Most people came to the Outer Banks to escape. And they wanted to escape all sorts of things. Responsibility. Work. Pressure. Relationships. But what if this was something different? What if they, or one of them, had come here to *find* something? Revenge?

He hated that he thought this way, but he had to. He wasn't like other people. He was a member of the Brethren of the Coast. No one was above suspicion, which is probably why he had no personal life to speak of. Most days, he was fine with that trade-off. But some days, like today, he came dangerously close to resenting it. After spending the morning with these people and seeing their easy banter and connection...it did make him question certain things.

He'd always thought of the Brethren as his family and friends.

But after what he had just witnessed on the dock at the Crab, he'd been reminded that secret societies bred...secrets. Damn. He hated when he got too inside his own head.

He'd been so lost in thought, he'd barely noticed that he was pulling into the driveway of the rental place. He contemplated backing out and heading back to the marina. Forget the whole thing. But he noticed someone at the window above the parking area, and at almost the same time, the front door opened, and Amelia stood there, beckoning him to come in.

"Your ears must have been burning," she called. "We've been talking about how great this morning was since we got back. Any chance you're here with some news for us? That would make the day perfect."

Grier stretched his arms over his head as he climbed out of the car and pushed his Chubby Squirrel Brewing baseball cap back on his head while looking up at the perfectly blue afternoon sky.

"No, I'm sorry to say," he called back. "Just wanted to set up a time with you all to check out Pea Island. And I did have a couple questions for everyone. Nothing burning." He reached back into the car and emerged with a pair of sunglasses which he promptly put on. "You all sure did hit the jackpot with the weather today. Feels more like June than April."

"Sure did," Amelia agreed. "Let's sit out back then. I could dip my feet into the pool and be happy. Sound good?"

"Sounds perfect," Grier replied, hating himself a bit for so easily manipulating the situation. Reaching in the glove compartment, he pocketed a couple of the vials he used to collect and test water in the sound for his work with the College of The Albemarle. Climbing out of the car he walked toward the door. He glanced up and saw Kirsten in the window, waving him in.

Sage checked her rearview mirror as she pulled into the bustling parking lot of Angus McTiki's. She had to avoid a mound of gravel, another of dark mulch, and a pallet of lumber, but she managed to find a spot and waited for Carlito to pull in next to her. She turned to tell the dogs she wouldn't be long inside. The late afternoon sun was starting its descent, and the temperature had dipped into the sixties. She put out some water and ruffled some ears.

There were hordes of contractors crawling over and throughout the space. The landscaping out front seemed finished and was truly stunning. Palm trees, hibiscus, and elephant ears created a lush welcoming yard. A water feature saw a waterfall burble from the top of an eight-foot volcano, creating a stream that flowed across the entrance and around the side of the building. A bamboo bridge led patrons across the running water and to the massive front door. The grass-covered roof lent shade and extended over the front deck and connected to woven umbrellas over tables and benches along the front of the property.

A crane was placing a large green and yellow sign along the roadway in front, a group of seven workers guiding it on its hoist into place. As soon as it had found some footing, half of the workers peeled off and rushed past the parked trucks into the building.

Sage and Carlito exchanged a look of surprise. What they were seeing was going to be one of *the* largest restaurant destinations on the Outer Banks.

"Serious bucks at work here," Sage muttered as she climbed out of her Bronco and checked herself in the side-view mirror and straightened a wrinkle out of her Local As It Gets t-shirt. She hadn't planned on a job application when she had left home and suddenly felt underdressed given the scale of the place.

"Seems like overkill to me," Carlito said, coming to stand next to her. His faded jeans and Chuy's t-shirt were no finer than Sage's outfit, but he seemed totally at ease. "Folks around here want something like this?"

"No clue," Sage answered. "No one's tried. Not like this. Shall we?"

Together they walked over the burbling stream and to the front doors where one of the workers held the door for them and they did their best to look as if they belonged.

As they stopped just inside the door to get their bearings, stunned by the extravagance of the space, the worker who had held the door entered behind them, and tapped Carlito lightly on the shoulder.

"You two looking for someone?" he asked. "Lots of moving pieces in here today. Friends and family later tonight. Mostly industry folks, but a massive trial run. Lots at stake. Best to stay out of the way."

Carlito glanced at Sage and, to her surprise, took the lead.

"We actually were hoping for some work," he said, thrusting a hand out to the man. "Carlito. And this is Sage. Long time beach bar folks."

"Right," the man replied, shaking Carlito's hand. "Name's Bill, but people call me John. Don't ask. You'll want to find Nancy. She's out back. Was the assistant manager, but there have been some shake-ups in the last few days. She's the manager now. You might get lucky. Tell her you talked to me. Technically, we're not supposed to let anyone in."

"Thanks, John," Carlito shot back. "Much appreciated. The place is gorgeous."

"Looks nice, but we have to make sure everything actually works, too," he said, glancing around. "Could use another week to fine-tune things, but no such luck. Speaking of. Good luck with Nancy. She's great but probably just a bit stressed at the moment. Hope I see you around."

With a wave over his head, he disappeared into a stream of workers headed toward the back of the dining area.

"There you have it," Carlito said, turning to Sage. "Let's go find Nancy."

The two of them wove their way through the throngs until Sage tapped Carlito's shoulder and pointed out another set of large wooden doors that stood half open toward the rear of the building. Picking their way there, they both stopped short when they reached the threshold. If the front had been impressive, the back gardens were doubly so. Tables shaded by enormous fronds were surrounded by all of the tropical plants seen out front. Multiplied. There were tiki statues and torches throughout, and multiple streams and fountains all surrounding the central feature: a massive swimming pool with a swim-up bar located on the far end.

Carlito let out a long, low whistle.

"You can say that again," Sage said quietly, nodding in the direction of a very harried woman holding a clipboard and arguing with one of the landscapers. As they watched, she took the worker by the arm and led him to a tiki statue that resembled one of the Easter Island *moai* figures that was partially obscured by a low hanging string of colorful lights. She pointed fiercely at the lights and to a series of bamboo poles that passed through that section of the gardens. The worker nodded and clearly offered some form of apology, but when the woman turned away to address other issues, the worker rewarded her with a very heartfelt one-finger salute.

"Must be Nancy," Carlito said, taking off in the woman's direction. "No sense wasting time. That interview in Manteo won't last forever."

"Hang on there, Sparky," Sage called after him. "I got this. I'm the actual bartender in this situation."

"Be my guest," Carlito replied, stopping and motioning her to go ahead. "I'll watch and learn."

"That's more like it," Sage answered, taking the lead. "Excuse me, miss! Are you Nancy?"

Sage waved at the woman and did a little stutter-step to catch up to her before she engaged with another of the workers who hustled around her.

The woman turned at the call and visibly deflated when she spied Sage and Carlito.

"You're not who I need right now," she said. "Yes, I'm Nancy. Whaddaya need? Everyone needs something today."

"Actually, John out front sent us back to you," Sage said offering a hand and pulling it back when the woman didn't look up from her clipboard. "We're wondering if you need any more help. Both of us are experienced. Longtime locals."

"What kind of experience?" Nancy shot back, still not looking up. "Your timing may be perfect. We've lost a few folks in the last couple of days, and I'm the only one making decisions."

"I'm a bartender and manager at the brewery, Swells'a," Sage said, earning a look from Nancy. "Been all up and down the Banks behind bars for a while."

"That's promising," she admitted. "What about him? He looks young to have much experience at anything."

"I'm a barback," Carlito said, stepping forward. "A good one."

"Hardest worker I've seen in a long time," Sage chimed in. "Wouldn't have let him tag along otherwise."

Carlito shot her a glance and turned back to Nancy.

"Do you swim?" Nancy asked, striding toward the end of the pool with the bar. "We'll need our best out here at the swim-up. Gonna be pretty crazy when we hit in season."

Carlito nodded in response and Sage said, "We swim like fish. Surfers, too. Perfect for out here."

Nancy turned her attention back to the pool bar and began sorting through some boxes of bar napkins, swizzle sticks, and elaborate tiki cups. Plastic with lids and twisty straws. The boxes were a kaleidoscope of colors. Sage reached down and ran her fingers across some of the merchandise. Picked out a napkin that was printed with a leprechaun standing tiptoe on a barstool stretching to smooch a beautiful hula girl.

"Cute," Sage said. "Someone has deep pockets. And a sense of humor."

"Yup," Nancy answered, tallying up how many boxes were scattered by the pool. "And while I admire those things, they're not my department. I just get things in order and ready for the public."

Carlito bent down and fished a small colorful cup out of one of the boxes. On this one, the little leprechaun stood next to the tall, beautiful hula girl, held her hand, and was teaching her how to Irish step dance.

"I love this," he said, holding it up to look at it.

"Yeah?" Nancy asked. "Keep it. Knock yourself out. Look, we have our friends and family tonight, soft opening tomorrow, and I have a million things to check off this list"—she held up the ever-present clipboard—"and this pool bar won't be open tonight. Waiting on permits and, honestly, it's going to be enough of a zoo without water everywhere. Tell you what. Come back tomorrow. I'll be here at eleven. Let's talk. We might actually need you. Stop by tonight, if you want. We'll have music. Herbie Knight and the Bad Puns. They're excellent. Just let John know on the way out."

"Hey thanks!" Carlito enthused, looking at the cup. "I love it."

"We'll have a full merch store up front," Nancy said, softening a bit. "Don't buy yourself anything, though. If you do work here, your wardrobe will fill up with Angus and Kailani there pretty fast. I have to run. You two seem decent. Let's try to make something work. Tomorrow."

"Tomorrow," Sage repeated. "For sure."

"Thanks again," Carlito called as Nancy turned and was almost instantly swallowed by a crowd of staff looking for answers. She waved at them without turning back.

As Carlito and Sage turned toward the main building, Carlito tossed his new plastic cup in the air, then stopped quickly, scooping some water from the pool and popping the plastic lid on top.

"What's up with that?" Sage asked, headed to the door back inside.

"Well, until now there was only one pool connected to the Keegan case"—he paused to glance back at the pool and its empty bar—"but now there are two. And we have a water sample from this one to run tests on."

Sage stopped, holding the door open for Carlito.

"Sonofabitch," she muttered. "I really do have to remember that you're a clever little bugger."

"I'll take that as a compliment," Carlito said, as he passed her and headed for John near the front door. "I really do like the merchandise, though."

"Yeah, have to admit it's pretty eye-catchy," Sage admitted. "And who knows. We might even get a job out of this and a new wardrobe. Let's get this water sample to Roger. No time to lose.

Carlito nodded, laughed as he passed a rack of bright t-shirts, then caught John's eye and approached. They had an industry night to attend tonight.

Grier was quite comfortable sitting on the side of the pool, his feet dangling into the cool water while his torso baked in the late afternoon sun. Amelia sat not far from him, while Kirsten lounged in the hot tub, steam rising from the surface making her hard to see until an inevitable breeze came in off the beach and swept it away.

"Gotta admit," Grier said, closing his eyes and angling his face to catch maximum sunshine, "it's moments like this that remind me why people love it here so much. It's easy to get caught up in the everyday noise, but it's a damn fine place to call home. Or just visit. Damn fine."

"Funny, I thought you made a good case for it here out on that boat this morning," Amelia said, as she leaned back on the deck and closed her eyes. "You sounded like someone who loved where they live."

"Oh, I do," Grier replied. "I find new things to get excited about almost every day. But sometimes, in slowing down, the simple things can take precedence. Like just sitting in the sun on a spring afternoon."

"You can't see me in here," Kirsten called from the hot tub, "but I can still hear you! Even over here in my steam bath, I have to agree with you. This is not a bad way to live."

"The others will be back from the beach soon, I'm sure," Amelia said, eyes still closed. "But feel free to ask us whatever you wanted, if you have to go. I honestly thought they'd be back already."

Grier, seeing an opportunity, quickly filled one of the vials with water from the pool. He didn't feel good about not being honest with the women, but if anything funny was going on, it would be better to handle this on the sly. If nothing was going on? No harm, no foul. The vial filled, he slipped it into a pocket of his pants.

"You know"—he checked his watch for effect—"I will have to push off in a bit. As much as I'd like to stay exactly where I am for the next three to five hours."

"Shoot," Kirsten said, as a gust of wind cleared the air around her for a moment.

"I was just hoping I could get more information on that incident at the bar?" Grier asked. "The one that spooked Elliot and, in turn, all of you. Any idea what year it could have been?"

"I mean, it was a while ago," Amelia said, sitting back up and squinting her eyes in concentration. "That would have put it somewhere around fifteen years ago, give or take."

"Any more thoughts on what happened?" Grier pressed. "Must have been serious to leave such an impression."

Kirsten floated over to the near side of the hot tub and draped her arms over the side. "Mark was the only one who was actually there," she said. "That's probably why we're all a bit fuzzy on it. It was bad. I remember that. It was more than someone just harassing a girl. She ended up in the hospital. Drugs were involved. That I remember because we were young and that just didn't happen in our circles."

"And the place?" Grier questioned. "On the sound? Something about a puffin?"

"Puffin Paradise?" Amelia said. "No, Puffin Isle. That's what it was. And you know, it's funny. Never thought about the double meaning. Puffin. Puffing? Man, were we naïve back then."

"The good old days," Kirsten said, resting her head on her arms.

"If only we had a device that we could carry with us, that holds basically all the accumulated knowledge of mankind in a box as big as your hand," Grier said as he reached into his jacket pocket and dramatically removed his cell phone. "Puffin Isle. Let's take a look."

He began to tap on his screen, whistling "Owner of a Lonely Heart" by Yes as he did.

"That's an oddly specific song to pull out," Amelia said with a chuckle.

"Always loved it," Grier answered. "Not sure why. Childhood memory—got it! Here we go. Puffin Isle. Open from 1997 until 2011. Closed suddenly. Let me dig a little more. And...here. 2010. A girl named Rebecca Willis was taken to the hospital after a night at the bar. Seems she had her drinks spiked. GHB. Problem was she blacked out and could never identify who gave it to her. Pretty surprising they got a positive test back, because that clears the system fast. That's why it became so popular. But no one would testify, apparently."

"That's horrible," Kirsten said. "That was more recent than any of us remember. Time flies, but one thing you can always count on is that there are predators around."

"Follow-up article here," Grier continued. "Poor girl. Emotional problems. Drug use. In and out of rehab. Finally got clean but passed away before she reached the age of thirty. Looks like her whole life went off the rails after that night."

"Oh, wow," Amelia said. "I don't think Mark knew any of the stuff that happened after. He was just there when she got taken out. It's so much worse than any of us ever knew."

"So bad it drove the bar out of business," Kirsten pointed out. "No wonder Mark never went back."

"I'll check with Deputy Goldstein," Grier said. "See if he has any more info on this. Sounds like the kind of thing people would remember. Damn shame. Waste of a young life."

"It is," Amelia agreed. "Like I said, we never knew the whole story."

"The good news," Grier said, "is that it *doesn't* happen here a lot. And there are folks here making sure it stays that way"—a quick glance at his dive watch—"and on that happy note, I hate to say I have to get going. When the others get back, talk amongst yourselves and let me know when you want to hit Pea Island. You'll love it. Trust me."

"Will do," Kirsten answered, climbing out of the hot tub and wrapping a towel around herself. "I hit my limit in there, I think. I'm prune-y. Thanks again for this morning. We'll definitely want to do it again."

"Excellent," Grier said, also rising. "You know where to find me."

As the two women walked him to the front door, the vial of pool water weighed heavy in his pocket and on his conscience. Did this new information put someone in the picture for causing this situation? Elliot himself? Whatever he had hoped to find out this afternoon, this hadn't been it.

Roger paced in the hallway outside of Interview Room One in the Manteo PD. He was feeling a bit nervous, if he was being completely honest with himself. He did his best work out in the field, not facing down high-powered business folks in a sterile interview room. It had been a while since he'd experienced this situation. Most cases here were more straightforward. Kids shoplifting. Traffic stops. The odd drunk driver. Maybe some unregistered boats or people fishing with no license. This was different.

No one would know from looking at him that his stomach felt like it was filled with molten lava. And that was the way he had to keep it. He doubted this was the first time Todd Lawton had been questioned by the cops.

But this was different for Roger. At least one man was dead. And with each passing hour, the chances of Mark Elliot being found safe, let alone alive, grew dimmer. The stakes couldn't be higher.

Chief Brady was in his office down the hall. Roger knew he could ask him to sit in on the interview, but that was the same as admitting he didn't feel up to it. He wasn't a kid. He was close to retirement, for cripes sake. He hitched his pants up by his duty belt and reached for the doorknob. He'd let Lawton and his lawyer stew for over a half hour. Partly to let them get itchy and frustrated. Frustrated people make mistakes.

As his hand touched the knob, he heard someone clear their throat at the other end of the hallway. He turned and was surprised to see Curt standing just inside the door.

"Forget about me? Thought maybe you could use some moral support," Curt said, nodding toward the interview room. "And I wanted in on this. I could watch through the two-way mirror. If you'd rather."

Roger was surprised at the wave of relief he felt at the sight of his friend. Even after the tense events of the afternoon.

"Actually, come on in," Roger said, his shoulders lowering a few inches. "More ears are better. I'm itching to get at him. Let's take this slimeball down."

"If he's guilty," Curt replied. "Need to be sure. Right, Deputy?"

"Of course," Roger sputtered. "What do you take me—" He stopped when he saw the impish grin spreading across Curt's face.

"Get in there, Columbo," Curt said.

As Roger turned to enter, the hallway door opened again. Grier appeared, nearly running into Curt just inside.

"Whoa," Grier almost shouted, "not the best place to stop, Mr. Man."

"Sorry about that," Curt answered, jumping out of the way. "Got caught up talking. You're here just in time for the fireworks."

"I don't know about any fireworks," Grier said, holding up a plastic bag with a vial of clear liquid inside of it. "I came to deliver pool water from the reunion rental house. Figured the sooner the better. And before you ask, no they didn't see me take it. No need to get them riled up if it's nothing."

"Mind reader," Roger said. "Can you drop that off with Russ? He'll run some preliminary tests, but it will eventually have to go to Raleigh. Trying to identify different pool waters is tricky. May take a while."

"We don't have a while. Like I said, sooner the better," Grier continued, moving past Curt and down the hallway toward Russ's office. He stopped mid-stride at one point and turned back to Roger. "Something I was going to tell you, but damned if I can remember right now. Getting old sucks. It'll come to me."

And he went on his way.

Mary stuck her head around the door of her reception area and waved to catch Roger's attention.

"I think you may be the most popular officer in the state today," she said. "Couple more folks out here to see you. They said it was urgent, but I wanted to see if you'd gotten into the interview yet. What should I do, handsome?"

"They asked for me specifically?" Roger asked, confusion splashed across his face.

Mary nodded, gave a wink, and he waved to have her let the new guests in.

"Interview could take a while," Roger said. "Let's take care of them first."

As Mary disappeared back to her desk, Grier's voice came from the direction of Russ's office in an exaggerated stage whisper. "*Hand-some*? You devil," he teased. "Did you two ever...?"

"No, now shut it," Roger replied, turning a particularly florid shade of magenta.

He was saved by the door opening yet again to reveal Sage and Carlito entering the hallway.

"Well, this is a cozy little reunion," Curt said. "You all didn't get enough of me at the Blue Crab? What brings you two here?"

They shared a look, both motioning for the other to start. Finally, Sage held a hand up and took the lead.

"We just came from Angus McTiki's," she explained. "Nice place. Like, really nice. We actually scored an invitation to the friends and family tonight. Looking good for jobs too, to be honest. But we came because Dick Tracy here pulled a fast one and—" She stepped back, giving Carlito the floor.

"Turns out they have a swim-up bar," Carlito started quietly before gaining momentum. "Swim-up bar means a pool, and that makes another potential scene for the Keegan case. And, well, here you go!"

He took the plastic McTiki's cup out of his pocket and presented it proudly.

"Looks like Russ is going to have a busy end to his day," Roger said. "Clean cup?"

"Took it straight out of the box myself," Carlito affirmed.

"Cute logo," Roger said, looking more closely at the cup. "If the food stinks, they'll make a fortune in merchandise. Head down to Russ's office. Since we're all here, you may as well come down to the observation suite after and give a listen. Just be quiet about it. Brady will blow a gasket if he gets wind of it. This case takes a turn now. I can feel it."

Carlito couldn't hide his excitement as he hurried down the hall, with Sage close behind.

Roger turned to Curt.

"Seems all is forgiven, if not forgotten," he said, nodding at the retreating others.

"For now," Curt said, his eyes following the other Brethren as they rounded the corner into Russ Wahl's office. "The best way to get us all back on the same page is to break this case. No pressure, though."

"Right," Roger answered, his hand now back on the doorway. "No pressure at all."

And while he knew that wasn't true, he felt much lighter with his teammates all in the building. He opened the door.

"Sorry about the delay, gentlemen," he said, with a smile that gave the lie to the statement. "Busy station. Lots of crime to fight. Shall we get to it?"

***

Carlito and Sage entered Russ's office to find the taller officer hunched over a table to one side, an array of test strips arrayed in front of him and a pair of goggles on his eyes. He was comparing various colors on the strips with a master list to one side.

"Hey, Russ," Sage said. "Roger sent us down here with another water sample for you."

"Oh, good," Russ replied, not turning around, "I was hoping for some more boring tests to run before I can go home to my wife and an adult beverage. Who's your friend?"

Sage startled, wondering how Russ had seen Carlito without turning around and then noticed the officer could see them in the reflection of a pane of glass on an inspirational print hanging in front of him. *See the Good.* Ironic, given where they were.

"Oh, yeah, this is Carlito," Sage said. "Curt brought him on as a kind of personal assistant. He's on probation, so we'll see."

Carlito shot Sage a dirty look before stepping to the table.

"Pleased to meet you, Officer Wahl," he said. "I've heard great things about you."

"I like him even more than I like you," Russ said, finally putting the test strips down. "Whaddaya have for me?"

Carlito placed the McTiki's cup next to Russs's arm and stepped back.

"This came from a swim-up bar at the new place up the beach. Roger thought it would be helpful to run it."

"Oh, Roger did, did he?" Russ answered, picking up the cup and examining it. "Clean cup, yeah? Didn't have a drink in it or anything?"

"No, sir," Carlito assured him.

"Right, well, give me a few minutes here," Russ said. "These tests are pretty rudimentary. Chlorination, pH level, stuff like that. Getting down to the finer points will mean sending it out, but I'll do what I can. Go bother Roger until I'm done. I'll shoot him a text when I have something."

"Thank you, sir," Carlito said, stepping back beside Sage.

"Enough with the 'sir' stuff," Sage said, with a nudge to Carlito. "He's got a high enough opinion of himself as it is."

"You could learn from him," Russ said, turning back to his table. "Good on ya, kid. With any luck, you'll rub off on this one."

Sage was laughing as she dragged Carlito back into the hallway and toward the observation room.

Roger settled into the chair opposite Lawton. Opposite Roger and to his left was Lawton's very high-priced lawyer, William Conklin. Conklin wore a suit that probably cost as much as Roger made in a year. If Roger was supposed to be impressed—or intimidated—it wasn't working.

Curt remained standing, leaning against the wall just inside the door, arms folded, and legs jauntily crossed.

"What's he doing here?" Lawton demanded with undisguised contempt.

"Hello, Mr. Lawton, pleasure to see you too," Roger said. "Thank you for voluntarily coming in. Mr. Stephens is here at the request of the Manteo PD. He's a liaison with Kill Devil Hills. We're cooperating on this investigation."

"Nice to see you again, Mr. Lawton," Curt said. "I'm just an observer. Forget I'm here."

"I wish I could," Lawton growled in response. He looked at his lawyer, and Conklin gave him a subtle shake of his head. This was not a battle worth fighting.

"William Conklin. With a C. And a K. Representing Mr. Lawton. Can you tell me precisely why we're here?" he said. "I'd like to hear how you justify dragging a highly respected businessman down here on one of the most critical dates of his new venture. A venture, I will add, that stands to bring a lot of money into your communities."

"So glad you asked," Roger answered, feeling his nerves settle as he faced the arrogance of Lawton and the condescension of Conklin. "First, just reminding you that we are being recorded"—he nodded to the video cameras in two corners of the room, leaving no place uncovered—"so let's get to it. Mr. Lawton, you were seen in the company of two men on this past Monday evening. Mark Elliot and Kevin Keegan. First at Bad Bean, and then briefly at the Lucky 12 Tavern in Nags Head. After that, things get a little less clear. You stated that you gave them a tour of your new bar, Angus McTiki's. Is this correct?"

"Yes, that's what I said," Lawton replied, folding his arms on the table in front of him and leaning backward, with his face up toward the ceiling.

"Can you explain exactly why this matters?" Conklin interjected. "For the record."

"Happy to," Roger answered with a saccharine smile. "We ask because the following morning Keegan's body was discovered in Alligator River wedged under a kayak, while Elliot has gone missing and has not been seen or heard from since. That makes you, Mr. Lawton, the last person known to have been in their company."

"I made it exceedingly clear that after we took the tour, I headed home. No idea what the other two did," Lawton said, but there was a hitch in his voice that hadn't been there a few seconds before.

"Right," Roger said, with a nod of his head. He pulled some files out from a stack of papers at his side and leafed through one. "You also *claim* that some time that night, your phone was stolen?"

"Or lost," Lawton said quietly. "But probably stolen. I don't lose things like that."

"And is this your phone?" Roger asked, reaching into a bag at his feet and placing the latest iPhone, secured in an evidence bag, on the table between the men.

Lawton paused for a fraction of a moment. The phone had a smear of mud across its side and dead leaves were strewn around the bag.

"Looks like it," Lawton finally admitted. "Lots of phones look like that. But like I said, I didn't have it, so wherever it was found, I had nothing to do with that."

Lawton looked ready to say more, but a restraining hand from his attorney stopped him. Clearly, Conklin had the final word in this situation.

"And you claim that you loaned your car the following day. Your EZ-Pass shows it traveling to Richmond, but you claim to have been at the construction site the following day. Mr. Stephens?" Roger turned to Curt. "Did you find Mr. Lawton on site when you stopped by the next day?"

"I did not," Curt said, pointedly. "Spoke to some folks there, but no one had seen him."

Roger turned a questioning look to Lawton, who in turn looked to his lawyer. Conklin leaned over and whispered something into his client's ear. Lawton gave a quick, sharp nod.

"I was there," Lawton insisted. "But I got in later that day. I'd been out for drinks the night before. Was a little slow getting started. Simple as that."

"And the car?" Roger asked.

"You've already answered that yourself," Lawton replied.

"We'll need to talk to whoever borrowed the car," Roger said. "And you have nothing to add about the two missing men? How did you end up in their company?"

"I already explained this, too," Lawton whined. "Keegan and I go way back. He was coming onto the team at the new spot. I'm devastated that he's dead. Devastated. And, as I've already said, I didn't know Elliot. He thought he remembered me from a long time ago, but I think he got it wrong. He seemed harmless enough and had clearly been around the Banks for a long time, so we just went with it. That's what we do here. I meet people every single day. Sometimes I buy them a drink. Sometimes they buy me one. This night was no different than any other."

"Except for the dead friend and the missing stranger, right?" Curt asked quietly from the wall.

If a look could eviscerate someone, that's what Lawton turned to Curt.

"Yes, of course," Lawton spat. "Except for that."

A buzzing from the phone Roger had placed next to him on the table interrupted whatever response Curt had to make. Roger took the phone, tapped the screen to life, and read. Next, he raised a hand and, without looking up, said, "Excuse us for just a moment. New information coming in. We'll be right back."

Lawton ran his hands through his hair and sighed as Roger and Curt exited the room. Conklin looked at his client and gave a shake of his head.

Grier already had his hands raised in apology when Roger came storming out of the interview room. Sage and Carlito hovered just behind Grier in the observation room doorway, confused looks on their faces.

"Who, whoa, whoa," Grier said. "This is on me. I remembered what it was I meant to tell you, and I really think you need to hear it before the interview is over."

Before Roger could respond, Russ came striding down the hallway from the other direction.

"Don't get too bothered," Russ said. "If he hadn't called you out, I would have. I have some very preliminary info on the water samples, and you need to hear this."

"Great," Roger replied, his anger slipping quickly away. "This better be good. That guy is cracking and the last thing I wanted was to give him some time to catch his breath and talk to that overpriced stuffed suit in there. Out with it. What do you have?"

Grier and Russ looked at each other unsure who should speak first.

"Russ, go," Roger demanded.

"Sure. Okay," Russ began. "As you know, I can't really tell much with the tests I have in house. One thing I *can* determine is the salinity of the samples. And let me tell you, the sample from the rental house pool has way too much salt in it to be a match with what drowned Keegan. Some of the high winds might have done it last week. Maybe they've been going straight from the ocean to the pool. Maybe all of the above. Don't know how, and it doesn't really matter. What matters is Keegan didn't drown in that pool. The McTiki's sample? Too early to tell, but I can't rule it out. So that one will be headed to Raleigh in just a little while."

"Thanks, Russ," Roger said, with a nod of his head. "Doesn't really clear anyone. Just clears one location. As we've mentioned, there are pools up and down the Banks. We'll need more to go on. Even if it turns out this happened at the tiki place, we need more evidence to prove *who* did it. Can you get the tiki place to forward any security footage from the night in question? Shouldn't take long. Place like that must have a solid setup for that. Especially with all those building supplies sitting around. Gotta keep an eye on them. But it is nice to see our reunion group one step closer to being ruled out. Glad I know, but I won't be sharing much of this with Lawton. The less he knows about where we're looking, the better. But I'm happy to rattle his cage a little"—he turned to Grier and raised his eyebrows—"and you?"

"Something came up when I was talking to Amelia and Kirsten, and I think it may be important."

"Make it good," Roger growled.

"Remember I told you about an incident at that Puffin Isle place that spooked Elliot a long time ago?" Grier asked.

Just then, Mary came around the corner with a tray of iced tea and cookies.

"Oh, my," she exclaimed. "I'm sorry. Bad timing. I was just going to drop these off in the observation room. I can come back."

"It's fine, Mary," Roger said. "You're fine. In fact, could you bring some to the interview room too? Might help to get their guard down."

"Thank you, Mary," Grier said. "Much appreciated."

As Mary scooted past to drop the tray in the room, Grier smiled after her before continuing.

"Well, I did some sleuthing," he went on, "and I found an incident in 2010. A young woman claimed she was drugged there, but no charges were ever filed because she blacked out and couldn't identify anyone. But a little deeper dive turned up that Keegan was a bartender there at the time and the man she claimed to have been with at her last memory was none other than—"

"Todd Lawton," Roger finished for him. "Well, damn. So now we have Elliot, Keegan, and Lawton all at the same place all those years ago when a crime was committed and never prosecuted."

"And I just pulled a load of drugs out of Keegan's apartment," Russ pointed out.

"This isn't a coincidence," Roger said. "Good work, Grier. Definitely worth pulling me out. Whatever happened to the girl?"

Grier moved to the side of the doorway to let Mary back out.

"Didn't turn out well for the poor thing," Grier answered. "Local girl. But no one could help her out. No evidence. She had a bad go of it. Spiraled out of control and died way too young."

"Aw, shit," Roger muttered. "Right. Text me all of that information.

Lawton is dirty and it sounds like he has been for a long time. Even dirtier than I thought. I figured it was run of the mill money stuff. This is even worse. We take him down now. No one else gets hurt. Or killed."

Roger walked back into the interview room, Curt just behind. Neither said a word as they took up their previous positions. Roger made a show of pulling out a new folder and placing it on the table, rifling through the pages. Curt remained by the door, swiping his phone screen, nodding periodically.

The silence hung in the air, growing more ponderous as the moments passed. Lawton turned to his lawyer, but Conklin just shook his head.

Roger muttered something indistinguishable to himself finally, made a show of checking the video cameras were recording, and finally sat back in his seat, fixing a stare on Lawton, who shifted in his seat.

"Right," Roger said finally. "Sorry about that. Some new information has come to light and needed my attention." Curt let out a little chortle which he stifled when Roger gave a glance. "First, just out of curiosity, when was the pool at McTiki's filled?"

Lawton was clearly caught off guard by the change in direction. "Uh, well. You'd have to ask the operations manager. I pay people to take care of that. No clue, myself."

"Mhm," Roger replied, leafing through some more papers. "Was it filled on, say, Monday, when you gave your private tour?"

Another look to his lawyer from Lawton. Conklin's face remained lowered to his notes on the table in front of him.

"We didn't go for a late-night swim or anything, so I wouldn't know," Lawton shot back. "Like I said, below my pay grade."

"That's fine," Roger said, shuffling the pages again. "We can talk to your staff, and I'm sure the security footage will tell us anyway."

At the mention of the security videos, Conklin finally looked lazily up from the table. "You'll need a warrant for that. I assume you have one, or you wouldn't be making empty threats like that?"

"It's in the works," Roger assured him. "We do things by the book here."

"Of course," Curt said quietly from the wall, "you could volunteer to turn them over yourself. You know, to prove you're telling us the truth. Like an innocent person would."

"As the officer here just said," Conklin replied, "by the books is best."

Roger nodded as if he'd anticipated that and pulled another file from the bottom of his stack.

"Couldn't agree more," Roger replied. "Warrant on its way very soon. I'd like to talk about something else for a bit. What can you tell me about bar called Puffin Isle?"

Lawton's face went completely slack. For the first time since he arrived, he seemed thrown. He looked to Conklin, who shrugged slightly in response. This was an unexpected line of questioning.

"Puffin Isle?" Lawton said, haltingly. "Don't remember it much. Long time ago."

"Yes, over ten years, now," Roger agreed. "Hard to believe. But you do remember it?"

"May have been there a couple times back in the day. Nothing really stands out to me. Just a bar."

"Just a bar," Roger said, more pages flipping. "Do you remember a young woman named Rebecca Willis?"

A pause.

"Before you answer," Roger broke in, "we pulled all the files on the case. We know the accusations. We know that Keegan worked there that night. We also know that Elliot was there that same night. Feels significant to me. How about you?"

Lawton slammed a hand on the table and pushed his chair back from the table.

"This shit again!" he burst out. "I've been over this a thousand times. It's ancient history."

"Ancient history last week maybe," Roger said, sliding a page across the table to Lawton. On it was a picture pf a pretty young woman. Blond hair, green eyes, a bright smile. "Not so ancient this week. That's Rebecca Willis. Pretty. She deserved better."

A quiet tap on the door was followed by Mary inching the door open and backing in laden with another tray of drinks and cookies.

The tension in the room was thick, and Mary noticed it before she was even halfway in.

"I'm sorry," she said. "I can come back."

"No, Mary," Roger assured her. "Come in. It's fine. We could use a refresher right about now, I think."

Mary circled the table, putting a glass in front of each man before leaving the platter of cookies in the center. Lawton gave a scathing look at Roger, trying his best, and failing, to not look at the picture the officer had placed in front of him.

Finally, Lawton broke.

"Deserved better?" he spat. "That girl was the one doing the stalking that night. She was on every guy in the crowd that looked like he had money. And I guarantee you, she settled on me because I had the most. But she got nowhere. Whatever happened to her, she brought on herself. But I had nothing to do with it. Tale as old as time. Small town girl wants out and thinks she can trap a guy and escape. But she was already on the wrong path. Sad? Maybe. But *nothing* to do with me."

Mary completed her delivery and, with a glance at Lawton, gave one of her tuts and slipped out the door.

"Seems like I touched a nerve there," Roger said with a crooked grin. "Have a sip of tea, see if you can calm yourself."

"No nerve," Lawton fumed, as he took a gulp of his tea. "I'm just sick of it being thrown in my face. Of *her* being thrown in my face. Another tramp gets what she deserves, it is not my issue."

"Pretty cold reaction," Curt said, barely looking up at Lawton.

"Sure is," Roger agreed. "Let's leave Rebecca Willis. For now."

"Thank you," Lawton said, sullenly.

"Let's talk about Kevin Keegan," Roger continued.

"What about him?" Lawton shot back, still fired up from the previous exchange. "He's dead. I'm sorry for him, but he ran with a bad crowd, and those things catch up to you."

"Tough crowd?" Curt asked. "Like you? You've been close to him for a long time. As you've repeatedly pointed out."

"Why is Stephens here?" Lawton said. "You're not even a cop."

"A valid point," Conklin interrupted. "Why is Mr. Stephens here?"

"He's consulting with us," Roger explained. "Would it surprise you to find out that we found a substantial amount of drugs in Keegan's apartment?"

"No," Lawton replied, finding his footing again after his lawyer had taken the heat off of him for a moment. "People do stupid things. Even good people. Even friends. If he was into drugs, that was his thing. Not mine. I'm a businessman. A good one. And when you're successful, people take aim at you. Which is what this feels like. Not the kind of fishing expedition I would choose to have at the beach. If you have nothing more for me, I assume I am free to go? From this *voluntary* chat?"

"If you aren't charging my client," Conklin said, "it seems clear he's done here, so we'll be excusing ourselves."

"No charges," Roger affirmed. "Yet. But stay in town. We'll have more questions."

"Whatever," Lawton muttered, as he stood and headed for the doorway.

Conklin stopped before he followed Lawton out of the room. "I do hope if we have another of these, that you'll have more evidence to share and not just hearsay."

"Count on it," Roger replied.

After the two men had left, the observation room emptied, and everyone huddled just outside the doorway to the interview room. Roger and Curt sipped the last of their teas.

"Warrant?" Roger asked Russ.

"Already on it," Russ replied. "Shouldn't be a problem. But there is something else. The Vollmerhausens."

Roger groaned. "What now?"

"They just called in. There's another truck at the trapper's shack. It's parked there, as of"—he glanced at his watch—"five minutes ago."

"Right," Roger said. "I'm tired of this. All of it. I'm not getting yanked around anymore. You all head to Lost Colony and get a table. This shouldn't take long. I'm going to get at least one thing checked off our list. And you all plan on being at McTiki's tonight. That's where the answers lie."

Roger led the others toward the exit, stopping to thank Mary for the refreshments, but she was gone. The clock on the wall in the waiting room showed after five. Good. She should be gone, although she rarely kept to her hours very strictly. But she should. The interview had taken longer than expected. He left a note to thank her and decided to speak to Brady about getting her a raise. She deserved it.

Roger turned back toward the offices and was shouting to Brady when he heard the door close behind the others. What he wouldn't give to be headed to the tavern himself right now.

CHAPTER 14

The friends had instinctually gathered on the deck overlooking the beach. The late afternoon sun was falling at their backs, and the pastel clouds were lighting up. Pink, red, purple, green. As the light faded, so did the day's warmth. The air held a chill that had been missing for the last few days, and they huddled under blankets and in hoodies, with chunky mugs of coffee instead of the usual happy hour wine and beer.

Francis was the last to emerge, closing the sliding door behind him and taking a seat. No one spoke. The endless rhythm of the ocean hypnotic. Comforting. Constant.

Silently, after a few minutes, Cathy reached out and took Terry's hand silently. Even now, no one spoke, but they all noticed. Amelia drew her legs up under herself, conserving warmth. Jaime crossed his legs and spilled some coffee on the beach towel he had draped over himself. He patted at it half-heartedly and then abandoned the effort.

"He's not coming back," Chris said, finally. "We all know that, right?"

"There's no way to know that," Kirsten said, her eyes never leaving the surf. "He could still be out there."

"Could be," Jaime agreed, "but the statistics are not good."

"We should have found something by now," Terry said, still clutching Cathy's hand.

"His car showed up," Amelia pointed out.

"Yeah," Francis replied. "Somehow that doesn't make me feel better."

"Man, I wish I'd said some things when I could have," Jaime said. "All that stupid stuff from when we were kids. Doesn't mean anything in the long run. But you just never think the last time is the *last time.*"

"Stop talking like that," Amelia persisted. "Until we have definite proof, I'm going to have faith."

"I can still wish I had done things differently," Jaime went on. "If, by some miracle he does come back, I'm turning over a new leaf."

"Everyone always says getting old is hard," Francis said, "but I thought we had more time."

"What will this place be now?" Cathy asked. "It was always our happy place. Our escape. Will it just always be a sad place now? Will we avoid it? Memorialize him? What?"

"Have to let life do its thing," Kirsten answered. "No way to know how we'll react. Or even what we'll be reacting to, at this point. For now, though, I'm going to let the sun set and appreciate my friends. Even the one who isn't here."

One by one, they put their drinks down and reached out to their neighbors until everyone was holding hands. The sun dipped below the house behind them and the shadows grew longer, reaching out until they stretched to the sea and the blue brilliance of the waves turned gray, and then grew duller until they were pale ghosts appearing and disappearing on the beach below.

"Love you guys," Terry said finally.

A chorus of "I love you" followed, and they fell again into silence.

Jaime was the first to break the hand-holding chain, rising and taking his mug with him.

"Wherever you are, Mark," he said quietly, looking to the emerging stars, "come back. Whatever it takes...come back."

As he left the deck and returned to the house, the shadows grew black, and when they could no longer see each other's faces, the friends slowly rose and returned to the living room.

Kirsten was the last to leave, and she paused at the railing to catch a last glimpse of the ocean as the light slipped away. A pod of dolphins lazily made its way north up the beach going wherever dolphins go at night. She thought back to Grier telling them about the dolphins segregating themselves and wondered, with a jolt, if Mark had been a sound side dolphin who had found himself surrounded by ocean dolphins. Had he wandered too far from his pod?

Finally, she turned and walked into the warm glow of the house and to the company of her friends.

Roger checked his watch as he passed Sawyer Lake Road on his way to Buffalo City and the shack. Again. The damn creepy shack that wouldn't leave him alone. As he drove further into the preserve, the shadows deepened, and the temperature dropped a good ten degrees while the wind was smothered by the forest. As the sun fell, he couldn't shake the feeling that something would happen tonight. The pieces were coming together, but he wasn't connecting them. Yet.

Lawton was a bad guy. That was clear. But being a jerk wasn't a prosecutable offense. More the pity. But he was hiding something. And if there was one thing Roger knew, it was that he would bring Lawton down.

But for now, he'd better get his mind on the task at hand. Someone was at the shack. Could be a poacher. Could be someone involved with Keegan's death and Elliot's disappearance. Hell, the cabin was on private property, it could just be whoever owned the place. But every cop instinct in his body was buzzing a warning.

He checked his belt. Taser. Cuffs. He switched on his body cam and stopped with his hand on his Glock. He hated carrying the thing, but something evil was prowling the Banks. Last resort only.

He let the cruiser glide silently up in front of the shack. It lay quiet and dark. He couldn't shake the feeling that someone, something, was staring out at him, but the shadows were impenetrable. The windows were black. Inscrutable.

He cursed quietly to himself as he gently swung his door open. Even the smallest noises sounded like firecrackers in the silent woods. The gravel under his boots popped loudly. Dammit.

He was halfway out of his car when an engine roared to life and a massive pickup pulled out from behind the cabin. As it rounded the corner, it hit its high beams and blinded Roger, who threw an arm up over his eyes and reached for his belt. Taser or Glock? Taser.

The truck roared onto the roadway and pulled across it, blocking any chance he had of escaping. The only route available to him was further into the preserve and to the dead end where Keegan had been found.

"Well, shit," he said to himself. He opened the rear door and half crouched behind it. It wasn't much cover, but better than nothing.

The truck stopped and idled. Roger swore he could feel it shaking the ground beneath him, but it was more likely the adrenaline shooting through his body.

The driver's door of the pickup slowly opened.

"How's it going, Officer Goldstein?" a voice called out.

The voice was familiar, but in the dark, and the surprise, and the nerves, Roger couldn't place it.

"No need to worry," the voice called. "We're actually here to perform a public service."

The passenger door opened, now, and another figure emerged. Another shadow behind the headlights. Roger draped his arms over the top of the car door and adopted a relaxed demeanor that was completely at odds with what was happening inside of him. He couldn't see who he was talking to, but he could see enough to know that both of them were tall. Taller than the F-150 they stood next to.

"Strange kind of public service that has you blocking my exit," Roger shouted back, probably a little louder than necessary. "Public *service* usually involves respect for public *servants*. You know, like me."

"Had to make sure we had your undivided attention," the driver replied. "This is the one and only time we'll be in touch with you."

A loud hissing sound emerged from the canal to Roger's right followed almost immediately by a sizeable splash. Must have been his little alligator buddy objecting to the ruckus happening in his usually quiet stretch of water.

The distraction was just enough for Roger's mind to click into gear, and he knew who he was talking to.

"Surprised to find you back here, Ben Hornigold," Roger ventured. "Last I saw you, you were up to no good out on the sound behind Bodie Island with that even less trustworthy Charles Vane. Heard you two took a shot later that day at my buddy, Roleth. Doesn't exactly inspire confidence in this current situation. And if that's Vane with you? Let's just say I'll stay where I am and see how this plays out."

"Didn't think you'd recognize my voice," Hornigold replied, reaching in to turn off the truck's headlights, and stepping in front of the pickup with his hands raised. "But I didn't take a shot at anyone. Not my way. In fact, it's partly why we're here."

"And I'm definitely not Vane," the other figure said, also stepping out with arms raised. "It's Eddie English, Roger."

"Eddie?" Roger asked. "This isn't sounding any better to me. Last I saw *you*, you were busting up the Blue Crab with Vane and his gang. Probably best you make your intentions clear before we go much further."

Something snapped in the woods beside the shack, and the

sound of a shotgun being pumped followed with a decisive chock. Before the echo had faded, a massive figure emerged from the trees and stepped toward the roadway.

"Hi there, Rog," Russ said calmly, both barrels of his shotgun aimed toward the truck and its occupants.

"Cutting it kinda close, Russ," Roger replied.

"Hello, Officer Wahl," Hornigold said. "The more the merrier."

Just then, the sound of tires crunching the gravel of the road crept up behind them. A pair of headlights came to life, lighting up Hornigold and English standing in front of their truck. A door opened and another, shorter, stockier figure entered the scene.

"Hey there, Chief," Roger said with a wave. "They just said the more the merrier, so I guess it's party time."

"Doesn't feel very festive when someone tries to trap one of my officers out in the middle of nowhere," Brady answered, his right hand hovering just above his service revolver.

"Easy now, Brady," Hornigold said, his hands still in the air.

"Yeah," English added. "It's because of Vane we wanted to meet you here."

"Wait," Roger said, now emerging from behind his car door. "Are the Vollmerhausens in on this? Did they help set me up?"

English laughed, and Hornigold doubled over, hands on his knees. It took them both a moment to compose themselves.

"Hell no," Hornigold finally managed to get out. "We just counted on them not being able to mind their own business. We had an alternative plan if you didn't show, but we figured you would."

"Get to it," Roger said, now leaning on the trunk of his cruiser. "And make it good. We have a busy night ahead of us."

"And this shotgun isn't getting any lighter," Russ added from the trees off to the side.

"Look, I've been around a long time," Hornigold continued. "I'm not a good guy, but I'm far from the worst. Been avoiding the likes of you for years. I walk along the line but rarely cross it. Made a lot of money from knockoff sunglasses, watches, sneakers. Fake fishing licenses. Off the record, moved a lot of weed over the years."

"No one cares about that anymore," Brady called from behind him.

"Still, off the record until it can be totally on the record," Hornigold responded.

"And as for me," English said, "that scene at the Crab was the last straw for me."

"Vane is out of control," Hornigold said. "I feel like a dinosaur hawking counterfeit Ray-Bans while he and his people are cutting down anyone who gets in their way as they destroy people's lives with that crap they sell. Hook young kids and don't care how many families are ripped apart."

"Fentanyl?" Roger asked.

"And worse," Hornigold replied.

"What? You snitch on him so we take him out and you can just move in and take over? That what's happening here?" Russ asked.

"Nah, man," English answered. "You got it all wrong."

"We're clearing out," Hornigold continued. "We don't fit here anymore. Maybe someday we will again, but not now. Look, in our way we love the Banks as much as you."

"I doubt that," Roger shot back.

"Don't try to paint yourself as some sort of man of the people, here," Brady said.

"It's not like that," Hornigold said. "Like I said, I've always been just on the wrong side of the law. But I never aimed to hurt anyone. Let alone kill them. Seems almost quaint now, with what's happening. But Eddie here and I belong to a different time. No one needs to hit us over the head with it anymore. We're not angels, but there were always lines we wouldn't cross. But someone moved the lines, and we stayed where we were. Vane is taking over. And we're not up to taking him down."

"Too many of these new young kids think the same way," English said. "Don't care about anything or anyone else."

"We're leaving," Hornigold admitted. "We're done. Maybe time to go straight. Or straight-*er*. But we can't do that here. Too much history. Not now and not with Vane. Nah. Our time is done. Maybe we'll retire here someday. Get one of those condos on the golf course."

"So why are we all here?" Roger asked, bluntly. "Because I'm not sure I buy any of this."

"That's fine," Hornigold replied. "Can't blame you. But it's true. We left something for you in the shack. All the details on Vane's next shipment. Tonight. Late. Time and place and what to expect are all there. You go grab that and we'll be on our way. Probably won't see us again. Not for a long time."

"How do we know it's not all a setup?" Russ asked, stepping further into the road but keeping the shotgun raised.

"Because this is way too much trouble to go through for that," English answered bluntly. "We could have taken you out one by one when you got here. You're really noisy in the woods, Russ."

Russ shrugged and lowered his gun. He looked at Roger who returned the shrug.

"Chief?" Roger called to Brady.

"Do we have enough to charge them with anything?" Brady answered.

"Not even a little bit," Roger admitted. "Could maybe come up with a boat registration violation if I tried."

Brady stood still and looked from Roger to the two confessed counterfeiters and then nodded.

"Thanks for your help," he said, as he climbed into his cruiser and backed it out of the way of the pickup's exit.

Roger raised his hands. "One last thing. Any idea why Todd Lawton's cell phone would have been in this cabin the other morning. Or any info on what happened to Kevin Keegan?"

"Sorry," Hornigold said with a shake of his head. "Vane took this place over a few months ago and we haven't been back since. Those are questions for him. Or Lawton. They've been cozying up together lately. We just picked this place because we knew it would get your attention, and Vane is busy elsewhere right now."

Roger nodded, lips pursed. Finally, he crossed the distance between his car and Hornigold and English. When he reached them, he offered his hand and each man, after a pause, stepped forward and shook it.

"Good luck," English said.

"You're going to need it," Hornigold added. "Vane is nuts. Don't trust anything about him. We'll see you 'round."

"I hope not," Roger replied. "No offense.'

The two men climbed into the F-150 and slowly made their way back out to Buffalo City Road. Their taillights eventually disappeared around a bend and faded into the night. Darkness and the sounds of the forest fell again.

"Here goes nothin'," Roger said as he turned on his phone's flashlight and tentatively went to the shack and in through the front door. It took almost no time for him to return with a large manila envelope in his hands. "It's all here. Goes down tonight. Late. Between McTiki's and this, we'll have our hands full."

The three officers met in front of the shack.

"This takes priority," Brady announced. "This is actionable. McTiki's is just playing a hunch and hoping something presents itself."

"Whatever you say, boss." A pause. "I think I understand what they meant," Roger said. "I feel like I don't belong in these Banks, either. The ones I fell in love with seem a long way off."

"Well, let's do something tonight to bring them back," Brady said, heading back to his car.

***

Curt and the others had been sitting in the Lost Colony Tavern for forty-five minutes. Grier was polishing off a Scotch egg and Carlito was nearing the end of what had been a massive shepherd's pie. Sage sat by a window, the dogs quietly curled at her feet. A cool breeze was whistling through downtown Manteo and something heavy hung over the town. It felt more like October than April, but none of them could explain where the feeling came from.

Curt checked the time on his cell phone, not for the first time. It was after six now, and with the official festivities at the tiki bar kicking off at seven, decisions would have to be made soon.

Gene O'Shea, the affable owner of the tavern, entered the dining room from the kitchen, spotted Curt and headed toward the table.

"Curt!" he called as he approached. "Always a pleasure. What can I get you? On the house."

"Gene, how're ya?" Curt replied. "Thanks, but no thanks. We're actually on our way to a business function. Of sorts."

"Offer stands if you change your mind," Gene said, taking in the table. "Grier, Sage. Great to see you. And you, young man! Congratulations on keeping some very fine company."

Carlito blushed and gave a half wave.

"I'm guessing you're talking about the McTiki event?" Gene continued. "Talk of the town. I'll look for a full report next time I see you."

"You guessed it," Curt said. "Just waiting to hear from Roger before we get moving. Look, Gene. Off the record, how are things going in town? We've been so taken up with the death in the refuge, I feel like we've missed some things. Manteo feels...tight, tonight. Coiled and ready to spring. You okay?"

"Ah, we'll be fine," Gene replied. "But you're not wrong. Whole place is spooked by these fentanyl cases. The kids in the hospital are good kids. I won't say the last ones you'd think could get caught up in stuff like that, but far from the first. Has everyone looking over their shoulder. And that Charles Vane has been around a lot. Was surprised to see him with you the other day. He's just bad news. Feels like it bodes ill for the upcoming season. But we'll be fine. We know how to take care of ourselves."

"I know you do," Curt said, "but you shouldn't have to. As soon as we take care of this other matter, you'll see a lot more of us. Promise."

"I won't complain, that's for sure," Gene answered. "I have to hit the office. Payroll and inventory tonight. Yay, me. Check out the store before you leave. Killer new t-shirts and some cool new books. Worth a look."

"Rain check, yeah?" Curt said, grabbing his phone as it vibrated and scuttered across the table. "I'll have my credit card ready next time I'm here. Promise."

Gene laughed and headed off to the back office, already calling to an employee behind the bar.

Curt looked at his phone and paused.

"Change of plans," he announced. "Roger is headed back to the station to file some paperwork and prepare for something later tonight. We're on our own with McTiki's. At least to start."

"Maybe not the worst thing," Grier chimed in, finishing off another Scotch egg. "Lawton would not be happy to see Roger as soon as he opens. Not after this afternoon's questioning."

"I think I'll hang back a little myself," Curt said. "I was in the interview room too. No need drawing attention right off the bat. I'll show up around eight. See how things are going. But I'll be laying low."

"Shall we?" Grier said, pushing back from the table and reaching for his wallet.

"I've got this," Curt said, motioning for the others to put their money away. "Maybe I'll even take a look at the store here before I head out. You have my number. Call if anything happens I need to know about."

"Another perk of the job," Sage explained to Carlito as they headed for the door. "The boss is rich."

Curt laughed to himself and reached for the check. He picked it up and grabbed his glasses to be sure of what he was seeing. The tab came to zero. He looked quickly for Gene to protest, but the owner had disappeared. Shaking his head, Curt hefted his credit card and headed to the gift shop.

CHAPTER 15

Grier took his own car and planned to attend the opening solo. He had no profile with any of the folks there and should be able to move freely among the guests and employees easily. Even Sage and Carlito had some baggage attached to them, having been there "applying" for work earlier. He knew people. That must qualify him for at least the friends' portion of friends and family.

He turned north toward Nags Head. Not for the first time, he felt isolated from his fellow Brethren. Sage and Carlito were closest in age and seemed to be developing a nice friendship. Roger had his colleagues on the force and probably spent more time with them than the Brethren. At least most of the time. Curt? Well, he was Curt. Devoted to the Banks in a way that seemed to exclude most other things. They'd known each other for years, but he knew little *about* Curt. He wanted to change that.

His time on the water with the reunion gang had reminded him how much he enjoyed the company of good people. People with curiosity, and humor, and goodwill. The Brethren served a noble purpose, but it was time to deepen those bonds. It could only help their shared goals. He hoped.

Briefly, he allowed himself to think about the group and their missing friend. What none of the Brethren had admitted to each other was that they had shifted, unspoken, to trying to expose and arrest Lawton for what they suspected he was hiding. There had been little talk of finding Elliot lately. If he was honest with himself, he had come to believe that Elliot was dead and the best they could hope for was closure for his friends and family and justice for what had been done to him. Somehow, it seemed if none of them spoke the words out loud that they could maintain the pretense that the outcome may be different.

He pulled into the parking lot for the new McTiki's. At ten past seven, the lot was already full to overflowing. There were parking valets, which surprised Grier. The Outer Banks were, on the whole, a much more relaxed place. Beach Town, U.S.A.

Seeing the line stretched out ahead of him, he reversed out and headed across the street to an empty lot. It had been a miniature golf course not long ago. Before the real estate had become too valuable for something frivolous that took up so much space. The lot had gained a reputation lately for some nefarious activity, but the arc lights across from it ensured that tonight it would be quiet. No doubt it would soon be home to a new McMansion or restaurant, but for tonight it provided an easy place to leave the car and get inside quickly. The fact that he was the only one to take advantage of the situation only confirmed his belief that most of the people in line for valets were more interested in being seen than in enjoying the night.

Grier strolled past the line of cars waiting and spotted Sage's Bronco parked down a side road. Smart, he thought. Different solution to the same problem.

He was impressed at the level of detail as he passed through the doorway. Palm fronds, brightly colored lights, replica puffer fish strung up around the walls. The staff was well dressed. Hawaiian shirts, but tasteful, and black dress pants. Much more like the classic Tonga Room, Trader Vic's, or even Three Dots and a Dash than the newer generation of tikis that were all flash and little substance.

Grier grabbed a coconut shrimp skewer from a passing server, while heading out back to the bar in the yard where the line was considerably shorter. He ordered a virgin mai tai, ignoring the raised eyebrows from the bartender. His was likely the only non-alcoholic drink ordered so far, but he knew the night was likely to get dicey later.

Herbie Knight was ensconced on a small stage on the far side of the pool, playing the most eclectic set list he had ever heard. He paused to listen to "Blue Hawaii," then smiled as it segued into "Margaritaville," and then "Whiskey in the Jar." The brilliance of the concept truly struck him then. Between an Irish pub and a tiki bar, there was something for everyone.

He spied Sage and Carlito in a cluster of people surrounding some high-top tables nearer to the stage. He tried to catch their eyes, but they seemed to be deep in conversation with a woman who was waving a clipboard in the air while directing a parade of employees.

Giving up on his two Brethren, Grier moved toward the Irish pub portion of the establishment. He spied a dark wooden door to the right of the larger entrance to the main tiki floor. As soon as he pushed his way in and the door closed behind him, he was enveloped in a hushed calm. Voices murmured. Employees wore white shirts with black ties tucked into them and moved calmly throughout. Grier immediately relaxed and found himself a lone stool at the bar.

He felt conspicuous with his heavily garnished drink and polished it off before ordering a non-alcoholic beer. The fact that the barkeep didn't blink an eye spoke to how popular alcohol-free beer had become. Even here.

Swinging himself around on the stool, he observed the pub in action. There were no televisions. No jukebox. Just folks talking. It was definitely more sparsely peopled than the tiki areas, but he suspected that would change as it got later.

He took another look around. The one thing he didn't see was

Todd Lawton. It seemed unlike the flashy businessman to not be the center of attention. Especially on an occasion like this.

He tapped out a message and sent it to Sage and Carlito, checking to see if they had seen Lawton. Within a few minutes, Carlito responded that they had not. Apparently, his absence had been noted as the woman they were speaking to, Nancy, was the manager and she was desperately trying to keep things on track. Thus, the clipboard calisthenics.

Grier wandered back out to the outdoor area. Herbie was just going on a break, so Grier approached and called a greeting to the local celebrity.

"Herb!" he said loudly, speaking over the crush of people. "Sounding great, as always."

"Why, thanks, Grier," Herb said, turning a genuinely pleased smile toward him. "Fun night. Trying to bring a little joy to the world."

"And succeeding, my friend," Grier replied. "Say. Have you seen Todd Lawton? I wanted to compliment him on this place. It's gorgeous."

"It really is," Herb agreed. "But, now that you mention it, I haven't seen him. Which is odd. Maybe he's planning a big entrance. That's something he would do. I was ready with 'Get the Party Started' for him, but no go."

"Yeah," Grier said. "Maybe he's still planning something. Make a big splash."

"I'm sure he's just taking care of business and working over-time," Herb said, with a wink.

"Good one, Herb," Grier said, "good one. Well, let me know if you spot him."

Grier was already scanning the crowd as he turned away. Carlito and Sage had barely moved, but the harried manager, Nancy, was nowhere to be seen. Grier circulated, but the night continued to pass with no sign of Lawton.

At nine o'clock, with just an hour to go, an army of servers appeared bearing massive bowls of rum cocktails with flaming ceramic volcanoes in the center. The crowd cheered. Herb launched into a conga and a dance line formed.

In the midst of this, Grier saw Curt arrive. He made his way to the newcomer's side, hoisting another virgin cocktail in salute.

"Don't worry, Mom," Grier teased. "No booze. Strange to say, also no Lawton. He's a no-show, and it's past time to be fashionably late."

"That's odd," Curt agreed. "He's been angling for this night for months. Maybe longer. What if this whole thing was a ruse? Get everyone looking in this direction and then pull something somewhere else."

"Like what?" Grier asked, as Sage and Carlito wandered up.

"Drugs?" Curt mused. "Moving Elliot somewhere? Alive or dead."

"Well then we fell for it hook, line and sinker," Grier admitted, nodding to welcome the others.

"I got a text from Roger a little bit ago," Curt said, changing the subject. "he's tied up with paperwork, but we've got more work ahead tonight. Vane is on the move. He'll fill us in when we meet. Maybe Lawton is with Vane."

"Only forty-five more minutes until closing," Sage pointed out. "I think we can call tonight a bust. At least if we wanted to nail Lawton. The place is awesome, though."

"I just don't understand where he is," Carlito muttered. "No way he would miss this."

"Well, if he's up to something, we were had and missed it," Grier said. "Should we find Roger and get ready for what's next?"

"Not much alternative, I guess," Curt agreed.

"Let's blow this popsicle stand," Grier said, heading for the exit and shooting a wave in Herb's direction.

Roger got back to the station and slowly ascended to the offices. Something was wrong. That same tickle in the back of his mind had kicked up. It didn't have to do with Hornigold and English. His gut told him they had played straight with him, and his gut was almost always right. Which is what made this loose thread bother him even more. In his experience, if something felt off, it usually was. Something was staring him in the face, and he just couldn't see it. With lives on the line, this was unacceptable. He had to do better.

He reached the reception area, glanced at the thank you note he had left Mary on her window, and let himself through to the offices. He flipped the hallway lights on and headed to his own office.

He paused in his doorway and looked into the darkened room. He could hear the trees outside scrabbling along the roof, like so many small creatures scampering just outside of his sight. Dammit. What was he missing? He knew if he didn't clue in tonight, it would be too late. He was out of time. Hornigold had made that clear.

He crossed to his desk and switched on his lamp. The small pool of light felt like a cocoon, keeping the world at bay and forcing him to pull in. Focus. Rethink.

Absently, he leafed through his notes from the afternoon's interview with Lawton. While it had felt like a waste of time, Roger knew they had rattled Lawton's cage. And rattled criminals made mistakes. They needed him to trip up. Because right now they had nothing.

The details of Rebecca Willis, the victim at Puffin Isle all those years ago, sat on top of the pile. And there was her photo. Young, clear-eyed, full of promise. Just before everything had gone wrong and she spiraled down.

There was something there. But what? He started his computer and, as he waited for it to boot up, stared closely at the photo. Rebecca Willis, long dead, was hanging on to some secrets still. When the computer hummed to life, he pulled up a search engine and entered Rebecca's name. A long list of hits appeared. All of the local papers had run the story. The alleged assault at the bar, but also the downward fall of one of their own that came later. An excellent student and long-distance runner. A life that should have been.

He dug deeper. No siblings. Ah, man. Even worse. Only child. Her parents, L. P. and Elizabeth M. Willis, had been longtime residents of the Banks. He searched their records. Nothing criminal. But they had split not long after Rebecca's death. He'd seen it so often. Relationships often collapsed under the weight of accumulated tragedy.

Luke had left the Outer Banks and started over in Richmond, remarrying five years later and working for an insurance company. Back to a sensible, low-key life. Elizabeth M. Willis, though, disappeared. The couple had last owned properties in Nags Head, Manteo, and Wanchese. Back in the days when average people could manage multiple investment properties through hard work and smart planning. Not possible these days.

The itch was growing stronger. He was getting close. He did a search for Elizabeth Willis. There was no record of her moving. She looked to have stayed local. Her ex-husband apparently left all of the houses to her. He must've really wanted out. Or felt guilty. Elizabeth eventually took a job at the Piggly Wiggly. Sold one house. Then another. Settling into the house in Wanchese.

And then...took a job with the Manteo Police Department.

What? Roger had never heard of an Elizabeth Willis here. He looked up her employment history with the department and froze. There it was. Elizabeth M. Willis had changed her name only a few weeks after starting at Manteo PD. Less changed than reverted. She went back to her maiden name and dropped her first name. Not unusual in people running from traumatic pasts. But there it was. Elizabeth M. Willis became...Mary Hallet.

Shit.

Roger's head swam. He replayed everything from the last few days. The clues had all been there. This is what he'd been missing. It all came flooding over him.

The ex-husband who wasn't discussed but had simply grown away from her.

The daughter she hadn't spoken to in years. Because she was

dead, but the pain of it was too hard to drop into casual conversation.

Dammit! Russ had told him about the mailbox at her house with the name "Willis" on it. How had he missed that?

She'd chosen the house in Wanchese. Not far from Keegan, who had been there the night her daughter had been drugged and assaulted. Staying close. Waiting.

She'd been at Bad Bean when Mark Elliot had recognized Todd Lawton. Maybe she had, too. She had lingered after Russ had left and her car didn't leave the parking lot until Lawton and the others had gone.

Oh, Mary. What did you see that night? What did you do?

He kept unravelling the strands.

She had appeared just this afternoon with the refreshments as they had been discussing her daughter. First in the hallway, and then in the interview room. Just as Lawton placed blame for everything on Rebecca Willis herself. With her dead daughter's face staring at her from the conference table.

And then she had been gone immediately after. He'd applauded her sticking to her hours for once, but what if she had been following Lawton?

All the flirting and the coy comments? They'd gotten more pronounced recently, and he'd been too egotistical to think it was anything more than her finally succumbing to his charm. Playing the game. Dammit, she'd used the old rope-a-dope on him to keep him off the scent. The same damn thing he'd used so often to lull suspects into making mistakes.

"What have you done, Mary? No, no, no."

He rushed out of the office and down to his car. He dialed Mary but it went straight to voicemail.

They'd been right. It was all going down tonight. They had just been completely off the mark as to *what* was going to happen.

Another call to Mary had the same result. As he pulled his seatbelt across himself and roared out of the lot and toward Kill Devil Hills, he called Curt.

They had missed what was going on. Badly. And if they didn't act fast, someone else would die tonight.

———

Back at the rental house, the evening had crept slowly past. No cocktails flowed. No music played. The house was mostly silent, with everyone scrolling on their phones, and Jaime watching cable news with the volume down. No one had even made dinner. They simply sat.

Just after ten, there came a quiet knock at the front door. It repeated itself two more times, before Amelia finally took note and walked down the stairs to see who could possibly be here at this time of night.

The others followed slowly, as baffled as she was. Jaime put a hand on her shoulder and stepped in front of her.

"We don't know who this is," he said. "Let me."

He opened the door, and a gasp escaped more than one of the friends at what they saw.

Mark Elliot stood on the doorstep. He was definitely the worse for wear. His clothes dirty and stained. His beard days old and his skin sallow.

"Boy, am I glad to see you," Elliot said quietly.

Without a word, the friends descended upon him and swept him into a hug. It was some time before any of them were able to speak.

———

The Brethren split up as they exited McTiki's to head to their respective cars. Curt, of course, had availed himself of the valet parking and was idling behind Sage's Bronco on the side street when his phone rang. Checking the incoming number, he saw it was Roger and answered.

Curt turned down his stereo as Roger launched into an explanation of what he'd pieced together. Curt sank deeper into his seat as he realized what had been going on around them the entire time. He killed his engine, climbed out of the Chevelle, and started toward the Bronco but was interrupted by Grier sprinting across the street from the empty lot where he had parked. He was waving his hands, shouting, and simultaneously trying to look behind him at the mostly deserted parking lot.

Mostly.

Grier joined Curt by the Bronco as Sage and Carlito emerged.

"You guys gotta come see this," Grier said, out of breath. "I just found out where Lawton is."

Without waiting for a response, he turned and ran back to where he had parked. The others exchanged a glance and hustled after him.

Grier raced past his car toward the farthest corner of the lot, well out of the lone working light that sat in the center of the parking area and illuminated almost nothing. It was a moment before the others noticed what had drawn Grier's attention.

In the deepest shadow, a sports car sat parked, facing away from the bar and the brightly lit festivities just across the street. The car was bright blue, easily spied now that everyone knew what they were looking at.

"Is that...?" Sage began.

"Yes," Curt answered. "A McLaren 750S. Half a million at a minimum. And it belongs to Todd Lawton."

The four approached the car cautiously, unsure of exactly what they would find. All four opened the flashlight feature on their phones, aiming at the car. The windows were open.

Carlito turned to look behind them, alert for any potential threat from that direction, but all was quiet. Too quiet.

Curt reached the driver's window and shone his light into the cockpit and stepped quickly back. Grier reached the passenger side, cautiously craned his neck around the edge of the door and stopped short.

"Holy. Shit," he exclaimed, before tearing the door open and crouching by the vehicle.

Sage and Carlito were next, and both recoiled as soon as they peered into the car.

Splayed out across both seats was Todd Lawton, arms zip-tied wide. His torso was bare, the letters "RW" splashed in red across his chest. An envelope was taped to his stomach, labeled in large letters. "Roger." His pants were draped over the steering wheel, and he sat in his boxer shorts, one leg on either side of the center console. His mouth was duct-taped shut, but his eyes were closed, and he looked in no condition to make any sound whatsoever.

Grier climbed in and checked for a pulse.

"He's alive!" he called. "Breathing is shallow, but steady!"

Curt moved to call Roger, when his own phone chimed. He tapped the green button quickly.

"Roger," he said, "get to the empty lot next to McTiki's. We found out why Lawton missed his own event."

He listened for a beat and then continued.

"No, he's alive," Curt affirmed. "But—well, you need to get here. And there's a letter for you. Taped to him. Speaker? Sure."

Curt switched his phone to speaker, and the others gathered around as Roger filled them in on everything he had just discovered about Mary Hallet. Before he was finished, the flashing blue and red lights of his cruiser lit up the lot and he skidded up next to them.

He jumped out of his car and rushed to the sports car, pulling on a pair of nitrile gloves. He climbed halfway in and slowly peeled the duct tape off of Lawton's mouth. Despite it clinging to his skin, Lawton didn't move.

"None of you thought to get this crap off him?" Roger shouted over his shoulder.

"We made sure he was okay, relatively speaking, and left the scene intact for you. It's only been a minute," Curt explained.

"Yeah, right," Roger grumbled in response. "That's good, I guess."

He grabbed the envelope from Lawton's stomach, leaving red angry stripes where the tape came away, then returned to his cruiser and called Brady and Russ to fill them in.

Carlito laid his hand on the car.

"Engine's mid-mounted on these," Carlito called. "This one's cool, so he's been here a while."

"I got here just after seven," Grier mused. "Wasn't here when I arrived."

"Brady and Russ are on their way. Ambulance too," Roger announced, returning. "They're looping Kill Devil PD in. Will cause delays. Pretty sure that was the plan."

He carefully opened the envelope bearing his name.

Slowly he began to read aloud.

Hi, Roger. By now, I'm guessing you've put things together. You were too smart to keep in the dark much longer, so I knew I had to take my chance. You've guessed, I'm sure, but just to make it clear, Rebecca Willis was my daughter. She told me many times before she died that Lawton was the one who had drugged and attacked her. Her inability to prove it led to her finding life unbearable. Even if people believed her, they weren't able to hold him responsible.

I didn't join the PD for revenge. I never expected to see Lawton again. And I did love the work. And being silly with you. If I hadn't been so broken, maybe things would have been different between us. Or maybe I flatter myself.

When Lawton walked into Bad Bean the other night,

I couldn't believe it. Keegan was there too, but Becca had been clear that he hadn't done a thing to her. Maybe he was part of the outfit that made it possible, but that was all. Elliot was just in the wrong place at the wrong time. Back then and this week.

So many people fighting so many ghosts.

I followed them when they left. When they reached Lawton's new place, I was able to watch through the fence. It was still unfinished, and they were drinking outside by the pool. When they started to argue, I started recording. There is a flash drive in this envelope. It will show you that Lawton fought with Keegan. They both realized that Elliot would be able to shed light on what Lawton had done to my girl. Keegan wanted to come clean. Lawton, not so much.

They fought. Lawton punched and then pushed Keegan into the pool and held him under. When it was over, Lawton pulled a gun and forced Elliot to load the body into his car. Not this one. A different one.

Elliot moved sluggishly, and I realized Lawton must have spiked the drinks the way he had Becca's. Keegan should have been able to take Lawton easily. But Lawton had stacked the deck in his favor. Again.

I followed them. This time to Alligator River. He dumped Keegan into the water, then turned on Elliot. Hit him with the gun and Elliot went down. I had parked up the road. They never knew I was there. I knew Elliot had minutes left before Lawton would kill him too. I hit Lawton from behind. A tire jack from my car. I had to get Elliot away, so loaded him into Lawton's car. I thought Lawton would still be out when I got back. I was wrong.

Apparently, he dragged himself to the shack, where you found his phone. He was working with Vane. I hadn't known that, but when I came back to get him, I saw Vane taking him out of the park. I took Lawton's car and parked it in McTiki's lot. No one paid it any notice, and no one was looking for mine, so I returned to Alligator River the next day and retrieved it. All easier than I expected.

I thought I'd missed my chance. Until he came in for his interview today. I put GHB in his tea. It seemed appropriate. The same drug that ended my beautiful girl would ruin him. I wanted him humiliated. Exposed. It was only fair.

Elliot is fine. I kept him hidden. I knew Lawton would kill him if he found him. There's already been too much death. I'm not a killer. Never was. I hope you never doubted that. But I was a mother grieving. I don't think there is any more powerful or tragic figure in humanity.

Don't look for me, Roger. Mary Hallet is gone. I'm finally free. I'll start a new life, now. Rebecca is letting me go, but I'll never let go of her. And I have delivered justice for her. You'll always be a what-if for me. If only life had been a little less cruel.

I've sailed away. No trail to follow. And no real

harm done, I hope. Other than to Lawton. And isn't that justice?

Roger shook the envelope, and a flash drive dropped into his open hand as his phone rang. Amelia Langley was calling.

An hour later, the Brethren sat in the living room of the rental house with the reunion friends scattered around them. All except Elliot, who had been put to bed and was sleeping soundly in his upstairs bedroom.

"He told us a nice lady had taken him to a house on an island," Amelia said. "He had everything he needed, but no phone or way back. She had taken his devices to keep him isolated. For his own good, she said."

"He must have been in one of the old duck blind places out in the sound," Chris mused. "One of the ones you showed us." He pointed to Grier, who pursed his lips and nodded.

"We might have been close to him out on your boat," Kirsten said, shaking her head.

"Or he could have been miles away," Grier replied. "We'll probably never know."

"She was good enough to return his car," Curt pointed out. "And his electronics. She was trying to send us a message. He would be okay. We just didn't know."

"He said she came and spent each night out on the island with him," Jaime said. "Just sat and talked. Looked out for him. He said she was...kind. But had been through a lot."

"That's an understatement," Sage said.

"She even had an Uber waiting for him when she dropped him off at the ramps under Virginia Dare Trail. Where we caught the airboat. Dropped him off and then took her boat out into the sound," Cathy said. "She did look out for him."

"Knowing her, that's not surprising. Hey. I'm sorry for all your trouble," Curt said, hands raised to the visitors. "I hope you won't let this ruin the Banks for you."

"Far from it," Terry said, grinning. "Before Mark fell asleep, we all had a talk and decided to spend more time here. He came back. It's our good luck place now."

"We're going to buy a house together here," Francis said, a hand on Jaime's shoulder. "Our own mini timeshare."

"We've seen we need to re-prioritize," Cathy continued. "And that means being with people we love in a place we love. So, you'll be seeing more of us."

"Good," Curt answered. "This place does have a way of casting a spell. I just hope future spells are a bit quieter."

"So do we!" Amelia agreed.

"The orbs!" Carlito exclaimed. "People kept reporting them. It was probably her, shuttling out to him each night and then back in the morning."

"Maybe," Roger said. "Partially. Which brings us"—he glanced at his watch—"to the rest of our evening. We'd best shove off."

The Brethren took their leave of the reunion group and headed south. Still work to be done.

EPILOGUE

At three in the morning, Curt and Roger stood on a rickety dock behind the Bodie Island Light Station by the Off-Island Trail. Behind them, the flashing lights of Russ's SUV were disappearing into the early morning gloom. Inside, cuffed and restrained was Henry Avery, the recent hire to the Park Service who had been using his position to meet smugglers across Route 12 on Coquina Beach and shuttling contraband through the park to pass to Charles Vane on the back of Bodie Island where the drugs crossed the Croatan Sound to disappear through Wanchese. The same Henry Avery who had been Kevin Keegan's landlord in Wanchese. The ties between Lawton, Keegan and Vane continued to grow stronger. Luckily, it was all about to end.

Tonight's haul had been massive. When all was said and done, probably the biggest capture in the history of the area. Hornigold had been true to his word.

A flurry of late-night calls, and Avery's involvement, had convinced the Park Service to leave it to Roger and Manteo PD. It had taken some convincing for Russ to leave with Avery and the shipment, aided by some Hatteras deputies, but he finally left, leaving the Brethren to themselves on the back side of the deal.

Brady had been needed elsewhere to get Lawton checked out at the hospital and then transferred to the station where he would be processed and begin his journey through the legal system. Good riddance.

And so, the Brethren waited in the dark for Charles Vane to show himself and discover that his operation was over. Curt stood silently beside Roger, the wooden box with the Blackbeard bowl in it tucked under one arm. Roger shot glances at it as they waited.

Finally, Curt couldn't ignore the looks any longer.

"What?" he finally asked quietly. "I couldn't just leave it in the trunk of the car here in the middle of the night with smugglers prowling around. It's probably the most valuable artifact on the entire Banks."

"Yeah," Roger answered, finally turning to Curt, "I just hope nothing happens to it if things get messy." He paused.

"What else?" Curt said. "Spit it out."

Roger turned his eyes back to the empty waters in front of them.

"You're not considering, you know, trying to use it or anything, are you? That would be bad. We've got this, Curt. It's handled."

"No, of course I'm not planning on trying anything like that," Curt said, with a laugh that sounded forced. "Relax. I'm just keeping it safe. I'm not about to do anything crazy."

"Right," Roger said, eyes still on the water. "Good. Glad to hear that."

Avery was a stooge. He carried out orders. Did what he was told. Vane was the danger. The boss. Enough of a threat that they had agreed that the Brethren would be needed to handle it. In case things took a turn for the extra-legal.

Just on time, at three fifteen, the quiet thrum of a boat approached. Then another. Two boats.

"All set?" Curt said quietly into the black night.

No response was needed. They were.

Two small boats rounded a bend and approached the dock, floodlights strafing the water in front of them until they slowed and glided into the dock. Charles Vane was alone in the first boat, the second lagging just behind held John Rackham and Mary Read. Every member of the Brethren recognized them from the fracas at the Blue Crab.

"Henry!" Vane called. "Time!"

"Sorry, Vane," Curt said quietly. "Tonight's delivery has been canceled."

A brilliant light flared off to one side, blinding the occupants of the incoming boats. Grier poled his airboat, floodlight fixed on the newcomers, out from the reeds by the island, his RIFFE speargun pointed at the drug dealers. His hand was perfectly steady.

Another light sprang to life from the opposite side, and a skiff with Sage and her two dogs slid into view. The dogs stood in the bow, hackles raised, teeth bared. Sage stood behind them, one hand on the wheel and another holding a flare gun low by her side.

"Sorry to say, you're done here. No delivery. No nothing," Roger said, without a hint of apology whatsoever.

Rackham spun his boat around as Mary Read cursed.

"Easy money, you said," she hissed at Vane. "And now no product? And cops? I'm not getting brought in for nothing. Get us out of here, John."

"Don't let these pathetic morons run you off," Vane answered. "Hold fast. We've got this."

But the boat peeled off and away, leaving a wake and disappearing into the inky night.

"Screw you, Vane!" Rackham's voice called back as the sound of the motor diminished and faded.

So much for honor among thieves.

None of the Brethren moved to follow.

"They'll get them on the other side," Roger assured Vane. "But you're ours."

"I don't think so," Vane said, pulling a rifle from under his boat's console. "No bunch of losers is getting in my way. Get lost or get dead."

"Not losers," Curt's voice was calm, measured. "We watch over these islands. And you're not welcome here. Ever again."

Roger's hand slipped to his service holster. Grier raised his speargun. Sage hefted the flare gun. The dogs coiled to leap, waiting only for a word from her.

"That the rifle you took a shot at me with earlier?" Grier called across the water. "You owe me for a repair."

"No clue what you're talking about," Vane said, with a laugh. "Sounds like you need to be more careful on the water."

"We're giving you one chance—only one—to turn around, leave, and keep going. Don't show your face in the Outer Banks again. Or it will end very differently."

"Please," Vane answered, "you don't scare me. He's a cop and the rest of you are just play-acting at being, I don't even know what. Superheroes or vigilantes or something? Piss off." He turned to Roger. "Take me in. You got nothin'. No merchandise, no evidence. I'll be out by morning."

As he finished, Vane noticed the box under Curt's arms, and something flickered in his eyes.

"Yeah, I think you misunderstand the situation," Roger said. "But just to clear things up."

Roger took a second, smaller pistol out of his belt and handed it to Curt.

"I need to check on the cruiser," Roger said, patting Curt on the shoulder as he turned and disappeared up the path.

"We're dealing with you, now. And we do things a little differently. Take this chance to go. And when you talk to your pals wherever you go to ground, tell them that the police here are the least of their worries. The Banks are under our protection. And we don't play by any rules but our own. I'm not a cop," Curt said, and took careful aim. One shot cracked into the night, and Vane's boat shuddered. "So, I'm perfectly willing to do things like that. I think you'll find that

I've hit just above the water line. But barely. The swell is coming up. Gonna be hard to stay afloat too much longer. Better get moving."

Grier took the pole from his boat and gave Vane's boat a hefty shove back out into the sound. "A helluva lot better chance than you gave those kids with your fentanyl," he said.

Vane paused and looked to the deck of his boat where a trickle of water was quickly becoming a stream.

"Dammit!" he cursed. "You can't do that! I'll kill you. After I take you for all your money!"

"I doubt that," Curt replied. "Unless you want to explain what you were doing here in the first place. Oh, and if you land in Wanchese, the cops *will* be waiting for you. And trust me when I say that you won't be safe in jail. I suggest finding a quiet spot somewhere else to dock and then get out of town. If I see you again, I won't aim for the boat."

"You're dead, Stephens," Vane growled. "You all are. No one does this to Charles Vane."

With a last furtive glance at the box under Curt's arm, Vane turned his boat with some difficulty and started back the way he had come. His curses could be heard echoing over the water as he struggled to control the rapidly filling boat.

The remaining Brethren all stood still, listening to the fading engine. No one moved. Curt thought, for just a moment, that the wake Vane left behind flared suddenly with the brilliant blue water that had seemed to follow him lately. He glanced at the box he still held, and when he turned back to the water, both Vane and the blue streaks were gone.

"You good, Carlito?" Curt said quietly.

A splash on the far side of Sage's boat gave way to two tan and muscled arms being thrown over the gunwale.

"All good, boss," the young man said as the rest of him followed, and he tumbled onto the deck of the boat with a laugh and a whoop.

"That shot came a little closer than we drew it up, but yeah, all set," Carlito said, pulling himself up onto one of the seats. "I got the tracker placed on the hull. We'll know wherever his boat ends up. No sweat."

"Good job, kid," Grier said, laughing. "I love it when a plan comes together."

"He won't stay away, you know that, right?" Sage said, calming the dogs and throwing a towel to Carlito.

"Probably not," Curt agreed. "But this should set him back for a while. And when he comes back, we'll be ready." Absentmindedly, he patted the heavy box. It did not go unnoticed. "I'll go let Roger know what happened. Meet you at the usual spot."

As he headed back toward the car, the two boats peeled off, and Grier called to Sage as they parted ways, headed to their berths.

"I heard the whole thing," Roger said, from the darkness by the path as Curt began to move. "Nice shot."

"Thanks," Curt said. "I wanted to aim higher. Self-restraint."

"Good," Roger replied. "That's my damn gun. Don't need it in a murder investigation."

The two chuckled as they walked wearily back to the cruiser.

Slowly, they all made their ways back north to Kill Devil Hills. Curt's usual spot. But not alone this time. Today had been a long day, but a good one. In the end. The Banks were always full of surprises. And that meant they had to be ready for anything. And anything covered a lot of ground.

They gathered on the beach and waited for the sun to rise over the Atlantic. It did. As it always did. And the new days would, of course, bring new challenges. New questions. But they were the Brethren of the Coast. And they were ready for whatever came. And they would have answers. They *were* the answers.

The End

The Brethren of the Coast Will Sail On.

If you enjoyed this book, please take a moment to visit Amazon or Goodreads and provide a short review or even just a rating. Every reader's voice is important for the continued life and growth of a book or series and vital in helping authors find their audience.

Look for Book Five of The Peripherals, *The Music of War,* soon and the next book in the Brethren of the Coast soon after. Keep up to date on all things related to my writing at:

www.markaldrich.net

where you can also sign up for a mailing list. Rest assured it will be used sparingly and only for announcements about the books.

Follow me on social media @marktheginger

SOME OUTER BANKS FACTS

First, there will be spoilers in these notes. If you are concerned about that, be sure to finish the book before reading on.

Blackbeard's history is inextricably linked with that of the Outer Banks. The pirate used the shallow and deceptive waters surrounding the Outer Banks to his advantage, prowling the local waters and establishing the area as a base for his exploits. He was particularly known for his relationship with Ocracoke Island and the city of Bath, North Carolina. His close friendship with the Governor of North Carolina provided him some security and frustrated many of the area's citizens.

On November 22, 1718, under the orders of Virgina's Governor, he was engaged in battle off of Ocracoke and finally defeated after sustaining over two dozen wounds and five gunshot wounds. His head was removed and displayed in Hampton, VA to warn off any prospective pirates.

Legends surround Blackbeard to this day. He was rumored to have buried his treasure on Ocracoke, which still attracts fortune seekers to the area. The inlet Teach's Hole on Ocracoke bears his name. And it is said his ghost still haunts the islands.

The stories around the silver punch bowl fashioned out of his skull are true. It was seen often in Colonial Williamsburg until it disappeared and remains lost. Or hidden.

It is still possible to find Blackbeard merchandise up and down the Outer Banks and his influence can be found in everything from t-shirts to restaurants to books and movies.

Much of the sound in the Outer Banks is indeed three to four feet in depth. It's possible to wade for great distances and never be in water over your waist. However, it is not recommended. It has also been known to host great white sharks (and many other varieties of sharks and snakes).

It is, indeed, possible to wade in the sound and pluck clams from the sandy bottom, which also happens to be the name of an ex-girlfriend.

There are a number of outfits that now offer airboat tours in the area. A relatively new addition to the local offerings. It's a truly unique way to get to know the Banks from a very different perspective.

Dolphins do indeed have a strange relationship with pufferfish. The neurotoxin released by pufferfish, called tetrodotoxin, can be lethal to humans in large doses, the dolphins manage to coax a small amount out of the fish while playing a slow and controlled game similar to catch, lasting up to thirty minutes. They lick, nudge, and gently nibble the justifiably alarmed puffers. The resultant feeling in the dolphin has been described as a trance-like, blissed out state. The often float just below the surface and are believed to be watching their own reflections. Because they are so so high. Many scientists believe this behavior, and the extreme control necessary to limit the exposure to the toxin, displays a high degree of intelligence and play. I have yet to hear a pufferfish offer their opinion.

There are many duck blinds scattered throughout the Outer Banks, including in around the various Sounds. For some time, they were largely left to themselves, although federal laws prohibit them on the protected areas of the Banks. Over time, they did become larger and more extravagant. The locals do like to tell the tale of one that had become so bold as to include power and septic service. Finally, the authorities could look away no longer and cracked down on the practice. The remains of these "blinds" can still be seen dotting the islands throughout the area.

The Alligator River National Wildlife Refuge is a 152,000-acre refuge in North Carolina's Dare and Hyde Counties. It happens to be one of my favorite places on the planet. It is home to many different wildlife species, and I have been fortunate to see coyote, deer, barred owls, otters, red-tailed hawks, merlins, snow geese, black bears, turtles, cottonmouths, water snakes, harriers, alligators, and the elusive and dangerously threatened red wolf. Alligator River is the only place where those wolves live in the wild.

There is also a small shack on Buffalo City Road in the refuge that lies on a small piece of privately owned land. It has a satellite dish, and a collection of bones and antlers adorns its front porch. I have never seen anyone entering or exiting, but it is clear it is still in use. And there is a small wooden bridge leading from the roadway into the marsh. I tend not to linger too close to it. I suggest you do the same.

Swells'a Brewing exists and I highly recommend it.

The Blue Crab also exists and does have some of the most beautiful sunsets in the Outer Banks. But don't tell anyone. We don't want the secret to get out.

Acknowledgments

No author is an island. We plow forward through the help of family and friends, colleagues, and collaborators. The list of those for this book is long, and I am deeply appreciative.

Once again, I begin with my family. My brother, Stephen Aldrich, and sister, Cindy Vollmer, have been sounding boards, cheerleaders, critics, publicists, and, above all, friends. I can't imagine this book, or any of my books, coming to fruition without them. Stephen, in particular, fielded many phone calls and emails about this book and always responded with wise advice.

Thanks, also, to my father. He introduced me to reading very early in life, sharing favorites of his long before I was of an age to appreciate them fully. Somehow, though, I found something in them to inspire me, beginning a lifelong fascination with storytelling. He's not here to see my books being published, but I know he would have been thrilled. Somehow, somewhere, he knows. My very own Peripheral.

Thank you to my mom. I know she *knew* I had a flashlight under the covers to read by long after I should have gone to sleep as a child, but she let me read on. She took me to the store to get the latest comic books and to the bookstore where she would let me roam and discover and dream. Look where it led. Thank you doesn't seem enough. She was always eager to let me imagine. I do so still because of her.

I'm also grateful to the many theatre artists with whom I've collaborated. They inspire and motivate me, and all of them have played a part in bringing me to this point. Theatre is a collaborative art. Writing can be very solitary. But the creativity that surrounds me on stage, inspires me when I sit in front of my computer.

Teachers. They impact us in so many ways and for our entire lives. I renew my thanks to three outstanding teachers who, to this day, inspire and encourage me—Ken Link, Brian Nelson, and Tom Watson. All were ahead of their times, and we students knew and were grateful. The simplest encouragement can give students wings. I remember them giving me mine.

Amy Gillespie has become a vital part of my author process. Thank you for your keen eye and tackling these manuscripts with intelligence, humor, and alacrity. Your willingness to stick with these, and me, is a gift I can never repay.

Profuse thanks to Chris Sorensen for his formatting and his cover design. Once again, he was able to create something that so wonderfully captures the tone of the book. He is a magician. I am grateful.

Gretchen Douglas, proofreader extraordinaire, once again provided invaluable insight both grammatically, logically, and thematically. She is a boon to anyone fortunate enough to work with her.

A heartfelt thank you to my beta readers, who took this latest venture seriously and offered excellent ideas, corrections, suggestions, and encouragement. Stephen Aldrich, Cindy Vollmer, Robin Lee-Thorp, Amy Gillespie, Jennifer Evans. Thank you is not nearly enough.

Once again, I single out two individuals for special thanks, Nick Sullivan, and Chris Sorensen. From practical help to encouragement to ridiculous banter via text or over a nosh and beer, they have been invaluable. Not just helpful, but friends and part of a burgeoning author network. Thank you.

Without doubt, my biggest thanks are reserved for my wife, Jennifer, and our new daughter, Stephania. Jennifer has encouraged me throughout, pushing when needed, handholding just as often. Stephania has opened my eyes to all the possibilities still surrounding us. The gift of being able to watch her grow and discover the world is the most magical journey I've ever taken. She's the sweetest. She's the smartest. She's the Nugget.

Lastly, I thank you, the readers, for taking another journey with me. I've always told stories, whether on a stage, a screen, or a page. None of it would have been possible without people willing to come along. People like you. Thank you for loving stories. Thank you for sharing mine.

About the Author

Mark Aldrich was born in Massachusetts and raised in Virginia. He lives in New York City with his wife and daughter. His debut novel, The Peripherals: Book One: *The End Is The Beginning* was published in 2022. Followed by *Red Sky, Chasing Today,* and *Beyond Darkness. Shallow Water, Deep Lies* is the first book in his Brethren of the Coast series, a spin-off from *Red Sky.* His writing combines a love of history, travel, folklore, and music. He has been traveling to the Outer Banks nearly all his life and his love for the area is the result of family and friends making it a home away from home.

He continues to travel extensively as an actor and singer. He has appeared in television, film, and theatre, including Broadway and many of the world's most famous stages. However, some of his favorite performances have been in pubs late at night on the west coast of Ireland.

Please feel free to follow and keep in touch at markaldrich.net and @marktheginger on Instagram and Twitter.